Heart and Skull

TEARS OF GODS & DRAGONS

BOOK 2

LV BARAT

HEART AND SKULL

Printed in the United States of America

First Printing, 2015

ISBN 0-9961770-2-7

WWW.LVBARAT.COM

PROLOGUE

THEY DESCENDED ON HORSEBACK and as they approached the harbor, Prince Kryst spied two ships, the color and construction of a type he had never seen—and he had seen many. Being the prince of the island nation of Maeltip, he had spent nearly his entire life on ships. The sails were black and the symbol in the center was red—the same symbol worn on the black, quilted tunics of the Linnsonians.

"Are those yours?" Prince Kryst nodded in the direction of the ships.

Angus beamed. "They are."

Kryst started to ask about the symbol, but was distracted when a large black tomcat ran out in front of their horses and hissed. Master Oscan and Angus pulled back their mounts, spat on their right and then their left.

"Is that a custom in Linnso?" Kryst asked.

Master Oscan narrowed his eyes, "The filthy get of some damned cunt to spy on us."

At first, Kryst did not understand what the man spoke of and then it dawned on him. "The cat?"

"I'd as soon kill it if I knew it didn't belong to one of your subjects." The corners of Angus's mouth turned down in an expression of disgust.

As if understanding the threat to its life, the cat bounded off into the crowd.

"Cats are familiars—the spies and protectors of the evil cunts calling themselves witches and wise women," Angus informed him. "They live halfway in the physical world and halfway in the netherworld."

Their assertions seemed absurd to the prince but he did not voice his thoughts. When they reached The Mystic Horizon, the heat and humidity weighed heavily upon them as the sun climbed, nearing its zenith. The island of Maeltip was known for its hot, humid climate and relentless sun. Prince Kryst wondered if these strange foreigners and guests of his father could look more uncomfortable.

After giving his horse to the stable boy, Master Oscan asked, "Tell me, Prince Kryst, what can we expect to find in this establishment?"

The Linnsonian sea captain's face was long, thin and hard with a pointed, clean-shaven chin and beady, black eyes. The top of his head was bald. The rest of his dark hair was neatly tied in a knot at the nape of his neck. When he smiled, he displayed long, erratically spaced teeth. But despite his appearance, the Linnsonian possessed a charming, lisping accent. Master Oscan's ugliness was made up for in his companion, Chief Mate Angus. The Chief Mate stood well over six feet, possessed a thick crop of sandy brown hair and had wide, grayish-blue eyes. A hint of brown stubble graced his jaw and upper lip. His muscular physique was encased in the same black attire as his Master, but whereas Master Oscan had a slight stoop to his shoulders, Chief Mate Angus stood proud and strong.

"Whores, good food and wine," Kryst replied impatiently.

"Anything else?"

"What more could you want?"

Angus appeared irritated. "Is there anything unexpected?"

Kryst did not understand what he meant. But rather than reveal his ignorance, he said, "Would you like a synopsis of the afternoon?"

The two Linnsonians nodded eagerly. They were a strange lot, but who was he to question their cultural quirks? Their eccentricity could explain the uneasy feeling Kryst had. Not to mention the queer manner of Titus, son of Milnit, who now fanned himself with a golden folding fan. Sweat beads sprouted from his forehead and trickled down his brow and face, leaving trails through his powdered skin. He was a small man but his flesh hung on him loosely without any definition, as if he had never taken exercise in his life. His lips were fleshy and always pursed, as if a sour taste lingered in his mouth.

"We eat and drink in the common room," Kryst explained. "After the meal, a special liquor is served. It is called *sim*, the same liquor you drank earlier. Then the girls are paraded before us and perform a provocative dance. The men bid on their favorite girl and then the real fun begins."

The reaction of the Linnsonians was quite unexpected. They

seemed to be disappointed.

They entered the establishment to loud, raucous laughter. The common room had filled up with merchants, common folk and some pirates. Kryst was recognized by a few patrons and heard their murmurs under the noise.

"...Prince Kryst..."

"...strange foreigners..."

The pirates regarded him with cool, smug expressions. Everyone else lowered their voices. Some bowed perfunctorily and some of the whores curtsied.

They sat down to a meal of baked sea bass, stewed tomatoes with kale in spices and wine, roasted turnips and honey pies. His Linnsonian companions voiced displeasure over the spice in the fish but ate greedily nonetheless. Kryst also ate with gusto, he had not eaten anything since the night before. During the meal, Mistress Lana—an overweight, middle-aged woman with curly brown hair and a double-chin—sang for them. Her voice was soothing if not a little low. While she sang, she winked at Kryst now and again. He knew her well as he was a regular patron.

"Are you betrothed, Prince Kryst?" Titus asked between bites of fish. He had nearly finished, leaving the head and spine on his plate. Spoonfuls of stewed tomatoes entered his fleshy mouth and he did not look up from his food to receive Kryst's answer.

"It's customary for a man in Maeltip not to marry until his twenty-fifth year of age. And we are allowed to choose our bride as long as she is of noble blood. My father will not dictate my choice. It's a very different custom than that of Corvasa."

"Quite!" Titus exclaimed between bites.

"Maeltipian men are encouraged to bed many women. But I prefer one or two rather than several chance encounters. In fact, my favorite is here. I believe that's why my father chose this particular place to entertain you."

"We anticipate gazing upon her beauty," Angus said.

"Are you an Adept, Titus?" Kryst asked.

An uncomfortable expression marred the Corvasan's powdered face. "Why, I possess some of the Talent, yes." He spoke slowly, seeming to weigh each word. "The Adepts of the Crystal Palace often send me to search for those who possess Talent in the rest of Perthia. That is how I was welcomed by your father and met these two fine gentlemen from the north."

The song ended and serving girls cleared their dishes. They brought an oaky, chocolate-flavored liquor. Serving girls drew the curtains over the windows, plunging the room into darkness. Wall candles flared to life at the end of the room where a stage was hidden behind red curtains. Mistress Lana once again stroked her lyre and was joined by a male piccolo player and percussionist. The red curtains parted to reveal two masked female figures standing at each end of the stage. A statue of the Maeltip fertility goddess, Rosa, was placed in the back. The hooded figures paraded several whores through the male audience. They were dressed in light blue amorphous fabric and naked underneath, accentuating their youthful, perky breasts and tender bodies to perfection.

Kryst spotted his favorite girl. She was a petite blonde named Simone with a high derriere and upturned nose. Since he was the prince, no one dared challenge his bid. When she saw him, she winked and smiled broadly. She was half-Knottian, so her eyes glowed the bright turquoise of the Knotts, but her hair was the color of straw as befit those from northern Corvasa.

The girls gathered on stage and provocatively undulated their hips to the rhythmic beat of the drums. Simone fixed her gaze on Kryst, making "ooh" and "aaah" shapes with her lips, half closing her eyes as if she was in the throes of ecstasy.

One black-hooded woman grasped Simone and gently pulled her forward. Speaking Corvasan, she announced, "Regard the lovely and sensuous Simone! Who shall place the first bid?"

The words were Kryst's cue to move forward and claim her. But just before he did so, the Linnsonians stood and raised their hands.

"We bid ten Corvasan gold."

Gasps and surprised murmurs passed through the crowd. Simone stared at Kryst in bewilderment. He had been the only man to enter her since being brought to the Mystic Horizon a month prior, Kryst had seen to that. But he only possessed around twenty Maeltip silver on his person and wondered where the Linnsonians had protracted such a sum. They moved forward in unison to claim her. Kryst stepped up, shoving between the Linnsonians and Simone.

"There must be some mistake, my good sirs," he said as Simone fell in behind him. "Simone is mine. I always choose her and she only goes with me. I will be taking her now."

Master Oscan took a step toward him. "Do you have the coin to claim her?"

Mistress Lana ceased playing and approached, an uncomfortable smile splayed across her fat face.

Angus put a hand on his shoulder. "Prince Kryst, don't defend her. She is just a whore. Albeit, she is the most beautiful of the group, but a whore nonetheless as are all women. Pick another because tonight this whore lies with my Master and me. You may join us if you like. After all, she is full of holes."

Kryst drew his sword. The musicians stopped playing and the room got quiet. Out of the corner of his eye, Kryst saw Titus rise from his seat and fold his arms in front, his eyes glowing in the semi-darkness. The sound of steel being drawn filled the room. Most likely the pirates, but whose side they would take was anyone's guess.

"Simone is mine," Kryst repeated. "She won't be going with anyone except me."

"Put your weapon away, Prince Kryst. This will turn out the worse for you," Angus said politely.

"Draw yours and come at me, if you would have her," Kryst replied.

A black-robed woman lightly touched his shoulder and spoke in a soothing tone. "Your majesty, please sheathe your sword, I beg you."

Something in her words made him hesitate, but he stood his ground. "If you would have her, come and get her."

Chief Mate Angus drew his sword quick as lightning and thrust it forward. But Kryst was faster. He pushed Simone backward where she fell to the floor as he dodged the Chief Mate's thrust. He turned full circle, swinging his blade high above him to come down hard where it met Angus's steel. They parried a few blows, and Kryst deftly jumped to his right, dodging the descending blade. He crouched low and swung with all his might, striking deeply into the Linnsonian's thigh. Blood gushed in rapid spurts as Angus stumbled backward and fell, his face a white mask of disbelief. Kryst pointed the blooded blade at Oscan.

"Draw your sword."

The man's face was unreadable. He did not move.

"Draw your sword!" Kryst shouted.

"The man who kills another man for a warm slit is no man." He answered so quietly Kryst barely heard him.

The Linnsonian gave the briefest of glances to Titus who quickly chanted in a language Kryst recognized as the True Tongue.

"Draw your sword, you coward, or I will be forced to cut you down."

The Linnsonian only stared at him with those black, beady eyes. Kryst raised his sword, dimly aware of the deathly quiet in a room full of men that had been so raucous just a few minutes ago. The only sound was Titus's soft chanting. Before he could strike, Titus thrust his hands toward Kryst, palms facing out.

Suddenly Kryst's legs buckled under and the room swam in an unfocused melding of images. His body went numb and he was unable to move anything. He heard voices but their words were distorted, garbled. Just before he lost consciousness, he distinctively heard the words *Ilnove Sii Dei.*

When he awoke, he was no longer in the brothel. He floated through air, surrounded by a yellowish light. Gravity pulled at his back but slowly shifted to his head. He realized he was upside down.

A copse of twisted, thorny trees came into view below him. The thorns were longer than his hand and the width of his thumb. Some of the thorny trees had people stuck to them, hanging upside down. Screams and moans came from some, others were silent. Giant red bugs the size of a man's fist buzzed around the bodies, occasionally landing.

I will be crucified on one of those trees like the others, he thought.

He braced himself as the sharp thorns pierced the flesh of his arms and legs and just above his left hip. He tried to wriggle free but he was partially paralyzed. Several giant flies, their fat bodies covered in cream-colored fur, buzzed around him. The pain forced screams to burst from his lips. His bowels went loose. Streams of warm blood ran down his torso and arms. His moans added to those of the others, culminating in a symphony of torture and death.

Suddenly, a man on horseback emerged from some bushes across a small field.

Through the excruciating pain and the inverted view, he saw the man approach, curious. His hair was dark and long, worn loose to the middle of his back. His eyes were unmistakably bright turquoise.

Am I in the Knotts?

Through the pain, Kryst was dimly aware of two people next to him. They didn't moan and he wondered if they were dead when the Knottian man pulled them off the trees.

Kryst cried out. "Please help me! Please...you can take me like these other two. Please, I beg you. Help me!" But the man ignored him.

In the end, the Knottian pulled him off the thorned tree but declined to heal him. The man and his companions disappeared into the surrounding bushes. Kryst lay among the trees of horror for hours or perhaps days, he could not tell. Screams of pain went silent only to give way to more screams when he saw others lowered by an invisible force onto the trees.

Deep within, he found the strength to crawl away from the thorny trees and into the forest. The cooler air among the pines and firs brought relief from the heat. He lay down on a bed of pine needles and stared up through the branches to the blue sky beyond. His wounds throbbed and he felt lightheaded, as if he was coming down with a fever but even in his semi-delirious state, he was thankful to be out of the blazing sun and away from the furry, blood-filled bugs. As he stared at the fir branches they seemed to meld into swirling shades of green. Why didn't the man who pulled him off the tree heal him as he had the others? Kryst cursed his fate. The wounds were serious. He had to get out of the forest and find a healer. He closed his eyes and must have dozed off because when he opened them again, it was twilight. Stars peeked through the branches and the moon gleamed full and bright on the horizon.

Somewhere in the distance, a screeching cry filled the air, a wailing like he had never heard before, not even in the torture chambers of his father. A few minutes passed in silence then transparent human bodies ascended slowly through the trees. They glowed slightly blue in the moonlight. Kryst felt warm urine release and gather underneath his buttocks and thighs. He wanted to get up and run but fear froze him. The wraiths were so numerous Kryst was sure he had been deposited in the belly of the underworld. Their cold, dead eyes were lost and forlorn. He knew they saw him but they paid him no heed, floating through the maze of giant conifer trees.

When most of the wraiths had ascended above the branches, he felt safer and crawled a few feet to a moonlit pond. The water soothed his wounds and tasted clean and refreshing. He splashed some on his face and neck. Through the drops, he caught movement and flickering light, followed by a rustling in the surrounding bushes. Kryst stared in the direction of the sound but was fairly certain it was not a wraith. A naked man emerged, his eyes wide in crazed fear. He took one look at Kryst and made some faint moaning sounds then turned his back.

"Hey!" Kryst called out. "Hey you! Wait!"

But the man ran, his white, skinny buttocks bouncing as he zipped through the trees.

The water eventually chilled him. The skin around the holes the thorns had made was red, swollen and sensitive to the touch. He knew what that meant.

I must find a way out but I'm so tired and need to sleep.

He crawled to the edge of the pond and lay down, drying himself with his quilted burgundy doublet. He washed his black wool breeches, twisting them to release as much water as possible. They still stunk of urine and feces but not as strongly. A giant gray boulder lay a few yards away. It was twice his height and many times his width. Perhaps it would shield him from the light breeze which blew from the north. Would he sleep tonight with the strange rustling sounds, the owl hoots and the fear of more wraiths emerging? Doubtful, but it did not matter. Finding a way out in his condition and in the dark was impossible.

He must have dozed off immediately because he dreamed of a powdered man in colorful finery, chanting in the True Tongue. The man seemed to melt into flesh-colored soup. Shapes formed and moved within the liquid. The last form to take shape had wings spread wide, a hooked beak and instead of black or brown eyes, its eyes glowed bright turquoise. It was some type of bird of prey and when it opened its beak to screech, Kryst realized it was a hawk.

SILLISNAE'S RETURN

THE ROOM WAS EXACTLY the way she had left it only a fortnight ago. But she gazed upon it with a different woman's eyes, the eyes of someone who had transformed into another person. Transformed *en totale*. The water basin stood in the same place where she had seen Hawk for the first time in a vision. That seemed like a lifetime ago. The linen-covered sofa occupied its place by the hearth. Fluted, rounded columns of white marble were interspersed throughout the two rooms. Her bed had been made or perhaps that was the way she had left it, she could not remember. The events of that fateful day ran together in her mind. An embroidered scene of cats frolicking among flowers and butterflies decorated her bedspread. The thought of Margot made tears well up in her eyes. Her little kitty with the yellow eyes and pink nose, the white and orange fur, the little friend who had been blasted to pieces by magic lightning meant for her. She realized she had not thought of Margot since she had left the Crystal Palace.

This room is dead and so is the girl who lived here.

Full length window-doors, covered by diaphanous white linen curtains, opened out onto the balcony. Outside, a cool breeze blew. The Palace Gardens were as immaculate as ever, the hedge bushes skillfully shaped into the likenesses of various animals. There was a squirrel, a rabbit and her special favorite, a winged horse. Rose bushes every color of the rainbow grew in geometrical patterns around the animal statues and also in long parallel rows leading to a glorious fountain. In the center, a statue of a tall, bearded man in a suit of armor held a sword pointing to the sky.

The First Sun King, Sillisnae thought, *pointing his sword to the sun.*

Tears ran down her cheeks as she stared at the garden she once loved.

Why did you make me return, Hawk?

An urgent knock on the door prompted her to wipe her face and take a deep breath.

A pale, thin man with a full crop of curly brown hair stared at her with wide, frantic eyes when she opened the door. His thin, white arms reached out and hugged her close.

"Sillisnae! What happened? They said you were a traitor."

She hugged him back numbly. "No, Ogeron," she whispered. "That's not true."

"Where is Lord Korodale?"

"Dead." Sillisnae sighed. "Please sit."

He folded his thin white hands and gazed at her expectantly. He wore a green, crushed velvet robe and a golden-leafed tiara. Ogeron had always been one to adorn himself.

She told him the entire sordid tale, from the time she left the city, to traveling to Ebro and killing Queen Nominthe, to passing through the netherworld into Westernaphalia, then defeating the Linnsonians. She told him about the Ghost Dragon. The only thing she left out was Sii Dei. No one could know about that until she spoke with the King.

While she told the tale, she changed out of her travel-stained clothes into a fresh gown, the color of yellow gold, with a bronze belt strung low on her hips. She did not mind Ogeron's eyes upon her as she bared her body for she knew the sight of a naked woman did not excite him. After she dressed, he brushed out her long, auburn hair, and then braided it.

"How did this woman, Sheena, break through the Globe spells?" he asked. His hands moved dexterously through her hair.

"She is half-Jaanaarian and was an Adept's Apprentice. She must have studied the spells of the Adepts of the Globes. In addition, she carried the royal blood of the House of the Sun. Apparently, she is the bastard child of King Emeril's ancestor."

"Ancestor?" Ogeron's voice was puzzled. "You mean his father?"

"No," Sillisnae replied. "Sheena is close to half a millenia old, born during the last war."

"That must be extremely powerful sorcery to cheat death for so long."

"Yes." Sillisnae felt gravely serious when discussing Sheena. "No doubt we will learn the secret and I have a feeling it involves blood sacrifice."

"Blood sacrifice." Ogeron moved in front of her. "Why do you say that?"

A loud knock at the door caused them to jump.

"Apprentice Sillisnae. It is Noctus Sern. I am to escort you to the King at once."

"Please enter."

A tall, thin man opened the door slowly. He was bald and wore the black and gold robes of an Adept. Sillisnae recognized him as one of the Adepts of the Council of Twelve and probably the next *Daimon Direttore*. He appeared to be in his eighties, but she knew he was much older. An Adept's magical power tended to make them look younger than the rest of the population. He had always been polite with her but she had never studied under him. Lord Korodale had always tutored her.

"You have the most talent of any apprentice I have seen in a while and my memory is long, Sillisnae," Lord Korodale had told her. "I am the only Adept that will train you."

Those words seemed strange to her now, knowing that the former *Daimon Direttore* was a traitor.

Had he been grooming me for Sii Dei?

Noctus Sern tentatively stepped inside. His hazel eyes, closely set under a prominent brow, were apprehensive.

"Apprentice Sillisnae, Ogeron." He bowed his head slightly in greeting and smiled.

She desperately wanted to trust this kindly old man. The Crystal Palace now seemed like a hostile place. She had to keep her head and be careful who she trusted. This frail, sweet old man could be Sii Dei. How many traitors were here? Even guards were suspect.

"Adept Sern." Sillisnae stood and curtsied. "How wonderful to see you. I trust you have been well."

"I have, Apprentice Sillsinae," he replied, "but the denizens of the Palace have been under great stress as you can imagine. We are all grateful to you for returning the Fire Globe. The King has been in quite a state. A few days after you, ahem, took your leave of the capital, the King agreed to marry again."

The news did not surprise her. King Emeril had been married briefly a few years before to a Lady Merrina from eastern Corvasa. She died under suspicious circumstances before producing an heir. The Healers said it was a wasting disease but there were rumors she was poisoned. After that, King Emeril enjoyed bedding the young maidens and apprentices that occupied the palace.

"The betrothed is one Lady Rubia, hailing from right here within the city." Noctus Sern cleared his throat and a worried expression suddenly clouded his features. "She will be with the King in the throne room."

He is warning me, thought Sillisnae. But in all truth, she did not care. Her head was somewhere else. She was thankful for his warning, though. Most of the palace knew about the King's lust for her.

"If you will excuse us, Ogeron. The King awaits." Noctus Sern offered Sillisnae his hand.

"Of course, of course," Ogeron said. "I will call upon you later, Sillisnae. We have much more to discuss." He kissed her on the cheek and was gone, the sound of swishing velvet trailing behind him.

Noctus Sern led her through the East Wing to the throne room. The last time Sillisnae had been in this section of the palace, she had almost become the King's mistress. At the time, she had relished the prospect of bedding the King. Love for him did not exist within her heart, then or now, but she had welcomed the protection afforded his mistresses.

The throne room occupied the end of the east wing hall, past the King's apartments. The doors were gold-plated and carved with ancient Corvasan runes. Butterflies leapt in her stomach as they slowly creaked open. She had been in the throne room only once before, when she was newly arrived at the Crystal Palace.

A guard announced their arrival. "Adept Noctus Sern of the Council of Twelve! Adept's Apprentice Sillisnae of northern Corvasa!"

King Emeril sat upon the throne, a giant gold-plated chair with griffins' heads as armrests placed a dozen steps above the floor. Emeralds and rubies decorated the rays of the golden sunburst that was the head of the throne. They created patterns of green and red lights on the wall behind him. He wore a gold crown shaped as a sunburst, encrusted with rubies at the tips of the rays. His wavy, dark-brown hair hung loose to his shoulders.

Men and women of the Council of Twelve stood in a semi-circle behind him with shaved heads and black and gold cloaks. They were fully-fledged Adepts, the position Sillisnae had been training for. The weight of their stares prickled her skin but she controlled her trembling. Many of their faces were unknown to her.

A woman in a simply tailored brown frock, with buttons up the sides of her torso to her shoulders, sat in a polished oaken chair on a platform beneath the throne. She possessed a pinched, anxious face with thin lips and a wide nose. Her hair was chestnut brown, braided and coiled high atop her head, forming a proxy crown. Pearls glistened within the braid. Much like the King, her dark eyebrows seemed to run together over the bridge of her nose, accentuating her light blue eyes.

That could be his sister, Sillisnae thought. When she entered, the woman lifted a dark eyebrow in disdainful haughtiness.

Sillisnae approached a dais well below the scowling woman and went to her knees in line with the throne.

"Rise, Sillisnae," the King commanded.

She rose slowly, keeping her expression vacant, unreadable. If the King expressed some semblance of affection that she could discern, she was determined to exploit it.

An older woman from the Council of Twelve stepped forward. A giant nose-ring nearly obscured her mouth but the rest of her face was leathery and wrinkled. Only the eyes were bright and alive due to the manipulation of *Od*.

"Apprentice, who is responsible for the Fire Globe's theft?"

Sillisnae kept her eyes on the King. "Sheena from Martine in northern Corvasa. She was an Adept's Apprentice in the Crystal Palace many years ago."

"Where is she now?" The Adept clasped her hands. "Why is she not here to answer for her crime of treason?"

I must temper my words, she thought. *How many Sii Dei are within this room?*

"She is currently in Jaanaar," Sillisnae said. Surprised murmurs sounded throughout the room.

"Jaanaar?" the King asked. "Why was she not brought by the King's Guard with you?"

"She was taken to Jaanaar as a catatonic hag. Her magic, youth and beauty have been stripped from her. She is half-Jaanaarian, so Hawk, son of Niall, thought she should be punished there."

"How was she able to break the protective spells around the Fire Globe?" the Adept asked.

"I-I am not entirely sure," Sillisnae stammered. "She was an Adept's Apprentice here in the Crystal Palace."

"I don't remember anyone named Sheena as an Adept's Apprentice," the King observed.

"She is five hundred years old, your Majesty."

Shocked gasps echoed in the chamber. Even the King held his jaw agape in wonder.

"Where is Lord Korodale?" a man's voice boomed from behind the throne. The Adept that spoke was so short Sillisnae could barely see him.

"Lord Korodale, the *Daimon Direttore*, is dead. Killed by the dragon fire of Renfala."

Silence followed that pronouncement. Had they already been informed of Lord Korodale's death?

"As are the Linnsonians," Sillisnae added. "Their entire camp was burned to the ground."

No one spoke. She could feel their eyes. Did they believe her? Or did they think her a traitor?

"And what part did you play in all of this?" the pinched-faced woman asked. "How do we know you did not take the Fire Globe? Are we supposed to take you at your word? And," she said loudly, lifting her dark eyebrows once more, "you may address me as Lady Rubia when replying."

"If I took it, I would not have brought it back, my Lady," Sillisnae replied.

"I think you are lying, girl," Lady Rubia stated. She lifted her finger and jabbed it in Sillisnae's direction. "You could have easily feigned innocence when your plans went awry. Isn't it convenient the mysterious Sheena disappears to Jaanaar where she can never be found?"

Sillisnae shook her head vigorously. "That is not what happened."

"I say throw her into the dungeon until she confesses. This is a very serious matter. We cannot just allow her to remain in her former quarters. What about the dragon attack on the south wall? She disappeared when that happened. Perhaps she had something to do with that as well."

"That is a little harsh, Lady Rubia," Noctus Sern said. "The Fire Globe disappeared before Adept Sillisnae left the Palace."

Lady Rubia rolled her eyes. "So what? That does not prove anything—"

"Enough of this!" King Emeril shouted.

Sillisnae jumped at the exclamation. In all her years at the Crystal Palace, she could not remember ever hearing King Emeril raise his voice.

"The Fire Globe must be reactivated at once," he pronounced. "Sillisnae, you will join me in the South Atrium with the Adepts of the Globe in an hour." The King stood and with a flourish of his robe disappeared behind a door at the back of his throne.

Lady Rubia appeared as if she had been slapped. Her sharp cheeks burned red. Gathering as much dignity as she could muster, she stood and with a swish of her woolen brown dress, followed her betrothed out the door behind the throne.

The Council of Twelve followed as well, their bald heads filing out like so many marbles through a hole.

* * * *

At the appointed time, a knock alerted Sillisnae to the King's guards, who brought her to Emeril in the South Atrium. The home of the Fire Globe appeared much like the Throne Room. It was at the end of the south wing, only a dozen steps away from Sillisnae's door.

The south atrium's dome was pure crystal and contained two levels with a circular balcony on the top floor. The crystal ceiling held the spell that guarded the Fire Globe. Sillisnae stared at it in wonder. How could Sheena break through a spell such as that?

King Emeril stood in the center of the room with two Adepts of the Globe on each side of him. He had removed his crown but still wore the royal cloak of red and purple. The Adepts of the Globe were completely hairless, due to a special herb they drank that made all of their hair fall out. No eyebrows, no eyelashes, nothing. Loose fitting green robes hung over their left shoulders and were cinched at the hips with a leather belt. They were supposedly the most powerful Adepts in the world, save Jaanaarians.

Lord Korodale had informed her they were directly descended from elementals and had small doses of human blood that allowed them to materialize their bodies.

King Emeril held out his hand and smiled. "You look exceptionally beautiful, Sillisnae."

A blush stole across her face and she glanced away. The intense desire in his eyes made her uncomfortable.

I must tell him soon.

A solid gold stand with four hands representing each direction occupied the center of the room. An Adept stood at the southern direction holding the defunct Globe, which was now black and as shiny as obsidian. No sign of life glimmered within, the glowing nucleus having been extinguished by Nominthe's heart.

"We will watch from up here." The King took her by the hand and led her to the balcony overlooking the small chamber.

The last two Adepts took their places around the stand. Now, four stood at each direction, softly chanting in the True Tongue. The Adept in the south carefully placed the black globe on the stand. The hand-shaped golden clasps moved to hold it in place. The globe slowly changed from black to gray to red. Then the red dissipated until it was transparent with a pinkish glow emanating from a center nucleus. The room was chilly when Sillisnae had entered but now it grew warmer by the second. Sweat trickled down between her breasts and gathered in her armpits. The nucleus pulsated waves of pink light throughout the room. A thin sliver of lightning sprouted forth from the nucleus and danced wildly upon the clear surface inside the Globe.

The King laughed in delight. "It is working."

The Adepts pulled their hands away, glanced up to the King and nodded in unison.

In his joy, King Emeril hoisted Sillisnae into the air and spun her around in delight. His spontaneity surprised her but she laughed as well. To feel the happiness of the moment soothed her fears. She now felt more comfortable in what she had to tell him.

"Your Majesty, I would like to speak with you in private," she said softly.

The Adepts exited the chamber, their bald heads shining with sweat from the heat of the Fire Globe.

"We are alone now. You may tell me whatever you wish." He still held her in his arms. Suddenly, he placed his hand behind her head and kissed her forcefully. He ran his other hand lightly over her breasts.

She broke away. "Your Majesty. I…I…"

"Don't say anything, Sillisnae." He moved in and kissed her again, this time he forced his tongue into her mouth.

She allowed him to kiss her for a few seconds then gently pushed him away.

"I must tell you something, your Majesty."

He let his arms drop and let out a deep sigh. She had practiced this dreaded conversation in her head a thousand times. What if he denied her request?

"Your Majesty, before I went searching for the Fire Globe, I came across some very disturbing revelations."

"Such as?" Emeril raised his bushy black eyebrows but his voice was breathless.

"I got a notion to follow Lord Korodale after the news broke of the theft of the Fire Globe," Sillisnae began. "I put my awareness into Margot, my cat. We followed him in the middle of the night, down into the catacombs beneath the palace. In a subterranean room, the *Daimon Direttore* met with a dozen other people in cloaks and cowls. He addressed them as 'Sii Dei' which means 'Shadow of the Gods' in the True Tongue. This group of people is a secret society of Adepts that stretches throughout Corvasa and probably Perthia as well. Lord Korodale indicated that Sii Dei had planned to steal the Fire Globe but someone else beat them to it. That someone else was Sheena. The gist of what I am trying to say, Your Majesty, is that there are several traitors within our midst and most of them, if not all, are Adepts."

He blinked at her, expressionless. "Those are very grave accusations, Sillisnae. And you did not see any of their faces?"

"Unfortunately, no." She lowered her eyes.

King Emeril folded his arms. "Sadly, this does not surprise me. The business of ruling and holding court is awash with intrigue, envy and betrayal. It has always been and will continue to be as long as human beings gather together in groups. How would I go about exposing the traitors? You are an Adept, how would you do it?"

"Adept's Apprentice," Sillisnae corrected him. "You can trust the Adepts of the Globes. They are not Sii Dei, otherwise they would have stolen it. Ask one or more of them to create a spell to monitor every member of the Council of Twelve."

He squinted his eyes and gazed off into the distance, considering her words. She thought him handsome at that moment. With the exception of a slightly protruding belly, he was not unattractive with his thick, curly brown hair and blue-gray eyes.

He must have read her mind because he said, "If you had royal blood, I would marry you, Sillisnae. But as it is, I am now betrothed to the Lady Rubia from Minosae, a distant cousin. As you know, those of the blood of the House of the Sun must marry their own."

She knew all too well and was thankful for it. Her request would hopefully fall upon ears willing to listen. Outside, a hawk screeched high overhead. The omen was clear. She swallowed and gathered her courage. "Your Majesty, I have a rather special request."

"My dear Sillisnae, I would grant you anything in my power. Ask away."

If he only knew what I was about to ask, she thought, *he would not say such a foolish thing.*

"My King, I request that I be allowed to leave the Crystal Palace and return to my home in northern Corvasa, where I may live out my life as a loyal subject of the realm and not as an Adept's Apprentice."

The King's enthusiastic smile deflated with disbelief. Dark clouds gathered in his light eyes.

"Leave your Apprenticeship? Why, you know that is forbidden."

"I understand. Since you are the King, I thought you could make an exception in my case, since I returned the Fire Globe…" Her voice trailed off. She would remind him of the Fire Globe over and over lest he refuse her request.

"But why would you want to leave one of the most powerful

positions within the realm? Leave me?" His voice rose.

She must tread carefully.

"I didn't ask for this talent and I don't have the fortitude for politics. I'm much more suited to the quiet country life. This adventure with the Fire Globe has taught me that. I want to return to my family in northern Corvasa and live out my days as a wife and mother, not an Adept's Apprentice."

The assertion was partly true. Not only had she tasted adventure and real unadulterated magic, but she wanted to learn the ways of the Jaanaarians and most of all, she wanted to return to Hawk.

"Is there anything you are not telling me, Sillisnae?"

Blushing, she gazed at her feet.

I am a very bad liar.

But how could she tell the King she was in love with someone else? She was a lowborn peasant, the daughter of a miller and his wife. The responsibility of bloodlines and marriage alliances was not for her. The magical talent she possessed was powerful but all the King needed to know was that she would never use it again as the Edict dictated. He looked at her in silence for what seemed like an eternity.

Finally he said, "Sillisnae, you put me in an impossible position. I cannot grant your request. You possess the talent to such a degree, it is imperative you serve the realm. And me, your King." He frowned at her, his blue-gray eyes sparkling darkly. "It is best to forget this foolishness. You will resume your studies with Noctus Sern—"

"But what if he is…" Sillisnae interrupted, forgetting herself.

"Sii Dei? Well, you should be able to discover that secret and inform me." He waved his hand in irritation. "Now off with you. I will summon you tomorrow."

Suddenly he reached out as quickly as a striking cobra and pulled the top of her yellow gown. The backs of his fingers touched her breasts and his face was within inches of hers.

"Oh, and don't think of running away again, even if it is for a good cause." He looked straight into her eyes, searching for something. His breath smelled of cloves the royals sometimes smoked. "I will overlook the good to punish the bad."

She took her leave quickly, holding back a sob. When she reached her room, the tears fell hot and salty down her face. The thought of making love to the King was not as bad as the thought of never seeing Hawk again.

If he makes me his mistress, I can never leave the Crystal Palace, she thought in a sense of panic. *I will be an outlaw if I go to Jaanaar with Hawk.*

Her balcony beckoned, promising comfort. The sun was low in the sky, forging rays of sunlight through the animal bush statues. The water of the fountain gleamed like crystal. A few gardeners trimmed hedge bushes and tended to the roses. Some children played with a kite, laughing and carefree. The day was slightly windy, blowing white and gray clouds across the cobalt blue sky. To the right of the animal statues, hedge bushes formed a maze she had loved to play in when she first came to the Crystal Palace.

She remembered her first lessons with her tutor, Lord Korodale. He had been polite enough but stern and demanding, as expected of the *Daimon Direttore*. Treason by his scheming was the last thing she would have expected. And Noctus Sern, the most likely candidate for the new *Daimon Direttore*? Did she trust him? At this point she did not trust anyone. If someone with as much power within the realm as Lord Korodale had schemed to betray the King, then any number of people with less influence could turn to treason.

Hawk had been adamant. "You must return the Fire Globe yourself. The Adepts that guard the Globe will know how to activate it. But you must go back. There is no other way." He had held her close and cursed the gods while she cried.

"I will come back for you, I promise it. You must know that I never break my promises." He had stroked her face, holding her close to his chest. Then he had kissed her forehead. "Look at me."

Gazing at him through her tears, she had clung desperately to the hope that fate would not intervene to keep them apart.

"I must bring Sheena to Jaanaar and cannot take you with me." Hawk had told her. "Firstly, I have to ask my *oide's* permission. If someone does not have Jaanaarian blood, they cannot enter Jaanaar. If you pass through the Golden Band, you'll become ill and die. But the druids know how to bypass the spell somehow. It's been done before. And I feel confident Akrae will give his consent. The other issue is the Fire Globe. It must be returned immediately. Who knows what is happening with it since its theft? No one has ever stolen an Elemental Globe before and we don't know what it will do or how it will affect elemental fire in the world."

Feelings of abandonment washed over her. Would he break his promise and not come for her? And what if he did not? Was it really so bad to become the King's mistress? She would have a place of honor among the entire kingdom and become an Adept for the good of the realm, for the good of people.

A gust of wind caressed her face and she wiped away a tear.

Oh Hawk, I miss you and want to return to you!

Only the soft wind and chirping of birds answered her wish.

THE OLD IS NEW AGAIN

THE GOLDEN BAND OF Jaanaar loomed in the distance. Sheena lay in front of him on her stomach, her limbs hanging loosely over Renfala's knotty skin. The rain beat down in icy drops but the dragon emanated heat that kept them as warm as if they were in front of a fire.

The Golden Band was a shimmery curtain of cascading light, kaleidoscopic and opalescent. It was created by a series of spells, over two thousand years old, in the age when druids and mages walked the land in vast numbers. The Golden Band kept all living things that did not possess magical talent at bay. A shimmery wall of astral light continued into the sky as far as the eye could see. The Golden Band could not be passed unless an extraordinary amount of magic was used, such as that of shapeshifting, and it was lethal to Jaanaarians attempting to leave their homeland.

Renfala flew high enough so Hawk could see the Western Ocean on his left and the Gulf of Jaanaar on his right. Beyond the Gulf lay the Land of the Osseks and beyond that, the Enchanted Lands, a vast red desert, resembling the Knotts but much more arid, with small cities clustered around oases. They had passed the tallest peaks of the Utild Mountain range, on the border of northern Corvasa and the Land of the Osseks, the tallest peak being in the farthest northeast corner, near the coast of the Straight of Jaanaar. Mount Moirae was home of the Weavers. Its craggy, sharply pointed summit reached nearly thirty thousand feet according to Akrae. The sharp spire of its peak was hidden under a dark gray cloud. When Hawk glimpsed it, he shivered despite Renfala's warmth.

The shimmery astral light of the Golden Band was much more transparent than he remembered. Usually, one could not see through it to the Jaanaarian island, but now he could make out the richly forested hills, the river valleys and the gigantic mountains.

Something is wrong, he thought when they approached the kaleidoscopic wall of light. He braced himself for the impact. Renfala did not hesitate, the muscles of his wings and back flexing and relaxing, flexing and relaxing. His wings made a loud *whoosh* as they flapped in the thin alpine air. When the raindrops hit Renfala's gray skin, they steamed away into nothingness.

In a split second, they crossed the shield of astral light and Hawk felt nothing, not even a tingle. The few times he had crossed the Golden Band in hawk form, he had always felt intense heat. He put his hand on Sheena's bony back to make sure she still lived. She did.

"*An ancient place, Shapeshifter,*" he heard Renfala say in his mind, the first words the dragon had directed at him.

Hawk had read the thoughts of the magical beast and given

commands, but the dragon never answered back. Until now.

The Terres River valley spread out beneath him, winding its way between two mountain ranges. A herd of elk cows ran, their bouncing backsides winking through tall grassland bushes. The air was noticeably colder and the rain still drizzled. Giant oaks and dark green yews littered the edge of the foothills, and then there was a steep climb into the mountains with several types of pine and firs. The smell of Jaanaar was different than any other place he had been. The scent of lilac, lavender and astringent pine always remained no matter what season it was. A clean, fresh smell.

"Descend slowly to the river," Hawk commanded Renfala with his mind.

The dragon slowed his flight and glided ten feet above the ground. An eruption of frogs, birds and deer greeted them as Renfala's feet hit the ground. The jouncing prompted Hawk to hold Sheena tightly. The dragon's feet made squishing sounds on the wetland floor. The smell of algae and wet, rotting foliage hung heavy here.

Sheena was light as a feather when Hawk lifted her. Her eyes still held the vacant, catatonic stare. Renfala curled his snakelike neck and regarded Hawk with eyes of blood. The top of the dragon's back stood twelve feet high with a sheen more dark gray than green. Sharp spikes protruded at the hunch which obliged Hawk to ride near the base of the neck. The wound where Hawk had taken his claw had already grown a new one.

The Ghost Dragon Claw.

He thought of Sillisnae, but it made his heart ache so he pushed her out of his mind.

"You may go where you like but avoid people," Hawk told him.

The dragon remained silent.

"I thank you great Renfala, for your courage and protection. For each time you have given aid," Hawk said aloud. Did the dragon help them because Hawk had taken his claw? He had given it to Sillisnae, to protect her in Minosae. Now that he no longer possessed it, would Renfala continue to heed his call? Hawk watched as he disappeared into the thick foliage of the wetlands, his spiked tail winding through the tall grasses like a snake.

Underneath a canopy formed by intertwining oak branches, Hawk carried Sheena to the center where stood the largest oak. Spiral staircases wound around the trunks and entered pod structures made of glass and wood. On top of the pods were wide, circular platforms with guardrails. The pods themselves had two levels, an eating area with a small iron woodstove and a sleeping area above, just below the outdoor deck. In addition to the spiral staircases, entrance to the pods could be accessed through a sophisticated rope and pulley system, but it was mainly used for hoisting food and supplies. Rope bridges hung loosely between trees.

Hawk, carrying Sheena on his back, ascended the spiral staircase of the center oak, the home of his *oide*, Akrae. Birdsong produced soft echoes throughout the highest branches.

Jaanaarians lived in loosely organized tribes with a druid the leader of each. Akrae was one such druid and also an *oide* to Hawk and a few others. The Ice People, as Jaanaarians were sometimes called, lived in complete communion with nature, most of them knowing the language of animals and plants. Procreation was performed through the druids' *pneuma* and mental projections rather than sex.

He felt a sense of pride as he climbed the circular staircase around Akrae's oak trunk. The mission was complete and the Fire Globe would function once more.

Hawk poked his head through the floor entrance to the pod. The dank smell brought back the feeling that something was amiss.

"Akrae?" he whispered.

The living space had a wood floor, a small hearth in the northern section with a curved chimney. The pelt of a white bear lay across the floor. Glass jars filled with nuts, fruit jellies and pickled vegetables littered the shelves of the rounded, wooden walls. The circular room was the height of two men. A dank smell permeated the air and that worried him. It was the smell of sickness. Hawk climbed to the second level which served as bedchamber.

He emerged through the wooden ceiling and climbed into Akrae's bedchamber with Sheena on his back. His *oide* lay upon a feather pallet, snoring soundly.

"Akrae!" he whispered forcefully.

The old druid smacked his lips together and slowly blinked his eyes.

"Hawk?" Akrae sat up slowly, blinked sleep from his eyes and folded his legs underneath him. He still wore the light blue and lilac robe he had worn the day he sent Hawk on his mission. The snowy white beard he was so proud of was matted and tangled and his eyes were red and glassy.

"Are you ill, my *oide*?"

Akrae coughed into his hand. "Perhaps a little. Most of us are, especially the Elders. The oaks have related we are weakening." His voice was thin and raspy. "Who is she?"

"The Fire Globe's thief." Hawk gently laid Sheena on the wooden floor, her glassy eyes staring straight up at the ceiling.

"How did she…" Akrae began, but then leaned closer. "She is Jaanaarian."

"Aye," Hawk replied. "I thought it wise to bring her here."

Akrae clasped her jaw in his hand and turned her head left and right. "You thought correctly, my apprentice. She is catatonic."

"She was stripped of the spell that kept her young and beautiful," Hawk explained. "The *Daimon Direttore* did this to her."

"Did he now?"

"We don't understand how she stole the Globe or broke through the protection spell. When I awoke from passing through the Earth Portal, I was taken to the village of Martine in Northern Corvasa by some peasants. She was the Healer in that village and had disguised herself with magic. When we trekked through the Renfala Forest, we were attacked. An attempt was made on two of my friends' lives and she was part of that, leaving us in the forest to die."

Akrae brushed a strand of gray hair away from her face. "I believe she is older than me. I do not recognize her."

Hawk laughed. "How old are you, my *oide*?"

Akrae gave a sly smile, glancing sideways at Hawk. "Older than you and younger than her."

Hawk had so many questions and things to tell his *oide*, he did not know where to begin, so he said, "We crossed the Golden Band on a dragon."

Akrae's reaction was not what Hawk expected. He hardly reacted at all and never took his eyes from Sheena. "A dragon you say? Where is he now?" Akrae ran his wrinkled hands over her body. His fingers were twice the length of Hawk's.

"By the river. Aren't you surprised?"

Akrae gave his apprentice a tired look. "At my age nothing surprises me. It is about time the dragons were awoken."

"I will tell you the entire story from beginning to end. But first I must ask—there is something different about Jaanaar. When we flew through the Golden Band, the astral light was transparent as if it was weakening. And then you say many of you are ill. I smelled sickness when I entered the pod. What is happening here?"

His *oide* sighed and pinned Hawk with his violet gaze. An expression that told him Akrae was about to reveal information more important than dragons.

"We are weakening, Hawk. The Golden Band is weakening. The magic that was impenetrable is now losing its power."

"But why?"

"The world desires us again, even if we do not want it."

"Can you be more specific?"

"The will to live is going out of us, the people of Jaanaar. Some do not know why there is a Golden Band. Because we have not had adversity for many years, we are becoming weak and apathetic. That is why the Golden Band is weakening and that is the reason for our sickness. This last time I sent you beyond the Golden Band, I knew it would be different. I knew you would face your most serious challenge yet. All peoples, nay all worlds, go through cycles and the cycle of the Golden Band is coming to an end. Why do you think I sent you into Corvasa? Why do you think I apprenticed you, who possesses mostly Knottian blood, to send on missions within greater Perthia?

"I have Jaanaarian blood—"

"Ah yes. You do. But it is awash with another blood, that from the Knotts. The reason we chose you is because full-blooded Jaanaarians are weak. We have not had to fight for our way of life in many centuries. When you don't have something to fight for, a common purpose or inspiration, you rot away from the inside and begin to harm yourself. The Jaanaarians need to be tempted, they need to cut their teeth against treachery, misery and pain. Without these things, individuals become lazy and indifferent."

Everything Akrae said, Hawk had intuitively sensed. But beyond the Golden Band, the world in general believed in the lofty, powerful magic of the Jaanaarians and those beliefs were not easily discarded.

"You both must be famished," Akrae observed. He stood and stretched, his joints creaking like an old wagon, and disappeared into the lower level. Within a few minutes, Hawk smelled the tempting aroma of bone broth. It was flavored with pieces of onion and garlic. Hawk ate greedily as Akrae sat Sheena up and held the bowl to her lips. She sipped loudly, all the while her eyes gazing straight ahead.

"We will take her to the hillnon tomorrow," Akrae said.

Hawk stared at his *oide* in disbelief. "The hillnon? She will live with the magi? Sounds more like a reward rather than a punishment."

Akrae lifted a finger. "Do you remember what I taught you about punishment and rehabilitation?"

"Death is not a punishment," Hawk repeated the phrase of which his *oide* was so fond.

"Correct. What is the most effective form of punishment?"

"When a man loses what he is," Hawk replied.

"Yes," Akrae said, "but why?"

He had the lesson drilled into his mind during his first years in Jaanaar. "Like taking a hand for thievery, a person loses what he is, he never forgets it."

"Putting a scheming, power-hungry, manipulative woman into an environment in which she must harvest, clean and hunt her own food, sew her own clothes, where she will perform chores night and day, her magical talent entirely blocked, how do you think such a woman will look on her time in such a place? She will have no power or influence and must learn to live with it."

"Yes, but perhaps she will cherish the desire for power, nurture it secretly in her heart, bide her time until the day she is free or can escape—"

"There is no escape from the hillnon," Akrae said with finality.

"But if there *were*," Hawk persisted, "she would still harbor the desire for power and scheme ways to cause mischief. She stole the Fire Globe, by the gods!" Hawk swore. "This woman is much more dangerous than I think you realize."

Akrae wagged his finger and smiled smugly. "She may be fearless in her imagination but not in physical reality. And only in her imagination will she ever be powerful again."

27

"Doesn't magic come from the imagination?"

A slight guffaw escaped Akrae's thin lips but he did not answer and Hawk understood the conversation was over. No matter what Akrae said, Hawk was not convinced putting Sheena in a hillnon was the best way to deal with her.

* * * *

The next day, Hawk bathed in the stream of the wetlands, something he enjoyed during the summer. The water was very cold, having just been frozen as snow on the high mountain peaks. The refreshing coldness tingled his skin. He had always bathed in rivers and lakes ever since he could remember, but in the Knotts, the water had been much warmer.

Renfala? Are you near?

He searched the immense wetlands for any sign of the magical beast.

No answer was forthcoming, only the sound of the stream, some frogs, and a few crows squawking overhead.

Akrae dressed in a pale green robe and a full-length, rabbit fur cloak. His *oide* gave him a fresh change of clothes: a boiled, brown leather jerkin, lambskin breeches the color of cream, a dark blue tunic and doublet.

Mid-morning they set out for Ocht Hillnon, a stony fortress built into the side of Mount Ocht. A strong mule carried Sheena and some provisions upon his back. The mountain was so named in the True Tongue because it was the eighth mountain beginning from the southern coast of Jaanaar in the Terres mountain range.

In the beginning, the climb was mild through the foothills and they made good time. But an hour later, the incline steepened sharply, and Hawk had to stop now and then to let Akrae catch his breath. It was not his age that slowed him, but the sickness. Akrae was usually spry in matters of physical exertion. The large evergreens of the lower mountain prevented wind, and sounds of various birds and squirrels echoed throughout. Sheena sat upon the mule, her back slouched and her eyes staring at the ground.

"I met an accursed fetch in the Renfala Forest, my *oide*. He was Jaanaarian."

Akrae stopped in his tracks and stared at his apprentice. "At one time, I would have said that was impossible but no more. Tell me."

"He said he was fishing off the coast and met with a boatload of women. Another boat came upon them and the next thing he knew, he was in the forest of the damned."

Akrae sighed and shook his head. "It doesn't surprise me. As I said, the Golden Band is weakening. If someone went beyond it, either the Jaanaarian man or his attackers, it seems completely plausible at this point."

"But their magic—"

"Hawk, it could have been Jaanaarians."

In all truth, he did not consider that possibility. "Jaanaarians from Jaanaar? Or somewhere else?"

Akrae glanced back at Sheena. He stared for a few seconds then said, "Somewhere else. In addition to the Golden Band, the Straight and Gulf of Jaanaar harbor dangerous whirlpools, huge random swells, tempting mermaids and giant sea creatures around its borders.

Sometimes Jaanaarian fishermen venture into these waters without being aware of it. Some magical creatures appearing as men must have possessed more powerful magic than the fetch or he wouldn't have ended up in the Renfala Forest."

And so they climbed. Both he and his *oide* were exhausted by the time they reached tree line. The hike had taken five hours. Akrae pointed in the distance and Hawk spied a dozen turrets jutting out from the craggy stone face of the mountain. Several gray stone steps led to two massive oak doors with sacred runes. The front of the hillnon was made of the rock of the mountain. Narrow vertical windows were cut into the stone face irregularly. The trail switched up the rocky side and posited them at the foot of the steps. As they climbed, some of the magi watched them through the narrow windows. Their heads were shaved and their faces beardless. Only the Honor wore hair and a beard. Seconds before they reached the giant doors, they slowly creaked open to reveal the man himself.

The Honor stood at least seven feet tall. His thin, white hair nearly reached his ankles. He beckoned them with a bony hand and a smile.

"Come, come. And be welcome," he said in a thin, raspy voice.

"Do you know him?" Hawk whispered to Akrae.

"Of course, my pupil. Ocht Hillnon is where I took my training as a young man. You don't think I would have brought Sheena somewhere unknown to me?"

The wooden doors were at least thirty feet high. Inside, a warm fire blazed in the center of the room, which an octagonal depression with three steps. Beyond the fire was a small hall, then large windows which led to a garden.

Bear skins and pillows surrounded the fire pit and the Honor indicated they sit. The mule was led away by a bald ascetic and Hawk gently placed Sheena on some pillows.

"May I present to you the Honorable Titae," Akrae said with a flourishing gesture of his hand. "He is my *oide* and dear friend."

Honor Titae bowed in Hawk's direction. "I am honored to meet the pupil of my pupil. Welcome Hawk. And who is the lady?"

"Her name is Sheena from Martine in Corvasa. She is half-Jaanaarian and was a very powerful Adept."

"It seems she has reached very advanced years," Honor Titae said with a chuckle. "Does she speak?"

"She has not spoken for a few days and remains catatonic. Not that it matters, don't the ascetics take vows of silence?" Hawk inquired.

Honor Titae nodded. "Some of the younger men do. The women do not for the most part."

"There is something else, my *oide*." Akrae nodded to Hawk.

Hawk retrieved the dried, blackened heart of Nominthe from his satchel. The muscle had hardened, giving it a rough, leathery feel. Honor Titae took it carefully and rolled it between his palms.

"That is the heart of the goddess Nominthe while she was in human form," Akrae explained. "It was able to neutralize the Fire Globe, so it must be kept in a safe, impregnable place until it disintegrates."

"Will it disintegrate?" Honor Titae asked.

"I believe it will."

Hawk suddenly thought of something. "Honor Titae, Sheena hasn't moved since her powers were stripped. Everywhere she goes, she is carried. She must be fed by someone. How will she be able to work if she does not move on her own?"

Honor Titae glanced at Sheena. "If she does not work, she will not be fed and will most likely die of starvation. We will not force-feed her."

The Honor whistled and two bald magi entered the stone chamber. Plain, gray woolen robes draped loosely from their skinny shoulders. Eyes downcast, they clasped their hands in front of them.

"Take this woman to the stone chambers," the Honor instructed them.

When they lifted her, Hawk searched her eyes for any reaction but there was none. Would she actually die from starvation rather than break her catatonic state? He wondered.

After Sheena had been carried off to her new home, Honor Titae led them through the rock garden behind the main chamber. A portion of the mountain had been cut out to allow sunlight to pour through.

"Has part of the mountain been cut away?" Hawk asked.

"Indeed, that is just what happened, in days long past, when the gods inhabited this place." Honor Titae explained. "See the blue sky beyond that opening? A thin film of transparent energy, much like glass, but alive and intelligent, covers the opening and allows sunlight but filters out cold, allowing these tropical plants to grow all year round."

Large, fan-leaved shrubs and exotic, multi-colored flowers covered the ground where a handful of ascetics tended to them silently.

"You will also notice the fruit trees." The Honor waved a hand. "Peach, apricot, apple. Over there, see? We also have blackberry and blueberry bushes."

Sheena will never passively tend to flowers and bushes, Hawk thought but he kept it to himself.

On the other side of the garden was a tall, vertical opening in the stone wall of the mountain. Honor Titae led them through a long torch-lit hall with wooden doors bound with iron locks on both sides. The smell was musty and ancient, reminding him of moldy manuscripts in a forgotten library. In no time they reached another opening in the rock. Passing through it, a tingle ran down Hawk's spine. A ward of some kind.

They entered a round, dimly-lit room with ghostly pools of water lining the walls. A phallic-shaped, opalescent crystal occupied the center. Along the length of the crystal were several outlined rectangles the size of a man's foot. The Honor waved his palm over a rectangle at chest height and it dissolved. He placed the heart inside where its girth caused it to lodge exactly in the center. Sparkles erupted around the edges of the rectangular opening, reforming the barrier of crystal. Nominthe's heart had found its new, permanent home.

"The power of this talisman will either wither and die or meld to that of this ancient crystal and become one with it," Honor Titae explained. "In any case, it will never again be held by human hands."

"What about a goddess's hands?" Hawk asked.

"Nor those," Titae replied, but Hawk thought he caught the slightest hint of doubt in his voice.

A MARRIAGE MADE IN
NATURE

THE AIR WAS DRY AND THIN, giving Lananell a chill in the morning until the sun rose overhead and warmed her. They had been climbing steadily higher ever since they left the burned-out camp in Westernaphalia. The alpine air tired her so much she had to stop every few minutes to catch her breath but Rosco would always wait patiently, smiling. She never asked, "How much longer?" because she did not want to bother him. He was so kind and sweet, much like Hawk. But unlike Hawk, she sensed his attraction.

"At one point it will flatten out, then we'll descend," Rosco told her.

He showed her berry bushes of the black, blue and red variety and they ate abundantly. Lananell quickly became enamored of their tart but sweet flavor.

"These are walnuts." He showed her the nuts in a particularly woodsy area. He broke the hard shell with his big hands and placed the light brown nuts in her mouth. They had a delicious, mild flavor. In Linnso, the nuts were called teardrops and they were harder and smaller.

"We could live for months on just these alone," Rosco explained. "I have two of these trees next to my cottage. Since my wife died, some days I'd only eat these and I could do farm work for hours."

They treaded along a well-worn wagon road.

"This road is used by merchants traveling between northern Corvasa and Westernaphalia." Rosco explained.

On a couple of occasions, they heard the wheels of a cart and Rosco pulled her into the surrounding woods and put a finger to his lips. As if she would shout! She was in a strange country and she trusted Rosco more than anyone she had ever met, except for Hawk.

The smooth object in her pocket was a reminder of him. She took it out and stared at it.

"You keep it," Hawk had told her.

"But it was given to you by the dryads," she had protested.

"For a purpose that has already been fulfilled. They'd want you to have it. You have a special gift with the nature spirits."

"Why do you even need that, Lananell?" Rosco asked, bringing her out of her reverie. "Can't you create a column of fire or blast lightning from your abdomen like you did when you first escaped?"

She had been expecting this question. "I can only create the column of fire with another Adept. I instinctively knew this. That is why I ran to Hawk in Minosae at the south wall and why I hugged Sillisnae in Ebro. I'm a catalyst for other Adepts' power. When I try to call forth fire alone, nothing happens."

"But in Ebro when you cut the space—"

"I didn't do that. I just showed them how. It was Hawk and Sillisnae's magic that opened the portal."

"Do you know the extent of what you can do?"

They descended into a copse of trees on the well-worn path. Lananell instinctively lowered her voice as if the trees listened.

"No, not really. I know I can heal others plus see and feel the spirits of the wood and meadow. The looking glass can help me call those spirits but I don't think I can do that without it."

"I see," Rosco said. He sounded pleased. Perhaps the idea of falling in love with an Adept gave him pause.

Yellow, purple and pink mountain flowers covered a meadow when they emerged from the copse of evergreen and oaks.

"The yellow flowers are alpine avers," Rosco explained. "We can eat them if we have to. The purplish-pink flowers are called fireweed. So named because they grow after forest fires. We can eat the stems of those but we must peel them first."

Curious, Lananell picked a fireweed, mainly because of the beauty of its color. She did as Rosco said, peeled the shoot and ate. The flavor was so bitter, it made her eyes water and she winced but swallowed all the same.

"Are you that hungry, dear Lananell?" Rosco laughed. "We only need to eat those as a last resort."

"We don't have these wildflowers in Linnso," Lananell stated. "We don't have such high mountains."

"Smell this." Rosco held up some light green leaves.

The smell was pungent but very pleasant. Bushes with the same leaves grew everywhere when they walked above tree line.

"It's mountain sage. A flavorful herb when dried," he informed her.

He carried a massive club on his back, the weapon he hit Lord Korodale with. He had told her what happened in the camp the first day they left Westernaphalia. Rosco had such big hands, she thought he did not need a club; he could crush a man's skull with nothing but those.

The trail they followed cleared mountain passes which were bordered by gray, craggy rocks jutting into the sky. She stared at them in wonder.

No one would be able to scale such a thing, she thought.

That night Rosco puzzled her. He made a bed of leaves and covered her with his surcoat but he never attempted to partake of her body.

Perhaps he wants me to initiate?

On the second night she lay next to him. He wrapped his arms around her but when she tried to unlace his breeches, he grabbed her hand.

"No," he whispered. "Not here. Not now."

The rest of the night she slept in his big, burly arms. His muscles were large and firm everywhere on his body. But his face was sharp, with high jutting cheekbones and a thin, pointy nose.

On the third day, they heard a wagon behind them.

"Hurry! Hide yourself. Into the bushes. Now!"

She ran as fast as her feet would take her and her lungs burned. The trees and tall bushes were woefully sparse.

They must have not hidden in time because a woman's voice cried out. "Who goes there? We come in peace."

Rosco drew his club and put a finger to his lips.

"We come in peace," she shouted again. "We are unarmed."

Rosco stood. "Stay here."

She watched him sprint to the road, crouching down as he got closer. The wagon slowed at the point where he crouched. Suddenly, he jumped up and let out a roar. The woman screamed.

"We come in peace!" a man yelled.

A few minutes passed and Lananell waited. Rosco stood next to the wagon, speaking with the man and woman. He put his club on his back and beckoned Lananell with his hand.

They rode the rest of the way in the cart, climbing higher as the landscape became rockier. Massive boulders lay inexplicably in the middle of the forest, as if the earth erupted from within. The peasants, a man and wife from a small hamlet near Martine, did not make much conversation and in fact, regarded her suspiciously. Her feet hurt from all the hiking, however, and she was glad for the rest. She and Rosco shared the back of the cart with a goat and a cage of white, long-eared rabbits.

Lananell stuck her fingers between the bars to pet them. Their tiny pink noses wiggled at her in curiosity. Before she realized it, she had spoken a few gentle words in Linnsonian and the peasant woman turned around quickly, glaring at her.

"What language that be?" she spat, directing the question to Rosco.

The woman's face had so many wrinkles; Lananell thought it resembled a crumpled blanket.

"She is from Maeltip," Rosco lied. "She does not speak much Corvasan."

The truth was the opposite. In Linnso, the women were taught Corvasan from a very young age, mainly to be able to communicate with merchants and fishermen from Perthia. Lananell had worked the brothels, as every girl was required to do after their first menarche, and spoke with many nationalities in Corvasan.

They rode the rest of the way in silence. Lananell tried to nap but sleep would not come. The sun was low on the western horizon when Rosco sat up suddenly and said, "We will leave you here, m'friends."

"Martine is another mile or two," the old woman said.

"My brother lives outside of Martine." Rosco pulled Lananell from the cart and the peasants watched them go.

She heard far away voices coming from the village. The sound made her ecstatic. Rest and repast would not be a long wait. Her stomach grumbled in anticipation.

"We are going around the village," Rosco told her. "I want to see Kurin before we go into town."

Lananell understood. The gods only knew what had happened since they had disappeared.

Kurin lived in a small dun built into a hill. The roof was made of earth and grass and the door was an arch of wood with a round window. Two other square windows were placed on either side of the door. Two goats and several chickens were penned up on the side. Atop the dun was a garden with vines and rows of leafy vegetables. Kurin's backside faced them as he dug in the dirt on top of his house.

"Kurin!" Rosco called out.

The old man turned. He was a medium-height, wiry man with the beginning of a stoop and a long, thinning beard. He put a hand over his eyes to shield the sun.

"Rosco?" The tool he held dropped to the ground and he ran down the slope of the dun.

Kurin's face was a twisted hodge-podge of shock, relief and anger. He clasped his brother in a tight embrace, a single tear falling from his eye.

"You're a damn fool!" he spat at Rosco when he pulled away. "What happened to you?"

Rosco shot Lananell a weary glance.

"Where is Sheena? Everyone has been asking for her. Did you see Sillisnae?"

"Brother, I have much to tell you."

Lananell thought his voice sounded tired. And why wouldn't it? They had been traveling for days.

"Of course, of course," Kurin mumbled. "Nella has made a goat stew." He glanced over his shoulder at Lananell. "Is she still mute?"

"No, my voice has been returned to me by the grace of a dragon," Lananell replied in a tiny voice. Old habits died hard. She still lowered her voice when speaking to men.

Inside, several large mirrors had been strategically placed on the walls to catch the sunlight and project it farther back into the dwelling. The first room contained the hearth where a small cook fire blazed. A pear-shaped woman stood next to it, holding a wooden spoon. All smiles and rosy-cheeked, she wiped her greasy hands on an apron that had seen many a prepared meal. A white linen coif was pulled over her blondish-brown hair with unruly tendrils falling into her face.

"Rosco!" she exclaimed, kissing him on both cheeks and smiling to reveal a gap-toothed smile.

"Nella! It is wonderful to be home."

"And who is this beauty?" she asked turning her hazel eyes to Lananell.

"My bride-to-be. Lananell."

Kurin's mouth fell open.

"Yes, brother. It is true. We want to be married as soon as possible."

Kurin and his wife gave each other a cryptic glance.

"Well, this is certainly unexpected." The smile remained on Nella's face but went out of her eyes.

"Tell us about that 'grace of a dragon' business," Kurin said.

And so they did. Rosco did most of the talking with Lananell interjecting here and there. Their hosts' expressions went from unbelieving frowns to wide-eyed wonder.

"Who would have thought that about Sheena?" Kurin shook his head.

"She healed many a malady," Nella lamented. "Where will we find another Healer?"

Rosco smiled. "Right here, dear Nella." He put a hand on Lananell's shoulder. "She has the Talent."

Kurin scowled but Lananell thought he always seemed to be scowling. It was his natural condition.

"You are from Linnso, dear?" Nella asked.

Lananell liked her immediately. She was a kindly lady, someone who had no ulterior motives. There were precious few like her in Linnso. Death was what awaited women somewhere between their mid-fifties and sixties. In Linnso, women were killed when they were no longer useful which meant when they could no longer reproduce or work. When women began to reach that age, the fear would take over and some would try to escape into the wilderness. The veneer of the kindly matron was not an option for those who had execution hanging over them.

"Yes," Lananell replied.

"What...what is it like there? Do you miss it?"

Lananell understood the woman was trying to make polite conversation but nowhere in her wildest dreams had she thought anyone would ever ask her if she missed Linnso. "No, Miss Nella. I don't miss it at all. It was a very difficult life for me because I am female."

Something in Lananell's eyes must have given away her extreme feelings about Linnso because Nella did not pursue the issue further. The cast iron pot smoked over the cook fire and Nella poured them all a bowl of goat stew. The aroma made Lananell's mouth water. She and Rosco had been living off foraged berries and nuts. Rosco ate his stew within four gulps without using a spoon.

"Hungry are we?"

"More than you know, brother. I have missed Nella's stew."

After dinner, Nella prepared two pallets in front of the hearth. Three large dogs, appearing to have hound mixture, slept on the floor next to them.

"They remind me of Tirag's dogs, the man who befriended us in Ebro. During the fighting, I lost track of him. I hope he got off the island safely."

Lananell did not remember Tirag. "It was chaos there, just before we left. I wonder how many survived?"

Somewhere outside an owl hooted. The fire was low and crackling and a soft breeze blew through the open window. She snuggled closer to Rosco, putting an arm around him. Within seconds she fell into a dreamless, restful sleep.

* * * *

The next morning, Nella gave them bread, cheese and plums for breakfast. Rosco bit into a ripe plum and juice squirted all over his face and clothes. Taking one, she devoured it greedily while Nella brought out a yellow silk dress with elaborate green and gold embroidery.

"Lananell," she said gently, smiling in her warm, matronly way. "I wore this when I married Kurin. I was much thinner then, almost exactly your size, dear girl. Come and see if it fits."

Lananell followed her down the narrow hallway. They entered Kurin and Nella's bedchamber and Lananell sat in a chair in front of a mirrored vanity.

Nella made polite conversation. She really liked to talk, Lananell noticed.

"Yes, I was thin and beautiful in my day, but youth and beauty are but a brief turn on the circle of life. Sometimes, I wished I was ugly because it lasts much longer. Yes, Kurin loves to eat and when Rosco's wife died..." Her voice trailed off.

"Do you have any children?" Lananell asked.

The woman lowered her eyes. "No, sadly. My womb has never bloomed a flower." Nella's voice quivered on the last syllable and Lananell felt guilty for asking.

"What was Rosco's wife like?"

Nella licked her lips. "She was my second cousin. Stout and strawberry blond with large breasts and hips. She could sing very well and would often entertain at the tavern. She and Rosco knew each other since they were children. Everyone in Martine is that way. We all grew up together."

"How did she die?" Lananell asked.

Nella's face became pensive. "Came down with a fever about two years after they were married, she did. Would not eat and lost most of her girth. Sheena said she could not be saved. At the end, she did not know who we were and she regressed back into childhood."

Lananell did not know what to say so she remained silent.

"It was very strange. She had always been as healthy as a horse. Everyone was shocked."

Nella gently brushed out the tangles in Lananell's brown curls, then combed it back and fastened it with some pins so she had a bun at the nape of her neck.

"Now we need some mountain flowers to accentuate your beauty." She disappeared and returned five minutes later with flowers of every color and weaved them deftly into Lananell's dark hair.

"In Linnso, we were encouraged to beautify ourselves by coal black eyeliner and juice from crushed berries to stain our lips."

Nella drew back, puzzled. "Were you, dear? Why?"

"For the men, they wanted us as beautiful as possible."

Nella ceased fussing over her hair and regarded her strangely. She realized she said something awkward but did not know what. The women were not expected to pleasure the men until they were married here in Perthia. That much she had gathered from just listening. Nella's puzzlement must have something to do with that.

"Well, you are ready. Let's get you into your gown."

Lananell lifted her arms as Nella pulled the yellow silk over her head. She tied a sash of purple velvet across her hips. Delicate lace decorated the ends of the long, fluted sleeves and the bodice was trimmed with the same white lace. Embroidered red, green and silver hummingbirds decorated the sleeves and sides of her gown.

"You are beautiful, Lananell." Nella seemed to force a smile.

Lananell noticed the change in her demeanor. She was trying to be nice, but something was bothering her. Hypersensitivity to others' moods—a change in timber of the voice, a deepening line between the eyebrows, the downturning of the corners of the mouth. Noticing these things and changing one's demeanor accordingly would mean the avoidance of a beating in Linnso.

But here in Corvasa, there would be no beatings, just disapproval and she could live with that.

"Clasdaq is here," Kurin yelled from the hearth room. "The ceremony will be under the oak tree."

"Who is Clasdaq?" Lananell asked.

"He is the Eldest of the village Elders. Healers usually perform marriages because of their special relationship with the dryads and the gods. But it seems our Healer betrayed everyone and everything." Nella gave her a sideways glance. "Are you ready?"

Nella led her outside where Rosco and Kurin were waiting. The back of the dun looked out on sagebrush, a meadow and then forest beyond. Mountain peaks cropped up in the distance, some of them already covered in snow. The sun was blazing in a corn blue sky and the air was dry and fresh as ever.

It is a beautiful day to get married, Lananell thought.

Another man with a full head of white hair and closely cropped whiskers stood under the giant oak. He wore a long white robe buckled at the waist with a leather belt. His eyes sparkled blue and gold.

"Is this the lovely bride?" he asked. "I am Elder Clasdaq." He kissed her softly on both cheeks and produced a garland of mountain flowers. He wrapped it around her wrist then Rosco's.

"I am Lananell," she whispered.

"What is your father's name child?" Elder Clasdaq asked.

"I don't know," she replied. "I never knew him."

Elder Clasdaq gave a curt nod and smile. Nella stood to her left and Kurin stood to Rosco's right.

The Elder lifted his hands in the air. "Selene, the mother of love and beauty, of sweet song and suckling babes, has blessed this union of Lananell from Linnso and Rosco, son of Connach. The elements of water and earth, the feminine forces, are receptive to those of Air and Fire, the masculine forces. Together, they culminate in the wholeness of man and woman..."

"Lananell," a voice whispered as Elder Clasdaq carried on, *"fairy lady..."*

She did not move her eyes to search for the source of the voice but stared into Rosco's face. Tears welled up within his eyes but he blinked them back.

It must be glorious to feel such emotion, she thought as she stared at her soon-to-be husband. She wished for such a talent.

I cannot feel anything except my duty. I am numb inside.

"Lananell...here..."

It was the oak tree. When Elder Clasdaq indicated they face him to pronounce a blessing, the oak was straight in her view.

"Don't fight them..." the voice said.

"And Selene takes a man and woman and binds them in commitment, duty and love, from which the fullest expression is children..."

Children, Lananell thought and hurriedly pushed the thought away.

"Children," the oak whispered. And then, *"Don't fight them..."*

"Who?" she projected the thought to the tree.

"You will know..."

"In the blessing of Selene and the elements, please join your lips in symbolic love and union."

Rosco bent down and planted a soft kiss on her lips. A rush of blood warmed her face. Perhaps she was feeling something after all.

A well-worn wagon road guided their way through tall, skinny pines and giant blue and white spruce on the way to Rosco's cottage. The smell of the needle leaves was intoxicating. Linnso had forests like this in the center of the island but she had never been there as it was uninhabited.

"It is still summer but the air is so fresh and dry. I don't sweat here at all."

"Yes, the lowlands have the liquid air as we call it up here. But the winters have blankets of snow in every direction and the sounds of the forest are muffled. You will notice how silent it is when the snow covers the ground."

Lananell had seen her share of snow. It fell thick and wet in Linnso, especially in the coastal areas where she had lived. The sea would turn black and gray and the waves would pound the shores, boats and harbors with terrifying ferocity. The wind would howl like a banshee, sometimes tearing one's feet out from under them. She was glad to be away from it.

Squirrels squeaked in high-pitched gibberish as they went by. Bright blue birds with tufts of feathers erupting from the tops of their heads cawed and encircled them. Lananell felt for the looking glass in her pocket. It was cold and smooth with a slight depression in the middle.

They rounded a corner on the path and Lananell got the first glimpse of her new home. She felt a burst of joy at seeing the humble cottage.

My new life awaits! She thought. And no fear or worry rested in her heart. The absence of those feelings was thoroughly unfamiliar.

* * * *

That night in their marriage bed, Lananell confessed. "You must know I am not a virgin. In Linnso—"

"No need, no need, my dear," Rosco said, brushing strands of curly brown hair away from her face. "We don't need to speak of the past again. It is dead and buried. You are with me now. And I will protect you. Do you believe me?"

Lananell ran her hand over his muscular chest. His arms were as thick as tree trunks. She laid her head on his chest.

"Yes," she whispered and she meant it.

He pulled her up to him and kissed her longingly on the mouth. Ever since she turned thirteen, she had been trained in the ways of bed pleasures so she put those skills to use. After considerable lovemaking using her hands, fingers and mouth, when her new husband entered her, he spent himself immediately.

The straw-filled bed felt like the bedding of a queen after nights spent on needle leaves and rolled up pallets but nevertheless, sleep would not come. Rosco fell asleep immediately. She extracted herself from his embrace and walked to the hearth room. The oak tree's words puzzled her and truth be told, gave her a bit of a fright as well. She thought of Hawk and Sillisnae and wondered if she would ever see them again. The looking glass seemed to call to her from where she had placed it by the hearth. Picking it up, it glowed with an opalescent brilliance. When she rubbed her thumb over the depression, she heard several low, whispering voices outside.

"Don't rub it unless you mean to call them," Hawk had told her.

"Them?" she had asked, puzzled.

"The dryads."

Naked as the day she was born, she opened the door to the cool, moonlit night. Goose pimples marked her flesh as she stepped barefoot onto the forest floor.

SEDUCED BY A GODDESS

H E AWOKE JUST BEFORE the first light of dawn. His sleep had been fitful and he wiped away crusties from the corners of his eyes. Every chirp of a bird or creak of a branch had jerked him from sleep into alertness. The infernal humidity still hung in the air.

"What is this place?" he asked himself more than once. "Am I in limbo in the Land of the Ancestors? Have I died?"

A squawk of a crow answered him, its large black wings beat against the lightening sky. The same sky that had welcomed the ascending wraiths.

Kryst was glad to be in the forest, though, rather than in the hot sand with the thorny trees. Pine needles were everywhere. He took a few from some branches overhead, crushed them with a rock and used his fingers to rub the juice into his wounds. He had done so every morning for at least ten days. It burned slightly but the wounds were still swollen and blue around the edges. They seemed to be healing, albeit slowly.

His tunic, surcoat and breeches lay on the sun-dappled forest floor next to him. The purse within his surcoat still held twenty Maeltip silver, but his sword had been lost in the brothel when the chanting Adept ensorcelled him. He still possessed a sharp dirk with an ivory handle that he had used to kill an injured bird. He had eaten the meat raw.

After he dressed, he tried to get his bearings by the position of the sun.

It was not the first time he had tried to find a way out. Every day he felt a tiny bit better and had set out through the dense foliage only to go in circles.

But today will be different, Kryst told himself. *Today I will exit this forest forever.*

He started out through the bushes and some branches hit his face. The dew soaked through his boots. He caught a whiff of something rancid and saw a half-eaten chipmunk covered with dirt and leaves. Kryst wrinkled his nose. The memory of the raw bird flesh brought bile into his throat. It would take a lot more hunger for him to touch the mutilated carcass.

Shifting patterns of light played across the forest floor. Strange birds with large blue bodies and black heads seemed to follow him, hopping from bough to bough, taunting him with their grating cries.

The forest was rich in scents of wet earth, pine and rotting wood. Golden mushrooms sprouted from the bases of giant firs. Squirrels watched him from aloft, some scurrying across his path. He walked slowly, every step carefully taken so as not to renew bleeding in his hip wound.

The sun rose higher and he sweat more profusely. It was hotter here than in Maeltip. He wiped the sweat from his brow and took off his surcoat.

I must be in the Knotts. Only the Knotts has heat and humidity to rival my homeland.

Every few minutes he stopped and listened for water or voices. But when the sun reached its zenith, it was not his ears that revealed a way out but his nose. He inhaled the unmistakable scent of woodsmoke and underneath that, a more subtle scent of roasting meat.

The lingering smell led him through dense foliage and over small ravines. Sap crusts formed on the pine and fir trunks, they felt knobby and smooth to the touch. Following the smell proved difficult. Sometimes he would lose it, then frantically turn his head this way and that, trying to pick it up again. Knobby tree roots reached for his feet at these times, causing him to stumble.

Once, he thought he saw one of the wraiths writhing among spruce branches but it was only the play of the light. He wondered if they had all ascended or if there were others left behind.

Finally, he reached a place where the smell was strongest. He saw the edge of the forest and a lush green meadow beyond the evergreens. His heart leapt in his chest and he sprang into a run, pushing through his fatigue and pain. Once his feet touched the soft grass and the forest was behind him, the stifling heat and humidity lifted. The day was bright, clear and breezy and in the distance, he spotted the source of the smells: A village with smoke rising from one of its chimneys. He raced toward it as fast as his feet would take him, ignoring the screaming of the wound just above his hip.

A village means a Healer or a Wise Woman. And I have good coin.

He stopped long enough to put his surcoat back on and take another glance at the haunted forest.

Where am I?

The village before him consisted of about a dozen buildings, most of them round and wooden with thatched straw roofs. A handful of people milled about.

A red-nosed farmer pulled a wagon heavily laden with carrots, onions and turnips. The man stopped in his tracks and stared at Kryst. He was burly, wearing a stained, loose brown workshirt and breeches held up by suspenders. He had curly strawberry blond whiskers that covered a typically peasant visage. Kryst took a step toward him and the farmer appeared alarmed.

"I mean you no harm, good sir." Kryst said with a smile. "I am a traveler lost—"

"I don't speak your tongue," the man said in Corvasan.

I am in Corvasa? But how?

"Could you tell me the name of this village?" Kryst asked in Corvasan. "Is there a Healer here? I am gravely wounded."

"Abomination!" a woman screamed. Off to the left, standing in front of a round, wooden building, a group of half a dozen people had formed. They pointed and stared. The woman who had screamed clutched a dirty child to her apron.

"He came from Renfala forest!" A tall man pointed. "He is cursed and will bring down the wrath of the gods upon us. Get him!"

The angry mob of peasants descended upon him, tearing at his clothes, hitting him in the face and torso, and when he fell to the ground they kicked him. All the while, yelling *fiend* and *abomination*.

"Stop! No!" he pleaded desperately. "I come in peace!"

The blows continued to rain down and he curled into a ball. "Stop! I am the Prince of Maeltip!" Someone pulled his hair, ripping it out from the roots. They kicked his lower back, shins and buttocks.

"Stop, I tell you! I am a prince!" But his cries were drowned out in the peasants' angry screams.

A foot stomped on the side of his head and the world spun around. He briefly lost consciousness and when he came to, he saw a tall, blond man in a motley robe pulling villagers off him.

"What are you doing?" the man shouted. "Leave him alone!"

Kryst felt a pair of hands grab his armpits and pull him to his feet. Now he was walking—being carried really—away from the mad throng. His vision was slightly blurred, probably because he had been hit in the eye. The tall man led him to a rectangular, two story building, fancier and sturdier than the surrounding round, wooden structures. Inside, the walls had been painted with bawdy scenes and naked women. He was led into a common room with a small fire in the hearth and hefty men sitting at long, wooden tables with large cups that could only be filled with wine or mead.

"Sit here," the man commanded. When he turned his gaze upon the other men, they got up and left without a word.

The pain in Kryst's head obliterated that of his wounds. "Where am I?" he asked.

"In Arthac," the man said. "My name is Locklin, son of Hap. I am the Healer here. You are a long way from Maeltip, brother."

"Is Arthac in Corvasa?" Kryst asked wearily. He felt steadier when he sat and his focus came back.

Locklin appeared to be in his mid-twenties with cleanly-shaven cheeks and chin and bright, blue eyes.

The atmosphere of the inn was musty and dank but Kryst was thankful to be away from the mob and to have found a Healer. A skinny, middle-aged wench with oily brown hair approached them.

"Bring some mead, Starla," Locklin instructed, "and some bread and cheese."

"Aye." She scurried off behind a curtained doorway.

"Why did they attack?" Kryst asked the Healer.

"Don't say anything." Locklin ran his hands over Kryst's face and head. "Hold still and close your eyes."

Kryst felt warmth move from Locklin's hands into the pain in his head. The pain quickly dissipated and the warmth moved downward through his neck. It was as if he had swallowed a cupful of hot liquid. The heat sought out the wounds from the thorns in his arms, legs and hip. The flesh tingled and itched as it knit together deep inside his muscles. In another minute, he felt the fatigue and lethargy leave him and sprightliness, as light and energetic as the first day of spring, filled his body. He opened his eyes when he felt no more pain and the last of the warmth left him.

"You are lucky those puncture wounds were superficial. The one above your hip bone could have killed you if just moved over an inch or two."

Kryst felt where the wound in his hip had been. There lingered a slight soreness but nothing more. He put his hands to his head and stared at Locklin, mesmerized.

"You are a miracle worker! I have heard of healings and I have had them myself, but you took all of the pain, I mean all of it. How did you do such a thing?"

Locklin waved his hand but also glanced side to side. They were alone in the room but the Healer lowered his voice. "Sometimes I have a little help."

"A little help?" Kryst asked.

Starla appeared with a platter of steaming bread, ripe cheese and some mead to wash it down. He drank greedily and tore into the warm, fresh bread. It was soft and white with some kind of seed mixed into the dough. The crust was hard and brown. He could not remember when warm bread tasted so good. The cheese was soft and ripe, the way he remembered Corvasan cheese. It was pungent and salty but the most delicious cheese he had ever tasted. The mead was thick and amber colored, flavored with cloves. He ate the entire plate within minutes.

"Might you have meat for a weary patron?" Kryst asked Starla when she returned.

Her smile revealed two long, overlapping front teeth. "Aye, we have some roast goat."

"Bring it." Goat was not his favorite but he was sure it would taste better than any goat he had before. She brought him a hindquarters portion, the skin blackened but the meat tender and juicy inside.

Locklin watched him silently while he ate. His eyes were light blue and far apart, his lips thick and fleshy. His long cloak was made of different colored swatches sewn together with embroidered runic symbols in each section. It accentuated his long blond hair which stood out more than any of his other features. Its luxurious curls and shine could rival that of a woman's.

Kryst took a silver Maeltipian coin from his purse and placed it on the table between them. "I must thank you for stepping in back there. Why did they attack me? Why did they call me fiend?"

"The villagers of Arthac are suspicious of strangers," Locklin explained. "You are a long way from Maeltip." He folded his hands in front of him where Kryst saw he wore a different gemstone on each finger. "You were shouting you were a prince. Do you have a name?"

Kryst hesitated. Should he reveal his true identity? Would it even matter, so far from home? But what of the manner in which he came to be here? How could he explain that?

"My name is Kryst, son of Olaf."

The Healer frowned. "Olaf? Do you mean King Olaf of Maeltip?"

Kryst leaned in closer. "Keep your voice down. I don't want to proclaim it, if you know what I mean. They already gave me a beating. If they think I am a prince they might get ideas about a ransom."

"You told them yourself you were a prince when they were beating you," the Healer whispered. "But do not worry, my lord. No harm will come to you under my protection." Locklin offered his hand and Kryst shook it. "By the way, what brings a prince to our small village in Corvasa?"

Locklin smiled broadly to reveal perfectly straight, white teeth.

Kryst took another gulp of mead to wash down the tender meat. If the Healer was worth his salt, he would be able to tell immediately if Kryst lied. And Kryst had never been a good liar.

Kryst studied him. He seemed friendly enough but there was something about Locklin that troubled him. He was too smug, too confident for a Healer of a small village. The man did not even blink when Kryst told him he was the Prince of Maeltip.

Locklin leaned in close. "Or more to the point, why were you in the Renfala Forest?"

"The Renfala Forest?"

Is that where I was? The thought made his stomach turn. Why am I not dead?

"Yes, you have heard of it, I trust?" Locklin asked.

Kryst nodded and took another bite of cheese. He was not ready to tell his tale to this man. Yes, the Healer had saved him from the mob and healed his wounds but there was...something. Something about his eyes. They reminded him of Titus, the man who had put him here.

"The wanderings of the living and undead from that forest will most likely cease now."

"Why?" Kryst asked.

"The dragon. Didn't you see it a fortnight ago? How could you have missed it? Anyone within ten miles would have heard that roar. He has arisen. The Renfala Forest no longer contains Renfala." Locklin chuckled.

"A dragon?" Kryst's mouth fell open for a few seconds. "But how...?"

"Someone must have freed him by killing his ghostly body," Locklin said. "Someone with a good dose of the Talent."

Kryst remembered the Knottian Healer, shook his head and changed the subject. "Can you bring me to Minosae, Locklin, son of Hap? I can pay you more silver." He glanced at the silver coin still resting between them.

"Aye. That I can, my lord." Locklin sipped from his clove-flavored mead. "I don't have another horse, just a cantankerous burrow."

Kryst was disappointed. He wanted to get to Minosae faster than a burrow's legs would take him but he agreed. "I am healed but I am still weary. Spent a fitful night."

"We sit within the village inn," Locklin said, "and brothel, although the whores are lacking. Starla is the most beautiful of them all."

"I am not interested in whores tonight. Hoping for sleep. And a bath."

He took leave of Locklin, agreeing to meet him on the morrow, and gave Starla a silver. She led him up creaking stairs to a small room with a straw mattress and coarse, gray woolen blankets to cover it. A table with a washstand and pitcher of water stood next to a narrow, floor-to-ceiling window.

"Might there be a place for a gentleman to have a bath?"

She stopped and turned her hazel eyes upon him. She would have been pretty if she had a little more meat on her bones and her hair was not so oily. Small, pert breasts were covered by a rough spun chemise. Her nose turned up at the tip and her eyes were round and wide, giving her the appearance of extreme youth.

"There are stalls in back, m'lord. I will warm the water for you. Come down after half an hour."

He sat on the pallet and looked out over the green meadow and forest beyond. The window faced north, the direction from which he had come, the Renfala Forest.

What does this all mean? He asked himself as he ran his fingers through his golden blond hair. *Why am I here? And still alive? I should have died in that forest if the legends are to be believed.*

In the stalls behind the inn, a large metal tub with steaming water lay in wait. He undressed slowly and slid his foot into scalding, soapy water. He sunk low and submerged his head. Starla appeared and gave him a stick of lilac scented soap. He vigorously scrubbed his body as the water slowly turned cloudy with dirt. The wounds on his arms and legs were slightly sore to the touch and small, reddish circles appeared where the puncture holes had been. The healed wound on his hip itched.

"Shall I wash your hair, m'lord?" Starla asked.

He eyed her up and down. Another time he would have partaken of her favors, perhaps, but his mind was too clouded and she was not even close to his standards.

"No," he replied. He lathered his hair and dunked his head underwater. By the time he finished, the water was dark gray. Thankful to be clean, he stepped out and dried himself with a giant brown towel she had left for him.

Back in the room, weariness overcame him and he lay down on the coarse pallet, with a full belly and clean body and let himself drift off. In the moments before sleep, he saw the faces of the Linnsonians,

Master Oscan and Chief Mate Angus. He wondered how they explained to his father what happened to him. Or would they place all the blame at the feet of the powdered Corvasan, Titus? What had happened to Simone? Thinking of her hurt the most.

…after all, she is full of holes…

* * * *

He awoke to a shadow standing over him. On instinct, Kryst lunged for his belt where his dirk was sheathed but the shadow darted as swiftly as a sand snake.

"You are jumpy in the morning, my prince," Locklin observed.

"Lord."

"What?"

"Address me as *lord*, not *prince*. I am not keen on everyone knowing who I am. I have no escort and am royalty in a foreign land."

"I am all the escort you'll need, my lord." Locklin smiled.

Kryst did not know how much he believed that.

The light outside was the pinkish glow of dawn. The sudden rush of reflex action had awoken him quickly. He pulled on his tunic and breeches.

"Forgive me." Kryst pulled on his boots. "I don't take kindly to being awoken by someone. Better to let me greet the morning in my own time."

When he was ready, he followed Locklin downstairs. Starla was nowhere in sight and the inn was completely deserted. Outside, the grass was covered with a sparkling sheen of dew. The air held a chill and the dawn spread its lightening fingers across a pale blue sky. It seemed he and the Healer were the only ones awake and stirring. The village was as quiet as the inn with no angry mobs of farmers and crafters to beat him to a bloody pulp.

Two mounts waited. Locklin's was a gray mare and the other was a brown burrow with vertical ears, big teeth and a mangy brown tail. Both animals had saddle bags loaded with provisions.

The Healer swung effortlessly into the saddle while Kryst tried to mount the burrow. It brayed loudly and moved away so Kryst lost his footing.

"Mother of gods!" he swore at the stubborn animal while Locklin laughed.

"Maeltipians are sailors and pirates, even the royals!"

He laughed again as Kryst felt his color rising. After three attempts, the animal relented and Kryst mounted.

"When will we reach the capital?" Kryst asked.

"We should arrive sometime on the morrow."

Kryst placed a silver coin into the Healer's hand. "Another one when we safely arrive in Minosae."

They rode through foothills covered in bright green ferns and brambles. The dew slowly evaporated as the sun climbed higher. They followed a path on which either side grew towering, ancient yews, oaks and elms. Kryst marveled at the majesty of the oaks. Yews proliferated in Maeltip but oak and elms were rare in his island nation. The path descended on a slight incline into another forest. The woods were alive with the fragrant scents of earth, pine, wet leaves and flowers. As the morning progressed, sweat soaked Kryst's tunic. The humidity was much more noticeable even though it was cooler than Maeltip. Flies danced around his head, occasionally delivering a bite. They rode in silence for a long while. Locklin's patchwork cloak fanned out over his horse's rump. Some of the sections of the cloak were embroidered with gold and silver thread in runic shapes. Many winked at Kryst when they caught the sun's light.

"What are those symbols on your cloak?" Kryst asked.

"The ancient runes of Jaanaar, a complete magical system whose methodology was lost over time. Now all we have left are the symbols."

"So this magic is something you are unfamiliar with?"

"Sadly, yes."

Kryst kicked his burrow closer. "There are no curved lines."

"No. It is the first written language of the True Tongue and it is unique in written languages because it does not use curves in its symbols. The correct use of the sounds and symbols could subdue dragons and give one the gift of flight, now they are mainly used for blocking and not by mere mortals."

"Blocking?"

Locklin changed the subject. "Tell me how you came to be in the forest? Maeltip is a long way away, my friend. It is an island country full of pirates, if I remember correctly. They have not a love of exploration on foot, I hear."

Kryst kicked his burrow to trot alongside the Healer.

"You should know the entire story," Kryst admitted. And so he told him. Everything from meeting the Linnsonians in his father's quarters to finding Arthac beyond the accursed forest. As he recounted his tale, he was shocked at the lack of Locklin's reaction. It was as if such tales of survival were commonplace for him.

"Did you say the man that freed you from the tree was Knottian?" Locklin asked after Kryst had finished.

"Yes. He had the unmistakable turquoise eyes. His complexion was between a golden and coppery tone and his hair straight and long, worn loose in the Knottian fashion."

Locklin stared ahead and did not speak for a long while. Kryst held his tongue. He did not like asking too many questions. It lessened one's position in others' eyes. Let the Healer think it made no difference to him.

The thick woods parted to reveal a meadow with a small hill in the center which did not appear natural. Kryst thought it man-made, perhaps an old dun. A very large dun. Or perhaps a burial ground. Locklin turned his horse off the path toward it. When Kryst followed, he glimpsed a ring of shiny, asymmetrical black stones about twice the size of a man at the top. They shone brilliantly when the light hit them. The grass surrounding and covering the hill was long and yellowish-green. The sky held billowy white clouds in a sea of summer blue. The day was thick and humid, nearly rivaling what he experienced in Renfala Forest.

"Where are we going?" Kryst asked.

"To the top of that hill."

"Why?"

"We must contact the spirit queen of these woods, else she will not let us pass unharmed."

Locklin's words irritated Kryst. He did not think such a thing necessary. "I'm sure she will look down upon us and smile with approval."

Locklin gave him a sharp look. "If we don't pay our respects, we may meet with bandits or other unforeseen dangers." His eyes conveyed that this was not negotiable.

Kryst's burrow made its way up the hill easily enough. When they were almost to the summit, he gazed down the way they had come and saw a canopy of green in the foliage below. Here and there the landscape was dotted with hills. Far in the distance to the north, he saw the mountains with a myriad of green, gray and brown across their summits. Soon they would be covered with something he almost never saw in Maeltip—snow.

The Healer dismounted, his blond ringlets bouncing, and beckoned Kryst with his hand. Something in Locklin's eyes made Kryst hesitate.

"The spirit queen will not be appeased unless we are both within the circle."

Kryst reluctantly kicked his burrow to Locklin's side.

"Dismount, my lord. I want to show you something." The Healer held out his hand and in the middle of his palm was a small blob of brownish-gray clay.

"A piece of clay?"

"Much more than that," Locklin replied. He unsheathed a dagger at his hip and sliced into the soft flesh of his thumb. Drops of blood welled up from the cut and dripped down onto the clay. He then spat upon it, rubbed it between his palms and placed it on the ground.

"Back away. Give it some room."

Locklin began to chant softly in a language Kryst recognized as Old Jaanaarian, also known as the True Tongue. The last time he heard such words, he was condemned to be crucified on a thorny tree.

"What are you doing?" he asked, striving to keep the alarm out of his voice.

"You'll see soon enough."

"I don't want to see. It was enchanted words of the True Tongue that sent me here, remember?"

Locklin ceased his chanting and gave Kryst an exasperated stare. "If I wanted to kill you or damn you or make you disappear, I would have done it already. This will greatly please you, Prince Kryst, I promise you. Know that I am your friend."

Minutes passed by while Locklin chanted but the clay remained unchanged.

Kryst glanced around impatiently. "Would you like me to piss on it?"

The Healer ignored him and continued. After a few more minutes, the clay began to move and separate. Spherical shapes formed and multiplied. In no time, the transforming clay was a few feet tall. The gray color lightened to yellow, at times shimmering with a golden glow, at others taking on a silver hue. The clay formed appendages which shaped themselves into arms and legs. Delicate hands and feet formed at the end of the appendages. The torso grew breasts and a waist formed as hips widened. Thin, unruly snakes sprouted from the head and separated at a rapid pace as they turned coal black. A nose grew and a jawline appeared.

As Kryst watched in fascination, what was happening did not really register in his conscious mind. He knew he was witnessing something extraordinary, but the overall magnitude of it was not grasped. The absurdity of the situation made him laugh. A spasm of light-headedness overtook him and he stumbled, barely catching himself before he fell. When he returned his gaze to the human shaped clay, he saw an extraordinarily beautiful woman.

She was nearly seven feet tall. The air around her sparkled with tiny points of bluish light. Her eyes were widely spaced and the color of the Ocean of the Sun, her hair fell to her waist in luxurious waves and was black as midnight. Her skin was pale as cream with a blossom of blush on her cheeks and chin. She wore a silvery, transparent gown that showed off her womanly curves to total perfection. Gazing on her body filled Kryst with desire at once, the better part of it against his will. When she saw him stiffen in his breeches, she smiled knowingly and slowly lay down on the grass, opening her legs provocatively.

Kryst felt he would go mad with lust. He went to her immediately, undid his breeches, lifted her shimmery gown and mounted her. She cried out in pleasure. As he pumped into her, her large firm breasts jiggled under a light sheen of sweat. It was not long before his orgasm was upon him and when he exploded within her, the last memory he had was collapsing on top of her.

When he awoke, he lay face down in the grass. He was dimly aware Locklin still chanted. The air around him was misty, yellowish, hiding the black stones from his view. It was as if the air was an opaque barrier. The sky above was overcast with dark gray clouds, the summer blue all but gone. He turned his head to the other side and there she was in all her naked glory. The sheen of sweat remained and the air continued to sparkle around her. She lightly pinched her nipple with her thumb and forefinger and Kryst felt himself stir again. She licked her lips and smiled. A faint breeze blew her black hair into her face and she laughed, the sound seeming to echo in every direction. She slowly brushed the wayward strand of hair aside with one long, thin finger. She gazed at him with her deep blue eyes but stayed silent.

"Who are you?" he asked.

She laughed softly. "I am Nominthe. And you would be?"

"I am Kryst. The Prince of Maeltip." He tried to lift himself onto his elbow, but was too fatigued.

"What do you want Kryst?" Nominthe asked, a smug smile enlivening her beautiful lips. She placed a light fingertip on his forehead and traced along the side to his temple.

"What do I want?" He was baffled. "Perhaps another go 'round in a few minutes." The orgasm was the most pleasurable experience he had ever had in his life. This strange woman's cunt fit upon his member like a vise.

"You can have that and more besides. May I ask something of you?" She transfixed him with her eyes.

They mesmerized him. He would do anything to have her again. She was the most beautiful woman he had ever seen. The desire he felt was all encompassing. He heard himself say, "Anything. I'll do anything." And he meant it. Sort of. It was as if an irresistible force occupied his mind. He wanted to help her but the urgency, the enthusiasm came from somewhere else. The knowledge of her creation was also not forgotten but it didn't seem to matter. All he wanted was to fuck her again.

"Do you recognize my name of Nominthe?" she asked him.

"A woman named Nominthe rules Ebro, the Island of Women. But no one ever goes there because the waters are treacherous, filled with mermaids and mermen, sharks, giant octopuses and kraken. So, most men agree Nominthe and her Isle of Women is a myth."

"I am no woman." She twirled a strand of black hair through her thin, white fingers.

"You are a goddess," he pronounced. He knew it even before he said it. That much was clear.

"Nominthe no longer resides on the Isle of Women. She has been stripped of her physical vehicle. And, oh, how I long for it again," she said wistfully.

"You are flesh and blood now," Kryst pointed out.

She lay back on the grass, staring up into the dark sky. "Oh, but not for long. I can only enjoy its sweetness for just a few moments on this physical plane." Her voice choked.

Kryst realized she was crying softly. Her breasts heaved as she sucked in air to release gentle sobs. It was too much. He made to mount her again but she put her hand to his chest.

"You must swear to find my heart. Swear it! And not only shall you have the lion's share of bed pleasures but also immense power. More power than you have ever dreamed of, *if* you find my heart and return it to me. Swear it."

"I swear," Kryst said, blinded by lust once more. All he wanted was to be inside of her again. Nothing else mattered. He had questions. Oh, did he have questions. But they could wait.

As he approached her with his cock hard, she deftly turned over and presented her full bottom. When he entered her from behind it was even more pleasurable than before. He thrust once, twice, thrice. She turned to look at him. He watched as her blue eyes turned to blood red and her teeth elongated into points. She laughed then, a high, grating cackle. That was all it took and his seed exploded from him, emptying all his strength. He shuddered and his spirit left his body and ascended into the sky. When he looked down, he saw himself collapsed on the ground alone. Nominthe was gone. Air rushed around him as he slammed back into his body. This time he did not lose consciousness but felt as if he had been wounded in battle. Delirious, he looked around and saw the mist had dissipated. Locklin walked toward him so Kryst rolled over and pulled up his breeches. He wondered if Locklin had watched them fuck. The Healer pulled him to his feet without a word and led him back to his burrow.

They descended the hill and rode in silence. Kryst was glad for it because his mind was a fog. All he could think about was his encounter with Nominthe. They rode on and another hour passed before Kryst felt coherent enough to speak.

"What happened back there?"

Locklin snickered. "Seems like you fucked a goddess."

Heat flooded Kryst's cheeks. "What did she mean by 'find her heart'?"

"She will give you clues, Kryst, son of Olaf. But now you are bound to the contract and must attempt to fulfill your oaths to the best of your ability. You must search for the heart of Nominthe until you find it."

"And if I do not find it?"

"Then you will die searching," the Healer answered matter-of-factly.

"And if I cease the search before I die?"

Locklin turned his gaze upon him. "Then she will kill you, Prince Kryst. Make no mistake. A pact with a goddess is not a matter to take lightly. If you forget your oath, she will hunt you down and kill you."

Anger rose within Kryst. The gods-be-damned Healer planned the entire episode. He lured him to the circle and conjured up the abomination. But why? To what purpose?

"You tricked me, evil druid! You tricked me into this. And that...woman. She tricked me with her charms and put a spell of lust upon me. How can a man resist such as that one? Tell me! And how am I to find this heart of hers?"

"No need to shout, Kryst, son of Olaf. Like I said she will give you clues. And you should feel privileged she chose you. She instructed me to seek you out in the village and aid you in any way. She was expecting your arrival. She chose *you*. A goddess. So you should not be complaining, but rejoicing."

Kryst was at a loss for words and then he suddenly realized the clothes he wore had transformed into the finest garments, the raiment of a King at court. When he touched his purse, it was inexplicably filled to bursting with coin.

A POISONED KISS

NOCTUS SERN'S LONG WHITE BEARD still possessed strands of dark brown. He had a habit of throwing it over his shoulder whenever he examined manuscripts. He pointed, directing Sillisnae's attention to a diagram of seven runes.

"This is called the Seed of Life. You use it to create golems but also to block the Talent."

"Block the Talent?"

"Yes. The Blocking Spell is the most powerful weapon used against Adepts by other Adepts," Noctus Sern explained. "But ages ago, it was used by the corrupted Jaanaarians to block everyone with whom they came into contact."

The room in which they studied was usually reserved for meetings of the Council of Twelve and private tutoring sessions. Sillisnae had been there many times before with Lord Korodale. Giant windows opened to a balcony that overlooked the palace gardens. Several books lay strewn across a massive oaken table in the center of the room. The rest of the walls were lined with books dealing with the Black Arts, therefore they were housed outside of the Palace library. Noctus Sern had been tutoring her all day. She wanted to linger forever learning about spells and symbols but knew what fate awaited her later. That night, King Emeril would make her his mistress even though he would marry Lady Rubia in a week's time.

"Block everyone? Are you stating that at one time, everyone had the Talent?"

Suddenly, Adept Sern appeared nervous. His hazel eyes darted this way and that as if someone watched them.

"At…one…time. Yes." He went to the windows and looked out, then peeked around the curtains, and finally went to the heavy wooden door, opened it and peered out into the hallway. Satisfied, he returned to the table, his expression still troubled but less so. He put both hands on her shoulders. "Sillisnae, one day I'll tell you about all of that. But today is not the time."

"Are you all right, Adept Sern?"

He smiled sympathetically, his wrinkled cheeks flushed. "Of course, my child. Don't you worry about an old man. An Adept of the Crystal Palace at that. Shall we continue discussing the Blocking Spell and its methodology? Its history can wait."

"Must I chant in the True Tongue?" she asked the old Adept.

"You may but it's not necessary. You can form a block with thought alone if your concentration is powerful enough. You must imagine it with all your senses, not exclusively sight. Place the seed of life with your thought form over the abdomen of the Adept you want to block. The magic exists in the breath and words, so once the block is mentally put over the diaphragm, the Adept can no longer call upon his Talent. Then you must lock it down in the groin area."

"Adept Sern, you say the magic exists in the breath in words. Would a block prevent an Adept from speaking?"

"Oh no." Adept Sern chuckled. "It is only the magic that is blocked, not the voice."

Sillisnae liked Noctus Sern much better than Lord Korodale. His manner was calm and sometimes even sweet, not stern and demanding like that of the former *Daimon Direttore*. She hoped beyond hope he did not belong to Sii Dei.

"Creating a Talent Block is one of the most complex spells of a magus. It takes many, many years to master it," he explained.

Noctus Sern had thankfully asked her precious few questions about Lord Korodale and the Fire Globe. He was a man of few words but when he did speak, he always said something profound.

"I will practice every day," she assured him. "Adept Sern, how did you come to the Crystal Palace?"

He gave a crooked smile and sat down in a foreign-made, gilded chair, booty from some far away land. "I hail from Aranhoe on the southern coast," he told her. "As an orphan roaming the streets, I performed magic tricks for the populace. At eleven I told fortunes just by looking at someone and then graduated to making healing charms. At twelve, I was levitating in the streets to cheering onlookers. On my thirteenth birthday, soldiers from Minosae arrived in Aranhoe searching for me. Too much talk among the city dwellers, you know. Somehow, word had reached the Council of Twelve that a boy in

Aranhoe could fly without training. They scooped me up and hauled me off to the Crystal Palace. Not that I minded or cared. To have a roof over my head, warm clothes on my back, delicious meals in my belly, seemed like a dream to a young boy who had lived on the streets ever since age five. My mother died from a fever, sadly," he said. "I never knew my father."

Sillisnae had heard his mother was a prostitute and died from a disease of the female parts. She was sure his mother would have been proud of her son to see him now, an Adept on the Council of Twelve and probably the next *Daimon Direttore*.

"Do you have any Adepts among your family or ancestors?" Sillisnae asked.

"I have an uncle who is a Healer in a small village outside of Aranhoe." His voice was distant.

"Why didn't you live with him when your mother passed to the Land of the Ancestors?" Perhaps she was prying too much but she was genuinely curious about the old man.

"He was involved with nefarious practices." The white eyebrows above his hazel eyes knotted together. "It was an impossibility."

She didn't press the issue but it raised some concerns. What possible nefarious practices could a Healer be up to?

Instead she asked, "Do you think you'll be made the *Daimon Direttore*?"

Noctus sighed. "I hope not but I fear I will be."

Crow's feet dug deep into the flesh around his eyes. Sillsinae thought he appeared too fatigued to accept any responsibilities of the

Daimon Direttore. He smelled of ancient books, mothballs and the faintest whiff of underlying sickness, so small it was mostly unnoticeable. She made a mental note to mention his health at another time.

"Will you hand me those manuscripts with the Old Jaanaarian?" he asked.

Sillisnae blew dust off the papers and handed them over. How long had it been since anyone set eyes upon them?

"The True Tongue is a most elegant language," he explained. "It is the language of the gods, the original word from which all things were created."

"Mmm-hmm." Sillisnae had heard this before and learned it well. Lord Korodale had been very strict in his tutoring of the True Tongue. He also put an inordinate amount of importance on the extinct language.

Noctus Sern rubbed his leathery, ancient hand over the hieroglyphs, took out a magnifying glass and read aloud. While he was occupied, Sillisnae lightly stepped toward a wooden cabinet laden with potions, tinctures, powders and oils. Lord Korodale had taught her the various uses for all of them. Noctus Sern was not watching when she slipped two tin canisters into her skirts.

A loud, fast rapping at the door made them jump.

"I am here to escort the Adept's Apprentice to the handmaidens," the voice behind the door announced.

"Enter." Adept Sern glanced at Sillisnae.

Sweat broke out on her forehead and her stomach churned. She thought she saw the faintest hint of pity in the Adept's eyes.

He knows, she thought. The entire palace probably knew. But it did not matter.

The guard led her to a special vanity room in the east wing where handmaidens prepared her. A bath was drawn and she stepped into the steaming water. The servants scrubbed her skin with a hard bristled brush. A plump, red-headed and freckled handmaiden named Gella washed her hair with a fragrant lavender soap, digging her fingertips into Sillisnae's scalp. The massage soothed her. When they finished, Gella combed out her hair while another handmaiden trimmed her nails and rubbed a rich, jasmine-scented cream into her skin. While they waited for her hair to dry, they dressed her in rose satin skirts and cream-colored chemise, bordered with lace from Maeltip. She slipped a gem-encrusted, light-green bodice over her head. The handmaidens pulled the strings and Sillisnae sucked in a breath as her breasts were shoved upward. When her hair was dry, it was curled into long ringlets and held in place by jeweled pins.

"You are so beautiful, Apprentice Sillisnae," Gella remarked as she applied black makeup to Sillisnae's eyes. She smelled of scented powder, her fat hands working deftly like a great artisan.

"Why are you crying, dear girl? Tonight, you become the King's mistress and probably get with child. You will be near to a queen's status once that happens."

Gella's words only released the floodgate of tears Sillisnae held back. She buried her face in her hands, ruining the freshly applied makeup. How could Hawk have sent her back here? She knew this was going to happen. There was no denying a king.

Sillisnae took a few deep breaths to calm herself.

Stop this! You are being ridiculous.

There was no need to cry. Out of thousands, perhaps millions of people, she was a commoner who possessed the Talent. She was an Adept. One in thousands could claim such a distinction. She would not act the fool and lament her situation. What must be done would be done.

"I'm sorry," she whispered to Gella as she wiped the makeup from her face.

"No need, no need, my dear girl," Gella said but she did not speak again.

The sun had just set when the guards summoned her. She remembered the last time she had walked into the same room of the King's apartments not a fortnight past. She had been so excited to become his mistress. Now it was the last thing she wanted. It was funny how a person's feelings could change so drastically in such a small amount of time.

The room possessed the same rich tapestries on the walls, the same wooden paneling reaching halfway up to the ceiling, the same rugs with golden tassels imported from Maeltip. But she was not the same. She was an entirely different person than she had been the last time she entered this room.

She sat at the table and the guard, who was a tall, meaty man, brought a silver platter with two crystal cups and a golden pitcher filled with warm, brown liquid. He slowly poured her a glass, his hands as big as bear claws.

"This is brandy."

Sillisnae did not recognize him. She wanted to speak, anything to calm her butterflies but before she could, the guard turned and exited without another word.

She took a small sip. The sweetness delighted her tongue but burned her throat when she swallowed.

A creak alerted her to the gold-trimmed door on the other side the room. Her breath caught. King Emeril entered, dressed in a long, light blue tunic with a bronze medallion belt. Soft, black leather boots adorned his feet. When he saw her, he smiled broadly, showing his perfect white teeth. Without speaking, he poured the brandy into a crystal goblet and drank, his eyes never leaving her. After he emptied the cup, he poured another for both of them.

The light blue tunic he wore accentuated his blue eyes that now rested on her ample cleavage. "You are the most beautiful woman in Corvasa." The King lifted his eyes to meet hers. "Tonight I will make you mine and hopefully sire a son."

Sillisnae conjured a smile. "Yes, Your Majesty."

The King took her hand, helping her stand. "Shall we?"

He led her through the gold-trimmed door into his bedchamber. A massive canopied bed graced the center of the room like a prophetic symbol of her future. Brown velvet drapes tied with golden satin ribbons hung from the bed posts. The sheets were also gold satin and the bed spread was wine-red velvet decorated with gold embroidery in the shape of leaves. Heavy, yellow damask curtains with images of griffins, dragons and oak leaves hung over the wall of windows that faced the gardens.

Beyond that is a balcony, Sillisnae thought.

"The handmaidens gave me an aphrodisiac that will prolong the act of love." From the folds of her skirts, she retrieved a tiny tin canister. Inside was a gloss that she applied to her lips. The King did not reply but cupped her face and kissed her hungrily. He tasted of brandy and she pretended to enjoy it, returning his kiss like she thought someone in love would.

"Mmmm," he said pulling back to look into her eyes. "It tastes of lemons."

"Yes," Sillisnae whispered, pressing her lips to his again. He shoved his tongue into her mouth even more forcefully than he did in the south atrium. He frantically loosened the laces of her bodice and her breasts spilled out. His eyes glassed over in lust as he stared at them.

"Ahhh…" he said in a trance and lowered his mouth to her left nipple hungrily.

"Oh!" she moaned. He bit down playfully then kissed her softly, his kisses growing ever fainter when she felt him go limp in her arms. She let him fall onto the bed, his breath coming in short, hurried gasps. She took off his boots, unlaced his breeches and pulled them off. His member was still stiff underneath his white underclothes. She removed those as well, trying not to look at his sex but her eyes wandered there anyway. Resting against a tuft of curly dark-brown pubic hair was a veiny shaft. Curiosity enticed her finger to reach out. She pulled back quickly, surprised at the hardness of it. She positioned herself behind the King with her hands beneath his armpits and pulled. By the gods, he was heavy! But she managed to move his body completely onto the bed and covered his nakedness with the bedspread.

With the amount of drug she had given him, he would sleep until noon of the morrow. She had taken the antidote while with the handmaidens to counteract any effects of the sleeping potion. Sillisnae did not feel the least bit sleepy and that meant the antidote had worked.

The balcony outside the King's bedchamber looked out onto the immaculate Palace gardens, just like her own. Sillisnae slipped through the yellow damask curtains and into the cool, moonlit night. A slight breeze caressed her face, blowing strands of hair into her eyes. It was an easy jump over the stone ledge and onto the ground below. Underneath a hedge of boxwood, she had hidden her satchel, but a throng of women now stood nearby, talking quietly among themselves. She crouched behind another hedge as they slowly made their way back toward the palace.

"I have commissioned a gown…"

"A distant cousin of…

"Lady Rubia is a cantankerous character…"

They were discussing the upcoming wedding of King Emeril to Lady Rubia. Sillisnae allowed herself to smile, but then it faded. The King's marriage didn't matter now. Minosae would be far behind her in a short time. The Palace Garden was lit by torches and moonlight but she moved deftly in the shadows to her hiding place. She pulled a plain woolen cloak with a hood from the satchel and fastened it around her shoulders. It would hide her elaborate finery from prying eyes. The night was calm and the stars twinkled mischievously. Remaining in the shadows, she ran toward a small gate embedded within the palace wall near the north entrance. It was ideal because it was very old, hidden by thick green vines and did not possess a latch. She discovered it years ago when she played in the garden with the younger Adept's apprentices. The swinging gate was held in place by the thick foliage, which she would have to remove to get out.

Where the moonlight fell across the yard, she crouched low and walked quickly. If, perchance, any member of the court were gazing at the garden in the moonlight, they would see a sinister, hooded figure and perhaps raise the alarm.

Don't think about that, she told herself. *It will only slow you down.*

When she got close, her heart sank when she saw three guards loitering near her secret gate. One, a tall skinny man, smoked a pipe while two shorter guards talked in low tones.

Closing her eyes, she pursed her lips and threw out a whistle about thirty yards to her left.

"Who goes there?" the skinny guard shouted, hurriedly extinguishing his pipe as his companions drew their swords.

Sillisnae threw out another sound, this one more ominous and threatening.

"Show yourself! Or we will come get you!"

Sillisnae threw the voice of a pain-filled scream.

The guards ran in the direction of the sound. Seeing her chance, she walked quickly, keeping her head down. The vine was thick and encircled each iron bar of the old gate. She pulled but it only gave a few inches. Taking a dirk from her satchel, she cut the vine frantically, all the while keeping watch for the guards. The vine was fibrous but she cut through the thickest strands and yanked it with all her might. It budged just enough for her to slip through.

At this time of night, the taverns and brothels were beginning their celebrations of vice. Sillisnae kept the hood of her cloak drawn over her face and made certain not to make eye contact with the revelers. The north gate was about a twenty minute walk from the palace.

A tavern door flew open to her right and two drunk miscreants were hurled forth into the street by another tall, muscular patron. The two men fell into a puddle only a few feet in front of her. Mud splattered all over her cloak.

"Aye, regard the pretty one!" One of the drunks leered at her, his dark, matted hair stuck to his muddy face. Long, yellow teeth, some rotting, protruded from his thin, crusty lips and his jerkin was threadbare with holes. His companion, a man dressed in a long, flowing robe like the style of those from Maeltip, stood up quickly, cursing in a foreign language and trying in vain to remove the mud from his clothes.

Sillisnae stepped to the side but the dark-haired, rotted-toothed man grabbed her ankle.

"The pretty one does not leave! Oh no. The girly-girl from the Palace stays with me." The man yanked her leg and she fell down, splashing into the mud, piss and horseshit. His hands groped at her legs.

"Get off me!" She kicked her legs and her foot struck the side of his head with a heavy thud. He ceased grabbing for her and seeing her opportunity, she stood but several onlookers had gathered around them. They were Minosae's poor, living near the city gates.

"You are not in the Crystal Palace anymore, missy!" an old, wrinkled woman screamed. She reached out and pulled Sillisnae's hair.

"Ow! Stop it!" She remembered the jewels the handmaidens had pinned into her auburn hair. In addition, her cloak had opened in the scuffle, revealing her elaborate silk and lace gown. The throng closed in around her, grabbing and pulling, beating and shouting. She fought back in a panic, trying to shield blows and discover a way out of the throng. A fist slammed into her temple, causing her to fall once more into the mud. Tiny lights danced in front of her eyes. Feet stomped on her torso. If she did not do something soon, the mob would seriously injure or even kill her.

A bright explosion of flame flew from her hands and slammed into two women and a man who were stomping her. They fell back, screaming and twisting, their bodies engulfed in flames. The rest of the mob immediately retreated, shouting and gaping in awe. She pulled the hood over her face and ran.

When she approached the gate, she casually walked through, half expecting a guard to call out to her. It was not a crime to leave the city late at night and usually citizens did so without any hassle. But Sillisnae was now a rebel, an outlaw who had drugged the King and if anyone tried to stop her, she had a surprise for them.

She passed through the gate and into the night without incident. More drunken revelers stumbled past but gave her no notice. A few other citizens meandered about but within half an hour of brisk walking, Sillisnae entered the surrounding forest, leaving the sight of the capital behind her. Putting the most distance between her and Minosae was her first goal. Once the King awoke, he would send out a search party. After that, it was up to her magic to evade detection.

The moonlight fell in bluish streams from the treetops, providing soft light to guide her. Tall, shadowed pines stretched like arrows into the sky. Patches of twinkling stars and the full moon peeked through breaks in the trees. Occasionally, the glow of animal eyes winked into existence from the undergrowth. The crisp night air smelled of earthy fungus and tree sap.

Her brisk pace caused a thin film of sweat to develop. The road steadily climbed uphill and steepened the farther north she went. It was called the Utina Road because it went north into the Utild Mountain Range, loosely following the Utina River, deviating west to go around the Renfala Forest. Now that the Renfala Forest no longer held its dragon, she thought of passing through but had not made up her mind. The idea of being alone in that forest was daunting even if its haunted status had been destroyed.

The night was eerily silent, the only sound a slight breeze passing through the trees. As she walked, her footfalls were muffled by the dirt road. She watched the moon travel across the sky as she gained altitude. Once she crested a hill, affording her a moonlit view of the city. The central spire of the Crystal Palace stabbed into the sky, a pink crystal monument to the ancient Corvasans.

When the moon set, the eastern horizon turned shades of coral, lavender and light blue. If the map she carried was correct, the road would take her past several hamlets before she arrived at the village of Arthac near the Renfala Forest before the Utina Road turned west.

The tall pines and a few birch created a canopy overhead with tiny drops of dew clinging to their needles. The sun had been above the horizon for about an hour when she heard the whinny of a horse and muffled conversation ahead. The road dipped down over a hill so she could not see the source of the sounds. She quickly retreated off the path into the thick foliage, hid behind a large trunk and waited.

"At least they are not coming from Minosae," she whispered to herself as some form of consolation.

Two men—one riding a large gray mare and the other a burrow—rode their mounts up the road at a fast walk. They were in deep conversation. The man riding the horse had the strangest appearance. His hair was blond, thick and perfectly coiffed, rivaling any hairdo of the many highborn ladies at court. He wore it loose over his shoulders and halfway down his back. The man on the burrow was also blond, of average height and possessed a closely cropped beard. He appeared to be about her age, but he wore finery Sillisnae had only seen upon King Emeril during elaborate ceremonies and celebrations.

The man with the long blond curls suddenly raised a hand for them to halt.

"What is it?" the man on the burrow asked. He had a foreign accent.

The man on the horse did not answer but gazed around suspiciously. Sillisnae stared. There was something very unusual about him. After a few seconds, she realized what she saw was a violet glow, the glow of an Adept. Probably a Healer from some village in the area, she tried to reassure herself. Crouching down even farther, she reached for the dragon claw.

It was gone.

What happened? Her mind screamed.

It was the scuffle. I lost it in the mob.

"Please show yourself whoever you are," the Adept commanded.

"What?" the other man asked, alarmed. "Is someone out there? Who do you see?"

The strange, metallic taste of panic rose up into her mouth.

The Adept dismounted and walked toward her.

"Hello?" he whispered. "I know you are behind that tree. Don't worry, we mean you no harm."

Sillisnae took a breath and stepped out from behind the tree. The man smiled gently and offered his hand. The gesture put her a little more at ease.

"I am Locklin, son of Hap, the Healer of the village of Arthac," he said. "And what is your name, miss?"

Sillisnae licked her lips. "Mallory." It was her middle name.

The foreign man appeared behind Locklin, son of Hap. He was dressed in such elaborate finery Sillisnae thought he must be royalty. A crease furrowed his brow. He regarded her with an expression of recognition but she could not remember ever meeting him. There was also something else underlying the recognition, a look which baffled her, an expression of hatred.

High overhead a crow cawed.

"Ah, Kryst, come say hello to Mallory." Locklin waved his hands in an elaborate gesture. "May I present Kryst, Prince of Maeltip, son of King Olaf. What is a beautiful young lady doing out here at the crack of dawn?"

"You are a prince." Sillisnae curtsied. That explained his fine dress. But why was the Prince of Maeltip traveling on a burrow with a lowly village Healer and not a proper escort?

The Prince of Maeltip stared at her strangely. "You are an Adept," he remarked in his drawling accent.

Sillisnae did not know what to say. How could he see it?

"Come with us, dear girl." Locklin's voice was soothing. "We have been riding all night and desire to satisfy our appetites. We have bread, cheese and apples."

The prince's eyes made her hesitate. It was as if there were two people looking out of them instead of one. But that was ridiculous, she was just being paranoid. These men had no idea who she was or what she had done.

"Why are you traveling to Minosae?" she asked.

"Our good prince needs an escort to return to Maeltip."

"Why not go to Aranhoe, then?" Sillisnae glanced between the two of them.

"I have family in Minosae," Kryst replied.

Of course! He must be kin of King Emeril if he is the prince of Maeltip.

Suddenly, she felt the pressing need to be gone, away from them, back on her way north.

"Come, and partake of nourishment," Locklin insisted. "We are very hungry and in need of pleasant company. As you can see, we are not bandits. I am the Healer of Arthac and can do no harm to another person. Come along my dear."

"I'm grateful for your hospitality, your Highness, Healer." She curtsied once more. "But I must be on my way." She slid past them toward the road. Her stomach grumbled in protest. Truth be told, she was hungry. Famished even. In her haste to pack, she had forgotten to bring any food. She glanced over her shoulder, contemplating accepting their offer. What could it hurt to break some bread for just a few minutes with harmless strangers? Then she could be on her way with a full belly and renewed strength for the journey. No need to gather nuts and berries, or hunt or fish.

At the edge of the road, she felt a heaviness in her feet, as if she was walking through thick mud. Her body became difficult to control. She realized in horror the Adept was trying to spellbind her. With extraordinary effort she turned to face him but to her surprise it was not the Healer but the prince who had his hand out, the fingertips pointed in her direction. She reached for the dragon claw and cursed, remembering it had been lost in her tussle with the drunks. She tried to summon her own magic to counteract his attack but her arms were heavy and numb.

"Wha…" she opened her mouth but her vocal chords immediately froze.

He is blocking me, she realized. Oh the cruel irony! Her legs went limp and the soft forest floor rushed to meet her.

SHADES OF A DIFFERENT TRIBE

"LANANELL, WE HAVE ANOTHER with that crazy sickness," Rosco told her in a whisper.

Shock ran through her. *Another? So soon?* "Bring him in, my husband."

Rosco led the older man by the hand into a makeshift room where Lananell now received patients. The pungent smells reminded her of Sheena's yurt before it was destroyed. The denizens of Martine had the foresight to salvage all her herbs, potions and salves. Lananell had taken on her new role as apothecary and healer with a minimum of fuss. The villagers were happy to have someone of the Talent back within their midst.

She and Rosco lived in a cottage made of wattle and daub. It was roomier than Lananell expected, including a hearth room, bedroom and another room where Rosco kept tools, farm equipment, weapons, projects and anything else that contributed to the daily life of a small farmer. While he had been away, Kurin and Nella had taken care of his sheep and pigs and tended the garden.

"I built this house myself after my parents died," he had told her on their wedding day.

"When did they die?"

"A dozen or so years ago. Both came down with the consumption disease. It hits mountain people the hardest. Their dun went to Kurin and his wife."

Rosco sat the sick man in front of her on a small pallet she had constructed. He was about fifty or so, short and skinny, with thinning salt and pepper hair. His cheeks and nose were bright red and his blue eyes bulged under an unbroken line of bushy white eyebrows. His breath came in short bursts and he had the smell of sickness about him. She wondered if Rosco could smell it or if that particular talent was reserved for Healers.

"What is his name?" she asked Rosco.

"Redrick, son of Dwayne. He is a sheepherder, like the young boy here yesterday."

"I am going to touch you," Lananell told Redrick. "Don't be afraid." When she reached to touch his face, he flinched back, whimpering.

"I'm not going to hurt you."

Redrick shook his head forcefully.

"Can you tell me what happened?"

The sheepherder licked his cracked lips and took a deep breath. "I was with my flock, beyond the town just east of Cryer's Hill. The dogs barked like they never have before..."

His words trailed off into silence and she patted him on the leg. It had been the same with the boy she treated yesterday. He had been in shock, so scared as to barely talk. Lananell had soothed him with her voice and administered a potion of nightshade and belladonna. The boy talked afterward but what he told her was so fantastic, she was sure the lad had an overactive imagination. Now this old sheepherder showed up with the same symptoms. And he was coming from the same general area as the boy, the foothills in the east, those that bordered the Utild mountain range which ran northeast for hundreds of leagues.

The Utild Mountains were said to have been formed when the gods fought their war of manifestation. The gods split into male and female halves and fell into the North Sea and the Gulf of Jaanaar. The split was so devastating the earth heaved forth and giant waves, taller than any mountain, had crashed into Perthia, forever altering the landscape. The Utild Mountains sprang up in a hail of fire and rock, the summits so steep and rocky that only the bravest of souls would attempt to pass them. The summits never knew a windless day or night. Oshii, the wind god, fiercely blew his sylphs over the craggy heights. It was said that if one did not die from the bone-chilling cold, then one would certainly perish by being blown off the side of the mountain. All explorers would seek the blessings of the druids, invoking the favor of Oshii and they would also be given a talisman to placate the sylphs.

Given these stories which Rosco related to her, Lananell found it hard to believe what the boy had told her.

Redrick's breathing slowed and his eye and face muscles relaxed. Good, the potion was working. She resumed her questions. "Redrick, did you see Osseks?"

The man shook his head. "I've never seen an Ossek, so I don't know who or what they were. But there were other...things with them. They were wild. *Wild!*"

"How do you mean?" Lananell shot a glance at Rosco.

Redrick swallowed and folded his dirty hands in his lap. "There was about a dozen of 'em. Men and women, both. They were dressed in fur and animal skins. Even their boots were made of fur—"

"Tell it from the beginning, Redrick," Lananell interrupted.

Redrick nodded his head, his bulging blue eyes trusting like a child's. "My dogs started barking and would not stop even when I called them. More often than not, that means a predator so I ran as fast as the old legs would take me, armed with my ax and bow. I would strike it down, whatever it was. I nocked an arrow, and then I would strike it down with my ax. The dogs were on the edge of dense woods. It was twilight and hard to see. I heard soft chanting in a foreign language. When I got close enough, I spied a few people gathered around a small fire. Some were dancing. Off to the side, I saw the carcass of some gutted animal. Some of the people were eating what could only be the flesh of that fresh kill. I took a few more steps to get a better look and I realized the carcass was no animal. It was a man still dressed in furs. His chest and belly were open and entrails were spilling out. Those people by the fire, his comrades were *eating him!*" Redrick paused and gazed at his folded hands. He swallowed and looked up.

"What happened next?" Rosco prodded.

"They stopped chanting but continued to dance. I stepped on a branch that made a loud crack. Those closest saw me through the trees. In the split second it took for them to raise the alarm, I glimpsed shades behind them.

"Shades?" Lananell asked.

"The spirits of the dead," Rosco clarified. "They have more substance than ghosts, their flesh is between this world and the next. They even eat and can sometimes move objects."

"A very distinct shade floated just above and behind a few of them. I saw a female shade, a young girl behind a man near my age and I saw a burly, bearded male shade behind a pregnant woman. My eyes took this all in within seconds. I was so scared, I froze. Then a shade behind a woman sitting by the fire opened its mouth. What came out was the most inhuman, accursed sound I have ever heard. I thought Labraid would take me then. The shade's mouth grew large, taking up its entire face. I called my dogs and fled for my life. I remember thinking they would kill some of my herd and eat them but at that point, I didn't care."

Redrick's eyes teared up but he wiped the tears away and spat. "Labraid and Romulus take those damned to the underworld unless they have unleashed the underworld upon us!"

The boy had related a similar tale.

Lananell gave Redrick a potion for his nerves and sent him on his way.

"Have you ever heard of something like that in Martine?" she asked Rosco.

"Never."

"Are those people Osseks?"

"Couldn't say. I've never seen one. They usually raid in the south. The mountain passes are too treacherous to cross around here. I don't know why they would be here."

Lananell could not venture a guess either. No matter where she went, ill luck seemed to follow. She was very contented living in the small mountain village. The villagers were curious about her and asked thousands of questions. She had obliged them politely, wanting desperately that they like her. When some villagers asked about Sheena, Rosco told them she betrayed the Sun King.

"Where is she now?" an old man with a flat face and bulbous nose had inquired.

"I don't know." Rosco was clearly uncomfortable discussing it.

In the end, they had accepted her and been welcoming. In addition to the kindness of the villagers, something else surprised her: her love for her husband. At first, she thought it due to his kindness but also because he did not beat her and would ask her advice about trivial matters. He would even ask her permission to go drinking in the tavern at night. But the longer she was with him, she came to realize their rapport was effortless and his laughter was contagious. He would do odd things, like run his fingers through her hair and tell her silly tales from local folklore. He would scoop her up in his arms and whirl her around. She was excited to greet him in the morning. She remembered her women friends in Linnso and how she loved them. Her love for Rosco was like that but she also loved him in several other ways. Loving a man was a new feeling. And when they made love she actually enjoyed it.

The townsfolk had slowly trickled in to partake of her vast healing and herbal-lore knowledge. She would venture into the wood, searching for roots and plants to begin her garden. Certain times of day were most beneficial for discovering the magic of plants and those times were just before and after sunrise and sunset. Once she walked north through the dense forest and happened upon bushes and shoots that appeared extraordinary. The fading light of the dying sun cast red and pink rays through the trees, dappling everything in a warm glow.

One day, she sat down under a giant fir with a few mushrooms for company and stared into the five pointed leaves of a bush with purple berries.

...beautiful lady...

"What?" Lananell asked, startled. No one was near but she was certain she had heard a voice. The bush she stared at seemed to grow a face with a distinct mouth created by darker leaves, holes in the bramble for eyes and a prominent branch as a nose. How could she have not noticed before? The face was unmistakable.

...my berries numb pain...

The face spoke without moving its mouth. She heard the voice in her mind.

...please take...

The berries were large, as big as her thumbnail and dark purple. They turned her hand a bright pinkish red. She brought some home and ground them into a paste with mortar and pestle. The next patient who came to her complaining of pain was an old miller with a headache. He ate the paste in front of her.

"Tastes like a fruit I had down south, once," he told her. The next day he returned to inform her the headache had ceased.

After that, many plants and trees revealed their secrets to her. There were lodgepole and ponderosa pines, giant firs and blue and white spruce. Near the river and streams there were cattail, bulrush, waterweed, sage, juniper, and aspen. The nature spirits whispered in her ears and even, on occasion, materialized. They could be small and green or very tall and whitish gray with long, thin fingers and branches and leaves growing from the tops of their heads. Lananell put their advice to practical use and experimented with the several different leaves and needles, nuts and berries. The dryads of the trees also showed themselves and she did not even need the looking glass Hawk had given her. It occurred to her that maybe they could give her information not related to the properties of the local flora.

"Are you familiar with the people who eat their own?" she asked a small flower fairy of the goldenrod the day after treating Redrick.

"Spirits that are bound are resentful," the light-green spirit answered in a tiny voice.

It was not really an answer to her question or perhaps it was a cryptic answer. She tried again. "Do any humans roam these woods that are followed by the shades of the dead?"

The tiny fairy giggled then disappointingly disappeared into the tiny, yellow flowers.

Another voice spoke. "These humans you speak of, they flee the creeping dryness of their land."

She did not see any spirit. "Who are you?"

"Your back is pressed against me."

She pushed herself away from the trunk but still did not see its spirit.

"The trees are dying far in the east. We know when our brothers perish," the deep, masculine voice told her.

"But why?"

"Heat is spreading throughout the world in strange ways."

She instantly thought of Sillisnae. Did she reach Minosae and return the Fire Globe?

"Why?" Lananell asked again but the tree fell silent.

That night, she and Rosco ate a dinner of cheese and vegetables from the garden and night fell like a blue velvet curtain with a glowing orb on the eastern horizon. Lananell lay next to Rosco on their bed. His breathing came in long-winded snores. She envied his ability to fall asleep immediately and he never woke during the night whereas the slightest sound would pull her from her dreams, which were nightmares more often than not. She could not escape the memories of Linnso: the beatings, rapes and general humiliations that awaited all women of that island.

Sometimes, her own screams would awaken her. But never Rosco. He slept as soundly as a baby, the rhythm of his snores uninterrupted.

A soft evening breeze blew the brown wool curtain back and forth. She slid silently from the covers and donned a worn yellow tunic with a fur-lined woolen cloak. The wooden door squeaked loudly when she opened it but Rosco did not awaken. The moonlit night swallowed her. The forest was bathed in an ethereal, bluish light. Somewhere in the east a wolf howled and she headed in that direction. An unfamiliar path opened up before her. Her footsteps fell on the soft forest floor.

A low hum grew steadily louder until she understood it was the whisperings of the nature spirits. Their cacophony was such that it was difficult to make out actual words but she intuited they urged her onward. She felt at her hip for the dirk. It was not until half an hour later when she realized she had forgotten the looking glass.

"By the gods!" she swore. If and when she came upon the strange people described by her patients, she would stay hidden behind a tree or under some bushes. The path started out at a slight incline but became steeper with each step. A chill hung in the air but she sweat due to the exertion. After climbing for awhile, she came to a grassy, flat meadow. The blades of grass shone in the moonlight with an extraordinary brilliance and the voices of the dryads slowly faded away. On the other side of the meadow lay a forest. Lananell remembered the herder telling her he had been in this meadow when his dogs came upon the strangers. To her right was an unmistakable hill...Cryer's Hill.

Her eyes focused intently across the ethereal sea of grass, searching for the slightest movement or even a fire in the forest beyond. There was no sound save for her breathing.

I don't want to go farther and I'm tired.

But rather than return home to Rosco, she continued to put one foot in front of the other. A force she had only recently become aware of awoke within her. It pushed her on and evaporated her fear. The force of courage.

A wolf howl caused her to jump. It came from the forest beyond the meadow. She walked quickly, almost breaking into a run but suddenly realized if anyone were watching the meadow, they would see her, so she crouched down low and crawled. Pebbles punctured her knees and the palms of her hands. When she reached the edge of the forest, she scrambled off the path into the tall grass and listened. There was no sound, not even the nature spirits of the meadow, nor was there any sign of fire. Perhaps the spirits slept here. Just as she was about to give up and curse herself for being such a damn fool, the tall grass rustled loudly on the path to her left. She froze in terror as the rustling moved closer.

It's probably just an animal.

But whatever it was, it sounded big. She slid her dirk from its sheath and held it in front of her. The grasses parted and she was face to face with a tall, skinny shade. His body and clothes were transparent with just the slightest hint of skeleton within his phantom flesh. The ghostly outline of a skull was visible. He was very tall—almost a giant—and his feet did not touch the ground.

The shade stood still as a statue, its vacant, glowing eyes transfixed upon her. She forgot her voice until the fetch blinked. That seemed to unleash a primal scream from the depths of her throat. When the ghost heard her scream, his mouth also opened wide until it obliterated his face. The sound that came out was a combination of growl and howl. Lananell was sure she had never heard anything like it, human or animal.

The fetch made no move to attack. His scream died out as his mouth slowly closed. She heard other voices on the path getting closer. The tall grasses parted once more and five people stopped dead in their tracks when they saw her. But it was not really five but three: two men and a woman dressed in animal skins. Two fetches hovered above and slightly behind the men. The shade that had come upon her moved to hover above and behind the woman.

She was a medium-height, middle-aged, stocky redhead, and her face was awash in freckles. She held a spear a foot taller than her head. Both men were tall and burly, with dark brown whiskers and long, curly brown hair falling into their eyes. Their uncanny resemblance marked them as twins or at least brothers. The taller of the two possessed a semi-transparent redheaded male shade with a red beard, who had the same facial structure and coloring as the red-headed woman, and a stooped, old woman shade hovered over his brother.

A few seconds passed in silence as the strangers and their shades studied Lananell. The taller man took a step forward. The red-headed woman shouted words in a strange language which stopped him in his tracks. She turned to Lananell and broke into a smug grin, revealing long, crooked teeth with a gap in front. She held out her hand. "We don't mean ye any harm, dear," the woman said in thickly accented Corvasan. "What is ye name?"

"Lananell." Fright constricted her throat and her response came out as a tiny whisper.

The woman moved tentatively closer, her hand still extended. "Don't ye be afraid, Lananell. We have warmth, fire. Sheath ye knife, girl."

The woman suddenly lunged but Lananell jumped as agile as a cat, turned and ran through the tall grasses. Thick pines were ahead but was it the forest on the way back to the village or the forest on the opposite side of meadow, from which the strangers had come? She had become confused in her directions. But it didn't matter. As long as she reached the forest, she could find someplace to hide or call the nature spirits to help her, looking glass or no. After all, she had done it before when she escaped the Linnsonians.

The strange foreigners called out but sounded far away. Was she outrunning them? The tall pines were not far, perhaps another fifty yards. Her lungs were on fire but she forced herself to run faster.

If they catch me, they will kill me and eat me, she thought in blind panic.

Just as she was about to reach the edge of the forest, three shades flew over her head and stopped in front of her, their feet dangling a few feet from the ground, above the grass. They howled and wailed, pointing their ghostly fingers and making such a racket that a pack of crows alighted from the trees ahead, angry at the interruption to their sleep, squawking loudly in protest.

Lananell screamed and fell onto her back covering her eyes. Someone pulled her up forcefully by her hair. It was one of the brothers, the shorter one. He shoved her face within inches of his. His breath smelled of blood and his eyes held the look of murder.

She grasped at his hand that held her hair. "Please don't hurt me," she begged.

"Aye, little mamie, I won't hurt ye." At that moment, the others appeared. The red-headed woman let out a high-pitched wail, ululating in delight. The others joined in and soon they were making more noise than the shade had made with its inhuman howl.

They are going to wake the dead, Lananell thought. *They already have.*

She laughed bitterly.

From beneath her skins, the red-headed woman produced a rope and bound Lananell's wrists.

"Walk!" she barked and pushed Lananell hard in the back.

Lananell stumbled but did not fall.

Moonlight spilled intermittently onto the forest floor. After nearly ten minutes of walking in silence behind the brothers and their shades, they approached a gathering of people. Only a few had ghostly shades hovering over them. Some were asleep and some stood around a fire pit with smoking coals. Off to the side, a dead woman lay on the ground with her entrails spilling out.

Lananell closed her eyes and prayed to the spirits of the forest.

KRYST RECEIVES A ROYAL GIFT

"**S**OLDIERS ARE COMING!"

The sound of horses' hooves grew louder with each second. The young woman, Mallory, lay on her stomach atop Locklin's horse in front of him. She had been silent the entire time. Locklin threatened her several times with torture but she never spoke. This Healer from Arthac was turning out to be someone sinister, perhaps even evil. But Kryst was glad he was getting closer to Maeltip with every minute and could abide the man's company just a little longer.

Kryst heard a feminine voice in his head as he studied the first approaching rider, a city guard from Minosae followed by about a dozen of his comrades.

Tell them who you are.

Among the soldiers was an old bald man in a black and gold robe. They slowed when they saw Kryst and Locklin.

"Hail there!" A city guard shouted. He was a young man with light brown hair and wore the Sun King's sunburst on his cloak and breast plate. "We are the City Guard of Minosae in service to the Sun King Emeril and the House of the Sun! We are searching for a woman who is a traitor."

"She is here!" Locklin called out.

The soldiers' party approached and Kryst saw a strange bluish glow around the old bald man. He stared, trying to figure out what he was seeing but finally understood it was the glow of his magical talent, the glow so much spoken of among Adepts and Healers. But why was he seeing it?

"Is this the woman you are looking for?" Locklin lifted Mallory's head by her auburn hair. "We found her in the woods. She attacked us with magic."

"That is her," the soldier kicked his horse to a trot. "She is a wanted traitor."

...*Speak up*... Nominthe's voice repeated in Kryst's head.

"I am Prince Kryst, first born son of King Olaf of Maeltip and cousin to King Emeril. How do we know what you say is true?"

The soldiers turned their eyes to Kryst and a few snickered. He became aware of how he must appear to them on top of a burrow but did not back down. "I insist I present this traitor to my cousin. We will be thankful for your escort."

All the soldiers looked to the bald man in the black cloak with the ethereal glow. The man rode forward on his massive black warhorse. As he approached, the shimmery glow formed an egglike structure around him.

"I am Adept Noctus Sern of the Crystal Palace." He eyed Kryst up and down and then shouted back to his comrades. "He is telling the truth. This man is who he says he is."

The young soldier lowered his head. "My lord, pardons. Your, er, mount, did not appear to be that of a prince. We will give you escort to Minosae. But we'll have the young woman ride on one of our horses because she is very valuable to the King, if it pleases the prince of Maeltip. Sir Berin, switch mounts with Prince Kryst."

The knight he commanded hesitated but did as he was bid. Kryst dismounted and gave Sir Berin the reins.

Mallory was transferred to another horse sitting upright behind a knight. She kept her head down when they led her there.

Adept Sern beckoned Kryst to ride next to him, just behind two men-at-arms. They rode two abreast with Locklin and Mallory behind them. Kryst smelled wood fires and cooking food the closer they came to the capital. Several hamlets littered the landscape when they crested a hill and spied the city wall with the Utina River snaking around its east side. The pinkish-white tower of the Crystal Palace gleamed starkly against the blue-gray sky. He remembered the half dozen times he had been there when he was just a young boy, when his mother was still alive.

"How did you come to subdue her magic?" Noctus Sern whispered. "You do realize she is an Adept's Apprentice. You are lucky to be alive."

Before Kryst could answer, Locklin replied. "I put the block on her."

"I see," Adept Sern said but Kryst thought he appeared confused.

Their party passed peasant farmers and merchants pulling wagons of their wares on the North Road. They gave the soldiers shy, curious glances.

Several men-at-arms paced back and forth along the rampart, their eyes visible through the slits in their helms. The black iron gate was open but was not as busy as Kryst would have expected.

After they entered the grounds of the palace, Adept Sern led Mallory away. Kryst met her eyes…and felt a brief burst of intense hatred. The emotion sprung up from his abdomen and was ferocious in its intensity. After a second or two, it was gone.

Within the central tower of the Crystal Palace, their escort barked orders at passing serving girls. "Bring these men mead, dried beef and cheese. Take them to the second level and find suitable quarters."

"Yes, sire." A pretty, brown-haired maid curtsied. "If you would follow me, m'lords."

Kryst climbed the spiral stairs of the central tower and the memories flooded in. He wondered if his cousin, King Emeril, would remember him and if he did, how would the King receive him?

They were shown to a luxurious room with a view of the palace garden. The furniture was an eclectic mix of woven rugs from the Knotts and Maeltip, classic Corvasan chairs with curved legs and arms, a semi-circular sofa in the fashion of Westernaphalia. Both Kryst and Locklin chose the sofa. It had been a long ride and Kryst's behind was sore.

Servants brought cheese, olives, jerked elk and flagons of wine. Locklin folded his hands and stared at Kryst with a wry smile. "If the King asks you how you came to be in Corvasa, how will you reply?"

"I will tell him the truth."

"Ah, the truth," Locklin mused, his fleshy lips pursed. "The truth that you escaped the Renfala forest? The fiends within it? The thorny crucifixion trees?" Locklin raised a blond eyebrow. "He will ask you how you came to be there. What will you tell him?"

Before he could answer, a pair of palace guards interrupted them. "If you would follow us, Prince Kryst, Healer Locklin. The Sun King Emeril desires you bear witness against the accused immediately."

The east wing of the Crystal Palace was the most elaborately decorated place Kryst had ever encountered. The sheer display of wealth and plunder was impossible to ignore. The floors were solid marble—mined from eastern Corvasa and the Knotts—with light blue, pink and black veins and polished to a lustrous sheen. Stained glass windows alternating to Kryst's left and right depicted scenes of the heroes of Corvasa, the warrior kings who, it was rumored, became post-mortem gods and were worshiped as such in the Corvasan pantheon.

I come from this bloodline, Kryst thought with a sense of pride. If he remembered correctly, the throne room was at the end of the east wing, just before the King's apartments.

"Prince Kryst of Maeltip and Healer Locklin of Arthac!" A guard announced them as the gilded doors opened.

A wave of nostalgia overcame Kryst when he entered.

The throne stood on a platform reached by a flight of steps that spread out like a woman's fan. On a smaller seat, a few steps below and to the left of the throne sat a stark, severe-appearing woman. Her thin lips were pursed, her blue eyes full of envy.

"That is Lady Rubia," Locklin whispered in his ear. "The King's betrothed and cousin through his mother's family."

Kryst was a little surprised. She was not ugly but by no means beautiful. In Corvasa, marriages were arranged among the nobility, a custom he did not understand. Yes, he would be obliged to marry a woman of noble blood but she would be of his choice, not his father's.

Lush, exquisitely crafted rugs from Maeltip covered the marble floors. Kryst recognized the handiwork immediately. The rugs were extremely dense with minute detail and a selection of colors only found in his homeland. The wall to his left was paneled in cherrybark oak. Suits of silver- and gold-plated armor stood along the walls, the empty slits of their visors gazing surreptitiously upon the gathering. Gorgeously adorned ladies of the court, their hair coiffed and molded into towering displays of domes and curls, lightly fanned themselves with handheld peacock feathers. In the style of Corvasa, they lightened their skin with powder and reddened their lips with juice of crushed geraniums and roses. Kryst smelled their perfume, a mixture of lemon and jasmine. He inhaled the enticing fragrance deeply. The expressions of the women were cryptically serious with a hint of amusement underneath.

...they revel in humiliation to their sex... the voice whispered, the voice of the goddess he had fucked.

King Emeril sat upon the Sun Throne, his dark facial whiskers cropped close and his sideburns sculpted to meet the hair on his jaw. He wore a golden cloak with white hare fur trim over a wine-red doublet, and red and gold striped breeches. He appeared older and smaller than Kryst remembered. The King was about ten years older than him and must have been sixteen the last time Kryst saw him. Their fathers had conversed together while Emeril played at swords with him. Purplish bags hung under the King's eyes and his skin was grayish-white.

By the gods, he looks like death, Kryst thought when their eyes met. *Is he sick?*

To his left stood Mallory, flanked by two guards. Her wrists were bound in chains. The beautiful auburn hair was mussed and one of her eyes was swollen black and blue. She stared straight ahead as if in a trance.

The King acknowledged Kryst's presence with a slight nod.

A bald old man wearing a black and gold robe stepped forward and went to one arthritic knee in front of the King. Kryst heard his joints cracking from where he stood.

"Rise, Adept Cortar," King Emeril commanded.

The Adept rose slowly, his joints popping anew, and said, "Your Highness, I wish to speak to the company gathered here."

King Emeril nodded and Adept Cortar turned to face his audience of lords, ladies and soldiers.

"Last night, the King was given a sleeping potion against his will. He was found unresponsive in his bed this morning. Once awoken, he was drowsy and had to be completely revived with smelling salts. By the grace of the gods, we are all very thankful and relieved his majesty has made a remarkable recovery."

Not so remarkable, thought Kryst. *He appears as if he is ready to vomit.*

Adept Cortar made a flourishing gesture with his hand, bowed, and resumed his speech.

"It is with great disappointment and shock that one of our own stands accused of administering the substance to the King against his will and of leaving the Palace as an Adept's Apprentice without permission." He lifted an arm and pointed at Mallory. "This woman, Sillisnae, daughter of Ellnis…"

Sillisnae?

"…was a trusted Adept's Apprentice who, a few days prior, returned the Fire Globe to us. She administered a potion that disguised its power through the dreamless, peaceful sleep of its victim. As time passed, it would have slowly worn away at the heart's power, eventually slowing it to such a degree it would have come to a complete stop."

The auburn-haired woman named Sillisnae shook her head violently. "*No!* That is a vile lie. I did not want to poison the King. I only wanted him to sleep while I slipped out of Minosae. I wanted to go home! I even told the King as much. Your Majesty, you must believe me. How could you believe I wanted to kill you? I am not that stupid—"

Lady Rubia leapt to her feet. "You will be silent, girl! You have not been called upon as of yet."

"Let her speak," King Emeril commanded. His voice was raspy and frail. Whatever potion she had given him, it clearly still wreaked havoc on his system.

The guards brought Sillisnae forward and shoved her to her knees. The chains clanked as she brought her hands up. "Your Majesty, all that I have said is the truth. I wanted to leave Minosae and the Crystal Palace. I never asked for this talent—"

"Magical talent is a great gift from the gods," Adept Cortar interrupted.

Sillisnae sighed and hung her head. When she spoke again, her voice cracked. "It was never my intention to poison you, your Majesty. What I wanted is that you sleep until the dawn so I could leave Minosae and make my way home under cover of the night. The only thing I am guilty of is giving you a sleep aide."

"And abandoning your post as Adept's Apprentice." Lady Rubia spat out the words. "You know it is forbidden to practice magic without the crown's consent after serving as an Adept's Apprentice."

"I understand but it was not my intention to practice magic again. I wanted to return home."

"Home?" King Emeril's voice was hoarse. "What is in that small village you could want, Sillisnae? And don't give me the excuse you want the simple life in the country. Your adventures with the Knottian man and your return of the Fire Globe prove that false. So, tell me, what is the real reason you left the Crystal Palace?"

A hush descended. Before, there had been whispers and idle talk but now all eyes were on Sillisnae and King Emeril. Kryst did not know their history, but when she spoke, the King's face contorted into an unmistakable expression of jealousy.

"I...I...I am in love with the Knottian, Your Majesty. I want to return to him so we may marry."

"Don't be silly, Sillisnae!" King Emeril shouted. "You have a duty here. *Love* has very little to do with it."

Adept Cortar laughed. "Women. They will throw everything good in their lives away for the tingling sensation of a lover's kiss. Small wonder I advocate for the abolishment of women on the Council of Twelve."

"My King, I am guilty of leaving the palace without permission. I am also guilty of giving you a sleeping potion. But these men lie when they say I intended to kill you!"

"The dose you gave His Majesty was massive!" Lady Rubia shouted. "He was still asleep when his squire came to wake him and if he had not, he would be dead now."

King Emeril turned his attention to Kryst and beckoned with his hand. "Step forward, cousin."

Kryst stepped next to Sillisnae, went to one knee and bowed his head. "Your Majesty, it has been a long time. I was hoping to see you again under more favorable circumstances."

"Rise," the King commanded. "I understand. I intend to feast you and your guest while you are here after we have dealt with this matter. Tell me what happened in the forest, cousin."

Kryst glanced briefly at Locklin who gave a slight nod. "I was traveling with this man, Locklin, the Healer from Arthac, when we came upon this Adept's Apprentice who then tried to attack us with magic."

King Emeril leaned on his right hand. "She is very powerful in the occult arts. How were you able to subdue her?"

"Healer Locklin of Arthac, is a first rate Adept. He was able to subdue her."

Adept Cortar laughed.

Kryst ignored his insolence and continued. "We decided to take her with us. She appeared to be of noble blood so we thought it prudent to bring her here."

"I am indebted to you, cousin," the King nodded. "Please ask a favor of me and I will grant it."

"How does a simple village Healer block the magic of an Adept's Apprentice?" Adept Cortar demanded. "The Blocking Spell is only known to advanced Adepts of the Crystal Palace and Jaanaarians."

Kryst swallowed but did not take his eyes from the King. He would not be berated by an unranked Adept, even if he sat upon the Council of Twelve. "I request, Your Majesty, that I be allowed to take the woman, Sillisnae, with me to Maeltip. She will work as a handmaid or serving girl in my father's castle."

The King's expression did not change but the two flanking Adepts appeared horrified.

"Your Majesty, I understand this fine gentleman is your blood, but Sillisnae is very valuable. After she is suitably punished, she perhaps could be returned to her apprenticeship. We can never be sufficiently convinced she will have her magic blocked satisfactorily," Noctus Sern pointed out.

Lady Rubia nodded her head. "Yes! Give the little trollop to your cousin, Your Majesty. I'm sure he will find suitable uses for her."

Kryst could see the homely woman was on fire with jealousy but the King ignored her outburst.

"We, Adept Noctus? Perhaps you cannot, but this is my cousin, the Prince of Maeltip. He and his companion have done a great service by capturing Sillisnae and returning her. They did not have to do this and the gods know it was not part of their plan." The King shot a furtive glance at Kryst. "Cousin, let me think upon this. Give me a day."

"Thank you, Your Majesty."

"If there is no other business, I will adjourn the royal session." No voices spoke as the entire hearing had only been for the fate of Sillisnae.

Kryst gazed at Sillisnae who still knelt, flanked by guards. Her beautiful green eyes met his stare. The bluish glow swirled around her as it had done with Noctus Sern. He felt a brief pang of lust when he saw the tops of her breasts displayed by her bodice.

...she will be yours... Nominthe's voice was in his head once more. *...and more besides...*

* * * *

The next day, he and Locklin were summoned to King Emeril's apartments.

The King sat in his leisure room in an oaken chair with golden cushions, almost as big as the throne, in front of a round oaken table. He ate from a platter of fruit.

"Ah, cousin! Healer Locklin. Please, sit, eat. I have decided to grant your request and give you Sillisnae," King Emeril informed them.

Kryst was shocked. He did not expect the King to assent.

"I have three conditions, however." King Emeril waved a hand. "You must return her within a year and you cannot unblock her talent."

Kryst was puzzled. "After a year, Your Majesty?"

A shadow of longing drifted across the King's face. "Yes. She must learn obedience rather than magic. And remaining in the Crystal Palace will not teach her that."

"And the last condition, my King?"

"She must remain a virgin. This is the most important one. She must remain chaste. I would recommend placing a maiden's belt upon her if she cannot be guarded at all times."

"Of course, Your Majesty. I will fasten a belt to her as soon as we reach Maeltip." Somewhere in his head, he heard a woman laugh.

Kryst and Locklin set out shortly after. Sillisnae was brought to them with chains still binding her wrists.

They were given mounts and a few provisions but the horses they could not keep. The ride to Aranhoe would take most of the day in Kryst's estimation. Sillisnae was put upon a fine white mare and they accelerated to a canter upon departing the south city gate.

Kryst took note of the massive hole and reined in next to Sillisnae. "What happened to the south gate?"

She stared straight ahead and did not respond. The guards riding ahead of them laughed loudly. If he allowed her insolence to remain unpunished, they would lose respect for him, especially Locklin. He hit her cheek with an open hand causing her to nearly fall from her horse. If he had met her just two days ago, before his encounter with Nominthe, he would have hesitated to strike her. But the goddess gave him full confidence; it was like she had become a part of him although he had heard her voice only a few times since their ritual.

"What happened back there?" he repeated the question.

"The dragon Renfala burned a hole through the gate," she said without looking at him.

"Why?"

"Because Hawk has control of the dragon." She turned and gave him a defiant glare.

He returned her stare and she averted her eyes after a moment.

They rode in silence along a well-worn, wagon-rutted road following the Utina River. The day was hot and hazy and Kryst was sweating. The humid air was replete with scents of earth and plants. The land was flat here, with dense foliage which seemed to grow denser the farther south they traveled. The river was calm and silent, moving slowly.

When they neared Aranhoe, the sun was in its golden hour, illuminating the trees and bushes with a bright glow. He smelled the city before he saw it. Small hamlets appeared with thatched-roof cottages and earthen duns. Underneath the smell of humid earth and plant, the fainter scent of the salt sea reached him. Kryst smiled. It was a familiar smell. He was almost home.

The smell of fish was overwhelming when they passed through the north gate. Merchants were everywhere with their carts and stalls. They called out to their party cautiously, not wanting to be too aggressive due to the soldiers. It was not a long ride to the docks but when Kryst gazed upon the sea, his heart leapt. Soon, he would be back in Maeltip, enjoying some spiced wine and a good read. Perhaps he would pay a visit to Simone.

They dismounted and Sir Morris said, "I leave you here, Lord Kryst. May you have a safe voyage, guarded over by Lir. May he provide you with sensuous but cunning mermaids."

At that, everyone laughed but Sillisnae. She stood stone-faced but Kryst saw a tear trickle slowly down her cheek.

THE INITIATION

"WE HAVE NOT ALWAYS BEEN THIS WAY." Akrae sighed. "There was a time when we had no sexual organs and were androgynous. There was no such thing as male and female. Even we have succumbed to the changes in the physical body. Only a select few of us can reproduce through parthenogenesis. The druids and the Honors of the hillnons, but the others have lost the ability. The world beyond the Golden Band calls to them, and they must go, I'm afraid."

They occupied a garden on a terrace within the hillnon. Several species of tropical plants and giant colorful flowers moved softly in a draft that descended from high above. It was one of several gardens in the distinct style he had seen when they first arrived: slabs of rock cut from the mountain to allow sunlight throughout. Akrae brought out a small crystal on a chain he wore around his neck.

Hawk's *oide* held up the crystal. "This was part of these mountains at the dawn of the world. Long before the Golden Band, just after the catastrophe."

The gem reminded Hawk of the Crystal Palace and that thought led to Sillisnae. "I cannot remain here long, my *oide*. I must return to Corvasa."

Akrae broke into a smile. "Your other half awaits?"

"Yes."

Akrae took the chain from around his neck and handed the crystal to Hawk. "Try to summon Renfala."

Hawk's mind went out of his body, up into the air and high above the hillnon. He saw streams and creeks forming in the amphitheater of the Terres mountains. He saw herds of elk and buffalo roaming through the wetlands and hawks and eagles flying above. But nowhere did he see Renfala. What was most disturbing was that he could not feel the dragon either. He felt all the animals, the fowls in the air, the fishes and amphibians in the streams, the elk, deer, bear and rabbits. But Renfala's essence was completely absent.

Where are you?

"Dragons are very mystical creatures," Akrae whispered.

The sound pulled Hawk's mind back into his body.

"They will only come to an individual's aide if it is fulfilling some higher purpose. You cannot command a dragon and especially, you cannot expect a dragon to involve itself in the day-to-day petty affairs of governments, rulers and populations."

The apprentice understood his master. "I will bring her back here, my *oide*."

"With a real woman, it will be much more difficult to create your mythic self, the goal of every Jaanaarian. It will delay the power to create life from thought alone which you may possess. I have seen it."

"I love her," was all Hawk could think to say.

Akrae took back his crystal necklace. "So be it." His *oide* raised his hands over his head, palms up. The air shimmered, he became exceedingly transparent and disappeared altogether. The air made a popping sound where he had been.

Hawk stood and felt a brief wave of intense heat throughout his body, then pain that always accompanied the metamorphisis. He disintegrated, but not completely. His arms shrank and grew feathers. His legs diminished into sticks. His neck shortened and grew into his head while beige and brown feathers sprouted all over his body.

The wings beat and the hawk took flight.

Flying through the Golden Band in the hawk's form was not what he anticipated. The astral wall barely flashed a spasm of heat through his body. It seemed to have weakened even further since he and Sheena, atop Renfala, flew through a few days past.

With the bird of prey's eyes, he saw several leagues beyond the Utild mountain range into the foothills. The wind filled his wings and carried him far distances without the effort of beating them.

When he was a young boy, the hawk was the first animal he contacted with his mind. One day, after he had completed eleven years of life, his mother had seen him shapeshifting into a hawk. The metamorphosis came naturally. Her laughter wounded him when he beat his wings ineffectively within their hut. That first time, he held the shape for only a few minutes. It took all of his concentration. Now, the transformation was second nature and he could hold the shape for a couple of hours. His clothes and anything upon his person would also be incorporated within his magic, enabling him to effectively carry anything—his sword, knives, money—while in the form of a hawk.

Once he had held the hawk's form for three hours but when he changed back, he could not understand language for the first five minutes. And the bird's thoughts continued to plague him. They were not actually coherent, detailed thoughts, but rather instincts. He realized if he stayed in any animal form for too long, the animal's mind may overtake his human mind.

The wind picked up speed, blowing him in a zig-zag formation across the sky. He floated effortlessly, gazing at the craggy mountains and yellow-green valleys. Frothy streams gushed hurriedly through the rocky, timbered sides of the mountains, a few of which still had snow cover on their jutting peaks.

Mount Moirae's summits were higher than the rest, hundreds of leagues away but still visible, occupying the northwest corner of Corvasa near the coast of the Straight of Jaanaar. A mountain of three peaks, the tallest being the center. On its eastern slope, the Othalla River began and flowed between Corvasa and the Land of the Osseks then finally into the South Sea bordering the Knotts.

Were the legends true that the Mothers of the World, the Weavers, lived there with the dragon Kefkinala and the Crystal Skull? No one currently alive had ever seen the Weavers and Hawk thought it a myth. Perhaps at one point the Weavers existed, but Hawk doubted they still did.

To the east, beyond Mount Moirae, dark, flat-bottomed clouds ominously lingered in the sky like massive giants searching for the perfect place to unload their water. A storm was brewing. The gray haze beneath the clouds told Hawk it was already raining in the Gulf of Jaanaar and probably Osseka as well. A flash of lightning cut the storm cloud, illuminating the rain in small reflective crystals. A couple of hours would pass before it entered the sky above Jaanaar.

All bird forms diminished his sense of smell while enhancing his eyesight. For the first few minutes, it was a strange sensation to have no sense of smell but he quickly forgot it when in flight. His eyes were so powerful they made up for the loss. A herd of elk grazed in the valley below and a predatory bear followed their movements from the cover of giant firs.

In no time he was flying over the foothills and was able to descend in altitude. Martine was not far and he thought he spied the small village a little to the east. The view was spectacular. Winding roads followed the Utina River. Some snaked off into the hillsides, but most roads went from small hamlets to the main road, the one which would bend around the Renfala Forest.

The valley formed by the Utild mountain range widened significantly. Here and there he saw small hamlets dotting the landscape. He spied a barn with a caved in roof and descended toward it. He was exhausted.

After transforming back into human form, he saw the barn was built on top of a steep green slope. Ancient wagon tracks led to its door. He pressed the wooden door and it creaked on its hinges to reveal a hay littered floor long since abandoned by any livestock. Hawk gathered some hay into a pile, laid down and fell into fitful sleep.

* * * *

They came in the middle of the night on his thirteenth birthday, the great warriors of his tribe, and bound him hand and foot. They threw him over the back of a horse. He bounced for what seemed like hours, until they came to a steep canyon into which they threw him. On the canyon floor, a circle was drawn around him in the red sand, the edges of which he could not pass beyond for three days. If he left the circle, he would be forced to wear women's clothing and would not be allowed to join the initiated in any activities. Hawk had not known of anyone that had left his circle. His second cousin died during his initiation when he was attacked by a mountain lion. He was given a hero's funeral and would exalt the Land of the Ancestors.

The tribal warriors gave him a rock the size of a large rabbit to defend himself. The first night nothing happened and his hunger and thirst were well under control. The Knottian warriors and adepts hid themselves somewhere in the forest but they still watched him from afar. At dusk the next day, he sensed several animals within the area. A few mule deer walked by lazily, eating what grass they could find. They gazed at him with their doe eyes while they ate, never making a sound.

The second night, his throat burned with thirst. Foregoing food had been easier than he thought but his mouth was parched, his tongue swollen and his need for water was nearly driving him mad.

At the break of dawn on the third day, he felt the beast before he heard it. A great lumbering black bear emerged from a copse of crack willows about thirty yards to his right. The bear trotted slowly through the red rock canyon. He sensed the bear's hunger but also its anger. Panic threatened but he willed it down into his gut. Pain would rain down on him but panic would get him killed. The large rock they had given him would make a formidable weapon but he needed something else. He sent out his mind and discovered his namesake somewhere close by, flying high above the canyon.

The bear was a few feet away, it lips pulled back to reveal white fangs like daggers. Its eyes were as black as its fur. Hawk smelled fear even though he was only a quarter the bear's size, if that.

Overhead, the hawk screeched.

Come to me, now! *Hawk commanded.*

The bear lunged. Hawk swung the heavy rock with both hands, hitting its temple. It sat back on its hind legs and let out a long, angry roar. The bear's breath smelled of rotting carcasses. Hawk crouched low as the bear swung, its six-inch claws meeting with flesh. He was only dimly aware of blood dripping down his leg. He raised the boulder but the bear was faster and swung again, this time ripping flesh on Hawk's rib cage and knocking the rock out of the circle where it was now useless. It was beyond his reach and if he stepped beyond the boundary, the initiation would be forfeit and he would not have another chance until the next full moon, in addition to the humiliation he would suffer.

The bear roared again, the sound deep, low and earthy. The sound of his death. The bear's roar would accompany him into the Land of the Ancestors. There was no shame in dying while fighting for one's life and no pain either. It was only when a person died in their sleep or from some ravaging fever that the pain came. That was what the tribal elders said anyway. He was about to find out if it was true.

The beast charged once more and swiped but Hawk rolled and hopped back onto his feet, all the while making sure he did not leave the circle. If he left the circle and ran, he would die anyway because he could not outrun the bear, but then he would also die in shame and that was not an option.

Perhaps he could tire the beast if he remained light on his feet. Claws half a foot long swiped out again, cutting Hawk's shoulder and knocking him to the ground. He quickly raised his hands in front of his face, as the bear straddled him. Any second now the bear would bite his head or neck for the kill.

The bird suddenly appeared within his line of vision, its wingspan massive, and its screech so high-pitched, he wanted to cover his ears. The hawk dug its talons deeply into the bear's head and eyes. The black beast swung its arms desperately, but the hawk ascended out of reach just in time. He saw the bear's eyes were dripping blood, the gelatinous bulbs leaking a smoky white fluid. Taking advantage of the bear's blindness, he rolled out from under him. The hawk's presence was now overwhelming in his mind. They were one and the same, the man and the bird of prey.

Kill him!

The hawk dove again and sunk its talons behind the bear's skull, thrusting its beak into the bear's skull and eyes. Hawk tasted the slightly metallic flavor of blood in his mouth. The bear roared and flung its arms hysterically. The animal stumbled and fell backward in its attempt to free itself from the attacking bird. When the bear hit the ground, the hawk let go briefly to avoid being squashed. The hawk did not linger in the air long, but dove again and struck forcefully with its beak. Hawk heard a crushing sound and the bear ran, sand flying from its feet.

Hawk's mind parted company with the bird.

The ordeal sapped his last scrap of energy. He lay panting in the circle, facing up into the sky. The sun was relentless and quickly reminded him of his thirst. The hawk rested somewhere nearby but he was too exhausted to search for him. Even though the sun shone brightly and his thirst was infuriating, he drifted off. When he awoke, the warriors of his tribe stood over him, the sun behind them and their faces in shadow.

* * * *

He immediately awoke in darkness, expecting to see the warriors standing above him. But he was quite alone, not a mouse or even a rat to keep him company. Sleep did not return and he decided to take wing once again.

The sun spread its pink dawn rays across the rolling hills below him when he spied the central tower of the Crystal Palace jutting into the sky as if pointing to the gods. The sight put his heart aflutter.

Sillisnae.

He pointed his beak to the ground and slowly descended, landing in a copse of willows next to a pond in the gigantic palace garden. He shapeshifted while still in the tree and instinctively put his hand on *Scartha's* hilt. The last time he was in Minosae, he had called Renfala and the beast breathed fire on the south wall, so he, Rosco and Lananell could escape. This time, he only disguised himself slightly because the only person who saw him up close and personal, Lord Korodale, was dead. The turquoise eyes that marked him as Knottian changed to a light brown. His long, dark brown hair, he tucked into the back of his surcoat. He lengthened his nose and fattened his lips.

The pinkish-white crystal spire loomed mightily overhead. A soft scent of jasmine hung in the air. The oasis was deserted but just outside the gates of the Crystal Palace, merchants called to potential customers to sell their early harvest fruits and vegetables. Three ducks flew into the pond beneath the willows. Their heads were a bright, emerald green with a white ring around their throat and a bright yellow beak. Their puffed out chests were chestnut brown. The water parted into a long "V" shape behind their tails. Hawk took their appearance as a good omen.

The Crystal Palace seemed to harbor less people than the last time he was here. He entered the central spire tower, avoiding the eyes of the guards. A well-dressed noble raised a hand in greeting as if he knew him but stopped mid-wave and passed on, realizing his error. Hawk ran up the steps of the central spire, taking two at a time. At the third level, he opened the southern door displaying the symbol of Selene.

Busts of Corvasan Kings lined the hallway. He walked anxiously through the richly decorated rooms with exquisite tapestries and finely made rugs.

A few servant girls carrying fresh linens passed him by with nary a glance. The morning sunlight streamed through massive windows to his right, those facing east.

A heavy oaken door at the end of the hallway marked the threshold into the South Atrium where the Fire Globe was kept. He wondered if Sillisnae helped the Adepts activate it. Funny, he could not locate Sillisnae's portrait. Next to the last door before the south atrium was an outline where a painting had been. The sight gave Hawk a chill. Something was not right. A sinking feeling rumbled his stomach.

He raised a hand to knock quietly and pressed his ear to the door. After hearing nothing, he said, "Sillisnae. It's me, Hawk."

Still nothing. He put his hand on the doorknob and turned.

The room was empty within. A water basin stood in the center of the room. She had told him of the first time she saw him, scrying into that water. He walked to the bedchamber and stared at the bedspread with embroidered scenes of cats playing among flowers and butterflies. The window-doors to the balcony were closed and bolted. Peeking through the white linen curtains, he saw the balcony was empty.

He quickly took leave of her room and the Hall of Adept's

Apprentices. A group of soldiers congregated near the entrance to the Palace Library, where he had exchanged fire with Lord Korodale in their battle at the south wall. He tentatively approached them.

"Exalted sirs," Hawk spoke with a Westernaphalian accent. "I am a humble servant of the King of Westernaphalia. I was sent here to deliver a special gift to his Majesty and the Council of Twelve, for their generous aide to the people of Westernaphalia after the attack we have suffered and the loss of one of our coastal villages. The relic has returned to its proper place, I trust."

The most senior in command, a tall man with dark brown whiskers, ran his eyes up and down Hawk suspiciously. "What is your name, sir?"

"My name is Salein, son of Dorak, the messenger for King Rogus of Westernaphalia. He sent me a few days after the garrison with the girl left for Minosae. I wanted to request audience with the King or failing that, an audience with the Council of Twelve will do."

"I am Sir Roque of the Palace Guard," the man said, his tone had lost its suspiciousness. "If you remain here, I'll approach the Council about giving you an audience."

Hawk bowed slightly. "Thank you, sir. And I'd guess the Fire Globe is back in its rightful place so we can all breathe a sigh of relief."

Sir Roque guffawed. "Ah yes, the ancient relic has been returned, but its savior turned out to be a traitor."

Hawk frowned. "A traitor?"

Another guard—a short, portly man with unruly hair the color of straw—spoke up. "The King's bed will be a little less warm, it will." He laughed along with the others.

"What?" Hawk was confused.

"Ah, it is novel news, Salein, son of Dorak. I don't expect a messenger from the northwest would have been made the wiser. Sillisnae, the Adept's Apprentice that returned the Fire Globe, has been discovered a traitor. King Emeril sent her to Maeltip with Prince Kryst."

Hawk attempted to feign outrage. "The Adept's Apprentice a traitor? What happened? Did she not return the Fire Globe? Isn't the penalty for treason death?"

"King Emeril gave her leniency because she returned the Fire Globe. His cousin, Prince Kryst, the son of King Olaf, requested her and the King relented."

"What did she do? It's shocking she would turn traitor right after returning the most powerful relic in the land."

"She was to become the King's mistress and the night the deed was to take place, she drugged him and escaped."

Hawk must have let his mask of composure drop because the guard frowned.

"Are you all right, sir?"

He swallowed. His mouth was dry. "That's very unfortunate. I hope the Sun King is faring well."

The Prince of Maeltip took Sillisnae? A pang of guilt clenched at his heart. It was he who insisted she return to Minosae with the Fire Globe.

Sir Roque disappeared up the steps of the central spire. The other guards chuckled and resumed talking among themselves, ignoring him.

He walked away, out of the palace and onto the grounds, his thoughts frenzied. One thing was certainly true; he could not stay in Minosae.

Outside the south gate was a tavern frequented by many men-at-arms, palace guards, and servants. In such an establishment, information in the form of gossip would be readily exchanged without having to ask a single question. The cobblestone street outside the iron gates was crowded with women, children, merchants, wagons and horses. He slipped unnoticed beyond the gate and made for the tavern, The Fox and Eagle.

The innkeeper was a plump redhead of around forty with a splash of freckles across her nose and forehead. She turned her kindly gaze upon him when he entered.

"A bit of mead and meat, good sir? There's a fresh batch of mead and roasting goat in the spit." She pointed.

"That would be most pleasant, kind lady." The common room was filled with loud voices and laughter even at this time of morning. Hawk sat at a wooden table and a serving girl placed a glass of mead front of him. He sipped and let the delicious taste of honey and cloves roll over his tongue.

A throng of four soldiers sat at the end of the table. Their laughter and conversation were loudest among the patrons. Hawk listened after the serving girl brought a plate full of roasted meat.

At first glance, he thought they were a group of four soldiers but were really only three. The fourth man was dressed in a black leather tunic with dark brown breeches. He had a massive belly, skinny legs and thick, black beard. The soldiers all appeared to be of an age with Hawk. The highest ranking soldier, evidenced by the pins on his surcoat, was towheaded with large blue eyes and a nose like a knife.

"...escorted them as far as Aranhoe."

"The King must be overjoyed to lose such a fine specimen as that beautiful Adept's Apprentice."

"Have you seen his betrothed?" the burly, black-bearded man asked his uniformed companion. "No wonder he keeps so many mistresses."

"Shh!" a short brown-haired soldier frowned at his blond commander. "There are ears everywhere."

Hawk ate about half the roast goat before he turned to the soldiers and lifted his mead. "Sirs," he nodded, "I have come from Westernaphalia to give King Emeril a message from my sovereign. Is it the Adept's Apprentice who rescued the Fire Globe that you speak of?"

The smiles and lighthearted expressions vanished from their faces.

"Westernaphalia, ay?" the burly, black-bearded man observed. He regarded Hawk with a beady stare and took a long swig from his giant horn. "What is your name, stranger?"

"I am Salein, son of Dorak, and in service to King Rogus of Westernaphalia. One of our coastal villages was destroyed by the Fire Globe. King Emeril sent aide and my King has sent me to give him special thanks and a gift."

"I am Tomas, son of Noor, from Minosae," the black bearded man said. "The Fire Globe was returned safely and now sits in its rightful place in the south atrium of the Crystal Palace. But the woman who brought it back was not so fortunate."

"Sillisnae?" Hawk asked.

"Yes. She drugged the King to avoid becoming his mistress and fled north. She was caught by Prince Kryst of Maeltip, cousin to King Emeril. He took her to Maeltip for service. The King was lenient because she restored the Fire Globe, but he essentially sold her into slavery to the Maeltipian prince."

Without a word, Hawk rose and threw some coin on the table, leaving the rest of the succulent, roasted meat untouched.

"My pardons, sir, for the wine or did you have mead? Not to your liking?" the red-headed innkeeper frowned as Hawk flew by her.

He did not hear. An old friend owed him a favor.

ROSCO TAKES A WALK

ROSCO AWOKE WITH A START and Lananell was not beside him. She liked to pick berries in the morning. She would return from her morning excursions with an apron full of blackberries and set to work preparing jam.

"I am making the acquaintance of the fairies of the wood," she had explained.

He hoped she returned soon, he was hungry and the woman could cook. Kurin had given them a sack full of boar sausage made from his freshest kill and Nella had mixed the meat with a generous heaping of fat from the animal.

His brother had also taken good care of his garden. The walnuts and apricots were ripe. After dressing, he took a basket outside and filled it. Lananell would no doubt make a nice apricot jam or even a pie. He climbed a ladder leaning against the tree and strapped the basket around his shoulder. The sun was hot today, and would only get hotter.

The basket was full in no time; he had always worked quickly and efficiently. But his wife had not returned yet. That was puzzling. It was nearly noon. He contemplated eating without her but decided against it. They would both be good and hungry by the time she returned.

Rosco fed his goat and chickens, collected eggs, and surveyed the garden. Harvest time was just around the corner. Lananell had sprouted and planted some herbs she found on one of her morning excursions. She had explained what they were for, but as he glanced at their unfamiliar leaves and branches, he completely forgot their names and functions.

The sun beat down and he wiped sweat from his brow. Brightly colored butterflies lazily flew from flower to leaf. The garden was alive with the sound of insects and birds. A stellar jay with its royal blue head and black neck squawked at him.

When he could put off eating not another minute, he still did not worry too much for Lananell as he cooked a few boar sausages in an iron skillet over the hearth fire. He ate them slowly, hoping she would walk through the door any minute and join him while the sausages still sizzled.

He washed his plate and put it away, wrapped the sausages to keep for his wife. Where was she? Another hour passed as he worked outside, pruning leaves and propping up sagging tomato vines. Lananell never returned.

That is when he saw the looking glass. It lay on the table next to the hearth.

Why would it be here? She usually never went anywhere without it.

He rolled it over his fingers, staring. The hairs on the back of his neck stood up. Something was wrong. Very wrong.

She should have been home by now.

Rosco put it in his pocket and walked out the door, moving swiftly. It would take half an hour to reach Kurin's, but perhaps Lananell had gone there.

When he arrived, their faces told him a different story.

"Lananell? No, Rosco, she has not been by here," Nella assured him.

"What happened?" his brother asked. "Tell us from the beginning."

"I awoke and she was gone. She was not in the house, nor outside. She often goes to pick berries in the mornings and *talk to the wood*, she says. So I thought that was what she was doing, but she would not stay gone so long. And I saw this on the hearth table." Rosco produced the looking glass.

"What is that?" Nella asked with a frown.

"A looking glass. Hawk gave it to her before we left Westernaphalia. He said she had the talent and should develop it with the help of the glass."

"Her healing talent?" Nella asked.

"No, talent in talking to the nature spirits and elementals."

Kurin shook his head, frowning. Rosco expected as much. His brother always saw the worst in every situation.

"Do you know the history of this girl, brother?" Kurin asked him.

Rosco felt a pang of anger rise. "I believe her history is my business alone, Kurin."

"Is it now?" Kurin moved toward his brother, squinting at him. "A man can never trust a wanton woman—"

"Don't you call her that," Rosco said calmly. He would not strike his brother in his own house but outside was a different story.

"You are my blood!" Kurin shouted. "You bring her here and marry on the spot without so much as a question as to my feelings. She is a foreigner from a country we know nothing of."

"You had best hold your tongue brother."

Nella stepped up, her face contorted in concern. "Rosco. I know—" She glanced at her husband. "We know you love her. She is kind, pretty and sweet. But she is not a virgin. She admitted as much to me before your wedding. Now, I don't know what the customs are where she comes from, but do you believe it was prudent to make such an important decision so hastily?"

Rosco saw red. He needed to take his leave before he lost his temper. He turned to the door. "So, you will not help me find my wife?" He slightly turned his face back toward them.

"Rosco, please, we meant no offense…" Nella's voice cracked.

But it was not her words he wanted to hear, but his brother's.

Outside, he walked quickly, his rage carrying him forward. Kurin had always had a sharp tongue and discordant character. He doubted everything and everyone.

The path to town led straight through the forest. The trees and soft bird calls mellowed his temper but when he reached the threshold of the thoroughfare, he felt more anxious than ever.

"Have you seen my wife?" he asked a plump, matronly woman named Carrae. She carried a squealing infant under one arm and a sack of potatoes in the other.

"No, Rosco, I haven't"

He moved away quickly. "Well, if you do, tell her I am searching for her."

The sun hung low on the horizon and Martine was emptying of its people going home for the main meal. Only those who frequented Martine's only tavern would be sticking around. It was a three story building made of wood and brick, painted white with crisscross of dark-brown wooden beams. The sound of laughter and merrymaking grew louder. Rosco entered and saw a handful of farmers and herders.

"Karl!" he called to a tall, hunchbacked man with big hands and a bulbous nose. "Have you seen Lananell today?"

Karl turned to the others, searching for an answer. "Your wife? No, Rosco. Sorry."

"Have any of you seen her?" he asked the others. "She has disappeared."

Merritt the farmer shook his head. Donal, a short, blond sheepherder who more often than not carried around a canister of snuff, spoke up. "Haven't seen her, Rosco. Have you lost your woman already, man?" He and the others laughed but it quickly died down when they saw he was not joining in with their jests. Donal swallowed. "When did you last see her?"

"Last night," Rosco replied. "When I woke up this morning, she was gone. I thought she had gone to pick berries or find herbs, like she does sometimes, but she has not returned and I am worried."

"Perhaps one of those shade people got her?" a man named Raffen, who Rosco knew since he was in swaddling clothes, asked. Raffen looked uneasily at the others. "We'll keep an eye out for her, Rosco. Selene knows Martine cannot lose another Healer."

Another Healer, Rosco thought. *Yes, the original Healer had been a foreigner, too, albeit a disguised one.*

Now Lananell had disappeared, just like Sheena. The men regarded one another uncomfortably. Rosco knew they were afraid of him. He was a bit intimidating with his height, big chest and shoulders, and he meant business. During the Spring Equinox, Martine would host games and bring in merchants from all over northern Corvasa. Rosco always entered the wrestling matches and tests of strength and almost always won. His brother Kurin was the only man in Martine to be disrespectful to his face.

Rosco half-heartedly nodded, thanked them and exited back out into the thoroughfare.

"Have you seen my wife?" he asked the shoemaker's wife, Mirae, a relatively handsome woman with thick brown hair and hourglass figure.

"No, Rosco I have not."

"Well, if you do, please tell her to go home at once. I have not seen her since last night."

His mind was a whirlwind now. He honestly did not know what to do. Should he go back home or stay in town in case she showed up?

What if she returned home and he was not there? He decided to go home and wait.

While he walked through the woods, he put his hand in his pocket and felt the looking glass. Just the touch of it seemed to calm him slightly. When he walked through the door, he called for her.

"Lananell!"

But there was no answer. The house was empty. He poured himself some wine and poked at the fire, stoking a flame. He spat into the fire. Where could she have gone? And why? That was the main question. She seemed happy with him and with her new duties. He sat and thought, staring into the fire, periodically getting up to pace around. Sometimes, he opened the door to see if she was walking up, but was only greeted with the rapidly fading sunlight. He kicked himself for not searching for her sooner. He should have begun the search that morning. Perhaps he would have had more luck.

He ran outside as the moon rose high. "Lananell! Lananell!" he shouted into the trees. The trees answered him by swaying gently in a breeze, the birds answered by singing and the gnats responded by swarming around him. He batted them and went back inside.

"Lananell, where are you?" he asked, slumping back down in front of the fire. That is when he noticed the looking glass he had set back on the table. A bright green glow emanated from it. Placing it in his hand, it was warm to the touch and emitted a low hum which Rosco had to strain to hear. He took a sip of wine and examined it more closely. When he turned, the looking glass went from glowing green to clear and the hum ceased. He turned again, rotating slowly in place, holding out the looking glass. Every time he turned past a particular direction, the looking glass glowed bright green. He ran outside and repeated the action.

"Northeast," he whispered. "It glows green when pointed northeast." Northeast was the direction of Cryer's Hill, the direction where the sheepherder and boy had been attacked. Had Lananell gone out to explore the area? He lifted the looking glass one last time and its green glow was unmistakable.

He hastily put a change of clothes in a knapsack. He fastened a giant club to his back, filled his pockets and the sack with some nuts, dried strips of elk meat, a boar sausage and apricots. A flaying knife lay on the window sill and he took it, plus a small spade, a piece of rope, a flagon of water and a torch. Kurin would no doubt come by soon. His goat and chickens were penned, so all Kurin had to do was feed them when he discovered Rosco had gone. He could trust him enough for that at least.

Rosco knew the trail that went northeast, through the meadow the miller described and over Cryer's Hill. It had been awhile since he had been there but he remembered well.

The moon was bright and lit his way. Every few minutes he held the looking glass in front of him to make sure he was continuing in the right direction. Maybe he was being foolish, perhaps he was not following Lananell at all, but his gut told him otherwise. The green glow continued to point in the northeast direction.

The meadow was calm and surreal under the moonlight. Someone had already cut through the tall grasses. The blades had been bent over and matted down in some places. Whoever it was, they were going northeast. In a clearing beyond the meadow, he discovered the remains of a fire. He waved the torch over the ground, searching for clues. A shiny object caught his eye. It was a silver clasp, used to hold a cloak or other article of clothing, in the shape of an eagle. The ground also had dark brown splotches which could only be dried blood. Seeing it threatened to raise panic but he willed it down. Another path—what appeared to be a game trail recently used by people—led off from the clearing and deeper into the forest, in the northeastern direction. The looking glass confirmed it. If it was indeed telling Rosco where Lananell was, she followed the trail out. The way led straight into the mountains, climbing up into the foothills first.

Now would be a good time to have Millena, he thought wistfully. He carried the torch and followed the path. Now and again, the flame would illuminate eyes staring out at him.

Crack!

Rosco froze. The sound came from somewhere behind him, but he couldn't tell how far.

"Who's there?" he called out into the darkness. Nothing answered as he stood there for how many minutes, he did not know. Whatever had made the sound was either gone or waiting for him to move again. He suddenly regretted bringing the torch. It announced his presence to everyone and everything within these woods.

He continued walking and had been for about an hour when he stopped suddenly and heard the unmistakable sound of footsteps behind him. He hurriedly dug a hole with the small spade and placed the end of the torch within. It would burn itself out or perhaps whoever was following him would take it. He quickened his pace. The tree cover blocked a lot of the moonlight but he could see well enough to make his way through the forest. Sometimes, he nearly broke into a run. He held the looking glass out in front of him once more and it still glowed when it pointed northeast.

The foothills were filled with giant boulders. Some existed unburied as if the hand of a giant placed them carefully among the trees, others were partly buried. Behind one of these boulders that glowed greenish-gray in the moonlight, Rosco hid and waited.

A few seconds passed and the footfalls got louder—whoever it was now ran. They had wisely not taken the torch. When Rosco was satisfied the culprit was close enough, he charged.

"*Rawr!*" he shouted, wielding his club in a giant arc.

"Rosco! No!" a familiar voice pleaded. The old man held up his hands. "It's me. Kurin!"

The power went out of him mid-swing and he dropped his club to the ground. "Kurin? What…why?"

"Why did you abandon your torch, fool?" Kurin spat.

"Let's go back and get it. I didn't know who you were. You are lucky to be alive."

They retraced their steps and Rosco clasped the still-burning torch. His brother's expression seemed to change with every angle of the flame.

Rosco did not ask Kurin for an explanation. Kurin hated admitting anything that would point to a soft heart or even optimism and hope. But he was glad for the help.

"Why have you come this way? Did those strangers get her? The Osseks?" Kurin asked.

"I don't know if they are Osseks. It is thousands of leagues from here to their territory and I have never heard them to raid this far northwest. They would have to climb over their treacherous mountain passes."

"Why have you come this way?" Kurin repeated.

"I used this," Rosco replied, holding up the looking glass. At the moment, it was clear. "I saw this call nature spirits for Hawk when that conjured dragon woman attacked Martine. He gave it to Lananell because she has a special gift with the fairies of the wood."

"Does it work for you, then, brother?"

Rosco held it up facing northeast and it immediately glowed green. Kurin watched in fascination. It was the most childlike expression Rosco had ever seen on his brother's face. If Kurin had not seen magic with his own eyes, he would have never believed it existed.

"It does this when I point it to the northeast, it turns green that is. Lananell carried it with her wherever she went so I take it to mean she's in the northeastern direction. It's showing me where she is because that's what she would have wanted."

Somewhere in the trees an owl hooted.

Rosco fully expected a rebuttal from his cantankerous brother. But Kurin surprised him and only nodded. Perhaps Kurin could sense his panic and his unwillingness to tolerate any doubt as to Lananell's disappearance.

After they had walked past the boulder where Rosco surprised his brother, Kurin asked, "How long do you intend to follow this trail, to search for her?"

"For as long as it takes. She is this way, I know it, and this small piece of glass will lead me to her."

And the biggest surprise for Rosco was in his brother's next words.

"Well, I will accompany you until we find her," Kurin said.

SHEENA SHOVELS SHIT

IN THE MORNING, SHEENA awoke to overwhelming sunlight in a room with no curtains. Stone walls towered over her. She lay upon a small pallet on the floor. Next to her was a pitcher of water and small porcelain wash basin. About twenty feet above was a hole in the stone wall with light piercing through. Two gray and white birds sat silently on the ledge of the natural window.

Two extraordinarily tall women entered through an off-white fabric hung over the threshold as a door. She pushed herself to a sitting position with difficulty. The women were surrounded by violet glows as if they moved within a colored egg. One of them squatted to look her in the eye. She had a blond braid forming a crown at the top of her head and wore a loose-fitting robe of white silk but it appeared lavender due to the glow around her. Her eyes were big and violet. In her hands she held a cup and raised it to Sheena's lips.

"Drink this." The woman's voice was musical and her beauty was so glorious it was almost painful to look upon her. "Ah, that is good, Sheena of Corvasa. I am Tessa and this is Raern. We are your guardians here in Ocht Hillnon."

Sheena swallowed the bitter substance and Tessa gave her more. Raern sat on her knees. She was not as beautiful as Tessa but was very striking in her own way. Her hair was dark brown and hung loosely, down to her knees. Her violet eyes were close together and her lips were overly full, giving her the appearance of a fish.

"Is she conscious?" Raern asked Tessa.

"Yes. And this drink will bring back her voice and memory."

When she said the words, Sheena suddenly remembered from the moment Simon Korodale took her power and beauty. Ever since then she had been in a state of shock. But now, all the memories flooded back. It was too much. She turned her face away from the Jaanaarian women and moaned.

"She is remembering," Tessa whispered.

A torrent of tears welled up and Sheena could not stop them. To release her anger, sadness, and rage, she was obliged to wail.

The women were silent as she sobbed uncontrollably. They watched her with their glows about them, something she would never regain and they made no move to comfort her.

"She is only half-Jaanaarian," Raern whispered to her companion.

Even though extreme emotion had hold of her, a tiny grain of rationality forced her to compose herself in front of these Jaanaarian women. One could still retain dignity even in the face of death. She would not let them get the best of her.

Tessa helped her stand and a rush of painful needles descended into her legs causing her to wobble.

"I have to sit for a moment," she said. Her legs were on fire. And her voice sounded weak, dry, her tongue thick in her mouth. The act of speaking took extraordinary effort. She wanted to push these giant women, who stood a full head and shoulders taller than her—and she was considered tall by Corvasan standards—away, but instead she was thankful for their touch and assistance. Perhaps she had lost height in addition to weight when Simon had taken her youth. Her arms were like shriveled sticks with dry cracked skin. Her hands were covered in dark spots and the nails were split and yellowing. She touched her scalp and only felt thin, scraggly tufts of hair.

"I will carry you," Raern said. The tall brunette scooped her up. "You are very light, Sheena."

Raern's touch was soft, soothing, full of comfort and warmth. Sheena heard her heartbeat through her chest. Tears threatened to fall again. It was as if she was a child back in her mother's arms.

They carried her down stone steps within a mountain cavern and then up another set of steps. They emerged into a fabulous garden with sheer rock walls of the mountain surrounding them. Rows of fruit and nut trees, flowers and crops occupied the entire open space. The colors of the fruits and flowers possessed every shade of the rainbow and seemed to possess a glow much like the one around Tessa and Raern.

If all I have to do is pick fruit and vegetables that will not quite be punishment.

But her escorts did not stop in the garden and continued through it. Only men were picking fruit. Their heads were shaved on the crown and they all possessed glows, but of varying colors. She tried to meet their eyes but they avoided hers at all cost.

"Where are you taking me?" This time her voice sounded strange, old, completely unrecognizable.

The women did not answer. A wonderful smell, like jasmine mixed with lavender, wafted past her nose and stayed with her as they neared the other side of the garden. Holes the height of two men penetrated the mountain rock in front of her. They entered a cave through one of these holes which connected to other caves and smaller caverns. The caves were living quarters Sheena realized. Another set of small caverns, some with men and women sitting in deep contemplation, possessed lime deposits jutting downward from the ceilings. Random steaming pools of water existed within the stone ground with a hazy light shining through the water.

They emerged into another open air garden surrounded by sheer rock walls, however the air in this garden smelled of shit and piss. Two small white tents with a ditch running alongside occupied the center of a field. Uncharacteristically green grass grew with a few flower bushes here and there. Sheena suddenly understood what her new job would be.

Tessa and Raern sat her down and gave her a shovel.

"Shovel the waste in the latrines halfway up the ditch then cover it with the dirt," Raern instructed.

"I cannot do that," Sheena protested. "I cannot even stand."

"Try to stand now," Tessa commanded.

Sheena pushed herself up with her hands and found the action surprisingly easy. Blood rushed into her legs but it was bearable. She gazed at Tessa in wonder. "How did…what…"

"Don't look at me," Tessa said. "It was Raern and the potion we gave you. She helped by carrying you. Now, the shovel, if you please."

She entered the white tent with the shovel. Inside, sections were divided with sheets of white linen as barriers. Each section contained a hole in the ground and the smell made Sheena gag but she held her breath and took a shovel full of shit outside to the ditch. After five trips, she was exhausted and had to sit down, panting from the exertion. Tessa and Raern silently watched. Their eyes held no pity. In fact, their eyes held nothing, they were violet pools of void. After a few minutes, they made a hand gesture, indicating she continue. She knew immediately what the gesture meant but did not understand how she knew.

The sun crossed the sky as she worked. Beads of sweat developed on her forehead and underarms. The work was slow going as she needed frequent bouts of rest. Every so often, Tessa would give her a drink of water.

When the sun was in its golden hour, Sheena let the shovel drop and went to her knees. "I cannot do anymore."

It was true. Her arms and shoulders ached, her back was sore and she was exhausted, gasping for breath through an open mouth. The women nodded and approached her. They floated rather than walked across the ground, their violet auras beautiful in the light of the sun.

"You must pick your own food so we will leave you here and you must find your way back to your room on your own. We will come for you again in the morning."

And so it went. Sheena would be woken at sunrise by Tessa and

Raern and led to the latrines where she worked for most of the day. Then she would pick her meals from the nut and fruit trees. One day, Tessa and Raern left her to do her work alone. When it was time to wash up and pick the night's supper, they reappeared out of nowhere to collect her.

In a bold display of confidence, while they walked through the gardens before the mountain caverns, Sheena asked "What is your purpose here?"

"To give our souls a face," Tessa said without hesitation. "The sacred teachings have become polluted in the south. They advocate for obliteration of individuality and disappearing into the void. It's a great corruption of the original teachings. And when they do teach magic without annihilation, it is only for power and manipulation."

Sheena remembered her time at the Crystal Palace as an Adept's Apprentice. She had learned all the ways of magic from elemental magic to runic magic to the magic of sound. But she had never heard of something called, "to give our souls a face".

"What do you mean?" she asked.

"Perhaps one day we will show you, Sheena," Tessa replied and neither of them elaborated further. They took on that eerie silence which meant they would not speak anymore.

Most of the Ocht hillnon existed within the mountain, in myriad caves and caverns where the inhabitants made their homes. Sheena had yet to see a gathering hall or any type of meeting place. Tessa and Raern always escorted her to and from her room, but there was no guard posted in the evening. And they left her alone now during the day, too. What would happen if she wandered off to explore? Would they punish her?

Her thoughts were rudely interrupted when she saw a man waiting for her in her room. He was very tall like the women, and wore a long white beard. His face was vaguely familiar.

"Ah, so you are not catatonic after all."

If Sheena had any blood left in her dried-out, emaciated body, it rushed to her face.

"Not anymore," Tessa said. "Raern and I gave her the drink."

"I'll have a private little talk with our newest guest," he told the women.

"Certainly, Honor," Raern replied. They bowed their heads and floated away, their auras glimmering in the dying light.

She noticed the women alternated between floating and walking, it was dependent on something, perhaps their mood, but she wasn't sure.

"I am Honor Titae, the druid leader of this hillnon. Do you remember me?" He sat cross-legged on the ground in her small stone room.

Sheena slowly sat, her bones creaking.

"No."

"Hawk and his *oide* brought you here. Do you remember them?"

A wave of anger came over her but she kept her composure. "I remember Hawk but not the other."

Honor Titae fixed her with his violet eyes. Eyes like hers. "How were you able to break the spell around the elemental globe?"

Sheena shifted uncomfortably. "I don't remember."

Honor Titae chuckled softly. His eyes were kind and for a brief instant, Sheena thought he believed her.

"You will tell me voluntarily one day." He stood. And vanished into thin air.

Sheena stared in shock and envy at the empty place where he had been standing. In all her many years of magical training, she had never mastered the skill of vanishing into thin air. What a talent! Why was a man with such power wasting his life cooped up in some mountain with a bunch of obsequious derelicts playing at being holy? By the gods, what a laugh! These Jaanaarians who inhabited this gods-forsaken island were weaklings. Outcasts. Unable to resist degenerative influences so they erected an astral wall to protect themselves! That was when they admitted defeat. Her mother knew it—that was why she left.

"It is the natural law, Sheena, my daughter," her mother told her. "All the peoples of Perthia are descendants of ancient Jaanaarians but they will not leave their land due to fear and fear makes one weak."

"Mother, will the Golden Band last forever?"

"That is the problem with spells, they do not last forever. Even those as powerful as the Golden Band. They decay just like everything else, perhaps not as quickly as other phenomenon, but they do decay."

Sheena remembered the conversation like it was yesterday. She knew the information would come in handy someday.

The next day while emptying the latrine, Sheena overheard a discussion between two women while they relieved themselves. She could not see them, but moved closer to the tents to hear better.

"…it caressed my body and renewed it. I could see and hear with more clarity than ever before. Only a few of us…"

The rest of what she said was barely discernible. Sheena moved closer.

The second woman spoke. "…the true fountain of youth. It took off decades."

"How many know its location?" The first one asked.

The wind blew the white linen flaps and she caught a glimpse of the women squatting over the latrine holes, their skirts billowing around them.

"…under the Heiro Needle…" she heard one say.

When they exited, both of their auras were blue with flecks of sparkling gold. Gray hair spilled over their shoulders, still thick and shiny.

The Heiro Needle.

When Tessa and Raern returned, she asked, "What is the Heiro Needle?"

Tessa began to explain, no questions asked, her blonde hair divided into two braids that she wore in front of her shoulders. "The denizens of Ocht Hillnon do not know if the Heiro Needle was natural or manmade. It is a large phallic stone protruding straight into the sky with an almost perfect four sided pyramid at its summit. The perfection of the pyramid capstone led some to wonder whether it was constructed by the gods. It occupies the center of one of the highest courtyards on the mountain. There are tunnels within the mountain that lead directly to it. It is the only way to get there."

"Is there anything below it?" Sheena asked.

"Underneath?" Tessa frowned which did not take away from her beauty but made her appear pouty. "I've never been there. Have you, Raern?"

"No. But there are legends about its power. It derives from the mountain. Why do you ask, Sheena?"

"I overheard some women discussing it—"

"Tonight, you will eat from one of the kitchens," Raern said, changing the subject.

Once they entered the mountain, instead of turning right, Tessa led her left and through a short maze of interlocking tunnels and caverns. The kitchen was adjacent to a larger room with a fireplace, thick, multi-colored rugs and silk pillows. Tessa went to a large iron pot and ladled out a bowl of meat stew with a slice of creamy white cheese. The soup was delicious and warmed her insides. The nuts and fruit she had been eating were also tastier than any time she could remember. Her limbs were beginning to fill out a little more.

That night in her room she waited until the last rays of twilight turned the sky a grayish blue. The full moon rose over the eastern horizon in all of its glory. All the better to light her way as she climbed through stepped tunnels and luxurious courtyards, up and up, through a myriad of passages. She was panting once she reached the courtyard with the Heiro Needle. It pointed upward into the starry sky like a giant stone finger. Another two tunnels led away from the courtyard into the belly of the mountain. Sheena decided to go left.

Darkness engulfed her. She pressed one bony hand against the smooth, cold surface of the stone. Her ancient eyes did not see well ever since the tragedy in Westernaphalia, so she kept her left hand out in front of her. A draft blew the fragrance of thousands of years past her nose.

She had been walking, tentative step by tentative step, for about fifteen minutes when she saw a soft glow of light. As she got closer, the light brightened and the tunnel took an abrupt turn to the right where a single torch burned in a lone sconce. The tunnel ended in a round room with two other tunnels leading off into the darkness. Taking the torch from its sconce, she sniffed the air at each entrance. The one to her left smelled of sulfur.

She stepped into its darkness and heard the sound of dripping water. Within a minute, the tunnel descended steeply into a subterranean cavern. The floor consisted of steaming, turquoise pools. Limestone crags hung from the ceiling like malformed fruit. The cave was illuminated with a strange golden light that seemed to come from everywhere and nowhere. She placed the torch in a sconce, hurriedly undressed and slid her foot carefully into the steaming, hot water. It was like a lover's caress after many moons of separation, like a warm blanket by a blazing hearth after trekking through an icy mountain winter. Her muscles had never felt so relaxed. She inhaled and spread her arms and legs, floating. The ceiling of the cave was covered in kaleidoscopic crystals that seemed to wink at her through the reflection of the water.

Millions of tiny bubbles floated from the bottom to the surface, tickling her skin. She must have looked a sight, an ancient old hag floating naked! Beauty did not matter here. If it was anywhere else, she would be treated with disgust, but would be expected to give wise counsel. If she did not feel so young, perhaps in such a situation, she would not care and would welcome the lack of attention and free time to rest her weary bones. But at the moment, she felt young again, she felt strength returning.

The water seemed to seep through her skin and into her flesh, caressing her bones, entering into and fortifying them. Small whirlpools appeared around her and sucked playfully at her flesh. The vortexes sucked, pulling something out, something foul and decaying. And then, suddenly, they disappeared. Sheena let her toes touch the bottom of the pool. Streams of water trickled down the skin of her arms and chest. Instinctively, she lifted a hand to her face. The wrinkles remained but were less pronounced and the flesh felt firmer.

The biggest difference was in her body. The aches had dissolved. When she gazed at the turquoise water, she noticed a whitish haze floating just above the surface. Looking closer, she saw it was not really a haze at all but the transparent, crystalline bodies of beautiful, tiny fairies. They possessed pointed ears and chins, with an opalescent sheen. Their eyes shifted colors like late afternoon sunlight through a window. Their faces twisted into smiles and she heard their tiny voices in her head.

...we are the fairies of these pools...

"Hello," Sheena said aloud.

...Hello, bright one...

They moved so quickly, intertwining with each other in a wavelike dance, that Sheena could not keep her eyes on one at a time. When one spoke, other tiny voices echoed.

...we have regenerated your essence...

My name is Sheena, she thought to them.

...Sheena. He has told us about your destiny. The essence of humans feed us...

She was perplexed. "What destiny? Who is he?"

...He is through the waters. Come, we will show you...

Through the waters?

Come...

Sheena inhaled deeply and sank back into the bubbling spring. The fairies swirled around her as tiny bubbles and pulled her body lower. A gap opened up beneath her and suddenly, she swam through a tunnel and out into a room with an extraordinarily high ceiling. The water was losing its density rapidly and she inhaled again. Air surrounded her.

The room was lit with that strange, golden light but in its center stood a huge cylindrical crystal with the top in the shape of a pyramid exactly like the Heiro Needle.

The crystal projected light into geometric patterns against the stone walls. In the center of the crystal was a dark shape from which waves of light emanated. Sheena felt a strange sort of awe while gazing upon it.

She took a step forward and reached out her hand. The object within appeared to be a human organ.

A heart.

An unmistakable presence was also with her in the room. A masculine presence.

"Who are you?" She whispered.

The crystal flashed and the emanations of snowflake-like images began to revolve around the room with a low, humming sound.

"If you take it, I will guide you," a man's voice boomed throughout the antechamber.

Sheena jumped. "Who are you?"

The man's laughter was low but taunting. The geometric patterns swirled around her on the black stone walls. She felt dizzy.

"Someone dearly in need of a human body, of a lover's embrace, of revenge."

Sheena froze, trembling. Back in the Linnsonian tent in Westernaphalia, she had felt a mild dread at facing her enemies. But she had never felt fear like this. "Where are you?" Sheena whispered.

"Where am I? Ah, but you are gazing at the most fundamental part of my being."

Sheena heard a whimper then a prolonged sucking noise as if someone were breathing air. The black heart within the crystal began to beat.

"I am Nolis, ancient warrior god of Perthia, a distinction now given to Neit. My blood has been spilled on the battlefields of Corvasa in the form of warriors who carry my blood in their veins. Ever since the separation, I have been searching for my other half and at one point, had found her. I was ecstatic at our reunion, but was soon tempted by human beauty and human women. I abandoned the other half, my other half, and when that is done, only disaster follows. She sought revenge against my descendants and enslaved them. She took human form and mated with them, her pure energy made manifest into blood."

Sheena was not the type to kneel before anyone. But the power in the room was undeniable, a force so unrelenting and brutal that she went against her own nature and knelt.

"I am at your service…ah, my lord." She had not the slightest idea how to properly address a god and her voice was trembling.

"Are you willing to grant my wishes?"

Sheena hesitated. The room was empty save for the crystal, the beating heart and its emanations.

"Would you like me to show myself?" It suddenly occurred to her this could all be a trick. Had Tessa and Raern set her up for this?

As if reading her thoughts, Nolis repeated his query. "Do you wish that I show myself?"

"Yes."

The air to her right shimmered and a transparent shape took form slowly. He was extremely tall, nearly twice the size of a full-blooded Jaanaarian. He wore a light blue silken tunic, with golden embroidered runes along the edges of the sleeves and collar. Golden sparkles danced around him like fireflies. Long, wavy curtains of shiny black hair parted in the middle to reveal a pair of sky-blue eyes. High cheekbones loomed over a slight, aquiline nose and full, sensual lips. Light suddenly beamed out of Nolis's eyes forcing Sheena to lower her gaze.

This is a god manifesting! she thought, awestruck. Surely, her luck had changed.

"Sheena, half-Jaanaarian and half-Corvasan daughter with the blood of the House of the Sun running through your veins. Your purpose is destruction." Nolis's voice boomed.

"Destruction?"

"Have you ever analyzed your motives?"

"No, I don't analyze motives. There is what I want and I take measures to get what I want. I analyze the risks of that." The frankness of her reply startled even her. Nolis obviously needed her for something, which returned a bit of her confidence.

Deep throated laughter rang out into the stone room and bounced off the wall. The phallic crystal visibly vibrated. "I like an ambitious and honest woman. You remind me of someone."

Sheena lifted her eyes to get another brief glimpse. The blinding light still shone from his eyes and a strange, golden glow shone from his body. There was something else, something she could not quite put her finger on, but then it came to her in a rush. Nolis did not cast a shadow and the lights illuminating from the crystal beamed right through him onto the wall.

He lifted his hand and a thin piece of the crystal fell away and shattered on the stone ground. The black organ was now unprotected and still emitted shimmering waves of light within the cylinder.

"Is that a heart?" Sheena asked.

"Take it," Nolis commanded. "And I will tell you what to do."

WARSHIPS AND VIOLET EYES

THE QUAY LEADING TO THE GALLEY was teeming with masses of people from all corners of Perthia and beyond. Merchants stood behind carts and within stalls that lined the quay. Brightly colored powders and liquids, tools, instruments and weapons, ship supplies and livestock, were all being sold. When their party passed, a pock-marked, thin man shouted from his stall, "Fine silks and satins for the beautiful lady…"

Sillisnae made the mistake of meeting his eyes.

"Hey ho, there, sweetness!" he thrust his tongue out and waved the tip like a snake.

Sillisnae turned away in disgust.

Fishermen had also set up stalls with the catch of the day. Some carried carts full of fish and dumped them into rectangular wooden bins, their silver bodies flapping in the sunlight.

Throughout the crowd, what could only be city watchmen patrolled the streets with sunbursts of the House of the Sun embroidered on their red cloaks. They carried swords and daggers and their eyes watched the throngs of people warily.

Some men of the crowd wore ballooned breeches of many colors tucked into leather or suede boots. Their hair was long and loose with close cropped beards and tattoos on their arms, chests and even faces.

Pirates.

Sillisnae stared, fascinated. She had never seen a pirate and only heard of them in stories. As soon as they glanced her way she turned her head.

The flood of warm, sweaty bodies shocked her. The capital was nothing like this. It was as if the entire city had crowded onto the boardwalk.

"That's it, over there," Kryst said to Locklin, pointing. "She is from Maeltip and will take us home. The *Crimson Treasure*."

The main mast boasted a red square sail with two fishes entwining each other and a bare-breasted mermaid graced the hull of the galley. Men moved about on deck shouting and carrying supplies. Sillisnae spied a long horizontal opening that could only be for oars.

Kryst pulled her by the hand to the gangway. In the throng, no one could see she still wore chains around her wrists. The reddish wood floor of the deck was wet with soapy water and the smell of lye mixed with the salty sea stung her nostrils.

When they boarded, Kryst produced a document with the King's seal.

"Ah, it be the Lord Prince!" a man exclaimed.

Prince Kryst's face dissolved into recognition.

"Samuel! This is Captain Samuel, an old friend of mine from Maeltip," Kryst said.

Locklin shook the captain's hand. "I am Locklin, son of Hap and Healer of the village Arthac in Corvasa."

"First time aboard a ship, Healer?" Captain Samuel spat. "Ye look a bit winkered. In any case, welcome aboard the *Crimson Treasure!*"

Before Locklin could answer, Kryst introduced Sillisnae. "May I present Sillisnae, a former Adept's Apprentice of the Crystal Palace."

The captain smelled as if he had not bathed in a year. When he smiled, he proudly displayed a mouthful of yellow, rotting teeth with a few missing from the bottom left side of his jaw. Above his beady, hazel eyes were two rectangular, black eyebrows and he had a hooked nose that pointed to the ground.

"Her magic is bound, correct?" Captain Samuel asked, giving Locklin a wary glance. "Don't want any trouble from rebellious Adepts. I have a disdain for the Black Arts, I do. Lost many a man to it."

"Of course," Locklin replied. "For all intents and purposes, she is no longer an Adept while she is bound and it would require a very talented druid to undo her bonds. No one will do that unless they are rewarded. We have King Emeril's seal and it is peacetime. No druid in Perthia will reverse her bond."

Captain Samuel's crew was as dirty and ill-kept as he was. Sillisnae knew they were pirates from the way they conspicuously leered without any attempt to hide it. Once, Lord Korodale had instructed her to read about one Salin the Strong Shoulders who captured a tribal queen from the Knotts to halt a war between Knottian tribes. He did it out of love and eventually married her. Knowing so little about pirates, she nevertheless understood the company she kept.

"Please release these shackles, my lord Kryst," she asked politely. "How can I escape a ship set sail? Where would I go? Please, please my lord, the chains have my wrists bruised and bleeding."

Before the prince could answer, Locklin's hand flung out lightning quick. She turned her head just in time and his open hand struck her ear rather than her face but oh, by the gods, did it smart! Captain Samuel chuckled.

"Spoiled bitch!" Locklin spat at her. "You are no longer in the Crystal Palace learning high magic. You will shut your mouth and only speak when spoken to. Or there will be more where that came from."

Sillisnae was incredulous. Why would a village Healer have such contempt for her? He had hit her on the deck in full view of the crew. Some of them tittered; the rest leered like they had done from the moment she stepped on board. Their hungry eyes made her stomach queasy. She would make certain not to venture very far from Kryst. Oddly, he was the only one she trusted.

"Are these men smugglers?" she whispered when Locklin was out of earshot.

"We are sailing to Maeltip, back to my home." He gave her a brief glance. "That is what is important."

"I be takin' ye to yer cabin, if it please the beautiful miss." Captain Samuel bowed with a flourish of his right arm in a gesture of supreme mockery.

Sillisnae blushed at the effrontery. A captain of a ship should not bow before a prisoner.

Kryst locked his jaw but his eyes were distant, cold. "That would be splendid, Captain Samuel. Please show us our accommodations."

Sillisnae's cabin was just under the deck and barely big enough for her to lie down. A basin of water and a pitcher had been placed on a stand near the doorway and she refreshed her face with the cool water. In addition to a heaping of straw, a pallet of colorful blankets lay on the floor. They appeared clean but the smell was rather musty. In a corner was a bucket for waste. The ship creaked and lurched. Sillisnae still heard the sounds of the quay. A small round window was just above her head. Straining on her tiptoes, she saw another ship docked next to them, its crew running about, readying themselves for voyage.

A sudden knock at the door followed by Kryst entering without being summoned reminded her she was still a captive.

"We are returning to the deck and will see you when we dock in Tovar," Kryst said. The splintered wooden door closed behind him with a thud and she was left alone in the cabin.

Her stomach rumbled. She had not eaten since they left Minosae. Would they ever feed her or just leave her to starve? And the chains on her wrists were painful.

A lurch caused her to lose her footing and she fell onto the pallet of blankets with a thud. Loud shouts from the deck heralded they had left the quay. She curled up in a ball and tried to ignore the pain in her wrists.

Soon they were sailing on the open water. The ship gently rocked and her stomach heaved but nothing came up. Lord Korodale had taught her breathing techniques when she first came to the Crystal Palace. She used them now to try to calm her queasiness.

"The breath is the final secret," he had informed her one day. "The *pneuma* contains the key to immortality. One day, I will explain more…"

Inhale. Hold. Exhale slowly. Inhale. Hold. Exhale slowly.

She must have dozed off because she awoke with a start when the door to her cabin swung open and banged against the wall.

Locklin swayed as he entered, drunk as a sailor in port.

"Is it night?" Sillisnae asked. She sat up, rubbed her eyes, and pulled the blankets around her. He stumbled over and slapped her full in the face. The blow was so strong she fell over, her head striking the ground. His hands groped clumsily at the laces of his breeches.

"No," she whispered when he grabbed her ankles, his unlaced breeches falling around his thighs. He pulled up her skirt.

"*No!*" she shouted, struggling. He grabbed the shackles that bound her wrists and the pain made her scream. He sat on her hips, her white linen bloomers the only barrier between them. She twisted and squirmed frantically, calling on every bit of strength to throw him off. Suddenly, his face was next to hers and he pulled her head by the hair.

"Best not to struggle unless you want a broken neck."

His breath smelled of wine and something else, some kind of meat. His greasy face was dark gray in some places from grime and dirt. His deep blue eyes were dead, vacant, and his thick crop of blond curls fell into her eyes. She took a deep, shuddering breath and let out a piercing wail as forceful as her lungs would allow. The bastard would not get away with this!

He abruptly backed away. "Bitch! If you do that again, I'll slit your throat!"

She sat up quickly to face him. "Hardly likely. What will your newfound master do to you then, fiend?"

The Healer's lips curled back into a snarl. He looked like a cornered, wild animal, ready to strike at any moment. "He is not my master."

"Ha!" Sillisnae erupted into taunting laughter. That seemed to enrage him even more and he slapped her again. Stars blossomed in a sea of black. Just as she felt the touch of his cold, clammy hands on her thighs once more, someone entered through the open door.

"What are you doing?" Kryst shouted. He yanked Locklin by the shoulders. "Are you mad, man? This is my prisoner. You will *not* touch her!"

Locklin glared at him. "How dare you touch me!" he slurred. "Don't forget who you are dealing with!"

"I have not forgotten." Kryst stood tall. "And I'll remind you to keep a civil tongue in your head, Corvasan. You seem to have forgotten who *you* are dealing with."

The Healer averted his eyes and stumbled as the ship lurched. "Why are you defending this split tail? Perhaps it was a mistake to bring you to that altar?"

"You and I both know it was not your decision," Kryst said, never taking his eyes off Locklin. "Now get out of here. And if I ever catch you doing this again, I'll have you walk the plank."

Locklin brushed himself off and spat. "Fat chance of that, prince. I am the only Adept aboard this ship." He stumbled toward the door and slammed it after him.

"Are you all right, Sillisnae?" His voice was sympathetic but he made no move toward her. "Did he hurt you?"

"No." She thought she may cry but she took a few deep breaths to stop the tears. "He frightened me more than anything." She pulled her skirt over her knees. "Why does he hate me so?"

"He hates everyone."

Sillisnae backed farther into the corner. Kryst stared at her like one would stare at an exotic animal.

"I'm very hungry, my...my...prince. Is it possible I could have some food?"

"Why, of course, Sillisnae. I didn't realize—"

The ship lurched wildly, throwing Kryst off his feet and sending Sillisnae rolling across the room. Panicked shouts from above penetrated the walls. The floor heaved upward again and they both were thrown in the opposite direction across the hay strewn floor.

"What is happening?" Sillisnae screamed. "Is it a storm?"

The Maeltipian got unsteadily to his feet and made for the door.

"Don't leave me here!" The ship lurched to one side. Sillisnae suppressed the urge to vomit. She managed to get to her feet and ran to Kryst, throwing her arms up and over his head from behind, in an embrace.

"What are you doing? Are you mad?"

"No!" she yelled. "I will not stay here if this ship is going down. I will not drown."

"You are not going to drown. Ships meet rough weather all the time. We are probably caught in some freak storm. That is why I must go on deck to see what is going on. Now let go!"

"Unshackle me!" Sillisnae demanded.

The ship continued to rock back and forth but less drastically. She had to shuffle her feet to keep balance but Kryst kept his easily.

"All right," he murmured. He produced a key from within the folds of his surcoat. The lurching of the ship made it difficult to fit the key into the small keyhole but on the third attempt he succeeded.

Kryst wasted no time. He bolted up the stairs to the deck with Sillisnae on his heels. Dark clouds obscured the bright moon and lightning struck in the distance, illuminating the black, roiling waves. The crew shouted commands in Maeltipian as giant waves crashed into the sides of the ship, spraying Sillisnae with water. All the men were soaked through already, some faces were panicked and others lined with determination. Captain Samuel stood at the helm, his long, dark hair plastered to his face, shouting orders to his crewmen. Sillisnae was shocked to see Locklin at his side with his hands raised in the air, chanting loudly in the True Tongue.

"What is going on?" Sillisnae yelled at Kryst but he ignored her and headed straight for Captain Samuel.

When he reached them, she heard him say, "Mother of the gods!"

Then she saw the cause of his curse.

Not far and directly in their path, the sea lapped against a giant black warship, the size of which took Sillisnae's breath away. The symbol of Neit, the god of war, graced the black sails.

"Blessed Selene," she murmured under her breath as her bladder threatened to give way. Fire balls flew from the warship's deck and slammed into the side of the *Crimson Treasure*. Several small boats filled with men-at-arms rushed toward them to the steady beat of drums. The smell of smoke hung thickly in the air.

Locklin chanted frantically in the True Tongue at the helm next to Captain Samuel. Sillisnae understood his spellbinding perfectly. He attempted to conjure a shield for the ship.

"If he doesn't stop them, they will board this ship in a matter of minutes." She grabbed Kryst's arm. "Unblock my magic. I can stop this."

Kryst was so mesmerized by the sight, Sillisnae was not sure if he had heard but then he turned to her. Light blue eyes peered out under a furrowed, blonde brow. "Locklin would never agree to it."

"This ship is on the verge of being taken! Stopping that is the priority."

The wind howled powerfully in her ears and a spray of freezing water hit her full in the face. She shivered violently at the shock of it. Their druids were the source of the blasting wind and rough waters. Whitish, transparent sylphs flew through the air in spirals and waves. If only her power were not blocked, she could take command of them.

Captain Samuel's hands were white from the force of holding the wheel and his face was a grimace of effort. But even with Locklin's chanting of the sacred words and the captain's efforts to physically turn the ship, they remained dead in the water. Sillisnae almost ran down

Kryst to approach Locklin. She pulled on his arm with all her might to bring him out of his self-styled trance.

"Whatever you are doing, it is not working!" She had to shout over the noise of the crashing waves, wind and sea spray. "Unblock my magic!"

Locklin gazed down at her with eyes of ice and a snarl. "Never," he hissed.

"You will kill us all," she insisted, "Your magic is ineffectual!"

He lowered a hand to her shoulder as if to shove her away but she thrust it aside. "Unbind me!" she shouted, grabbing the edges of his motley cloak. "Release me now or you will get us all killed!"

A loud crack ripped through the air when part of the starboard railing ripped apart. Two crewmen who had been standing against it fell screaming into the sea, their cries echoing through the air.

Sillisnae shook Locklin. "Release my bonds now and you may have a chance. If you do not, there will come a day when you wish you had, *if* you survive!"

The Healer lowered his hands and stared at her, bewildered. It must have been something in her eyes. But before he could answer, there was another sound of wood splitting and the deck lurched upward to meet them. When she hit, she saw men in black climbing over the railing with swords drawn and shouting in the harsh, guttural language she had come to know as Linnsonian. Locklin lay next to her on his back, his eyes dazed. Sounds of swords joined in battle, war shouts and cries of pain surrounded them.

"This is it, Locklin," she spat. Water had soaked her dress and the ice cold made her teeth chatter. Her hand cupped his jaw and turned his face toward her. "The Li-Li-Linnsonians are taking the ship. Wi-with their druids, you are no match. Unblock me now!"

"I can't," he said.

"What do you mean you can't?"

"It was Kryst who blocked you," he shouted, "or rather, the entity that enlivens him."

"The entity?" She had no idea what he meant. Two hands pulled her up from behind and roughly spun her around. A man with penetrating black eyes stared at her severely. A long black cloak with a cowl obscured parts of his face. Wispy tendrils of white hair fell into his eyes. All of a sudden she was aware the wind had ceased its relentless howling and the sea had calmed. But men shouted and fought all around her. Some of the crew fought the Linnsonians but only half-heartedly. Many others threw down their weapons, went to their knees and bowed their heads before their new masters.

"All here are now under the jurisdiction of Captain Oscan of Linnso!" a black-clad Linnsonian shouted at the top of his lungs.

Kryst winced when he heard the name. Black-clad men continued to climb over the railing of the deck. A tall man with a sharp nose who appeared to be in authority stepped up to the helm and a circle formed around him. Kryst pulled Sillisnae back, away from the thronging bodies of men, Linnsonians and Maeltipian crew alike.

"Where is the woman?" Captain Oscan asked the throng.

All heads turned in the direction of Sillisnae and Kryst. A path formed through the crowd, creating a human hallway leading to the new captain.

"You!" he said when he saw Kryst. "But how?"

A hushed silence fell over the crew. The only sounds were of waves lapping against the hull. The clouds had parted again, allowing the moonlight to illuminate the scene. Captain Oscan beckoned with his hand but when Kryst tried to pull her forward, she resisted.

"Don't do that if you want to live," he barked. "These men mean business."

He did not have to tell her that! She knew damn well who *these men* were. But she did not understand why they wanted her or how they knew she was on the ship. Perhaps Renfala had not killed all the Linnsonians in the camp, allowing some to escape. But how could they recognize her? She had been in the tent with Sheena for only a short period.

"Captain Oscan!" Kryst called, pulling a reluctant Sillisnae behind him. "The last time I saw you, you had sword in hand ready to strike me down."

"Approach, Prince of Maeltip. Your father will be overjoyed to see you are alive and uninjured. He has sent many a man to search far and wide over the lands of Perthia. That vile Adept who chanted in the Misty Horizon, called upon the Black Arts and you disappeared."

"The vile Adept? You mean Titus, son of Milnit? For some inexplicable reason, I think Titus was bid to do as he was told."

Captain Oscan guffawed and spittle flew from his lips. "Why Prince Kryst, your father was so generous to give us ships and an army of pirates and you think I repay him by harming his son? You have gravely misjudged my character!"

Sillisnae detected the minutest trace of sarcasm in his voice. But she doubted Kryst did. His eyes told her he wanted to believe the Captain. The crew stood transfixed, staring back and forth between Kryst and Captain Oscan.

"Why have you taken this ship, Captain Oscan? If you honored my father truly, as you say, you would not have put the lives of this crew in danger."

"I did not know you were on this ship, Prince Kryst. Now that I do, I see you have this lovely young woman with you. What is your name, my dear?"

Sillisnae cringed. She wanted to be invisible. If only she possessed her magic!

"Her name is Sillisnae, Captain Oscan," Kryst said defiantly. "She is a former Adept's Apprentice from the Crystal Palace, given to me by the Sun King himself."

Whatever the Captain thought of Kryst's words, he carefully hid beneath a stoic mask.

"Wonderful. Then you will not mind if we reroute this ship toward our destination. Your father would welcome a chance for you to prove yourself in battle."

Locklin appeared suddenly behind them. "You must go with them, Kryst. You have no choice."

"Who is this man who would not show and introduce himself properly?" Captain Oscan asked loudly.

Locklin quickly stepped in front of Kryst and went to one knee. "I am Locklin, son of Hap, Healer of Arthac in Corvasa, Captain. My services are at your disposal."

The Linnsonian chuckled. "One quick to change allegiance when he is faced with no other choice. I like that. A practical man. Stand, Locklin of Arthac. What kind of powers do you possess?"

"All manner of talents, Captain. Healing, divining, summoning of gods and demons, creation of golems, and other things. It all depends on what you ask of me."

"I see. I may, in fact, have use for you. Stay within sight." Captain Oscan nodded curtly then threw his hands high into the air. "Hi oh! Anric! Set a course for the mouth of the Othalla! All of you men! You are now under the command of Captain Oscan of Linnso. We sail north, up the Othalla. If you obey, you will be treated well. If you do not, it will be all the worse for you. Our druids are highly trained, the best in the realm. Unless you desire to meet Labraid on this journey, I advise each and every one of you to obey because insubordination will be punished severely. Any type of rebellion will be swiftly crushed."

As he spoke, several Linnsonians surrounded them with curved longswords drawn, large axes secured to their backs and daggers at their hips. About a dozen extraordinarily tall men, almost twice the size of an average man, stood equally spaced among their fellow countrymen. Cylindrical-shaped hats with several unfamiliar runes sat arrogantly atop their heads. All had their foreheads tattooed with a winged disk. And their eyes were violet.

Violet eyes?

They can't be...

That was not possible. But their height was another giveaway.

Sillisnae also saw an Adept glow surrounding each of them.

Captain Oscan approached and offered his arm to her. "My dear, you are a sight for battle weary eyes. You will be my very special guest."

Kryst quickly shoved between them. "She remains with me, Captain. She is a gift from King Emeril of Corvasa, his most treasured prize I promised to keep safe."

Something powerful illuminated Kryst's eyes at that moment. Her breath caught in her throat. A moment that seemed like an eternity passed while all eyes watched, waiting. Captain Oscan slowly broke into a smile and bowed with a flourish.

"Of course, Prince Kryst. You are my very special guest as well. Won't you accompany us?"

RIDDLES FROM LITTLE GIRLS

"WHERE ARE WE GOING?"

The river was incredibly wide, at least a mile. Kryst recalled the source of the Cthalla was in a valley on the eastern side of Mount Moirae, the legendary home of the Weavers. Many leagues to the south of its source were three haunted cities called the Triad in what was now Osseka, a frightful place where the tribes ate man flesh.

"There are two possibilities. But suffice to say, our destination may be much closer than previously thought," Master Oscan replied.

They sat in Captain Samuel's cabin. His head had been posted on a spike on deck as a reminder to those who would think of mutiny. The quarters were cramped and smelled of stale ale and rum. Two bunks with maroon blankets hung from a wall. A giant square table took up most of the room. Burning candles illuminated a map and two manuscripts.

"And the destination would be?" Kryst pressed.

Sillisnae sat next to him; her flowing auburn hair was freshly brushed and hung down over her shoulders in cascading waves. Master Oscan had provided a female servant to beautify her. The woman's name was Tanell and she would not look a man in the eye. Sillisnae stared straight ahead with her hands in her lap. The ship did not rock nearly as much as it had on open sea. The windows behind Oscan framed a foggy green landscape.

"You could not possibly want to go to the Triad," Kryst observed.

"Because it is haunted?" Master Oscan folded his hands in his lap. "That is not our destination."

"Then where?"

The Master's black eyes beamed with a mischievous deviance. "To Mount Moirae."

Sillisnae sucked in breath next to him.

"The home of the Weavers?" Kryst was incredulous.

The Master guffawed. "You don't really believe that do you? Three old women who weave the fate of the entire world, who are older than the gods and even created them? What rubbish. Oh, the gods exist all right, but not in human form and must be pulled into those forms by humans.

"Something spectacularly phenomenal exists in Mount Moirae but it is not three old hags with supernatural powers. And what exists there, we will take."

"Which is?" Kryst asked. He was infinitely curious. "Is it the dragon?"

Master Oscan pressed his fingertips together and shot Sillisnae a brief glance. "Yes, that and the crystal it guards."

"The Crystal Skull?" That was also a legend. "If you don't believe in the existence of the Weavers, why would you believe in the Crystal Skull?"

"Oh, the Skull exists as does the dragon." Master Oscan's beady black eyes rested on Sillisnae. The ship creaked and Kryst heard the sound of ropes tightening.

Kryst knew about the Crystal Skull or at least had learned about it in his studies. All children in Perthia had heard stories of the Weavers and the Skull that created the world.

"The dragon guards the Skull because it has the power to create worlds and the power to give them life. If it fell into the wrong hands, it could wreak havoc. It was said the skull belonged to the first god to become a man after having discovered the secret of creating matter from light. No one knew his name, it was forgotten through the mists of time, but some say he was a Jaanaarian, having been sent to earth from the stars. He then procreated through his thought forms."

"What exactly does the Crystal Skull do?" Kryst asked.

"Ah, Prince Kryst. Guard well the information you are about to receive. The Adepts in the Crystal Palace of Corvasa do not even possess it. They are clueless and wandering around in the dark. But those of us in Linnso know its value, therefore we pursue it."

"And that is?" Kryst wished he would get to the point.

"The Crystal Skull holds all magical knowledge within it. The one who wears the Crystal Skull and is not killed by its power will initially feel they can read the thoughts of all the people in the world simultaneously. But that is only the beginning. The real power lies in the wearer's ability to control it. And that cannot be done without divine intervention—"

"Divine intervention?" Kryst interrupted.

"—that will facilitate the wearer to control the thoughts of the most powerful men in Perthia. In addition, control the thoughts of entire populations! And they won't have a clue they are being manipulated." Spittle flew from Master Oscan's lips and his voice got higher when he spoke the last two words. He must have realized he lost control of his emotions because he quickly cleared his throat and took on a less excited tone. "Originally, the Crystal Skull was meant to communicate with the other Jaanaarians that came from the sky. But somehow that communication was broken and the method of its implementation lost. Before the Golden Band, some Jaanaarians hid it within Mt. Moirae and a dragon was bound to protect it."

Kryst could only imagine what such a force could do in the hands of these strange Northerners, these men who had cursed him to the Renfala Forest.

"Why did you have Titus send me away?"

"Simone and your stubbornness—"

Kryst waved a hand. "I'm here as your prisoner, Master Oscan. You don't need to lie. I've the distinct feeling the entire episode was planned."

Master Oscan's face suddenly became gravely serious. He lifted a hand and pointed at Sillisnae. "When you stand against your fellow man in defense of these life-support systems for orifices, then you deserve a horrible death. Do you realize what such creatures are capable of?"

Kryst glanced sideways at Sillisnae. She stared straight ahead, out the windows behind Oscan.

"No, please inform me."

"Chaos," Master Oscan replied. "The elevation of the mediocre and the rejection of aggression, a masculine virtue. Women abhor violence because they invariably lose when it's employed against them."

"That may be true, but it still doesn't justify challenging me to a duel. I fail to see the connection. Simone was mine."

Master Oscan chuckled softly and shook his head. "All women belong to every man. All women and children have a psychological mechanism that allows them to love their oppressors. If they are not given a firm hand they quickly sniff out weakness and use their powers of emotional and psychological manipulation to gain the upper hand, to secure their safety. When men hoard women through attachment, jealousy, prestige or all three, other men suffer. Men that would be their mentors and comrades. A healthy society does not suffer the wiles of women. And who are women's enablers? Weak men. That is why they must be eradicated."

"So you don't have a particular woman, Master Oscan?"

"Of course I do. I am married. And I partake of any woman I have a fancy for. And if any man tries to stop me he will meet with death."

Kryst was slightly confused. "What about your wife? Do you share her with other men?"

"Of course. My wife's biological function is to procreate and raise male children until the age of four, and satisfy the desires of men who are her superiors. If one of my comrades wanted her, they may partake, because I and all other Linnsonian men realize the true nature of women and do not make distinctions between *good* and *bad* women. They are all the same, only different faces. They are filthy, nasty creatures and are not on the same level as us. They must be dealt with through physical force and rigid codes of conduct. In Linnso, we breed them for beauty and educate them in the erotic arts after their menarche. They are pleasure vehicles of the highest quality."

Kryst could not imagine allowing other men to lie with his wife. The thought made him cringe. He didn't want anyone to touch Simone and she wasn't even his wife. But they had their culture, possibly an unfortunate outcome of their slavery in Ebro, as the legend went, but that was over a thousand years ago and could not possibly have an effect on their worldview now. Or could it?

The beautiful woman sitting next to him never spoke during their conversation. It was as if Master Oscan had her tongue pulled out. But just the slightest sigh gave him a clue she was listening and coherent.

On deck, a horn blew.

Master Oscan frowned and stood. "That's odd." The windows behind him only revealed a thick fog. It had become much denser during their conversation.

The horn blew again. This time, accompanied by shouts and a hair-splitting wail.

"If you will excuse me..." Master Oscan rushed out of the room.

Kryst and Sillisnae rose without a word and followed him out onto deck.

Several Linnsonians had gathered and pointed over the bow. The fog beyond had an unnaturally rectangular hole within it, the edges sharp and distinct. Through the hole they saw a gleaming city, its crystal spires sparkling in a light that came from the city itself.

"By the gods!" Kryst swore under his breath. "That is one of the Triad."

"It cannot be"—Master Oscan moved toward the bow—"my calculations had us nearing the Triad after a full day. We only entered the mouth of the Othalla mere hours ago."

"The Triad exists half in this world and half in the other; therefore it can move or fold space." Sillisnae said matter-of-factly.

They were the first words Kryst heard her speak since they had been captured.

The eight-foot tall Linnsonian druids, who appeared Jaanaarian, moved among the astonished men, their bodies gliding across air as their black robes trailed behind them. The crew members moved to give them room at the head of the bow and they raised their hands to the sky and chanted.

"They are chanting in the True Tongue," Sillisnae said. Her tone was shocked. "How could they know the True Tongue in Linnso?"

The galley was pulled by an invisible force as there was no wind and no one rowing. The druids continued to chant but it did not stop their trajectory.

"Why do they not stop it?" Master Oscan asked Sillisnae.

She turned to him, her face devoid of expression. "No terrestrial magic will be able to stop that."

"How do you know?"

135

"I was an Adept's Apprentice in the Crystal Palace." Sillisnae rolled her eyes.

Master Oscan hit Sillisnae in the mouth with an open hand. She fell but got back to her feet immediately, her expressionless stare unchanged.

"Don't attempt to show me insolence, girl. Remember who you are dealing with." He hit her again, this time harder, and when she fell she remained on the ground.

"She is my prisoner—" Kryst stepped closer.

"You are a prisoner yourself, Prince Kryst. Be glad I treat my captives with such kindness."

Sillisnae was slow to stand and when she did, an angry red welt had blossomed high on her cheekbone.

A loud *boom* rang out from the druids' direction. One had sent a blast of lightning into the orifice but to no avail. The ship continued on its course toward the sparkling, ghostly city.

"Do something, Svarlat!" Master Oscan yelled. "Free this ship, now!"

Another blast of a fireball from the gray-haired giant called Svarlat. The ball flew into the hole but was progressively extinguished, as if layers of shimmering air reduced its power as it neared the city.

All around them fog whirled, sometimes forming into human shapes only to disintegrate when the crew touched them.

Some of the human shapes approached Sillisnae and she flinched back. When she saw Kryst try to touch one, she hissed and pulled his hand back. "Don't touch them! They are between this world and the next. If you touch them, they will suck your life force and drag you into the nether world."

Master Oscan stood at the helm and waved his hands. "We are moving faster. Druids, to me! Everyone else, to arms! We will meet whatever is here with magic and steel." He disappeared in the fog with the giant druids.

Shouts came to them distorted, at times far away, as if some of the Linnsonian sailors had left the ship and were already within the city.

To Kryst's surprise, Sillisnae hugged him.

"Stay close to me," she said. "I'm afraid."

"What do you know about the Triad, Sillisnae?"

The ship seemed to speed up. Kryst saw islands in the water as the fog thinned. They were rocks of steel gray and off-white cliffs covered with palm trees that were common in Maeltip. The islands were connected by arched, marble bridges that glistened with a light of their own. Tiny hovels and duns littered the small islands but Kryst saw no people.

"The Triad exists on a ley line as the legend goes—" she whispered in his ear.

"A ley line?"

"A place on the earth where the barriers between the worlds are thin. That is why the city can appear to us. The earth mingles with the otherworld and the city manifests in the general area. The powers of the druids aren't working because the city is only half here in this time and place."

The turrets and spires lorded high above the ship. They were worn and run-down. Vines grew in lazy swirls throughout the marble and crystal buildings. The city sat on a slightly jutting peninsula. Weeds grew everywhere among the tiled courtyards. Warped docks and crumbling quays splayed out like the fingers of a hand into the wide river.

"It is deserted," Kryst observed.

"I wouldn't count on it," Sillisnae replied.

As they neared, Master Oscan gave the order to drop anchor and have a boat prepared.

"You," he said pointing to Kryst. "And bring the snatch."

A small boat with oars was lowered into the water.

"Climb down the rope ladder and get inside," Oscan said. "I'll be going as well. Tomat, you are the Master until I return. And Karvis, Svarlat, Jovnar, you come with us."

Three giant druids turned from the bow, climbed down and stepped into the boat. The big men were all gray of hair and beard. Their jaws were as big as Kryst's entire head. Their lips were flat and thin, their noses were long and slightly upturned at the tip, and their brows displayed identical tattoos of a winged disk. Kryst thought they could be brothers or even triplets; the resemblance between them was so striking. Then he noticed their violet eyes.

Jaanaarians.

But how could that be? How could Jaanaarians be in service to Linnsonians?

"I am Prince Kryst of Maeltip." He introduced himself, hoping to get a feel for these strange creatures. They did not answer but stared in silence.

Master Oscan got in and two of the druids took to the oars.

They came to a small dock, its wood rotted in places, the walkway twisted and warped. A couple of boats with multiple holes lay capsized on the river's shore. A thoroughfare of cobblestone ran perpendicular to the withered quays and docks. It appeared as if no one had walked these streets for centuries. The only buildings left to stand were large, made of the ubiquitous marble and crystal. Along the quay, what at one time had been sturdy brick and wood buildings most likely housing merchants' goods from all over the world, now stood in decay and disarray. Some had signs of fire damage while others stood with empty windows staring out like forgotten eyes. Kryst wondered what gazed out at them from those holes.

"There is a presence…here," the druid called Svarlat said.

His voice was deep; just what Kryst thought a giant's voice would sound like.

"What is it?" Master Oscan asked. He had unsheathed his sword which was shorter than the swords of Maeltip and Corvasa.

Jovnar the druid moved forward and beckoned them to follow. The fog obscured the sight of the ship but the view of the city was clear. Hills with several stone ruins lay beyond the abandoned buildings. A few cobblestone streets led off from the edge of the river. Jovnar's legs took massive strides and Kryst, Sillisnae and Master Oscan had to walk quickly to keep up with him. No wind blew and the ruins were deathly quiet. The buildings along the street appeared the same as those along the thoroughfare, some were burned with no roofs, some were dilapidated and all were abandoned.

"What is the history of this place?" Master Oscan directed his question to the druids.

"These are the cities of the Egirins, a people from far in the East, beyond Osseka and the Knotts," Karvis began. His voice was nearly identical to that of Svarlat's.

He continued. "They were highly advanced and also fierce fighters. They fought their way through the Knottian barbarians and settled on the Othalla River bank. They called their city, Ellis, named after their patron god and their progenitor. Most lands east of the Othalla River do not have cities and are mainly roving bands of nomadic tribes. But these people built the most beautiful cities the world had ever seen. The Crystal Palace in Minosae is modeled on their former King's Palace."

The druid suddenly stopped and held up his hand indicating they do the same. He and Jovnar walked quickly ahead. A relatively intact building stood high on a hill. It had the customary columns surrounding all four sides like the ancient architecture of Corvasa. Sillisnae touched Kryst's arm.

"I don't want to go there," she said. "Nothing good is in there."

"I thought she was blocked," Kryst heard Jovnar whisper in Corvasan.

"She is." Master Oscan gazed at Sillisnae curiously. He approached her but she did not flinch away. "How do you know that? Tell me and be quick about it."

"I feel it. I don't know how. It is a dark place, an evil place."

And so Master Oscan insisted they walk toward it. The sky above hung low with dark, ominous clouds. As they approached the columned palace, the clouds roiled dark blue and gray as if anticipating their entry.

In contrast to the buildings along the banks of the river, the palace gleamed. It seemed to sparkle from within, beckoning them. Kryst could have sworn the structure was crumbling when he saw it from the riverbank. The fog had returned and obliterated the view below. They climbed a switchback trail. The river and buildings had disappeared into the fog which was now enveloping their party as well. It swirled, creating a tunnel, pulling them toward the palace as its columns glowed in opalescent colors.

Jovnar led the way with Master Oscan, Svarlat and Karvis behind him. Sillisnae and Kryst carried the rear.

What do the Linnsonians want from this accursed place? he asked himself.

Suddenly a young girl stepped out of the fog, blocking their path. Her hair was chestnut brown, decorated in curls and tied back with a blue ribbon. She wore a light blue satin gown that covered her feet. She had doe-like brown eyes and porcelain skin. She resembled a doll more than a young girl living in an abandoned city.

"What is the secret of the Crystal Skull?" she asked in a tiny voice.

They stared at her in silence.

"What is the secret for that which you seek?" She directed her question to Master Oscan.

He stepped around the druids toward the young girl. "How do you know about that, little one?"

The little girl repeated her question. "What is the secret of the Crystal Skull?"

Master Oscan attempted to bypass her but stopped short.

"You cannot pass onto the Syril until the riddle is answered," the young girl said.

"What is it, my Master?" Svarlat asked.

The druids were visibly nervous, gazing around in every direction as if they thought someone watched them.

"I cannot move forward. There is an invisible wall here." He made as if to shove the little girl but Svarlat hissed.

"Don't touch her, Master. She is a glamour and the spell is impenetrable. We must answer her question."

"Well, get on with it then. Answer it," Oscan commanded.

"I don't know the answer."

Oscan looked hard at his other two druids and raised his eyebrows. "Well?"

Jovnar and Karvis glanced at each other and shook their heads.

...the secret is: to remember who you are...tell her...

"To remember who you are," Kryst said loudly.

The little girl rested her doe eyes on him and nodded slowly. She turned and beckoned them with her hand. They walked through the watery, magnified wall following the blue-clad girl.

"How did you know the answer?" Sillisnae whispered to him.

"A voice told me."

"What voice?"

"Another time."

The little girl led them up wide marble steps numbering in the hundreds. The clouds over their heads seemed too low. Kryst thought he could raise his hand and touch them. They were dark gray now and a trick of the light revealed angry, demon faces baring their fangs. Sillisnae saw it too because he heard her gasp.

"This is a trap," she whispered to Kryst. "There is death in this place. It reeks of it."

But she followed anyway. When they reached the first columns, the young girl pointed one small finger. "The oracle has been waiting for you."

The druids nodded and went in, quickly followed by Master Oscan, Sillisnae and Kryst. He hoped he would hear Nominthe's voice again. When she was near, he felt invincible.

They meandered through the opalescent columns. At once, Kryst thought the fluted columns were made of the finest marble and then others seemed to be made of solid glass or crystal with tiny sparkles shimmering within. When they had walked a few yards into the building, the columns seemed to move and shift as if mirrors had been placed all around to fool their eyes. His focus went in and out as the columns did the same thing. Master Oscan and the druids would be obscured from his view, would seem far away and then suddenly appear very close.

"What is happening?" Sillisnae asked in an alarmed voice.

"I don't know."

A low moan erupted from every direction. The druids froze and placed themselves in a squat-like stance with their knees bent and their backsides halfway down to the floor. They spread out their arms then crossed them over their chests.

"They make runic signs to fend off the warding spell. Take the apprentice and follow me."

Kryst never thought he would be so relieved to hear Nominthe's voice.

"You. Where are you?" he responded in his mind.

"Right here."

A tiny light—much like a firefly—hovered in front of his face. It moved quickly and Kryst grabbed Sillisnae's hand and pulled her after it. Kryst did not see Master Oscan anywhere and the three druids remained in their runic poses.

"Hurry!" Nominthe insisted.

He yanked Sillisnae hard and followed the tiny ball of light. It led through the shifting columns and through one of a series of archways. They entered a room with a fountain. A statue of a naked woman—her arm reaching for the ceiling—stood upon the mouth of a jumping fish. Water, which was an unnaturally bright turquoise, sprayed out of her mouth and eyes in three different arcs.

"By the gods," Sillisnae swore. "Who are they?"

At first he did not know what she was talking about. Then he saw.

A gathering of people sat in chairs in a circle behind the fountain. It took Kryst a few seconds to realize what was so strange about them. Shadows cut halfway across their faces, leaving just one eye visible even though they were not wearing hats. The group was equally divided between men and women. In the center of the circle stood the little girl in blue who had led them to the strange building.

"Do you seek the Crystal Skull?" a woman asked.

Kryst suddenly understood these strange people would pass judgment on them. Where was Nominthe? The tiny light had disappeared.

"I don't seek the Crystal Skull," he told them. "I don't know why I've been asked this."

"Those who have come from the North seek it." The woman's voice was deep and raspy like a man's. "Why are they seeking—?"

"I don't know!" Kryst shouted.

A shuffling sound caused him to turn. Behind them stood Locklin, a dagger raised high in his hand. Kryst moved just in time as the momentum of Locklin's swing made the Healer stumble face first. Kryst shoved him to the ground. The man sprawled out onto his stomach and his body disintegrated into ash in a matter of seconds.

Kryst was vaguely aware of someone pulling him away. It was Sillisnae. When he saw the panic on her face, he understood. The strange people with shadowy faces moved toward them. They glided on air like wraiths, their feet hovering a foot from the marble floor. Their mouths worked in and out making strange sounds. When they were within a yard of Sillisnae and him, they clicked their teeth in a chattering cacophony like an ensorcelled skull.

"Come on Kryst!" Sillisnae shouted.

He did not understand why she pulled him. These strange people did not mean them harm, they would show them the way out of this place, this haunted city of the dead. They would lead them away from Master Oscan and his giant Jaanaarian druids. But where were they? He had forgotten all about them.

Shadows played across the walls of the room in a hurried, frantic fashion. The shadows had weight and density. They swirled around his head and around the strange, chattering people. *Click, click, click,* their teeth chattered. They gathered around him. He felt his life force exiting through his eyes, nose and mouth, but he did not care, the feeling was warm and comforting.

A pair of massive hands grabbed his armpits and pulled. It could not have been Sillisnae. The scene dissolved into the black mists he thought were shadows. It was replaced by a large room with a domed ceiling and marble walls. In the middle of the room stood four fluted marble columns around a pool of water. But the water was strange. It was opalescent and shimmered, not transparent or blue. The three giant druids and Master Oscan stood between the marble columns, gazing into the pool of…well…what exactly?

"It looks like mercury," Sillisnae said.

How did she come to be next to him? They had just been in the room with the shadows and now they stood in this bright room lit from a skylight in the top of the dome.

The Jaanaarian druids raised their hands skyward. The tattoos on their foreheads glowed red. Master Oscan gazed into the pool.

He is waiting for something. But what?

A hissing sound that came from the mouths of the druids filled the room. A small lump appeared on the surface of the liquid and grew in size, taking many shapes as it enlarged vertically from the pool. The liquid finally settled into the shape of a giant hand that swayed back and forth and then suddenly, grabbed Jovnar and pulled him into the pool. The druid did not scream but tensed and disappeared into the liquid. The other two druids hummed in low tones and made hand signs with their fingers.

"That is runic magic," Sillsinae whispered. "They are conjuring life to transport them through that substance."

"The mercury?"

"I think so."

The hand grew to an enormous size and grabbed all of them in one fell swoop. The liquid felt cold and possessed a metallic smell. He instinctively held his breath and closed his eyes as the frigid liquid metal touched every part of him. His body was jerked violently from side to side and he heard moans coming from the others but the sound diminished quickly and he realized they were separating from him. The metallic liquid was suddenly gone and he felt cold air on his skin and opened his eyes.

Kryst stood on a broad plain covered with snow. In the distance, ice sheets covered sides of gray, rocky mountains. A frigid wind blew and it was almost impossible to distinguish where the ground ended and the sky began. Sillisnae and the druids were gone. He was alone. Goose pimples erupted on his skin and he shivered, his teeth chattering much like the shadow-faced men and women back at the Triad. He curled his cloak around him.

How cold is it here? I will freeze to death.

As soon as the thought entered his mind, the wind subsided and he felt warmth. Movement in the periphery of his vision caused him to jerk to his left. There, crouched low as if to strike, was a naked man with gray skin and yellow eyes. Something was strange about his head. It took a minute or two to see that he had sharp horns growing out of it like a goat's. His grayish, purple lips drew back into a clownish smile. His teeth were honed into sharp points like the giant icicles that hung from the jutting crags of the mountains ahead. His pupils were vertical slits. He made no sound, only stared at Kryst with his bright yellow eyes. His mouth slowly opened wide. It got wider and wider, until all he saw was the demon's tongue and tonsils. But that did not last for long. A vortex appeared within the cavernous mouth and as Kryst gazed into it, he understood his death was imminent. The gray, lizard-skinned fiend would kill him.

What he saw in the demon's mouth at first confused him. A ship was anchored in the river near the shore of the abandoned, ruined cities. It was the ship he had sailed upon, the *Crimson Treasure*, captured by the Linnsonians. The scene rushed at him and he saw the Linnsonians fighting for their lives. But it was of no use. What they fought against were the undead and their swords fell not upon solid matter but smoky apparitions that whirled around them like tornados. The apparitions took form only to disintegrate when struck by Linnsonian swords.

Giant snakelike creatures with slimy, whitish bodies arose from the river surrounding the ship. They had bald heads with no eyes or noses but giant mouths with teeth like swords. The back half of their bodies slithered back and forth to propel them forward. Their long, pink tongues unrolled and wrapped around the terrified Linnsonians, bringing them into their toothy mouths.

Some men jumped into the river and swam frantically for shore. When they arrived, coughing and panting, a bluish fog that had gathered in the ruins of the buildings spilled onto the river bank. At first, the Linnsonian survivors did not pay heed to the strange fog but then bloody slashes appeared on their bodies. Kryst saw the fog form long claws and slash the helpless survivors. One man was ripped to shreds, his skin falling away from his flesh as he flailed wildly, screaming.

Just when Kryst was about to look away from the carnage, the scene abruptly changed. He saw a translucent skull with an abnormally large brain cavity. The skull slowly turned to face him. Rainbows sparkled on its surface. When he gazed into the hollow eye sockets, Kryst felt as if he was being sucked into light and could feel the entire earth and the thoughts of its creatures simultaneously. He lost himself for a brief moment, thinking he had died with this newfound awareness. The beauty! The rapture! The bliss! He had never experienced anything like this in his entire life, but was he still himself? It seemed as if he had disappeared and he just *existed,* along with everything else in perfect, glorious timelessness.

Suddenly, he was again aware of his body and being an entity called Kryst, complete with a personality, past, and set of likes and dislikes. He was no longer on the broad plain covered with snow but in a giant cave. Water flowed somewhere close and a strange green light glowed somewhere behind him. His thoughts were jumbled, incoherent.

The beautiful image of Nominthe appeared before him. She stared with a knowing smile then a bluish-gray mist enveloped him and he drifted into unconsciousness.

MOUNTAIN PASSES AND
LONGING GLANCES

A WOMAN WRAPPED IN SHAGGY bear fur handed her a cup full of steaming liquid. Lananell took it cautiously. The woman, who had deep lines cutting into her cheeks and whose skin was gray like old parchment, gestured for Lananell to drink. The broth smelled of meat and marrow and she let it touch her lips but only pretended to drink.

When the old woman was satisfied Lananell had sipped a bit, she nodded and grunted.

"Tara," she said, pointing at her chest.

"I am Lananell. Do you speak Corvasan?"

Tara shook her head.

Her captors had thrown her into an animal skin tent and set a guard outside. To her relief, the guard did not have one of those shades hovering behind him. Neither did Tara. The tent was small, just big enough to lie down and stretch out her legs. The floor was covered with a deerskin.

Tara stared at her with rheumy eyes. Her silver hair hung over her shoulder in a long braid. Lananell set the cup of broth down, pointed at her nether regions and then the tent flap. Tara nodded and smiled, revealing dark pink gums absent of teeth. Lananell marveled at her age. She still was not accustomed to seeing very old women.

Even here, they let them live.

Tara opened the tent flap and crawled outside. Lananell followed. The old woman said something to the guard in their language. He nodded, spat and waved his hand in the direction of the forest.

While she relieved herself, she studied the camp and the people in it.

Not all were followed by shades, only a small fraction. Some shades had closed eyes and were larger in size than their human hosts. They appeared to wear the same style of clothing, a motley of animal skins sewn together. The amount of people in the camp seemed to have grown exponentially. Granted, she did arrive in the middle of the night but now it seemed there were nearly half a hundred men, women and children milling about.

A large fire pit occupied the center of the camp. At the moment, only coals smoldered within. The dead woman with her entrails spilling out had disappeared. Lananell wondered what happened to her. She remembered the broth and shivered.

After she relieved herself, she approached her guard cautiously. He held a long staff with a curved blade securely fastened to the end. She made a noise before she got too close so he would not be startled and attack. He turned toward her.

The bottom half of his face was covered by a wool scarf the color of wheat. A pair of piercing black eyes stared at her. His hair was brown and tied back in a tail.

"Sir…" she began in Corvasan.

He suddenly lunged as swiftly and as agile as a cat and struck her in the face. Pain exploded in her lip but she did not fall. Her hand flew to her mouth and she re-entered her tent without saying a word.

Pain is only a sensation. It is only a sensation. It is I who assigns good or bad to the feeling.

Tara was waiting for her. When she saw Lananell, she motioned that she lay down and mumbled in her language. She moved Lananell's hand away from her lip. The old woman flinched back, her eyes went wide and her toothless mouth worked in and out. She muttered a few words in her language and produced a metal container from within her animal pelts. The salve smelled like mint and made Lananell's lip tingle.

"We move," Tara said and placed her two fingers on the floor pelts, mimicking a man walking.

"You speak Corvasan?"

Tara shook her head again.

Outside, men shouted and the sound of clanking metal and wood caused her to peek through the tent flaps. Indeed, everyone was decamping.

"Where are we going?" she asked Tara, but the old woman did not answer and moved past her, out into the camp.

The masked guard with the black eyes grabbed Lananell's arm and roughly pulled her out of the tent. In a matter of seconds, he took it down, rolled it up and fastened it to his back. Tara reappeared riding a brown mule with massive ears that pointed to the sky. The guard rebound Lananell's wrists to a rope fastened around Tara's waist. The three of them fell in behind a procession already departing the camp.

For the first time since she had been captured, Lananell saw other prisoners dragged behind mules at the end of the line.

The procession climbed. And as they did, the air became thinner and colder. Whenever a breeze blew, which it often did, she shivered uncontrollably. But she did not complain and forced herself to keep going, putting one foot in front of the other.

The procession entered a thickly wooded forest that followed a well-worn trail which switchbacked up the side of a mountain. The trees provided welcome relief from the bursts of wind. Blue and gray birds perched high within the evergreens called to them. Lananell tried to feel them, to get into their minds. For a brief moment, she saw the procession winding along far below, the view obscured by branches. But the vision only lasted a few seconds.

"Are you from Corvasa?" a man's voice loudly whispered behind her. He was older than her but still young, with a thin, muscular frame, wavy brown hair and bright green eyes. He wore a cream colored chemise and brown woolen breeches tucked into suede, knee-high boots. The donkey's rider to which he was tied was a fierce-looking man that wore a giant cat's head as a hat.

Once he heard the man speak, the rider dismounted and beat him with a staff much like her guard's, only there was a metal ball at the end. Lananell wanted to call out, to tell him to stop but the words melted in her throat before they could reach her lips. The man with the cat's head forced the Corvasan to remove his boots.

They resumed climbing as if nothing had happened. They stopped to make camp at a level meadow after many hours of hiking. The sun peeked just above the western horizon and shone through a gap between two hills. The men set to making a bonfire as the women and older children erected tents.

The fire raged in no time as the last rays of the sun died in the west and a smattering of stars twinkled in the east. The temperature dropped significantly and Lananell moved as close to the bonfire as she could. A hierarchy existed in the order of proximity to the warmth. All of the men who possessed shades sat in the inner ring. Behind them were women with shades. Behind those were men with no shades, then women and children. Lananell sat in the outer ring of the prisoners and their guards. She spied the Corvasan man who had spoken to her but he stood stock still with his head down and his bare feet bloody. A throng of bodies gave her a limited view of the men in the inner circle but she recognized the two brothers who had captured her and their shades. It was the first time she had seen them since that night.

She wondered if Rosco searched for her. The thought that she had lost her freedom once more was almost too much to bear. Tears welled up in her eyes as she stood among the crowd, shivering. If she had only remembered the looking glass, none of this would have happened! Suddenly, she did not care if she got warm. The grief was so overwhelming, her legs felt weak, almost numb. She swayed and Tara caught her.

The old woman hissed and propped her up. The masked guard was nowhere to be seen in the press of people. Fragrant meat aromas teased her nose, causing her stomach to rumble and her mouth to water. She had not eaten anything all day, having pretended to eat the broth with the mystery meat. Tara tugged the rope and instantly they were meandering through the crowd as morsels of meat were being passed around. Tara gestured toward the bonfire with her wrinkled hand then brought it to her mouth. Lananell nodded eagerly.

When Tara handed her a seared piece of tough meat, greasy and dripping, Lananell tore into it without the slightest care if it was human flesh or not. Truth be told, it tasted like deer or elk, a hunting party must have been sent out.

After she finished, Tara led her to the same tent, the mysterious guard still absent. After the long climb, and a full belly, sleep came easily and was dreamless. She awoke to the sound of Tara snoring next to her, the dawn threatening to break with bluish light.

Outside, her guard had reappeared but slept soundly a few feet away with spear still in hand. The rope around her wrists had been removed. Carefully stepping around the guard, she slipped into the surrounding woods. No one stirred within the camp.

Her knees creaked when she squatted to empty her bladder. Taking a deep breath, she quieted the voices in her mind and listened for any voices from the wood. There were only the sounds of birds awakening and singing to the sun's arrival. She did not understand why they were silent now and had spoken with her when she was alone before her capture. Perhaps they were afraid of the strange people with whom she traveled. What other explanation could there be?

I'm so sorry, Rosco, my husband, she thought sadly. *I am stupid and forgetful. If only I had remembered the looking glass...*

The nagging thought of escape crossed her mind but she quickly dismissed it. She could probably find her way back to the meadow where she was captured but it was the shades she feared. She didn't know the extent of their power or what they could do to her. Lananell had never heard of ghosts killing humans but that did not mean it couldn't happen.

Tara and her guard were awake when she returned, along with a few others. The guard rolled up her tent and fastened it to his back as he had done the previous morning.

The amount of people that formed a column to march up to the mountain pass was significantly less than the night before. Many of the men with hovering shades had disappeared.

This time their party ascended above tree line onto rocky terrain with small shrubs as the only cover. The wind blew relentlessly. The line of mules and people on foot looked like a slow snake slithering ever higher.

When they finally reached the lowest point in the mountain's summit—the pass between two jagged slabs of gray rock—Lananell shivered uncontrollably in her lightweight tunic and cloak. The blasts of wind seemed to freeze her solid. Her lips, hands and feet felt numb. Why was it so cold? It was still summer. In Linnso, the cold fronts coming off the sea would howl and thrash as if the wind god wanted to destroy the island. The rain would beat down in sheets of gray. She thought that was cold but it was nothing like this.

The pass provided a spectacular view of the mountains and valleys beyond. One such valley held a sprinkling of small dots which appeared to be tents, at least fifty of them.

A hand touched her shoulder. When she turned, she met with the black-eyed guard. Lananell knew the look in his eyes well. She had seen it many times before. A forceful pull ripped her cloak from her shoulders. She stumbled back and fell into a sharp rock that pierced her backside. The pain made her cry out which seemed to anger him. He grabbed her more forcefully, turning her onto her belly in the sagebrush. She did not fight him. The blows would come if she did and she had learned at a very young age not to fight. The men of Linnso never left marks when they hit. They liked their women perfectly beautiful.

Lananell went to a place far away, a safe sanctuary in her mind. The sooner he finished, the more quickly they would be off again and she could bask in some safety for a little while. But the special herb she took in Linnso to avoid pregnancy might not grow here, she thought in a panic. The color was yellow and light green with small, blue flowers. She had seen perhaps one or two in Martine but now they had ascended so high, Lananell was doubtful she could find it.

The constant wind blew a sage brush next to her head. Somewhere she heard Tara yelling and then the guard was gone, pulled off her from behind. A man on a horse loomed over her. She recognized the taller brother who had captured her in the meadow near Martine. His red-headed shade loomed behind him with its eyes closed. The angle of the sun was such that his face was in shadow.

"Naton! Naton!" Tara ran to him. The rest of her words flew from her mouth in a torrent while she pointed at the guard who was being restrained by another man with a hovering shade.

Naton dismounted, picked up the guard's spear where he had let it fall before he attempted to rape her and struck him in the head with the wooden end. Tara screamed as the guard went down, an angry red welt blossoming on his forehead.

"Oshal mannekip! Oshal mannekip!" Lananell's guard held up his hand to fend off any more blows. Whatever it meant, Naton helped him to his feet, returned his spear and shoved him forward, farther up the line.

A crowd had gathered to stare. The Corvasan prisoner, who had been beaten for speaking to her, leered. She slowly became aware that her calves were cold and realized the guard had torn through her tunic. The sagging piece of cloth was easily ripped away but now she had a hole in the front, exposing her legs from the knees down.

Naton shouted commands and the line formed up again. He kicked his horse to a gallop and disappeared to the front of the line.

The descent seemed more difficult than the climb. The path was steep and tiny rocks caused her feet to slip more than once. When she fell the first time, she was not quick enough to regain her footing and the rocks painfully cut into the back of her legs, pulling her torn tunic up her thighs.

The mule Tara rode deftly maneuvered down the scree and steep terrain. Its large, split hooves never slipped. Lananell was envious and tried all the more to concentrate on placing her feet so as to avoid the loose rocks. Her neck hurt from staring down for so long but she managed to descend for another hour before she slipped and fell again. This time, her right foot slid out to the side, causing her to hit the ground shoulder first where a sharp rock hidden by a tuft of grass cut her. Lananell bit her lip in a gasp, trying not to scream. She had already called too much attention to herself. Tara roughly pulled the rope and

Lananell got to her feet, her shoulder dripping blood through the fabric.

At tree line, the severe incline gave way to switchbacks. The line moved more quickly and Lananell had to run along behind the mule at times. She was as careful here as she was on the steep slope. Downed trees covered with lichen and moss could twist an ankle or send her flying to the ground face first. Small streams trickled out from the earth and they stopped to drink each time. The water tasted fresh and was the coldest water she had ever tasted. Several species of birds watched them from the tree heights. Sometimes they swooped in an arc from tree to tree. Lananell tried to contact them but to no avail. The cover of the evergreens blocked the breeze and kept the air slightly humid. Sweat trickled down between her breasts and wet her armpits. She was glad for it. Being warm was uncomfortable but bearable; being cold and shivering amounted to slow torture.

They had been descending for hours—Lananell did not know how many—when the path finally leveled off and led them straight through the forest instead of switchbacking down a mountainside. Oak, ash and yew trees appeared amongst the pine and firs. Sunlight dappled the pine needle strewn forest floor. Wildflowers blossomed in every direction and filled the air with floral aromas. She inhaled the fresh scents deeply. The beauty of it reached out to her, taking on a life of its own to comfort her.

Uneasiness grew among the tribe as the sound of horses' hooves pounding the earth reached them. Riders shouted in their language to those who walked. A commotion of blunt shouts and whinnying horses up ahead gave way to laughter and signs of greeting. Those men with hovering shades she had noticed missing, returned. She glimpsed a rider with a body thrown over his shoulder but her view was quickly blocked by the ensuing melee.

Whatever had happened, the men with the shades seemed more anxious to get to their destination because they shouted to the line behind them and Lananell felt a rough shove in her back. She stumbled forward and turned reflexively to see the source of the shove. It was her guard. That was the first time he had touched her since he had been punished. The welt on his forehead was purplish blue.

When the sun sank behind the mountains, the riders in the front raised their hands to halt. They reached a small clearing with a brook running off to the side and the line broke into a circle to make camp.

Naton rode to the center with the body and let it fall to the ground. Lananell gasped when she saw it was a small child. He moaned when Naton prodded him with a spear. The boy got to his feet and she saw he was not a boy at all but a fully grown man with whiskers past his throat and beefy arms with copious amounts of hair. He was the smallest man she had ever seen in her life. If he stood on his tiptoes, he might have reached her waistline.

Naton and a few other riders with shades circled him with their horses. His hair and beard were red and he wore a leather jerkin. His face appeared to have been flattened with something. His nose was tiny, almost non-existent with two holes in a small lump of flesh. Beady golden-green eyes stared out from beneath an extremely prominent brow.

No one has eyes like that, she thought. The pupils were vertical slits like a cat's.

One of the riders unfurled a whip at his legs and the small man fell, eliciting a roar of laughter from the onlookers.

"What are they doing with him?" she asked Tara. The old woman just shook her head without looking at her. Lananell did not know if Tara could understand but she would not give up trying to communicate.

The Corvasan prisoner who had tried to speak to her caught her eye by waving his hands.

"Gnome," he mouthed in Corvasan.

Gnome? Lananell thought. She had heard stories of them but that was a long time ago in a childhood she wanted to forget. The problem with memories is that one could not selectively choose one without other, more unpleasant ones streaming in.

Gnomes are the elementals of earth, a voice deep within informed her.

When Tara had erected the tent, she untied Lananell's wrists and beckoned her inside.

"What will they do with him?" Lananell repeated.

Tara did not reply but set to grinding some herbs and roots she had picked nearby. Lananell took off her leather shoes and rubbed her feet which were raw and sore from walking. Tara motioned for her to pull down the sleeve of her chemise. The herb poultice stung when Tara rubbed it into her shoulder wound. Outside, men gathered wood and made a fire, an exact repeat of the previous night but without the roasting meat. In its place, a ration of dried meat was dispersed among all the tents. Lananell quite liked the taste. It was savory and tangy, bursting with flavor when she chewed it.

The night was warm and she was exhausted. Once the jerky was finished, she lay down next to Tara and must have dozed off immediately because the next time she woke, the bright moon was high overhead. All the sounds of the camp had gone silent, except for an owl hooting nearby. Tara had unleashed her ropes and she went outside to empty herself of water.

The guard slept a few yards away, his snores deep throated and angry. Consumed in a nightmare, his eyelids jerked and his face contorted. Lananell eyed the staff that lay next to him. She imagined herself quietly picking it up and shoving the curved blade into his exposed throat. What would happen then? They would seize her and probably feast upon her flesh. Or would they? She knew they set sentries at night but she had never seen them. She could also go back in the tent after killing him and feign ignorance when he was discovered. No, that would not work. She was the only one in the camp with a serious motive.

Pondering the guard's murder, she strolled into the trees and squatted down. The moon was bright and its light glistened off the warm liquid as it left her body.

A branch broke behind her.

At first, she did not think anything of it. Probably a chipmunk that had been disturbed.

But then she felt the earth move.

The jerk made her fall over. To her left, a rolling sound, like that of thunder, boomed and a gigantic mass of earth heaved up and rolled toward the camp. Huge trees, probably more than two hundred years old, were uprooted and thrown down like twigs. Lananell bolted as one massive pine fell where she had relieved herself. The powerful force caused the trunk to bounce when it hit the ground. Screams erupted from the tents and ghostly shades flew in circles overhead, shrieking inhuman cries. Another mass of earth exploded, as if something long dead and buried awoke with a big appetite and a sore arse. The mound of earth moved, or rather rolled, flipping more trees onto the tents. Some of the flying shades blew at the trees with their mouths, causing them to fall in the opposite direction.

Lananell ran farther into the woods. She had seen about a dozen trees fall onto the tents. Whoever occupied those tents was surely dead now.

Stinging branches whipped at her face and arms. Her feet became lodged underneath a fallen, rotted tree, causing her to fall. She got up and ran even faster, pushing her hands in front of her to block hanging vines, towering bushes and branches. Her lungs began to burn, forcing her to stop. Screams could still be heard but they were far away. Her knees gave way and she knelt, panting, her chest heaving. How long had she been running?

"Now there's a good girl. Ye remain still…"

Lananell jerked her head up. A man she had never seen before stood over her. He wore the animal skins of the Osseks. The moonlight glinted on a curved dagger he held at hip level.

"This won't hurt ye." He grabbed her by the hair and lifted the knife.

She screamed, throwing her hands above her head. The ground beneath her jerked wildly, throwing her attacker to the ground. Pain exploded in her scalp as he took a large tuft of her dark hair with him.

She hopped to her feet and ran, following the sound of moans and screams, this time slowing down to make sure she did not trip over any felled trees. Every other second she glanced behind her, but her attacker was gone.

When she reached the camp, a giant hole in the earth existed where they had taunted the gnome earlier. Tents had been flattened by massive trees. Bodies of men, women and children also lay under the felled trees. Some were still alive, moaning in pain, blood covering their faces and soaking their animal skins, others were clearly dead. The survivors wandered around in shock, some trying to lift the massive trunks off their loved ones in vain.

She searched for Tara and found her lying on the ground with a bloody ankle.

"What happened here?" Lananell asked but Tara made no reply. Her breath came in short gasps. The guard was nowhere to be seen, nor was the gnome they had captured. Lananell took a deep breath and laid her hands on Tara's wound. The old woman let her. Lananell did not know if it would work but she had to try. She reached down into her gut, felt the warmth there and attempted to raise it.

THE PIRATE AND THE
SHAPESHIFTER

RUNKEN SHOUTS AND BAWDY JOKES burst from crowded taverns and brothels along the quay. The Lightning Rod was Hawk's destination, a mead and dining hall teeming with pirates, merchants and sailors, foreign and domestic. He hoped to find his friend there, someone he had known since his first trip beyond the Golden Band at age fifteen. Aranhoe was always teeming with multiple expressions of humanity, especially pirates and foreign merchants, as trade from all over the world entered the port. The sun had set a few hours since and most of the denizens were good and drunk. Hawk had to tread carefully among them, the street along the bay being too narrow for the reveling crowd.

A tall, comely, dark-haired woman stepped in front of him unexpectedly. She had large, wide-set brown eyes and when she smiled, her teeth were perfectly straight and gleaming white. "Are ye in need of a companion, sir?"

"No."

"Aw, c'mon now. Give a lady a little time of yer day, y'know what I mean?"

"I'm doubtful you're a lady."

Hawk sidestepped her. But she deftly maneuvered in front of him again within a second.

"Ye be from the Knotts with those turquoise eyes." She snickered and winked.

Hawk cocked his head to one side, studying her. "Are you from Aranhoe or somewhere else?"

"From Aranhoe, born and bred," she said, smiling even more broadly. "My name is Sylvie."

"Do you know a pirate by the name of Ragnar Stellic, Sylvie?"

Her face flashed instant recognition but she quickly hid the expression with coyness. "I might know such a man…might be."

Hawk reached into his brown suede tunic, pulled out a Corvasan gold coin and held it in front of her big brown eyes.

She slipped her arm around his. "I'll lead you to him."

He let himself be led down the thoroughfare. Her dark hair smelled of cloves and he understood why when she retrieved a hand-rolled cigarette and thrust an end into one of the many torches that lined the busy street. The spicy, sweet scent of the smoke brought back memories of his first encounter with the pirate, Ragnar, all those years ago.

About twenty paces in front of them, three drunks with their arms entangled belted out notes of a sentimental ballad. Their faces were brown with dirt and sweat. Hawk counted a dozen teeth between them. A lanky man in the middle seemed oddly familiar. One pirate's arm brushed the side of Sylvie's breast. She hissed at him and picked up her pace.

"Do you know them?" Hawk asked.

She took a long drag on her clove cigarette and pointed to a rowdy tavern. "In there."

It was not the Lightning Rod but the Steel Pike. The common room was filled to the brim with all types of bodies dressed in every style and color of the rainbow. Greasy pirates with scarred faces and stolen jewelry about their necks laughed loudly while drunkenly spilling their mead and wine. Merchants and smugglers, their clothes darker and blander, sat huddled together, discussing their trade in hushed tones over ale. Big-breasted serving women hauled jugs of drink and trays full of roasted meat, shouting commands and maneuvering through the crowd. Scantily clad whores hung off the arms of every type of man, feigning amusement at stale jokes. Even through the cacophonous din, Hawk heard Ragnar's unmistakable voice. It boomed in a full-throated baritone.

The Maeltipian pirate stood at the back of the room, a drinking horn raised high over his head, shouting and laughing with his companions. He was hard to miss. He had jet black hair plaited in a long braid that reached his waist and stood so tall he towered over his companions. His nose pointed to the ground with a giant bump on the ridge from where it had been broken many years ago.

"A man's hair affords him the psychic senses," he had told Hawk the first time they met.

He was pleased to see the pirate had not cut it.

Ragnar wore striped brown and gray breeches tucked into knee-high, black boots. A curved sword hung from a wide red sash that encircled his waist. A soft brown, sealskin vest covered a faded red chemise. Necklaces of every metal, with pendants honoring gods from all over the world, hung from his neck. Hawk recognized a jade torque that Ragnar had bragged was taken from his first kill at age twelve. It had been too big for him then, but now the jade slightly punctured the flesh between the collar bones.

"Why are you stopping?" Sylvie exhaled clove-scented smoke "That is the man you seek right there." The sweet smoke was a nice distraction as the tavern smelled overwhelmingly of sweat, dirt, fish, urine and certain female odors.

He remained still and did not approach the rowdy Ragnar but watched the big man drink, laugh and shout for a good five minutes. Finally, he caught Ragnar's eye. Hawk was amused to watch recognition slowly dawn over his face.

The big pirate pointed, mouthed "You!" then threw his head back to emit a deep, guttural laugh. When he met Hawk's eyes again, he shook his head in disbelief. They moved toward each other and Ragnar thrust out his big hand. When Hawk took it, Ragnar pulled him into a bear hug, almost fully knocking the wind from his lungs.

"Knottian!" he shouted in his Maeltipian accent. "The Knottian from beyond the Band has returned! Ha ha!"

"Ragnar. It's a great pleasure to see you!" Hawk beat Ragnar's back with his hand. He genuinely liked the big pirate even though he was as deadly as a cobra and as wily as a scorpion. Hawk had seen him kill innocent men and rape village women, but it did not stem the affection he had for the fellow.

Ragnar let go and gave Sylvie an appreciative glance. "This one will warm your bed to a toasty heat, I can vouch for that, my old friend!" He slapped Hawk on the shoulder. "What are you doing in Aranhoe?"

"I need to sail to Maeltip as fast as possible."

"Ah! To the land of my birth! Ha ha! And what is in that island paradise that you so desperately seek?"

Hawk had to shout to be heard over the voices and laughter. "I'm searching for someone. A former Adept's Apprentice of the Crystal Palace."

Hawk felt Sylvie's hand release his arm and then she slowly walked away.

Ragnar arched an eyebrow. "An Adept's Apprentice?"

"A *former* Adept's Apprentice, Ragnar. She was given as a slave to Maeltip's prince."

A concerned expression stole over the pirate's features and he pulled Hawk to a corner of the room where they could hear each other better.

"You should not advertise that information, old friend. This coastal town is crawling with spies and traitors." The old pirate's beady black eyes gleamed. "The prince had been missing for a fortnight. Vanished from a brothel. Some said due to the black arts. The word went out in Maeltip and a reward was offered. Then he showed up in

Minosae with a Corvasan Healer and King Emeril gave him the Adept's Apprentice."

Hawk rubbed his chin. "Do you know where they are now?"

"Why, sailing to Maeltip I would presume. And with Lady Luck, we will be there tomorrow if that is your wish. And will locate your Adept's Apprentice. Now we must drink to friendships old and new!" Ragnar raised his horn. "Wench! Bring more wine!" he shouted at a passing serving girl.

Hawk was disappointed Ragnar did not want to leave right away. He was anxious to get to Sillisnae. Something was wrong, he could feel it. But he swallowed his desire. The pirate would not let him down. They would set sail on the morrow for the island nation and he would find and free Sillisnae and then return to Jaanaar.

"Do they have good mulled wine here?" he asked.

"Excellent, my friend. They also brew special cloudy liquor that tastes like licorice. You must try it."

Ragnar passed the horn and Hawk took a swig. The taste was very sweet, almost unbearably so, but the more Hawk drank the more he liked it. In a few minutes, a comforting, warm feeling came over him. He did not drink spirits a lot but when he did, he never regretted it. A quick scan of the room did not reveal Sylvie. She had disappeared. Being what she was, he was glad for it. He had no desire to partake of pleasures of the flesh and less to deny her favors. Perhaps Ragnar wanted her.

"King Olaf is harboring a bunch of foreigners from the North. A strange lot. But very disciplined."

A creeping fear suddenly seized Hawk. "From the North? Where?"

"They are from Linnso and have an impressive fleet of black ships."

Hawk listened, keeping his expression neutral. "Have you actually seen these Linnsonians?"

Before the pirate could answer, a loud commotion in the front of the tavern near the door caught their attention.

"A black ship has captured the prince of Maeltip," a skinny merchant sailor shouted. "They captured them aboard the *Crimson Treasure*, we saw it! They used the black arts, they did!"

"Where did they go?" a gruff voice called out.

"The galley headed for the mouth of the Othalla River and the black ship changed course for Maeltip."

"The Othalla River?" A tavern wench asked.

The Steel Pike began to empty out, to shed Maeltipians like cockroaches fleeing the light. No doubt ready to sail in search of their kidnapped Prince.

"Sillisnae was on that ship," Hawk told Ragnar. "We must sail immediately."

The old pirate shook his head, his black braid wagging behind him. "I cannot do that, my friend. The seer hag has forbidden travel until the morn. Those men that left to set sail will encounter a trap."

Hawk knew it was useless to argue with a pirate when the black arts were behind their decisions. They were a very superstitious lot. All sailors were. The seer hag was an ancient woman that sat in a chair on the quay with her equally ancient white mutt. All manner of captains came to her for advice and foretelling of the weather. She was right most of the time or her business would have dwindled down to nothing. Sailors and captains were very unforgiving when their Adepts made mistakes about the weather. Not only was life lost, but valuable cargo and ships. Hawk could not remember the hag's name but she always seemed to have a client sitting in front of her, listening to his fortune.

He was tempted to threaten Ragnar, so great was his desire to be in pursuit of Sillisnae. But he knew his protestations would fall on deaf ears.

"You are welcome to my quarters aboard the *Tawdry Maiden* as always," Ragnar said, interrupting his worries. "It will be like old times."

"I'd be grateful, Ragnar. Where are you sleeping tonight?"

"Why, here of course. With a port whore if Selene smiles upon me. What happened to yours?"

"She seems to have departed."

Ragnar chuckled. "Maybe she sensed you are not fully human!"

The pirate was referring to how they met all those years ago. Hawk had shapeshifted to save his life. Ragnar was just a stranger then, but after that became a lifelong friend.

"Do you know her? Sylvie?" Hawk asked.

"She is a port whore. Fairly well known among the men. Pretty girl. Nice firm titties and a high bottom. I've had her a few times meself."

"When I mentioned the Adept's Apprentice, she disappeared. Is she a spy for someone?"

Ragnar caressed his beard. "I don't know much of her except what she can do in the bedroom. It wouldn't be the first time a whore has spied. It's quite common, Hawk."

His answer did nothing to assuage Hawk's anxiety.

"Do you remember what my galley looks like?" Ragnar asked as Hawk stood to go.

"How could I forget such an exceptional vessel?" Hawk said, firmly planting his tongue in his cheek. "I'll see you at the break of dawn on the morrow."

Torches burned brightly all along the quay, lighting his way to the familiar trireme galley. The seer hag sat forlornly in her wicker chair, her rheumy eyes searching the passers-by for clients. She clucked at them, not even speaking words, assuming they already knew who she was, so vast was her reputation. She looked exactly the same as when he had been in this port city four years ago.

When he had saved Ragnar's life…

* * * *

It happened during one of his many excursions beyond the Golden Band. Akrae sent him on relatively easy missions within the realm of Perthia "to familiarize you with the territory" he explained. On these excursions, Hawk shapeshifted into his namesake and crossed the Golden Band, in search of an object Akrae commanded him to bring back to Jaanaar. The object could be anything—a blacksmith's apron, an emerald ring, a legionnaire's short sword, a gaoler's whip—it did not matter as long as Hawk brought it back. The point was to survive with just the clothes on his back, the wits in his head and the Jaanaarian magic he had learned.

It was on one such excursion Hawk met Ragnar Stellic, the Maeltipian pirate. Akrae sent him to retrieve an ivory staff from the Lord of Aranhoe—a Lord Abril at the time. He lived in a castle on the hill overlooking the city. The castle was a rectangle shape with fluted columns, a leftover relic from the time of the ancient Corvasans. They built their residences with layers of columns instead of walls, the warm weather of southern Corvasa allowed for it. Luckily, the design made Hawk's assignment extremely easy. He waited until the Lord—a cousin of King Emeril—and his household fell asleep then flew through the columns, his wings making rhythmic swoosh sounds, and found Lord Abril's receiving room without too much difficulty. He shapeshifted into human form and attached the ivory staff to his person. He shapeshifted back into the form of a hawk and flew out into the clear night without ever seeing another person in the castle.

The Lightning Rod, a tavern filled with noises of loud drunks and amateur fiddle players, caught his attention as he circled overhead. Landing in an alley, Hawk shapeshifted into human form and entered the establishment. The patrons were mostly pirates, some merchants and a scattering of whores. The noise and stench of sweat changed his mind about socializing. The ivory prize he carried was too valuable to risk theft. Once outside, he happened upon a man being beaten in an alley. Usually Hawk would not have interfered, but the man was sorely outnumbered.

"Hey! What are you doing?"

Two men stopped kicking the bleeding victim and ran toward him. In a split second his limbs shrunk and sprouted feathers, his nose and jaw elongated into a beak and his chest puffed out. He took wing just before they were upon him and flew over their heads, down the alley. Opening his talons, he sunk them into the face of an attacker. The man screamed and waved his arms, grabbing Hawk's body and pulling. Hawk sunk his beak into the man's wrist and twisted. The man screamed and let go. Hawk flew to another attacker and sunk his talons into his eyes, making sure not to miss his mark this time. The man they were beating stood and swayed, his face a bloody mess. When his attackers saw that, they ran.

The injured man fell back on his haunches and Hawk metamorphosed back into human form. If the man was shocked at what he saw, he made no indication, but stared blankly, breathing through his mouth.

Hawk helped him up and put his arm around his shoulders.

"Where do you live?"

The man mumbled something but his mouth was full of broken teeth.

"What?"

"The quay," he said in Corvasan with an accent. "Ship…"

The first time Hawk saw the Tawdry Maiden, he thought it was some cruel joke. The ship was painted a variety of colors and the "tawdry maiden" that decorated the hull had been painted every color of the rainbow. Her face was blue, her hair green, and her lips purple. Her breasts had been painted yellow and the rest of her torso, orange. Her arms were chartreuse. It was the gaudiest site he had ever seen. The injured sailor stumbled on the gangway but Hawk caught him. Several of the crew appeared, cursing.

"What happened to him?" a young sailor of thirteen or fourteen asked. He was Corvasan but dressed in filthy rags.

"He was beaten. They could have killed him."

"You," the kid said pointing at Hawk. "You stay."

And so it was that Hawk befriended Ragnar Stellic, the pirate from Maeltip. He stayed with Ragnar and his crew for a month, sailing on the

Tawdry Maiden along the shores of Corvasa and Westernaphalia, west of Aranhoe. Hawk saw Ragnar raid other ships and small coastal villages but he never participated. When they raided along the coast, Hawk remained onboard and watched Ragnar return with loot and booty. He would relate his adventures over casks of Maeltipian wine.

"You must accompany me sometime," Ragnar demanded.

"I am not suited to raiding and raping," Hawk explained.

"Then what are you suited for?"

"The recovery of the heroic, of the mythic."

Ragnar frowned. "Is that what they teach you in Jaanaar?"

"They don't teach me anything in Jaanaar. They point me in a general direction and I must discover the rest for myself."

* * * *

He was jolted from his reverie by a couple of drunken sailors bumping into him. They mumbled something in a language Hawk didn't recognize and continued on, stumbling and burping. Up ahead, Hawk saw the *Tawdry Maiden* under the light of the full moon and brightly burning torches. The sight of it made him smile.

Two men who smelled like stale beer and old sweat greeted him on the gangway. They were both short with coppery skin. One had yellowish, light green eyes, like the color of olives. He had never been south of Maeltip but knew they were from lands beyond the Ocean of the Sun.

"Who are ye?" one asked in thickly accented Corvasan.

Hawk judged him to be about sixteen. His long dark hair hung loosely in his face and he had a thick scar from below his left eye to the corner of his mouth. He unsheathed a dagger and folded his arms in front.

Hawk flashed the key Ragnar had given him. The young pirates nodded and bid him follow. They led him down one level to Ragnar's quarters. Potent smells of rare spices and pungent herbs hung in the air. Sacks of salt, onions and potatoes lined the inner wall. Map scrolls, candles and a half empty bottle of rum littered a blackwood, round table.

"It smells a lot different down here than on deck," Hawk observed.

"Ragnar smuggles the spice from ports in the Knotts," the scar-faced pirate informed him.

At the mention of his homeland, Hawk thought of the herbal concoctions his mother made. She sold them to coasters, as they referred to people who lived on the coast in the Knotts, and the coasters sold them to the merchants from all over Perthia and the lands south of Maeltip.

"This is the captain's quarters. May your goddess, Selene, take you."

They left him in the wood-paneled room with a large feather bed and round port window. A trio of doves were locked in a cage, cooing. Hawk communicated a thought of greeting and they replied they wanted to fly.

I cannot do such, dear friends. I am a guest here.

The doves did not respond but he sensed their disappointment. They cooed for him as he lay down. Once he closed his eyes, sleep overtook him.

He dreamt of Sillisnae. It was her face but she was someone else. Her expression was completely out of character. He realized in horror she was Nominthe. And she laughed at him. Laughed and laughed. Her face melted and he tried to scoop up the liquid flesh but it fell through his fingers until all that was left was a skull. And it laughed at him.

He awoke at dawn in a sweat and heard shouts on deck. The ship lurched, prompting him to look out the window. Ragnar had not lied. Leaving at dawn was what he said and leaving at dawn was what they were doing. He found the pirate captain on deck at the helm, barking orders to his crew and chewing a piece of dried fish. When he saw Hawk he smiled broadly and patted him on the back.

"Good sleep, my friend? I, for one, did not do much sleeping." Ragnar winked. "Sylvie returned and she sure did ask a lot of questions."

"Such as?"

"Oh, who you were, how I knew you, where we were going on the morrow. I lied about it all, of course. I don't pillow talk with port whores but after what you mentioned, I didn't want her to be suspicious."

The quay slowly diminished from their sight. Was Sylvie standing somewhere, watching forlornly as they sailed away? Ready to run to the first Corvasan Legionnaire or Crystal Palace man-at-arms she could find and relate that a Knottian man was asking about a certain Adept's Apprentice?

The rising sun shone pink and orange through low clouds to the east. The light reflected off the tiny ripples of the bay, causing Hawk to squint from the glare. They sailed due east in the direction of the

Knotts, with the oars going at maximum capacity. For most of the day, he stayed on deck with Ragnar and reminisced about old times. Gray dolphins swam briskly alongside the ship, occasionally leaping into the air. Hawk related to Ragnar of their voyage to Ebro and how he was enticed into the waters by a mermaid.

"Hah! I've seen many mermaid and mermen in these waters. They like the warmer temperature. Never been enticed by one though and cannot say I would mind."

"I never reached her. Perhaps she would have killed me but I will never know." He then told his friend about their adventures in Ebro.

"Ebro!" Ragnar exclaimed. "The spells around that island make for very uncomfortable sailing. No one has gone near for centuries. And you are saying you did?"

"That and more. The Queen of that island is no more and her slaves freed," Hawk said. He thought of his dream the night before and how Sillisnae transformed into Nominthe.

"So, it is all true then, and not just a legend?"

"Oh, yes, it is true. Legends are always true but just hidden in the mists of time and spatial isolation."

"It was rumored she was a goddess?" Ragnar frowned.

"Yes."

"How did you defeat her?"

Hawk told the entire tale from the time they were captured in the boat to when they stepped through the elemental portal. Ragnar listened attentively, interrupting to ask questions about Renfala and Lord Korodale. As Hawk explained, a pensive expression overcame the pirate's features.

"I'm not sure she is really dead," Hawk said at the end of his tale. "I don't know if mortals can kill the gods."

"If anyone killed her, it sounds as if the dragon did," Ragnar pointed out.

Renfala.

Where was he now? Still in Jaanaar? Sillisnae had possession of the Dragon Claw or did she? Had it been discovered? When he thought of Sillisnae, a creeping worry gnawed at his heart. The strange dream he had the night before did not help.

King Emeril would not give her to someone who meant her harm...

"Keep telling yourself that," he said under his breath.

"We will make good time, my friend. I told you before, the *Tawdry Maiden* is the fastest galley of its size in Perthia and probably in all of the south seas."

The wind pounded their faces with salt spray as the galley raced through the waters. The docks and quay of Aranhoe gave way to untouched coastline with dottings of small coastal hamlets. These possessed tiny harbors of small fishing boats with a few longships and galleys here and there. Here, east of Aranhoe, the *Tawdry Maiden* was by far the largest ship. The other boats hurried to shore when they saw her. After a couple of hours, the hamlets and boats disappeared and they sailed alone.

The Othalla River was a natural border between Corvasa and the Knotts. Hawk spied a west and east jetty protruding out into the wide open bay as the *Tawdry Maiden* approached. The dark gray rocks of the jetties glistened with sea spray. On both sides of the river's mouth were reddish cliffs and birch trees with light green leaves. From that point eastward, the shoreline of the Knotts moved farther southward. If one continued southward along the coastline, they would soon meet with a very tropical climate. Atop the red cliffs were bright green, rolling meadows dotted with wildflowers. A slight mist hung in the air evincing a foreboding, mystical atmosphere. Some of his former countrymen could be hiding in those mists, ready to fall upon the ship.

Ragnar called out some words in Maeltipian and the ship turned port as the crew maneuvered the sails. The galley sailed through the center of the river's mouth and into the fog without incident.

When they had set a new course, Hawk approached Ragnar. "How long until we reach the Triad?"

The old pirate spat out tobacco juice from a bulging wad housed in his lower lip. "Half a day, possibly more. It may be dusk when we reach it."

They both stared apprehensively into the thickening fog. It was unusual that it did not dissipate with the powerful sun.

Something awaits us in there, Hawk knew. Something nasty.

THE REGENERATING HEART

S HE FELT THE BLACK MUSCLE tied to her waist. The first time she had touched it, she was consumed by a black anger, a rage so great, it threatened to burn her body to ashes.

"What was that?" Sheena asked awestruck.

"You are experiencing the residual feelings of the owner of the heart."

"By the gods, the rage—"

Nolis raised his hand that she be silent. "It is best not to speak of such things."

He showed her a tunnel she had somehow overlooked. Was it possible he created it while they conversed? The interior was lit by ensconced torches.

"This will lead you under the Straight of Jaanaar beneath the Golden Band."

"Beneath the Golden Band?" Sheena was incredulous. "Aren't there ancient spells that prevent all Jaanaarians from crossing?"

"You possess the heart of a goddess. Its magic will be enough. You will pass through unharmed." His face shone with golden light.

At that moment, Sheena felt an indescribable love for him. Kneeling, she kissed his boots. The intensity of the feelings shocked her. She had never bowed before anyone in her life. But he was a god, and he was freeing her. His giant hands enveloped hers and he pulled her up.

"Your magic will return to you in increments once you cross the Golden Band." His form brightened, if that was possible, and he appeared to shine as brightly as the sun. The light reduced to a small sphere the size of Sheena's hand, followed by a *pop!* and Nolis vanished into thin air as Honor Titae had done.

"Nolis," Sheena whispered. "Are you still here?" All she heard was the dripping of water and her own echo.

The tunnel had a low ceiling, forcing her to bend down. It smelled of wet stone and ancient metals. Water streaks lined the walls under the torchlight. She walked with her head down for what seemed like hours but then the tunnel suddenly widened. It contracted and expanded alternately, sometimes becoming so narrow she was obliged to walk sideways.

At a certain point, after hours of walking, elaborate pictures and ancient runes appeared in white, black and red paint. The fragrance of roses permeated the air. She inhaled deeply.

A type of spell exists here, she realized. But she felt no heat of a ward. If the spell still existed, either the heart blocked it or it had weakened significantly.

The tunnel twisted and turned sharply and she soon lost her sense of direction. A strange, blue light appeared ahead. Her strength had returned enough so she could walk quickly, nearly run in fact. Within minutes, she was in a domed room with a round, stained glass window in the ceiling. Blue light formed a shimmering curtain she intuitively understood to be the astral barrier. Perhaps she was underneath it but that would not explain the window. With Nominthe's heart grasped firmly in one hand, she reached out toward the shimmery bluish light. Just before her hand made contact, she heard a soft step behind her. Whirling around, she came face to face with Honor Titae.

"Sheena. You cannot leave." His long white beard was doubly braided, hanging to mid-chest level. His violet eyes glowed and one hand was lifted with the first two fingers pointing upward. The gesture tickled her memory just like those made by Tessa and Raern: Runic symbols made with hand gestures. She once possessed the knowledge and according to Nolis, it would return over time.

Her lips drew back in a snarl then she spit in disgust. "Get out of here, old man! You and the filthy Jaanaarians are an emasculated, docile people. You have no fight left within you."

"You are Jaanaarian," the old fart pointed out. He stepped toward her.

The heart quickly grew hot in her hands, nearly causing her to drop it. It glowed blue and suddenly a thin string of lightning shot out and ripped through Honor Titae's chest. The impact threw him high against the wall where he fell to the ground with a thump and toppled over. The smell of burning flesh hung heavily in the air. A black hole existed where his chest had been. The periphery of the flesh singed black and smoke tendrils swirled lazily into the air.

Sheena studied the heart with fascination. What was it Nolis had said?

"It knows what it does and still contains the owner's desires."

Perhaps the heart knew Honor Titae would inhibit its owner's fulfillment. The thought made Sheena tremble.

The stone wall was cold against her back as she leaned against it, inhaling deeply. After a few breaths, the trembling stopped. She took one last look at the dead druid. His violet eyes stared at her in accusation, his mouth open in an expression of shock. The two white braids of his beard were gone, burned to ashes. The lightning had also singed some of his long white hair.

How could such a powerful sorcerer meet such an unexpected end? she wondered. The Jaanaarians were capable of reproducing themselves through thought alone. They were nearly gods.

Well, apparently not enough like them...

An overwhelming feeling of guilt hit her like a wave washing over a sandy beach, destroying the sand castle of her ambition.

"He was of your people," a voice whispered. It was not her voice but that of Nolis.

He is not like me. His heart was pure, she thought. *On the contrary, the heart I hold in my hand is something else.* And then, *Can Nolis read my thoughts?*

The blue wall of light hummed and shimmered. She thrust the heart through it.

Her hand slightly tingled but nothing more. She easily stepped through the curtain of light to the other side and was surprised by the lack of sensation.

Beyond the light curtain, the room was a mirror image from whence she had just come. Instead of a tunnel leading out, there were ancient, crumbling steps that descended into darkness.

With Nominthe's heart firmly clenched in one hand, she stepped tentatively forward. The ubiquitous sound of dripping water followed.

The tunnel was spacious and airy, a welcome change from the tight, twisting tunnels that led her to the domed room.

The idea that tons of water flowed somewhere above, that she was traversing the earth underneath the ocean floor, brought a smile to her lips. The smell was ancient, as if no one had been this way in centuries.

The stairs seemed to go on forever. Intermittently, they would give way to smooth, flat stone but would appear after a few steps.

She flinched back and screamed as a black spider the size of her foot went scrambling past on the wall to her right.

Do not fear, you jumpy old woman! It cannot harm you…

But in actuality, she did not know if that was true. If it had bitten her, it very well could have killed her. She was not on the surface any longer; living things in these tunnels may have more power than those on the surface.

Underneath the irritating sound of dripping water, her ears picked up something else. Flowing water. The sound gave her encouragement and she walked faster, trying to make herself as small as possible lest she brush up against a spider or something even more threatening.

Within an hour, she reached a stream with dark blue waters. The tunnel turned sharply to the right and followed the stream, progressively opening up into various caverns. The ceiling lifted to a height of more than fifty feet with beige crags jutting down like the gods pointing fingers. The steps ceased and the stone floor gave way to squishy earth. She put the heart inside a fold in the robes Nolis had given her, bent down and scooped up some of the ice cold water, half expecting to taste salt but it was fresh and pristine.

She came to a place where the stream frothed over rocks and something long and slimy lay in front of her where the light was dim. Sheena stopped and swallowed.

What had Nolis said?

"You will walk for several hours and then come to an underground river. Follow it and soon you will see their city."

"Whose city?"

"Everything cannot be explained or it will cease to exist."

"What?"

But the god did not reply. During her excursion into the bowels of the earth, she came to understand what he meant. The shapeshifter, Hawk, had been given a mission of which the instructions were disguised in poetic verse and his own imagination had to discover the clues. Perhaps it was a better way than forthright explanations.

The slimy, gray body expanded and contracted, as if breathing. A tail appeared, divided into two sections and disappeared into the darkness. She waited then stepped forward with great caution. The light revealed a small opening within a wall leading to another cavern. How many of these caverns would she have to pass through? And then she noticed something extraordinary. She put her hands to her face and felt smooth skin. If only she had a mirror, or a calm pool of water to gaze upon. Then she could see if Nolis was correct. Anxiously, she leaned over and gazed into the flowing stream, desperate to get any glimpse of her reflection, even if only fleeting.

"You will want to go to the surface before you reach Mount Moirae," a baritone voice said behind her.

Sheena jumped, nearly falling into the water. She whirled around and what she saw left her speechless.

A young child stood in front of her. But no, it was not a child but a grown man with a full, gray beard. His beady eyes were chestnut brown with no whites and vertical black slits for pupils. The little man wore dark green stockings and a velvet jerkin with a leather belt and dagger at his hip. At full height, he could not have reached Sheena's thigh.

"Did the giants call you?" he asked. "You resemble them but do not have the height."

Sheena licked her lips which were bone dry.

He is a gnome, an elemental Earth spirit.

His gray hair was split into two braids and he wore a steel conical helmet. His arms and legs were stunted and tufts of auburn hair sprouted from the backs of his hands.

"Giants?" she asked.

The little gnome cocked his head to one side, studying her intently. "Are you from the surface?" The deep voice did not match his diminished stature.

"Nolis has sent me," she informed him.

The gnome's eyebrows shot up. "Oh, please follow me. I will take you to your kind."

"My kind?"

But the gnome was already making use of his stunted legs. They carried him with an unexpected speed and grace. Sheena had to run to catch up and followed him under an arch in the stone wall of the cavern. She was expecting yet another cavern but what she saw made her stop in her tracks, her mouth agape.

She gazed upon an underground town with grass, flowers and trees. A meadow with blooming wildflowers separated her and her new companion from the town of cottages and duns. A soft, golden light shone everywhere, but Sheena could not see from whence it came. A giant grove glowed with green light in the distance. The oaks were huge, probably ten times larger than oaks in Jaanaar. Sheena spied tall beings walking among them. Judging from their size, she guessed they were nearly twenty feet tall.

Other gnomes emerged from behind glowing flowers and shrubs. They all looked the same but some had amber colored eyes instead of brown with the same vertical black slits as pupils.

"I am Hoffgarn," the gnome told her. "Don't mind them. They find those from the surface rare and fascinating."

He took Sheena's hand. His skin was rough and his grip firm. He led her toward the oak grove. Duns made of earth surrounded the grove in a semi-circle. Behind the grove were green hills of varying height, some of them with doors at their bases.

"What is this place?" she asked.

Hoffgarn did not reply but continued to lead her. The stream twisted through the wetlands and crystal bridges crossed over here and there where the width of the river was widest. A pack of mule deer grazed lazily through the lush meadow and pairs of doves cooed from the branches of cherry blossom trees whose fragrance permeated the air.

"Is this the Land of the Ancestors?" she asked Hoffgarn but he still would not reply. He seemed rather intent to get her to the grove as soon as possible. The flowers, grass and bushes also possessed a glow much like the fauna of Jaanaar. Now that she could see the giants better, she noticed their strangely shaped heads. The skull was elongated at a diagonal angle and all of them had varying shades of red hair. Otherwise, they appeared just like Jaanaarians only much taller.

Hoffgarn waved at the nearest giant whose eyes glowed bright purple. He smiled warmly and approached. The smile made Sheena feel guilty but she did not know why.

When he came closer, he emanated an unmistakable intense vibration. He offered his hand in greeting and Sheena took it. When she touched him, visions exploded within her mind's eye.

She saw a human skull made of crystal, then a dragon's head. She instinctively flinched back, remembering the dragonfire in the Linnsonian camp.

"*The precious cargo will not be activated without that which you have seen,*" the giant told her in her mind without moving his lips.

"What?" she asked aloud.

His eyes glittered gold and silver. "A man awaits, a twin for your soul, he awaits as if in a garden."

"I…" Sheena began but her words melted in her mouth. The giant's kaleidoscopic eyes were hypnotizing her. "A twin soul…" she whispered.

"What is this place? Who are you? Is it the Land of the Ancestors?"

"Yes, this is the Land of the Ancestors but not in the way you are thinking," the giant replied. *"I am Ulfinir and this is the place we came to when the world was young, many ages ago."*

"Are you gods?" Sheena asked.

Ulfinir laughed, an airy, soft sound. "Perhaps we may seem that way to humans." He spoke now with his mouth and his eyes remained a glowing violet. They turned silver and gold when he projected thoughts.

"What do you mean that a man awaits me?"

"Everything cannot be explained," Ulfinir said in his airy voice, "because then—"

"It will cease to exist," Sheena finished for him. That seemed to be a very popular saying.

From behind the giant oaks in the distance, a figure clad entirely in black appeared. His face was obscured by a large cowl and he floated rather than walked, reminding her of Tessa and Raern. She briefly wondered if they had been punished for her disappearance.

When he was within a few feet, he reached up to his cowl and pulled it down. Sheena gasped in horror.

"Hello, Sheena," Simon Korodale said. "It is lovely to see you again."

Her mouth went dry. "Simon...but how...why?"

Several different emotions fought for control. Fear, rage, sadness, curiosity, guilt, shame...even love, all bubbled within her consciousness. She instinctively clenched the heart, fearing he would attack her again. He appeared younger; the same as when she fell in love with him those many years ago in the Crystal Palace. She wanted to speak but could not find the words. Aware that the gnome and Ulfinir watched her, she was embarrassed when tears fell from her eyes.

Lord Korodale relieved her by speaking. "How did you break the spell of the Adepts of the Globes?"

It was a fair question and one which she knew she would be obliged to explain one day. But she thought that day would come later rather than sooner. Her former lover still wore the golden helmet of the *Daimon Direttore*. He had grown some whiskers but they were closely cropped. His dark brown eyes still possessed a ferocious intensity and his thin lips were pursed in an uncomfortable line.

He is as afraid of me as I am of him, she realized. She had a few questions of her own to ask.

"I took a section of the crystal dome in the South Atrium when I still lived in the Crystal Palace. The dome holds the spell that protects—"

"That is common knowledge, Sheena," Lord Korodale interrupted. "Tell me something I don't know. Did you have help from another member of Sii Dei?"

"No. The piece of crystal was all I needed. It took me several decades to work out the spell embedded within. I had all the time I needed in the tiny village."

"How were you able to unwork the spell in the dome?" he asked.

"That was the easy part. Crystal possesses a nature so that it remembers and can hold any spell, any information put into it. It can connect to its source via the earth and her energies. When I was convinced I had discovered the spell, I simply entombed myself in the Earth for a few minutes with the crystal and worked the spell backwards. The earth carried the counter-spell to its source, namely the dome of the south atrium. When the protection was neutralized, I simply cut space and pulled the Fire Globe through the ether."

"Why go to Minosae after you stole it? You had what you wanted, why risk being discovered?"

Sheena laughed at that. He was still always one step behind her even in death. If one could call him dead.

"I had to make certain you did not suspect me. Or Sii Dei. And I wanted to see you one last time." It was true. She had loved him once, many years ago, but as she grew older she realized the futility of love. For her, there was only power and love made one vulnerable.

"How do the Linnsonians fit into all of this?" he asked.

That was the question she was most afraid of. She shot a glance at the giant who stood listening in silence.

"I don't know," she replied.

Lord Korodale laughed loudly. "You're lying."

"How did you retain your form here, Simon?" she asked, attempting to steer the conversation away from the Linnsonians.

"Now Sheena, you already know the answer to that question. No need to state the obvious."

"Since you were burned to ashes by Renfala..."

"My physical body, lover, not my astral body. That was completely intact and could not be burned. I am the *Daimon Direttore* after all. Do you think the Jaanaarians can keep such a secret for themselves? Come on now, I expect more from you. All of Sii Dei knows the secret kept from the Council of Twelve and Adepts throughout the realm. The secret to which the Jaanaarians think they are exclusively privy."

"Yes…but…you betrayed…well…"

"I *betrayed?*" Lord Korodale snickered. "Sheena, stop now. Did you forget all of your knowledge?"

He had a point. She had indeed forgotten a lot and less than half of her occult knowledge had returned.

"Do you live here now?" she asked.

Lord Korodale folded him arms. The crimson cloak he had worn in physical form was now black as night. His expression softened and for a brief instant, she thought she saw some of the old love flash in his brown eyes.

"I can show you the way to the surface." He floated closer until he was only inches away. She thought he might try to kiss her, so dense was his body. In fact, she could not tell the difference between his physical body and the vehicle he now occupied.

"You will exit exactly where you need to be."

Sheena nodded and took a step back. The giant had disappeared. In fact, she could not see any more giants within the grove, only a few gnomes lounging among the wildflowers. Hoffgarn had disappeared as well.

Butterflies that glowed every color of the rainbow gathered around them. Simon floated slightly in front of her. He pointed. "See the entrance into that dun? Enter and you will be on the surface in no time. What you have failed to reveal about the Linnsonians will only be your undoing."

Sheena stopped and took one last look around at the strange golden light and meadow beyond. "That is something I will never reveal, Simon. If you only knew—"

"I already do. I wanted to see if you would tell me." He nodded toward the entrance. "Goodbye for now, sweet lover." He planted a kiss on her lips. It felt like a soft breeze, so light was it. And then he was gone.

A CANNIBAL'S FEAST

A PARTY OF THREE RIDERS met their procession at the edge of a meadow across which lay the camp she had seen from the mountain pass.

Lananell stood on her tiptoes to watch the approaching riders. Naton headed the procession and he presented a white, squirming sack with rope tied around it in sections. Lananell understood it was the man they had captured in the woods, the man who tried to kill her.

The gnome had disappeared. The camp had burned their dead, all in all, nearly a dozen people perished. She did not understand how the earth could explode like it did. And the hole in the middle of the camp…had it swallowed the gnome? She would probably never know.

Naton pointed to the back of the line, explaining something to the riders from the camp. For one brief instant she felt her stomach drop when she was sure Naton pointed in her direction.

You're just imagining things. Why would he point at you? You are now just a lowly slave, no better than you were in Linnso.

But her fears were confirmed when one of the riders galloped to where she waited. Tara kicked her mule to move out of the way.

He wore the skin and head of a big cat, its eyes polished amber, its fangs the color of ivory. Strawberry blond hair tumbled about his shoulders and dark blue eyes stared out at her beneath a scarred brow. Brown leather was laced to his forearms and he wore a dented and scratched breast plate.

He pointed at Tara and said a word. The old woman made a face, dismounted and untied Lananell's hands.

Before Lananell understood what was happening, the rider lifted her up onto his horse.

She clasped the saddle horn as they galloped past Naton and toward the camp.

"I am Stogar of the Grenta clan," he said in Corvasan.

"Are you Ossek?" she asked timidly.

He slowed the horse to a trot. "You aren't Corvasan."

"No," she whispered. Is that why they had kidnapped her? Did they think her Corvasan?

The pavilions in the camp were unlike any she had seen before. They were giant conical shapes, sewn of different types of pelts and held up by wooden poles with a smoke hole at the top.

Stogar dismounted and led her into one of the larger tents where several people gathered around a small fire in the center. Men lounged on pillows and furry pelts covering the ground.

"Hentra," Stogar called to a woman even older and more shrunken than Tara. A hunchback forced her to walk awkwardly with a cane. Thin, gray hair sprouted from her pink scalp and her eyes were light gray with rheumy yellow in the whites.

"Speak to her in Corvasan," Stogar commanded gruffly and took his leave.

"You are a healer, child," Hentra said in a papery, congested voice that attested to her age. She reached out a withered, spotted hand to touch her cheek.

Lananell nodded. "I cannot heal myself."

"Aye." The old woman sat her down on a furry brown bear's pelt surrounded by pillows. Next to them, two men sat smoking from tubes attached to a glass vase. The smoke smelled of dried flowers as it drifted lazily across the tent. When Hentra made eye contact, they left without a word. After they had gone, Hentra grabbed the long tube and inhaled deeply. She let some smoke slowly ooze out of her mouth and nostrils then blew the rest into Lananell's face.

"Inhale, my dear," she instructed in that ancient, raspy voice.

Lananell inhaled and almost immediately, the pain in her lip and her scalp subsided.

"What is your name, child?"

"Lananell," she responded meekly. Her own voice sounded distant, as if belonging to someone else. Her head felt light and woozy, like it was detached from her body, ascending through the smoke hole high above her.

"Where do you hail from? You aren't Corvasan."

The thought of Linnso was also distant, an amorphous wall of fog blanketed over the memories.

"A place called Linnso."

Hentra was mid-inhalation when she withdrew the snakelike pipe from her mouth. "Linnso?" The old woman frowned and exhaled the smoke through her nostrils like Renfala did when he blew fire.

A young girl of five or six, dressed in the ubiquitous pelts, set a tray of black bread and cheese in front of them. Lananell was famished and tore into the bread hungrily. It was a bit stale but tasted delicious all the same.

"Are you from Osseka?" Lananell asked Hentra.

The old woman narrowed her eyes. "Osseka is not a place, but a people. Wherever the blood of the Osseks runs through live veins, that is where Osseka exists."

"Oh." She could not think of anything else to say.

Hentra smiled a toothless grin and inhaled deeply from the pipe. When she exhaled, she once more aimed the smoke in Lananell's direction. That was all it took to bring her to the brink of consciousness. She stretched out on the bear fur. All the muscles in her body relaxed. Hentra carefully propped her head on a pillow and covered her with another fur hide.

She dreamed of Rosco. His face was twisted and lined with worry as he walked through the moonlight of the forest calling her name. Kurin was with him carrying a torch.

"I'm here!" Lananell screamed but he did not hear.

"Rosco! I am to the north and east, over the mountain pass!"

But Rosco was oblivious to her cries. The distress on his face broke her heart and she must have cried because when she awoke, her cheeks were wet with tears. Hentra was gone but a man with a spear stood behind her and her wrists had been tied again. When he saw she had awoken, he pulled her up by the arm and shoved her roughly outside.

A woman wearing a long dirty chemise and maroon bodice stood alone next to the pavilion as if she waited for Lananell. "Are you Corvasan?" She had a pox-marked face and lanky brown hair.

"I...I...live in Martine. What's your name?"

"Faria. Pleased to make your acquaintance." She offered her hand and Lananell took it. "I'm from Newhouse in the far east of Corvasa, near the Othalla River."

Faria's eyes were tired and her face was worn and haggard but she managed to produce a smile. "You have an accent."

Lananell lowered her voice, ignoring her statement. "My name is Lananell. Do you know what they intend to do with us?"

"The Osseks take the women for breedin' and the men for work. I have been here for six moons." She undid the rope around Lananell's wrists.

She stared at Faria, incredulous.

"You're allowed to roam free here, Lananell."

Lananell carefully chose her words. "Have you ever tried to...es...I mean, er, return to Corvasa?"

Faria managed to laugh. It was a pathetic, beaten sound. "The mountain passes would be impossible to cross alone."

Lananell expected that response but was not sure she completely agreed.

Faria led her to the center of the circle of pavilions. Massive logs were arranged by muscular men heaving axes and women carried kindling they had gathered in the forest. The last rays of twilight faded slowly and a few stars twinkled in the east. She and Faria stood and watched the entire tribe of Osseks form a circle. Men in black and red robes emerged from the nearby pavilions wearing the heads of animals. One man wore a horse's head, another that of an elk, another a bear's head and so on.

Two young boys carried a wooden plank and a thick wooden pole twice the height of two men. Another boy lit the bonfire with a torch. A man wearing a wolf's head led out a prisoner with his hands tied in front of him. Lananell's breath caught in her throat. It was the man who tried to kill her.

"A man captured from a different tribe," Faria observed. "He was their Healer. The Osseks do not make slaves out of prisoners. They make slaves of prisoner's shades."

"How?" Lananell asked.

"Just watch. And they take those with magical talent."

"You mean the shades behind their leaders are all Healers?"

Faria gave Lananell a queer look. "Healers and Adepts."

Lananell was confused. But before she could clarify, drums began beating in low, ominous rhythms.

The Osseks began to dance. Soon Lananell and Faria were caught up in the dance which moved the participants in a counter-clockwise direction. The prisoner was tied to the pole secured on the plank. An

Ossek with a brown bear's head unsheathed his dagger and held the blade in front of the prisoner's eyes but the man did not react. He gazed sideways to the ground. The drums continued to beat and Bear's Head danced around the prisoner, holding his dagger high above his head and ululating in high-pitched tones. His demonstration seemed to excite the bystanders into a frenzy and soon everyone was jumping up and down and ululating at the top of their voices. Faria encouraged Lananell do the same.

Bear's Head danced around the prisoner, behind the pole to which he was tied, and suddenly, faster than a striking cobra, swiped the dagger across the man's throat. Blood erupted in pulsing globules and the prisoner made a brief gurgling noise as his eyes went wide.

Lananell could not help herself. She screamed. Not that it made a difference in the wild cacophony. The two young boys who had set up the plank held a wooden bucket with tar-sealed seams underneath the man's throat as his head fell forward, effectively capturing his life's blood as it gushed from his throat.

"Why did they do that?" She asked but Faria did not hear her. The bucket was passed around to the Osseks in the innermost circle. Lananell judged they were boys on the verge of manhood.

She put her hands to her face and felt wet tears there. Bodies pressed all around her. The smoke from the bonfire stung her eyes. All she wanted to do was break away, to run, where did not matter but the crowd prevented it.

The prisoner was cut down and his body laid out on the plank while Bear's Head knelt over him. He lifted his dagger once more and plunged it into the corpse's chest just below the collar bone. The chants and screams of the crowd reached an ecstatic crescendo. The elk's head stood and gestured for silence.

Through the commotion and her own horrified state, Lananell had failed to notice a small fire had been lit under a black iron pot.

"They will eat his organs," Faria shouted in her ear. "The young warriors and necromancers will partake and the rest will get a taste of his blood. The drinking of the blood insures the man's spirit stays with the tribe for protection. The person who eats his heart, however, will have the full power of his shade until the captor's death."

"Why do the Osseks eat his other organs if it's only the heart that gives the power?" Lananell asked.

"It's not only the heart," Faria pointed out. "Those who eat the other organs acquire the knowledge those organs represent. But the person who eats the heart gets the lion's share and consequently, the shade."

Bear's Head dexterously cut away organs and placed them into the black pot. The crowd stomped their feet in unison and lowered their voices to a rhythmic hum. The youth gathered around and Bear's Head used a spear to stab a cooked organ for each of them. When the last had been given out, Bear's Head retrieved the prized heart which had not been cooked. He bit into it and the crowd roared all around them.

"It is a great privilege to be eaten by an entire tribe," Faria explained after the noise died down. "The one sacrificed knows he will act as a magical talisman for his conquerors before he returns to the Land of the Ancestors. For the Osseks who have shades following them, they receive special powers."

"How?"

"Remember, I told you they only cannibalize ones with talent. The shade will provide his master with all the powers he had while alive. The longer his master lives, the more spiritual advancement the shade will receive once his service is finished."

"I have magical talent," Lananell told Faria as they were shoved and pushed by the dispersing crowd.

"You aren't Ossek. They only eat those of Ossekan blood. They feel the peoples to the west are weak so they don't want their blood."

"I see," Lananell said but she was not listening anymore. Her head was filling with plans on the best way of escape. Her captors were monsters.

She was so weary. So, so weary. How could she have let herself be captured again? Was it her destiny? She thought back to escaping her own people on that fateful day in the forest. She had not even wanted to escape. Soraya had convinced her to come along and it all began from there.

During the cold night, she and Faria slept in the massive pavilion with nearly two dozen others. She fully expected the men to come to her but they did not, even though she noticed some of them gaze upon her longingly. During the days, she took the habit of wandering into the surrounding forest. The camp was always cold and windy. Hentra gave her a cloak made of white goat fur. When in the trees, the wind did not blow so harshly and the chill did not goose-pimple her flesh. The first couple of days, she sat with her back against a giant fir tree with a reddish-brown trunk and flaking bark. Back in Martine, the tree had spoken to her but the plants and trees were strangely silent after her capture.

Birds landed on branches and tilted their heads, watching. They were small and white with black stripes down their backs. Sometimes, they would fly down and hop around the trunk, chirping. On the third day, while she sat nearly consumed by sleep, she heard the soft whisper of a male voice.

...our kind will give power only to you...

"What?" Lananell asked aloud. The voice had surprised her but she was relieved as well.

...later...

"What? What do you mean?" But the tree did not answer if it had, in fact, been the tree speaking. She tried to reach the contemplative state in which she had been when the tree spoke, but her mind was racing. The birds continued to hop and chirp. A slight breeze swayed the tops of the pines and the smell of tree sap was heavy in the air. Mushrooms with red and white tops littered the bases of many of the thicker trunks. Lananell had seen Hentra picking some of them.

"These mushrooms open the special sight and the destiny of the clan can be revealed," she told Lananell.

Hentra also told her the clan would remain camped at their current location until the winter came.

"Naton wants to stay here for three moons. There are lots of big game and many roots and nuts to gather."

Lananell was thankful to hear it. Traveling with the clan was exhausting on foot.

Sometimes in the middle of the night she would awake thinking of Rosco. Was he searching for her? She missed him so much.

"Do you love me, Lananell?" Rosco asked on the night of their

matrimony.

"What is love?" She countered. He only stared at her. He did not have an answer.

In Linnso, there was no talk of love. But in this new, strange land, everyone seemed to talk of it. In Linnso, there was only duty. The women had the duty of raising small babies and toddlers, providing sex for the men, cleaning and preparing cuisine. When Rosco asked her if she loved him, she had been taken aback. She felt if she did not say yes, she would disappoint him. He was kind, never hit her and seemed to care about her opinion. For that, she would be eternally grateful. But she had come to love him for all of that and more. And she missed him terribly.

In Linnso, she had become pregnant after her menarche at age thirteen. Almost all of the women did. She raised the male child until age four, and then he was taken by the men to be raised by them. From birth, women were encouraged never to develop attachments to their children, only the other womenfolk they lived and worked with. When the child was taken away from her, Lananell cried in secret. But the boy was the one screaming. To remember it now brought tears to her cheeks.

She listened to Faria's steady breathing. The Corvasan woman slept so soundly, sometimes Lananell thought she passed on to the Land of the Ancestors. Shouts and wailing, accompanied by sounds of steel clanking and horses whinnying, brought Lananell out of her sleepy stupor. She shook Faria. The woman snorted and moaned but did not awaken.

Pulling back the flap of the pavilion, Lananell peered out into the dewy soft light of morning. The camp was awakening. The pavilion in the northernmost part of the circle always housed their leaders, including Naton and his woman. The shouts had come from the tent in the north.

Later that morning, when everyone had awoken and Lananell took a breakfast of goat cheese and pine nuts, she heard talk of Naton being mortally wounded by a spear from an ambush. They had summoned their most powerful Healers, Hentra among them.

Later that day, when the sun had set over the mountains in the west, the north tent's flap finally parted and Hentra emerged. Her expression was despondent. Smaller fires burned in the center of the circle of pavilions. Hentra joined Lananell and Faria with a group of a dozen Osseks as they warmed themselves and prepared to cook the night's meat.

"Naton will pass on to the Land of the Ancestors," the old woman informed Lananell. "The herbs don't work the healing power. I don't know why. My talents are failing." The old woman's voice broke and a tear streamed down one dry, lined cheek. "The others are failing as well. Our gods have forsaken us!"

Faria eyed Lananell but all she could do was stare into the fire. The flames flickered and danced in their oranges and reds then slowly took on human shapes and the shapes formed faces, faces she knew. One a middle-aged women with long, light brown hair holding a black object high over her head. Lananell recognized Sheena, as she was when she first encountered her in Martine. The sight made her sad. Even though she knew Sheena was a traitor and the thief of the Fire Globe, Lananell still had a soft spot for the Jaanaarian sorceress. Sheena had given her refuge when she escaped the Linnsonians.

Lananell stared more intently. What was Sheena holding? In her other hand she held an iron chain which led to a man whose face Lananell initially could not see but when he turned his head Lananell sucked in breath. The man was Rosco with an iron collar around his neck.

"What is it, young one?" Hentra asked, frowning.

"I…I…cannot stay here," Lananell stammered.

Hentra did not answer but Faria eyed her up and down. "They will never let you go," she said.

"You cannot heal Naton," Lananell told Hentra. "But I can."

The wise woman lifted her eyes to Lananell's. Lananell saw trust there.

She knows that I can as well.

"Take me to him."

The chief's tent was gargantuan and opulent. A plethora of feather pillows were piled against the northern side of a round wall. Naton lay upon them with a bear skin covering his body to his chest. His shade appeared more transparent than Lananell remembered.

He is near death. The shade will disappear just before he dies.

To the right of Naton, lounging on pillows, lay a man Lananell knew as Evanton. The shade of the druid she had seen sacrificed hovered behind him.

So he had been the bear's head in the ceremony.

Hentra took Lananell's hand into her dry, withered one and led her gently toward the dying man. The left side of his chest showed an oozing hole where a spear had penetrated just below the last rib. The hole was too wide to be that of an arrow. Lananell wrinkled her nose at the smell. In addition to dark blood, whitish-yellow pus lined the edge of the wound.

"It is festering," Lananell said.

"Yes, and it will not close. I have tried every type of herb I could find. Something is wrong. It is some cruel magic." Hentra spat on the ground.

…our kind will give power only to you…

"Show me which medicines you used, Hentra."

Hentra grabbed a gray mortar and pestle with her curled, arthritic hand. Within was a bright green paste with a pungent pine smell.

"The needle leaves of the evergreens," Hentra said, "with Murdock root and nightshade for pain. The healing power is in the smell so it is not lacking but they will not clean or close the wound. I have never seen anything like it."

"Let me try," Lananell said. She dipped her fingers into the paste and approached Naton.

Evanton stood and put his arm out to block her but Hentra hissed like a cobra. He sat down immediately with a shamed expression.

The paste slid smoothly over the wound. Lananell held her breath because the smell brought her close to fainting. She carefully applied the green salve in slow, sweeping strokes. Naton's eyes were half open and glazed over but she knew he was aware of what she did. She smiled at him to soothe his nerves and—to her shock—he smiled back ever so slightly.

Hentra produced some soft cloth to dress the wound and keep it in place. Lananell felt Naton's forehead, dimpled with beads of sweat. She kept her palm there and called upon the energy within her. His forehead did not get cooler, but the green salve underneath the bandages glowed with bright green light. Hentra marveled at the sight with wide eyes and an open mouth.

Lananell withdrew her hands. "Your wound will be healed on the morrow."

"We'll see about that, foreigner!" Evanton hissed. "If our own Healers cannot close the wound, then one such as you can hardly heal him."

"He will be healed on the morrow," she responded calmly. The shade of the druid behind him regarded her with sad, knowing eyes. Suddenly, she felt a pang of extreme pity and turned away.

The next day at sunrise, Hentra came to her tent and shook her awake.

"Naton wants to see you, Lananell."

"Is he healed?"

The old woman's wrinkles parted for a slight smile. "You shall see for yourself."

When she entered the tent, Naton sat up on his pillows and color had returned to his cheeks. His shade had also become more material and hovered over him with renewed vigor. "Here is the only woman that could heal me!" he boomed.

Evanton frowned at her but Lananell did not care.

She knelt in front of him. "Chieftain."

"Look at me, Lananell from Linnso."

260

She did as he bid. The cloth, held in place by a wrap of bandages over his shoulder and around his torso, still stuck to his wound. A young girl unwrapped the bandages and Lananell gasped at what she saw. The wound had completely healed! Not even the slightest scar marked the place where it had been. The Osseks marveled in awe all around her.

"You have healed me where others could not, where my own blood could not. What is this power you have that others have not?"

Lananell bit her lip. *Power?* "The power is not mine, chieftain. The power comes from the spirit in the plants."

"My own Healers, the blood of my people are familiar with the spirits of the plants, Lananell of Linnso. Why is it they could not use them?"

Lananell knew why but dare she express it? "My chieftain, the plants have given me their power because they wish for something in return."

An "aha" was shouted from somewhere behind her.

"What is that, Lananell from Linnso?"

"I want to return home."

Evanton laughed loudly. "Chieftain, this slave has just made a demand of us. Are you going to stand for such insolence? The woman must be punished. No woman dares give commands to chieftains of the Grenta clan."

"Leave us!" Naton shouted. His voice boomed throughout the pavilion. "Everyone out! Except for you," he indicated Lananell.

"Chieftain—" Evanton began.

"Out!"

Evanton bored into Lananell with a gaze of death. When he passed, he spat in front of her. He was one of the men she saw eying her provocatively when she first arrived in camp. No doubt, Naton or someone higher in rank, had foiled his intentions and now his thwarted desire had turned to venom. Or perhaps his newly acquired shade had turned him against her. The man had tried to kill her after all.

"Come closer, Lananell of Linnso."

Naton sighed and glanced back at his shade then focused intently on Lananell. "When I was a boy, my father noted I excelled at prophecy. Sometimes I saw things in water or fire, sometimes in the clouds. In objects made of glass, I saw scenes play out that would come to pass. One such time, I saw a beautiful young woman with a strange accent and curly brown hair. Men hunted her because she was valuable. I saw her with two other women, also being hunted and without seeing anything else, I realized they would be used by other, nefarious forces to bring about something monstrous, something beyond tyranny, but what it was, I couldn't quite say then and still can't. But I'll tell you this, Lananell from Linnso. The woman I saw was you. And I didn't realize it until we brought you back to camp. The first time I saw you, you were terrified and I thought, just another one to breed but then I came to understand who you were. That's why no one has touched you, Lananell. If you were just another Corvasan, you would have been pregnant by now."

"But the Ossekan blood…"

"We only use pure blooded Ossekans for the ritual. But those numbers are dwindling and we need warriors."

"Warriors for?"

"Something is coming Lananell, a great showdown of massive proportions. And the Ossek tribes will be ready!"

ROSCO MEETS THE OSSEKS

THE TENDER LIGHT OF DAWN caressed them through the oak branches beneath which they slept, waking Rosco from a nightmare. The earth was wet with morning dew; small drops glistened on the blades of grass and sparkled upon the pine needles. Somewhere nearby a spring flowed. Rosco followed the sound to a brook where he washed his face and upper body.

The oak they slept under was one of a dozen that formed a grove, most likely an ancient ritual place for druids. When he returned, Kurin had awoken, his mouth hard.

"What's for breakfast, dear brother?" Kurin took out his pipe.

"I don't think you'll have time for that. I want to get going right away."

"Breakfast?"

"I brought some elk jerky and blood sausages."

Kurin made a fire and roasted the sausages over it. Rosco loved the subtle taste of blood sausage. Lananell had grown fond of it as well. Thinking of her, he took the looking glass into his hand. Last night, it had led them along a well-worn path.

She must have come this way.

At one time, the path had probably started out as a game trail. If he didn't find Lananell by nightfall, he would hunt tonight. He had attached his bow to his back along with a quiver and arrows. A skinning knife hung from his belt. The jerky and blood sausage wouldn't last very long for the two of them.

They ate in silence except for the occasional birdsong from orange-chested robins. The looking glass continued to glow green when he held it in the direction of the untraveled path. They would follow it until they found her or until the glass ceased to glow.

Walking through this northern alpine territory was much easier than what he had done in Westernaphalia. The path was devoid of rich foliage hiding felled trunks and twisted roots. The ground was firm with short grass and rock. In some places they crested false summits which were notably colder and windier than in Martine. Occasionally, he saw a herd of elk cows or marmots scurrying across open terrain. The marmots were portly with a long coat of golden fur and brown faces. They waddled away when they saw Rosco and his brother. He wondered how they would taste. Marmot meat couldn't be too tough.

Kurin was old but he kept a pace Rosco struggled to keep up with. The man had always been a superb hiker and fast runner where Rosco was always admired throughout Martine for his strength and grappling skills.

"Do you know anything about the Osseks?" Rosco asked Kurin. "I believe that's who gave those herders such a fright. And possibly who took Lananell."

"If they're Osseks, they are many leagues from their homeland. And I've never heard them to raid in northern Corvasa, only in the south."

"Perhaps something drove them this way. Perhaps they tired of the southern lands."

Kurin let his staff swing in front of him as he walked. "Possible. But they aren't anyone I would want to meet with."

Rosco's heart sank but his brother was right. If the stories told by the boy and the herder were true, the people out there were murderers and possibly man-flesh eaters. The most serious of transgressions against the gods of Corvasa. He didn't know about their gods, however. Perhaps they required the flesh of men and women?

"Are they nomadic barbarians?"

"From what I can remember, yes," Kurin said. "Like most peoples of Perthia, they are descended from a Jaanaarian who strayed many centuries ago."

They crested another hill covered with pink monkshood and purple larkspur. Beauty abounded in every direction. The view was of gently rolling hills.

"Lo! There!" Kurin pointed. They hadn't seen any person or sign of settlement. Until now.

A smoke plume rose against the gray sky. The whitish plume formed a gentle swirl against the backdrop of semi-dark clouds that blocked the rays of the sun.

"How far away would you say that is?" Kurin whispered. Of course, whoever was the source of the fire could not hear them but his brother had always been overly cautious.

"An hour's walk. Perhaps two. It's hard to tell."

"The trail leads in their direction. Should we go around?" Kurin asked.

Rosco drew his bow from his back. He hated using the bow on anything other than game. But it wouldn't come to that. He would avoid any danger if possible and if they needed to go around, they would. He would not die today, not until he found his wife.

"This is what we're going to do"—he turned to his brother— "we'll continue until we get close enough to hear them or at least see them—"

"What if they posted sentries?"

Rosco pondered that question. "They won't have sentries until dark. From the plume, it's a small fire. No doubt, they believe themselves to be out here alone."

A copse of evergreens with some aspens and elms lay ahead of them. The plume seemed to come from beyond it or perhaps a clearing within. Instinctively, once they reached the trees, they slowed. Birdsong was loud and abundant. A few royal-blue stellar jays called out with their rankling squawks. Rosco felt the looking glass glow hot within his hands which worried him. The plume of smoke slowly fizzled out in the sky.

He put a hand on his brother's shoulder and a forefinger to his lips. "Slow down," Rosco mouthed.

They crept along slowly, half that of their previous pace. Rosco tried to be as quiet as possible, at the same time listening intently for any branches breaking or bushes shifting.

Kurin stopped so suddenly Rosco nearly ran him over. "There's something ahead there," he whispered.

"What?"

"I don't know. But it's big."

"Not human?" Rosco nocked an arrow.

Kurin drew his short sword but truth be told, the old man had not used that thing in ages. Rosco saw the dust on the hilt.

About ten yards ahead of them, hurried footsteps crunched through fallen branches. Rosco was tempted to unleash the arrow but there was a slight chance it could be Lananell.

What emerged was a gray and white wolf, twice as big as the largest dog he had ever seen. It stood nearly to his waist. Something was wrong, though, because it didn't bare its teeth or growl, but traipsed off the trail at a trot and then fell into a canter. Rosco had only seen a wolf one other time in his life, when he was a boy and had gone north with their father hunting moose.

He thought the wolf should have been more aggressive. The animal seemed spooked.

"Keep moving slowly," he whispered to Kurin. "There may be more."

Bushes moved ahead and Rosco heard a sound like gurgling or gulping, like something feasted.

One step, then two. They crouched low and lengthened their stride, carefully placing each foot as silently as possible.

Kurin held up his hand and Rosco stopped. "Something else is there," he turned his head slightly toward Rosco and whispered out of the side of his mouth. "It's a man...and he seems to be eating."

Rosco squatted to see better through the trees. Kurin was right. A dead wolf lay on its side, its icy blue, lifeless eyes stared at him. His intestines and abdominal viscera were splayed across the ground in a banquet of red and sickly yellow. A blurry figure crouched over the animal's guts, eating it off the ground in large gulps. There was something off about the man. He was sure it was a man; he was taller than Rosco by a head or two. Rosco stared, attempting to understand what it was he was seeing. Then it slowly dawned on him. The man who feasted like he was at a wedding banquet was partly transparent, Rosco could see through him to the trees beyond.

A cold shiver ran down his spine. He motioned to Kurin they move back. They would go around, way around.

Kurin's foot hit a felled log and he landed on his backside with a thump. The slurping noises stopped.

Rosco pulled his brother up with one hand. "Run!" he yelled. Panic threatened as he ran off the path deep into the copse. Branches scratched his legs, and leaves hit him in the face. Kurin's panting was right behind him, which gave him some comfort.

An explosion of dirt erupted in front of him. Unable to stop his momentum, he fell into it, his mouth, nostrils and eyes filling with dirt and pine needles. The world went black for a brief moment then a blood-curdling screech forced him to cover his ears.

"Kurin!" he spat and rubbed the dirt from his eyes.

"I'm here!" his brother called back somewhere to Rosco's left.

Rosco drew his dagger because he had dropped the bow somewhere back on the path.

It didn't matter, though, because what stood or rather *hovered* in front of them was not made of man-flesh. It was the shade of a man, a rather tall gentleman. His mouth hung open and part of the skin and flesh of his jaw was missing, revealing yellow, rotted teeth. Transparent rags hung off his rail-thin body and long tufts of white hair jutted chaotically from his scalp. His gaping mouth opened even wider and he let out another deafening screech.

A mangy brown dog appeared and barked at them and they heard some human voices as well. The progenitors of the plume of smoke, no doubt. Rosco cursed himself. Why had he not gone around?

Two men and a young boy approached behind the barking mutt. The dog growled and lunged at Rosco. He quickly stood and kicked it in the face, sending it yelping toward its masters.

The men were tall and well-built but not nearly as tall or muscled as Rosco. If it were not for the skinny shade, he would've challenged the bigger one to a grappling session. They carried no weapons as far as he could discern. One was older, about forty, with a thick, graying brown beard that reached the middle of his chest. The younger man looked in his mid-twenties and wore a black leather jerkin, a smith's garment. He was handsome with dark brown wavy hair and a closely trimmed beard. The boy was about ten and was a younger version of the smith.

"Delinal cheka." The oldest pointed. "Delinal cheka."

Rosco and Kurin looked at each other.

"We only speak Corvasan," Kurin said.

The five, or six of them, if the shade was counted, stood in silence and stared at each other. The strangers were not armed. He and Kurin were. But what of the shade, what could it do?

"Ye come with us," the smith said.

"We are searching for someone who is lost," Rosco spoke up.

"Who?" the smith asked.

"A woman, about this tall with curly brown hair. Very pretty."

An unmistakable, cryptic glance passed between the smith and older man. The shade that had frightened him glided behind the long-bearded man.

"Is she kin?" the oldest asked in thickly accented Corvasan.

Rosco nodded. "She's my wife."

The smith lifted his eyebrows in surprise.

These people know her. He was sure of it.

"Have you seen her?" he prodded.

"Ye come with us," the smith repeated. "I am Tonek." He motioned to the old man with the shade. "My father, Ongus. And Wylt, my son. We've knowledge of yer wife."

Rosco regarded the shade suspiciously. "If you'll point us in the direction, I'd rather not accompany you."

"Not yer choice," Ongus said.

Rosco dug in his heels. "And if we do not?"

The shade flew over Ongus' head and swirled around Kurin and him in a frenzy, so fast it was a blur. Rosco became dizzy, all he saw was the swirling of the shade, the twirling of Kurin's face and the surrounding trees. The dizziness caused him to fall and wretch. Kurin landed on top of him, forcing him into his own vomit. Hands were upon them within seconds, pulling them up and slapping their faces. The entire world was in a green spin. Rosco felt his stomach rising and retched again, this time onto someone's garments. Whose, he did not know.

Next thing he knew he was being led by the hand because he couldn't walk by himself. Someone wiped his mouth and tunic with a leaf. A few minutes passed and the green swirls became light golden and blue swirls. By now he felt a little better and noticed for the first time his hands were tied with a rope that connected to Kurin's waist which then connected to his brother's wrists. Tonek and Wylt walked behind them while Ongus and his shade were in front. And his bow and dagger were gone.

Wonderful, Rosco! If I had kept my mouth shut, perhaps we would not be bound. But he couldn't be so sure.

They walked the trail for another two hours and stopped when the last rays of the sun died out over the mountains in the west. Tonek and Ongus built a fire while Ongus's shade looked on. Rosco's eyes were being drawn to the ghost more frequently. The shade had a perpetual gaped-mouth expression. Was it possible to speak to him or did he only speak to his master?

"Does he speak?" he asked the young boy while Ongus and his father made camp.

Wylt looked at the ground then shot a glance at his father. The boy nodded his head.

"Will he speak to us?" Kurin asked under his breath.

"He's not supposed to." The boy's voice was musical without a trace of accent.

"Were you born in Corvasa?" Rosco asked.

"Yes."

"And your father? Was he born here too?"

"No, my father was born in Osseka." The boy again glanced in his father's direction. He lowered his voice even further. "The Honor said we must go west before I was born. Our homeland is a wasteland."

"The Honor?"

"Wylt!" Ongus stood over them with his shade. The big, bearded man grabbed the boy by the arm, pulled him up roughly, and shouted something in their language.

The Osseks ate in silence. Cooked meat on skewers. Rosco heard Kurin's stomach grumble at the enticing aroma. Rosco wouldn't touch whatever they ate even if offered. Thankfully, they didn't offer.

Kurin attempted to taunt the shade by sticking out his tongue and waving his hands over his ears. The shade's expression never changed with his eternally gaped mouth.

After the meal, they began their trek anew. A rope linked Rosco's and Kurin's wrists and was tied around Ongus's waist. It was long enough for the brothers to make their water without disturbing the old man. Rosco walked into the periphery of the clearing, on the edge of dense woods. After relieving himself, and making sure they were not watching, he took out the looking glass. It was as clear as a mountain spring. He pointed it toward the path and it glowed green. Rosco exhaled a sigh of relief.

A flash of light in the distance off to the right made him look up. All he could see were the many varieties of conifer trees and large bushes swaying in the breeze. The light was almost gone but he saw something dark move through the trees. He couldn't tell if it was a bear or elk, it was too far away. Something about it made his hair stand up on the back of his neck.

"It won't come near us. Animals are terrified of shades," Tonek said when Rosco told him what he had seen.

"They always run away. That's why we don't hunt with them," Wylt added in his perfect Corvasan.

"What if it isn't an animal?" Rosco asked.

Ongus guffawed. A low, guttural sound that sent a few gray jays squawking through the air. "Humans don't like shades either. No humans will bother us."

And apparently they all agreed because when it came time to retire, the Osseks didn't set a watch but the shade remained in the air hovering, his eyes never closing. It was good enough. Whatever was out there, he was convinced it would not approach the shade and if it did, they would all know about it plenty of time in advance.

* * * *

She emerged somewhere on the side of a mountain after climbing through a series of gray rock caves. The first thing she saw below her was two men. Their forms seemed familiar but were still too far away to see them clearly. She followed and watched as a giant wolf surprised them. Their fright and disorientation pushed her to move closer and get a better look.

Suddenly four other men emerged from the thick copse of trees. These men were tribal, dressed as they were in animal skins. Something was off about one of them…then she saw it. His feet did not touch the ground! He was a ghost or some type of spirit.

"These men are Osseks," Sheena whispered to herself. She had learned about them briefly in her studies back at the Crystal Palace. "Savage cannibals, they are."

But why would she be following Osseks? What did that have to do with the blackened heart she carried within her robes?

The shade flew at the first two men in a frenzy. They turned and ducked. In that instant, Sheena saw their faces: Rosco and Kurin!

Suddenly what Simon had told her made sense. *You will exit exactly where you need to be.*

But why Rosco and Kurin? They were just peasants, although it was entirely possible they would lead her to Hawk. She decided to follow them after the Osseks took them as prisoners.

When they made camp, Sheena tried to disguise herself as an animal to get closer. Her magic was still very difficult to control and she didn't know what these ghosts that followed the living Osseks could do. The transformation gave off a flash of light when Rosco went to relieve himself.

"Damn the gods!" she swore under her breath and hurriedly made her way through the trees. He did not follow.

When she had run to a safe distance, she lie down and felt her body. It had returned to its original shape. She was now in the form of a middle-aged woman, the form she disguised herself with while in Martine.

"Use the heart to bind the shade," Nolis whispered through the air.

Sheena bolted upright. "Nolis? Are you there?"

But the voice she thought she heard was just the wind through the trees. Or was it? The words were distinct and she clearly understood them.

But how? How would she use the heart? Nolis told her that her magic would return in increments. Some of it returned, but she could not control it, which made it next to useless.

She must have sat in the woods for an hour or two, pondering the magical method of the heart and what Rosco and Kurin could possibly have to do with Nolis, when she heard the unmistakable sound of footsteps on loose branches. The heart seemed to vibrate against her body and she quickly grasped it.

* * * *

Rosco fell asleep immediately but awoke with a jolt, the rope chafing his wrists. The wraith was howling like a wolf baying at the moon. Tonek was already on his feet, spear in hand. Ongus rubbed sleep from his eyes. He mumbled something in their language and Tonek went down the path with the shade trailing behind. The big man didn't even get up and snored soundly within a minute after Tonek and the shade left.

Rosco moved closer to Wylt. "I thought the shade could only serve his master?"

Wylt gave him a tired smile. "If he gives permission to kin, the shade will obey. It's like having a slave—"

A deep howl in the woods followed by a scream forced them to their feet.

"That was a man's scream," Kurin pointed out.

"And the howl was my shade," Ongus said. The big man stood and picked up his staff, this time appearing fully alert. He took a pouch from the animal skins and spread a black paste on a small log. He lit the torch with what was left of their fire. "Follow me."

"Tonek didn't have a torch," Rosco said.

"The shade glows in the dark with an otherworldly light," Wylt explained.

"Can you untie our wrists?" Rosco asked Ongus. "We'd be much more effective to an enemy."

The big Ossek regarded him suspiciously. "You are my enemy."

"Am I? It seems that whatever is out there is your enemy."

Ongus moved out of the clearing and into the woods, ignoring Rosco. Wylt followed closely behind. Rosco and Kurin had no choice but to follow together or stay near the fire and wait. The curiosity got the better of Rosco so they followed the Osseks in silence. The moon was half a quarter and did not shed much light. They made their way slowly through the dense forest, stepping carefully to avoid rocks and felled branches. Ongus called out to his shade and Tonek but to no avail.

When he heard the screams, they sounded far away. They would never find them tonight. The torch illuminated only so much area.

Kurin and Rosco joined in calling their names but after what seemed like a few hours, they gave up in exhaustion, with nary a glimpse of Tonek or the shade.

"We won't find them tonight," Rosco told Ongus. "We should wait until first light."

Ongus turned toward him. Rosco saw uncontrolled panic in his face. The sight unnerved him. Why was he so afraid?

As if sensing Rosco's thoughts, Wylt spoke, half of his young, handsome face illuminated by the torchlight. "A shade is never lost. It ceases to exist when its master dies. Some type of magic has been done here if we can't find the shade."

"Magic?" Kurin regarded his brother strangely.

Was he thinking of the looking glass? Rosco wondered. How could the looking glass make a man and a shade disappear, especially since its current owner, Rosco himself, had no magical ability whatsoever. No, it was not the looking glass.

"Tell me again..." Ongus spat out, his face turning red in frustration, "...about..." He spoke the rest of his sentence in his own language and Wylt translated.

"He wants to know everything about what you saw. He wants to know where you saw it, how big it was, what color, as much as you can remember."

"I told you everything already, Wylt." The old man should've listened better instead of disregarding it. "I saw a flash of light. Then I saw something moving among the bushes. It was black and about the size of a human but I can't be sure." At the time, he had thought it was an animal, but now he wasn't so certain. And what of the flash? Rosco rubbed his chin. There was something...something he had thought strange at the time but soon forgot within seconds. Now it came back into his mind. "Whatever it was, it was unusually black, like a shadow." He glared at Ongus. "Yes, it was as black as deepest midnight. But since it was partly hidden by bushes and trees, I didn't think that very unusual at the time. It could've been a black bear. They're all over this region, I'm sure you know."

"Black bears do not kill shades," was all the old man said. He walked back to the fire, easily seen through the trees.

They slept fitfully the rest of the night. Rosco dreamt of the looking glass. He took it out of his pocket and it was completely black. A voice within it laughed. A woman's voice.

* * * *

He awoke to Kurin shaking him.

"Rosco...Rosco! Hurry, the others are up and searching."

The dawn had only begun to peek through the trees, casting everything in a gray-blue light. Birds of all varieties were singing their homage to the sun. The day was cloudy, with holes of sky here and there. He wiped sleep from his eyes and followed Kurin into the wood. This time it was much easier to see. They searched in a radius of several yards. It didn't take long before a wail full of despair reached his ears. He and Kurin ran awkwardly to the source.

There they found Ongus crying hysterically over the body of Tonek. Tonek's mouth was open and his eyes wide, as if whatever killed him was the surprise of his life, or death, as the case was.

Kurin knelt over the body. "I can't see any wound or blood."

"For the love of Selene, stop wailing, man!" Rosco shouted. "Think of the boy. This was his father!"

They were in a copse of aspen trees, their round leaves winking as they blew in the soft morning breeze. Ongus made an attempt to control himself.

"Have you found the wound?" Rosco asked.

"There is no wound! This is the Black Art. I told you this before. The shade is still missing and we won't find him. He has been returned to the Land of the Ancestors by the Black Art, the same thing that killed Tonek!" Ongus let out a fresh sob.

Suddenly, Rosco was very nervous. He looked around the forest apprehensively. Nothing unusual caught his fancy, no shadows lurking in bushes or behind trees. But not so! He saw a figure running but it was only Wylt. When he came upon them and saw his father, he stared at Rosco.

"How?" The boy went to his knees and sobbed.

Ongus untied their ropes, finally containing his grief. They undressed the body but still did not find any wounds. From Tonek's expression, it was as if he died of fright, as if whatever he saw stopped his heart immediately.

"Our custom is to burn our dead," Ongus said, closing Tonek's frightened eyes. "But we don't have the means here or the time. We bury him."

THE VIOLET-EYED TRAITOR

"WHERE IS KRYST?" SILLISNAE ASKED.

They were in a foggy, green valley of sagebrush, monkshood and purple larkspur. She could not remember how they got there. Jovnar sat at her side, staring at her with violet eyes.

"I don't know," he replied. "But I'm certain we will see him up there." He tilted his head toward the giant mountain, its peak covered in low clouds. The day was gray and overcast. A light rain hit Sillisnae's face and the smell of wet earth and stone filled the air with a luscious fragrance.

"Where is here?" Sillisnae asked.

"We must wait." Jovnar regarded the mountain with a frown. "It is not yet the proper time. And we must wait for the vehicle."

"The vehicle?" Locklin's multi-colored coat was ragged and torn and his blond curls were in disarray. His expression was anxious, impatient.

Sillisnae thought he would climb the mountain alone. "Do you mean Kryst?"

The druid didn't answer and sat down, his back to the mountain, and gazed out into a green valley with a newborn river winding through it.

"You are Jaanaarian," she pronounced.

The giant druid's winged disk tattoo wrinkled on his forehead when he frowned. "I am."

"What are you doing with these men from Linnso?"

"I was born there." He stared ahead into the valley, his violet eyes expressionless. "I have never known Jaanaar and I never will."

"You were born of a Jaanaarian mother?" Sillisnae was confused. Lananell had mentioned that the women had no control over their own lives, in effect reduced to pleasure vehicles for all the men that wanted them. Surely a Jaanaarian woman would have the magical power to resist, even kill them.

"I was born whole, from the thought forms of my father. We don't procreate like the peoples of Perthia."

From the thought forms of my father?

She wanted elaboration but had more pressing questions. "How did Jaanaarians come to be in Linnso in the first place?"

"We were there from the very beginning. Before the arrival of Linn and his Ebron women. Jaanaarians inhabited the entire North in those long ago times, not just the island of Jaanaar."

A realization surprised Sillisnae. "How old are you?"

The druid lowered his head and sighed. "I'm not really sure. I lost count at four hundred."

Sillisnae stared at the man. She had heard such tales of the longevity of Jaanaarians. The legends were in the ancient manuscripts Lord Korodale had given her. And Hawk had told her that Sheena was five centuries old. "Were you alive when the first Linnsonians arrived?"

The druid shook his head, wet strands of gray hair sticking to his face. "Oh no. I'm not that old. I believe that was at least one thousand revolutions ago."

She glanced at Locklin who was listening intently. The man repulsed her.

"I thought Jaanaarians didn't involve themselves in the struggles of other peoples? Have the Linnsonians bound you?"

At that, Jovnar laughed. "Bound me? No one binds Jaanaarians."

"Then, how…"

"Sometimes what is honorable is the opposite of one's expectations."

Sillisnae was shocked. "So you are not slaves of Captain Oscan? You do his bidding of your own accord?"

"Of course. We may leave anytime we want. We live separate from Linnsonians but give aide whenever needed."

"Why?" Sillisnae was perplexed.

When the druid turned to gaze at her, the winged disk tattoo glowed orange. His violet eyes seemed to glow as well. "The

Linnsonians were begot from an unnatural order, from the sin of a goddess copulating with enslaved men to perpetuate a race of semi-divine women. Even though Ebro was destroyed," and here Jovnar gave her a quizzical look, "its influence spread through Perthia, especially through Corvasa where the art of blocking spiritual power has been perfected."

"But the Linnsonians block the powers of their women from puberty onward," Sillisnae pointed out.

"Who do you think does the blocking?" Jovnar asked with an upturn of the corners of his mouth.

She thought of Lananell then: Her fey features and brown curls, her demure demeanor and fear. She wondered if she was in Martine with her uncle Rosco and if they had married. Oh, to live a quiet, pastoral life in the mountains without danger at every turn. How she envied them! She wondered if she'd ever see them again.

Jovnar stood and made runic gestures with his fingers toward the mountain summit obscured by clouds. He did not bid they follow but Locklin and Sillisnae fell in behind him anyway.

"Where are we going?" she asked.

"That," Jovnar tilted his head toward the mountain, "has been our destination all along."

"What is there?" She thought she had asked that question before but never got an answer.

"It is Mount Moirae," Lockin replied.

Sillisnae stopped in her tracks. "The home of the Weavers? Don't they live within the mountain? I don't see an opening."

"It's obscured by the clouds," Jovnar said. "A horizontal opening exists just above tree line."

"I...I...thought they were just a legend."

"Well yes, they are a legend but at the same time very real."

Sillsinae hesitated.

Jovnar gazed at her with an unreadable expression. "You must come, Sillisnae of Corvasa. Your destiny lies on that mountain and beyond."

An invisible force pulled her, made her feet move in the glistening wet grass and mountain wild flowers. She followed the men, Jovnar's form a good three feet taller than that of Locklin's, and the Corvasan Healer would be considered tall among his fellow Corvasans.

They hiked in silence for a long time. The end of Locklin's multicolored robe dragged along the rain soaked earth. Jovnar's long legs obliged them to walk faster as his stride encompassed two of Locklin's and three of Sillisnae's.

They climbed for what seemed like forever. Even through the chill of the altitude and wet drizzling rain, sweat poured from her armpits. The valley landscape quickly turned to evergreen trees and soft ground covered in pine needles. They did not follow any game trail but wove their way through the trees randomly. Jovnar seemed to know where he was going. Periodically she stopped to catch her breath, so exhausting was the pace. Jovnar casually waited but Locklin would sneer and roll his eyes.

As they climbed higher, the fog ran thicker and it was hard to see her companions. Their forms appeared and disappeared in the fog.

Something wet and slimy brushed against her arm.

"Jovnar?" she called out. A muffled shout was the answer. She couldn't tell if it was Locklin or Jovnar.

"Wait for me!"

Her immediate environment was ghostly white. She had never seen fog so thick in her life.

"Keep shouting! I'm losing my direction!" she called.

Other...*things*...moved in the fog. She caught a glance of something dark, greenish-gray, with snakelike skin but the fog obscured most of its body.

"Sillisnae!" It was Locklin and he was close but she couldn't tell his direction.

"I'm here!" She backed up into him. "Praise Selene, Locklin!"

Something growled in her ear and she whirled around. What stood in front of her was not Locklin.

Its head was the shape of a bowl, the top flat, as if it had no brain. The eyes slanted sideways, and were completely black, devoid of pupils. Two holes served as a nose. The mouth was wide and full of white fangs. Its body stood upright, resembling that of a human, but the hands and feet possessed three long tentacles for fingers and toes, with black claws twice the length of her middle finger. The skin was what she had seen moving through the fog: dark greenish-gray with scales and a coating of slime.

Her voice wouldn't work when she tried to scream. Her heart thumped wildly and for a brief second she thought she would lose consciousness. The monster stood nearly the same height as Jovnar.

The demon pulled back its lips to bare its fangs and growled again, then abruptly lunged.

Just in the nick of time she found her courage to dodge its swipe. The black claws caught her shoulder and she screamed. The impact caused her to stumble but she didn't fall. In a panic, she ran downhill, her mind a whirl of thoughts but the foremost was to get away from the thing that chased her. She heard its panting behind her. Through the fog, she caught another glimpse of slimy, green-gray skin and she stopped, panic flooding her mind. She let out a long, piercing scream. The footsteps were almost upon her. She bolted to her right and screamed again. Out of nowhere Locklin appeared and she ran headlong into him.

"Locklin!" She embraced him as if he was Hawk come back to her. "Th-th-th…" Words wanted to rush out of her mouth in a torrent but she couldn't speak them properly.

Locklin put his hands on her shoulders. "Calm down. I'm here. What's wrong?"

"Th-the-there are these things"—Sillisnae attempted to catch her breath—"demons…uh, monsters."

Growls pierced the fog only a few feet in front of them. Locklin pulled Sillisnae to him. Two of the monsters materialized out of the fog and bared their fangs.

"By the gods," Locklin whispered. The fiends suddenly lunged and Locklin thrust Sillisnae into them.

She fell to the ground face first, fully expecting the strange monsters to begin slashing at her back. She made one last attempt to call upon her power but it was useless. Somewhere behind her, Locklin chanted in the True Tongue. Something stepped on her back, briefly knocking the wind out of her, and then she heard a man scream in excruciating pain followed by growls and the sound of flesh tearing.

Sillisnae found her breath and ran diagonally uphill, away from the screams. Her heart felt as if it would explode in her chest. Her lungs screamed in burning pain. She was dimly aware of more shouts in the distance but it hardly mattered. The survival instinct had surfaced and the most important thing was to get away, far away. The screams abruptly stopped and the silence was followed by eerie wolf howls that sounded partly human.

The fog suddenly thinned, too quickly to be completely natural. A few yards ahead was a giant fell tree and underneath it, a hole covered with leaves and pine needles. She dropped and rolled into it. The smell of rot filled her nostrils. Leaves and dirt clung to her exposed skin. She righted herself and gazed out the opening, now wider since she had forced herself through it.

Footsteps approached and a face suddenly appeared. The sight scared her into a scream but it was Jovnar, his large jaw gaping. Without a word, he offered his hand and pulled her out.

"The screams…"

"Were Locklin's," he finished.

"Is he…"

"Dead? Yes. Treachery is something rooted out when the source is approached."

"He…he…tried to kill me." The tears could not be denied any longer. Sillisnae burst into sobs.

The druid pointed to a copse of aspens. "Locklin's body is over there. We must bury him."

"You could have saved him," she whispered faintly through her tears.

"No. My magic doesn't work here and neither did his."

Sillisnae wiped her nose and glanced around. The creatures had disappeared with the fog. Her body still trembled and she took a few deep breaths to stop it. "How are we supposed to bury him, Jovnar? We have no shovel."

"We'll cover him with leaves and pine-needles from the forest floor."

Locklin's torso had been ripped open and his right arm hung by threads of muscle and skin. Blood soaked the ground beneath and its metallic smell hung in the air. Sillisnae stared at the gore in fascination. Locklin's mouth hung open; his eyes stared off into a distant land, most likely the Land of the Ancestors. She never liked him, in fact detested him, but seeing his body with his guts scattered activated her sympathy, even though he tried to feed her to the scaly fiends. She picked up some fallen branches and placed them over his torn body. Jovnar did the same. When they had finished, the fog was completely gone.

"I already knew one of us would die up here. It could've been you or me. The mountain demands blood," the druid said stoically.

He glanced toward the top of the mountain. There, revealing itself as the fog cleared, was a thin horizontal opening halfway up between the tree line and summit. The edges were angular, too perfect to be natural.

Within the opening, blackness beckoned. Sillisnae shivered.

Without a word, Jovnar hiked in sweeping strides toward the opening. She had no recourse but to follow. Locklin had given his life for something he so vehemently desired. But what was that exactly? What did he think he would acquire on this mountain? And the Linnsonians? What did they want? She asked as much to Jovnar in between deep breaths.

"They are here for the Crystal Skull."

What is the secret of the Crystal Skull?

"Why? What will they do with it?" Master Oscan had told Kryst what its capabilities were but she wanted to hear it from the druid.

"Sillisnae of Corvasa, they will control the thoughts of the most powerful Adepts in Perthia. The Adepts will do their bidding."

"And how will they do that? Master Oscan said something about 'divine intervention'. Are you divine, Jovnar?"

The druid cracked a wan smile. "No," he said. "The Jaanaarian race has not been divine for centuries. But with the Crystal Skull, that may change. For those of us outside of Jaanaar anyway. We must bring a god or goddess through a human vehicle, to possess the body and mind, otherwise the person will die from the Skull's power. It is a very complicated affair. There must be a man and woman to do it."

"What is the point of controlling the thoughts of the Adepts of Perthia? What about those who aren't Adepts?"

"They are irrelevant. The masses will follow the Adepts and the royals like they always do. But they will succumb to mass slavery not even realizing they are slaves. It is all a matter of controlling thought processes. And that is only the beginning; the first part, if you will. The next step is finding the female triate."

"The female triate? What's that?"

"You will know soon enough, Sillisnae of Corvasa."

"But I want you to tell me, Jovnar of Linnso." Might as well have a bit of fun with the druid. Unfortunately, he ignored her plea.

When she stared at the opening, she felt an odd sort of exhilaration that propelled her feet faster. Fear was there, sure, but so was curiosity and that outweighed the fear. It was only an entrance into the mountain and the demon fog had receded.

As they got closer, a strange sound like a sigh was heard, as if the opening was a mouth and the mountain was breathing through it. The sky was still gray and flat but the rain had stopped. They passed tree line and the landscape resembled the valley below with more slate gray rock piles. Tiny pikas squeaked at them from behind rocks.

"Are you ready?" Jovnar asked when they reached the slit in the mountain.

It was much larger now that they were upon it. When she saw it from below, she thought they would have to duck to enter, but now it was at least four times the height of Jovnar.

The strange sound persisted and when she stepped into the darkness, it felt as if she moved through a curtain of falling water or a wall of frigid air.

The druid overtook her as they walked into a low-ceilinged cave. A dim light came from deep within and it took a few minutes for Sillisnae's eyes to adjust. Somewhere, water dripped and flowed. The stone ceiling was as flat as the floor and the room was a rectangular shape. Jovnar walked quickly toward the source of the light and Sillisnae followed.

The druid stopped suddenly and held out his arm to prevent her from going farther. The floor gave way like the edge of a cliff. In front of them was a yawning abyss, the bottom of which she could not see. A faint draft blew up and ruffled the edge of her dress. She could only guess as to the depth of the crevasse that lay before her.

About one hundred paces to their left, Sillisnae saw a bridge as her eyes adjusted to the small amount of light. It arched over the gaping chasm and led to an island where something green glowed.

"What is that?"

The question seemed to surprise Jovnar. "Oh yes. That is where we are going."

"Over the bridge."

"Yes."

"And the green light…"

"Comes from the Crystal Skull."

She was suddenly terrified. "I don't want to. I don't see the Weavers. Where are they? And the dragon Kefkinala?"

"I didn't know what to expect, either, Sillisnae—"

"Your magic doesn't work here. We have no protection. This is too easy. It's a trick."

The giant chuckled softly. The sound was infuriating. Somewhere overhead she heard the sound of small wings. Bats flew in their meandering, sloppy way in the space above them which disappeared into blackness like the crevasse below.

"It may be a trick but we must go. We cannot remain here."

He pulled her along but her feet refused. The fear of falling into the crevasse—falling for what would seem like an eternity, with every bone in her body breaking and her limbs and head separating from her torso in an explosion of bone, blood and muscle—froze her where she stood. Maybe she wasn't as brave as she thought. Jovnar must have sensed her feelings because he scooped her into his arms as if she were a child's doll.

The bridge had no railings to protect them and was made of a black, shiny material, with gleaming sparkles. Jovnar tentatively stepped onto the bridge. Another draft suddenly blew from the depths below and caressed Sillisnae's face. It grew stronger as Jovnar walked.

My magic does not work here...

Sillisnae turned her head away and closed her eyes.

Oh dearest Selene, please don't let him fall. Protect us, dearest mother, if your power extends to this place.

She kept her eyes tightly shut for what seemed like an eternity but the druid never faltered or altered his pace.

"We're almost there. You might want to open your eyes."

A green ball of light sat on an elaborate rug in the middle of the island, which was really a crag jutting up from the depths of the crevasse. As they got closer, what seemed to be a ball was really a transparent skull emanating green light. Captain Oscan, Kryst and Karvis stood around it. Svarlat was missing.

Jovnar stood Sillisnae on her feet. They were well beyond the edge of the top of the crag but still surrounded by a vast sea of air. The rock beneath her feet was slate gray and solid. A slight breeze continued to blow from the depths and ruffle her auburn hair. Captain Oscan did not seem to notice they had arrived but Kryst stared at her, terrified.

Where were the Weavers? Or the dragon? It all seemed too easy. And she still could not remember how they got to the base of the mountain.

"How did you get here?" she whispered to Kryst.

His light blue eyes carried such fright, he appeared to be on the brink of screaming, and that made her very afraid. But then his eyes changed. The terror in them turned to hatred as he glared at her and grabbed her by the shoulders in a fit of rage. The whites of his eyes went black and she saw within them something familiar. Then he spoke, but the voice that came out was a woman's voice, a goddess's voice.

"I knew we would meet again."

AN UNLIKELY REUNION

EVANTON ENTERED THE TENT with a smirk on his face. "It seems some of your countrymen have been searching for you."

Lananell had just awoken from a nap on the bear skins and pillows. It was customary among the Osseks to take naps when the sun was highest in the sky.

"What?" She rubbed her eyes.

Before he could answer, the tent flap opened wide and a man she only knew by sight entered. He was older with a long beard and if she remembered correctly, he possessed a shade. But the shade wasn't with him and that was odd.

He lowered his head when he saw her. Her fame had grown throughout the camp after healing Naton. "Corvasan Healer," he said, "I am Ongus. We found someone on the mountain pass who claims to know you."

Lananell got to her feet. "Where?" She followed the big man outside.

The camp was teeming with activity. Many of the Osseks gave her a wide berth and suspicious looks. Even though she healed their leader, she was still a foreigner and this nomadic people distrusted foreigners. The day was overcast and the dark clouds threatened rain. Lananell was thankful for a break from the relentless sun. At this altitude, it beat down with a peculiar intensity. Her heart pounded in her chest as Ongus pulled back the flap to one of the smaller tents.

"Rosco!" She fell into his arms, tears of joy and love sprouting from her eyes. He smelled of sweat and earth, his customary fragrance. A kiss was planted on top of her head. "I knew you would come."

He cupped her face to look at him. "What happened, Lananell? How did you come to be here?"

Kurin sat next to him, his scowl as prominent as ever but she saw in his eyes a softness she had never seen before.

"Kurin," she said. "You accompanied my husband?"

The old man nodded. "Now I wish I hadn't. Who are these filthy people, Lananell?"

Same old Kurin, as cantankerous as ever.

She told the entire sad tale, bursting into tears when she spoke of the cannibalistic ceremony. Ongus sat in silence listening but she didn't care. They would let her return home now, she knew it, no matter what she said about them. Naton had promised.

"Tell her what happened," Kurin said.

Rosco kissed his wife softly on the lips. "I'm just so glad to see you again. Thank the gods you're safe."

Ongus stood up abruptly and left the tent. The light from the opening flap revealed a young boy. His eyes appeared red from crying.

"What happened?" she asked Rosco. "How did you find me?"

Her husband cleared his throat and he gave the young boy a sympathetic glance. "The looking glass. I found you with the looking glass."

"Oh!" She hugged him tight and kissed him again. So something good came out of her forgetfulness. "But how? You don't have any talent, or do you?"

He chuckled lightly. "No, I don't, dear one. But it did glow green when I pointed it in a certain direction. I understood that to mean you were in that direction. I followed it and soon I discovered a path. The looking glass glowed green all along the path so I knew you had taken it."

He went on to tell her about discovering the shade and how they had been captured. When he got to the part about Tonek, the boy left the tent.

"That was his father?" Lananell asked.

"Yes and he was the son of Ongus. They are very distraught."

"And you said Ongus's shade is missing?"

"Yes."

"That's odd," she frowned. "The shade belonged to Ongus and Ongus is still alive. The shades return to the Land of the Ancestors only when their masters die."

Kurin rubbed his bearded chin. "Lananell, when can we go back to Martine? My wife has probably run off with the one of the village Elders by now."

"Of course, dear Kurin. We'll return soon. I must inform the Chieftain."

The boy waited outside in the flat overcast light. A slight breeze blew and Lananell shivered when they exited the tent. "What is your name, little one?"

"Wylt," he replied confidently. He stood up straight and nodded.

In the pavilion, Naton sat propped up by pillows, as she had left him. Evanton was disappointingly at his side. Perhaps he would object to releasing her. Well, soon enough she would find out.

She instructed Rosco and Kurin to wait near the entrance while she approached Naton.

"Chieftain"—she knelt—"my husband and brother-in-law have arrived in camp. They were captured on the path to Corvasa by Ongus, Tonek and his boy, Wylt. In the middle of the night they were ambushed and Tonek was killed."

"What's this? How?" The Ossek chieftain sat up and frowned.

"If it please you chieftain, Ongus and his grandson can tell it better because they were there."

Naton nodded. "Bring them forward."

Wylt approached the chieftain and knelt next to Lananell. "My chieftain. My grandfather is sick with grief over my father."

"Tell me what happened, dear Wylt."

The boy recounted the entire tale. When he came to the part of the missing shade, Naton held up his hand. Evanton's expression was one of shock. That made Lananell nervous.

"It was Ongus's shade that was wailing and that is why Tonek went to check in the wood?" Naton asked.

"Yes," Rosco spoke up. He stood behind her and knelt. "I was there."

"How dare you speak to the Chieftain without being summoned," Evanton shouted but Naton shushed him.

"Go on, Corvasan."

"Tonek was found with a shocked expression and we couldn't find wounds of any kind on his body."

Naton appeared puzzled. "Removing the bonds of shades is impossible while its master lives. I've never heard of such a thing. Or…" Naton became pensive, staring at the ground with his finger to his lips.

"Were you followed?" He asked Rosco after a minute.

Lananell saw her husband hesitate. Unfortunately, so did Evanton.

"Chieftain, he hides something. This man can't be trusted. He is Corvasan and of course desires that we return his wife."

Rosco got to his feet but kept his head low. "I'm not hiding anything. At the time, I didn't think anything of it. Tonek and Ongus had tied my brother and me, so I could only go so far to relieve myself. While there, I saw a flash which made me look up. There was a shadow but it was so obscured that I was certain it was an animal so I thought no more of it."

"A flash you say?" Naton asked.

"Yes, a flash."

The Chieftain bid him come closer. "Lananell, you approach as well. The rest of you, leave us!"

Evanton snarled. "Chieftain—"

"Go!"

The other Osseks were already exiting the tent. Evanton bumped into Rosco and stared him down. His shade also regarded them with its transparent eyes. Her husband didn't flinch and returned the stare.

"Evanton!"

The warrior slithered away, never taking his eyes off Rosco until the tent flap had closed. Naton chuckled.

"It seems your husband has made an enemy, Lananell of Linnso." He turned his gaze to Rosco. "Beware of that one. He is young and desiring to prove himself." Naton sighed and his shade ascended slightly, its red hair sparkling.

Lananell thought it strange.

Naton continued. "But on to the reason I sent away the others. It has to do with my bloodline. My father to be precise. You see, he is none other than Honor Othar, the Jaanaarian who left his people in his other form, his doppelganger. He understood many things. And loved many women, realizing the terrible loss he perpetrated only later..."

"The terrible loss?" Rosco asked.

"That is for another time." Naton scratched his dark beard. "Othar told the secret of the blockage to his descendants and in some cases his wives. The secret of the blockage was the most important information my father brought with him or so he said. At the time, he explained why the first Jaanaarian traitors abandoned Jaanaar which was the reason the Golden Band was created in the first place. Unfortunately, they took with them much mystical knowledge and blocking the inherent magical talent was one of them. Far back in the mists of the beginning of time, a spirit imprisoned in matter, a goddess was formed. She was called by many names but the one we Osseks use is Gerda and she was the earth, the very ground we stand upon and the nature that sustains us. In all of her creatures, she put a form of herself and that form was magical. The Jaanaarians, due to their exceptional magical ability, discovered a way to block the magic of Gerda in humans. The blockage is heritable, meaning it would repeat itself in each successive generation. Currently, we now have most people without any magical power whatsoever, and the Adepts are soon taken by the ruling families of Perthia, except for in Osseka, of course."

Lananell wanted to know more. "How do they block the power, Chieftain?"

"It is a complicated affair and one which I've never attempted. It involves a negation of imagination, and the use of Od, and magical runes of one against another. Once someone is blocked, usually their offspring will be blocked and after successive generations, it will seem normal."

Lananell put a hand to her abdomen. "It was magical lightning that unblocked me." For some strange reason, tears welled up in her eyes.

"Yes!" Naton exclaimed, a smile arising upon his face. "Magical lightning comes from the inner dragon. The Dragons are the physical manifestations of the power of Gerda. But everyone has the dragon within them. It just has to be ignited. All of the Jaanaarians still retain the knowledge of the inner dragon. They also retain the knowledge of how to block it.

BOOM!

The force of the blast knocked everyone to the ground. Lananell had a brief flashback of the battle at the south gate of the Crystal Palace as her shoulder exploded in pain.

"Rosco?" she called out in panic.

"I'm fine," he lay on the ground near her feet.

Screams rang out all over the camp. Naton hobbled for the exit. When he lifted the flap, several panicked Osseks ran inside.

And old, stooped man pointed his cane at the flap and said something in the Ossekan language.

Naton listened attentively. His shade hovered over him and ascended even higher, still with a strange sparkle about him. The Chieftain's eyes widened as if he suddenly realized something.

He limped outside, past the group of Osseks that had gathered, all shouting and waving their hands. Rosco pulled Lananell and his brother to their feet and gave pursuit.

Outside, several people lay on the ground. Lananell recognized Evanton lying face down in the dirt, his shade also in a horizontal position but still present. In the center of the camp, next to the smoking coals of the previous night's bonfire, stood a man, or rather a giant, dressed in black robes. Lananell's heart leapt into her throat. She knew exactly who he was.

"That's a Linnsonian druid." Her mouth was dry as ashes. "Run!"

She nearly fell, tripping over her own feet in a panic. All she could think of was to get away.

Just get to the tent, only if I can reach the tent, I'll be safe...

But she knew it wasn't true. She would never be safe. Not now, not ever. They would never let her be; they would drag her back to Linnso in chains and execute her as an example.

But to her surprise she made it inside. It was as if some supernatural power made her feet run faster. The darkness engulfed her. She stumbled around, still running, trying to find a pelt or some pillows to hide beneath. A pair of hands grabbed her shoulders and she fell into the bosom of a woman.

"Oh, Hentra!" she exclaimed.

But Rosco! Where's Rosco? Did he follow me? I told him to run.

"Rosco!" she tried to extract herself from Hentra's arms but the hands that held her were vise-like in their grip.

"Hentra, let go! My husband..."

"He cannot help you now." The voice was not Hentra's but a voice she recognized, a voice she had trusted at one time.

"Sheena?"

"Well, now. I'm so glad you remember me, Lananell."

"But, I thought...you were..."

"In Jaanaar? I was. But I decided to leave them behind. Captivity doesn't agree with me."

Lananell squirmed but Sheena's grip would not give. The light that usually flowed into the tent from the smoke hole was completely gone. Sheena's face was indistinguishable.

"Let me go!"

"Oh, you're a sought-after prize, dear Lananell."

Suddenly, light flooded her eyes so intensely, she was as blind as she was in the darkness. Sheena's hands fell away and Lananell immediately ran, in which direction she did not know. Everything was blindingly bright. After a few seconds her eyes adjusted. All around her lay bodies. She recognized Rosco who laid face up, his chest covered in blood. Kurin was next to him, face down.

"Rosco!" she screamed. Blood seeped out of his ears when she shook him but he was still breathing. Blood bubbles formed in his mouth with each breath. The field was unnaturally quiet. Were all these people dead or so seriously injured they did not moan? No sound came from Kurin either.

"Rosco...Rosco...can you hear me?" She wiped away tendrils of brown hair that stuck to his face. The muscles of his face didn't move. He grabbed her wrist.

"What? What do you want my darling?" Tears streamed down her cheeks. "Tell me what to do. Where does it hurt?"

He felt within his surcoat and placed something in her hand. It was cold, smooth, familiar.

"Hide it," he whispered with great difficulty and turned his face away from her.

A shadow fell over them. "He can't hear you, Lananell."

A giant stood over her with the sun at his back. She couldn't see his face. She wasn't familiar with this particular druid but did it matter? Obviously he was sent here for her.

Dust and dirt hung in the air all around, making her cough. The winged disk tattoo glowed orange as he held her eyes in his violet gaze.

"Did you kill all these people?" she asked. "My husband?"

The druid surveyed the fallen that littered the rocky ground. One body, dressed in silks in the fashion of Corvasa moved slowly, moaning. A shade hovered just above. The hair was long and light brown but matted with ash and dirt. The head lifted and Lananell saw that it was Sheena. The druid turned to face her, never releasing his grip from Lananell's arm. Sheena had retaken the form which Lananell had first met in Martine, that of an attractive, middle-aged woman. Her movements were slow but her eyes were alight with mischievous awareness.

She fakes injury…

The second she thought it, Sheena pulled something from her robes as quickly as a striking cobra. She held it in front of her and it sizzled with lightning, one beam leaping out toward them. Lananell screamed but the lightning divided into several smaller beams and enveloped them in a cocoon of light. The druid held the lightning in a matrix through a smoky beam that protruded from his abdomen. The smoke formed a protective shield around them. The lightning lost power with each passing second. When it was all but gone, the beam of smoky light protruding from the druid's abdomen burst forth with renewed power and blasted Sheena into the air where her body somersaulted wildly. The shade that hovered over her followed. Whatever she was holding was sucked toward them by the druid's abdominal beam.

He caught it mid-air and examined it.

Lananell gasped. "That's a heart."

Sheena's body lay prostrate on the ground but the druid was not finished with her. He tucked the heart into his robes and pulled Lananell to where Sheena lay. The shade above her was fading fast. Lananell guessed it was male.

"Heal her!" he commanded, forcing her to her knees.

Sheena's body was splayed at unnatural angles. She looked like a broken doll.

"I want to heal my husband!" Lananell shouted through tears. "My husband first!"

The druid grabbed her by the back of the neck. The motor function of her body immediately ceased like she was paralyzed but she could still feel sensation. He dragged her by her neck along the ground and sharp rocks cut into her skin. The pain was enormous.

"Stop!" her hands clasped at small rocks, dirt, anything she could grasp. The sound of low, amused laughter filled her world.

He dragged her back to where Sheena lay. "Heal her or do you want more of the same?" The grip on her neck was as tight as ever and she knew it was futile to resist. He would torture her until she obeyed. That was the way it was done in Linnso.

Some of the injured moaned, others screamed. Lananell blocked it out and raised her hands over Sheena's broken body. The force from her abdomen wouldn't come. Instinctively, she knew it was because she was terrified. She tried to calm her nerves with deep breaths. If she didn't heal Sheena, the gods only knew what he would do to her. But oddly, she understood he wanted her for some reason, either to return her to Linnso or something else. For the Linnsonians to send one of their giant druids seemed like an awful lot of trouble just for her.

"What's the delay, Lananell?"

"I can't call forth the power."

"Yes, you can and you will. Don't send it through your hands but your abdomen. Now do it."

She tried again, this time the power moved and with extraordinary effort she brought it through her belly button. Sensations that could have only been Sheena's life experiences entered her thoughts: A young girl holding her mother's hand, standing in front of a man sitting upon a throne...then a man with a golden helmet—Lananell recognized him as the wizard that attacked them in Minosae—stood in front of her, his eyes full of admiration and love, then peasant villagers being treated with a potion she administered...a young boy blasted with lightning and falling down, unmoving.

Sheena convulsed violently, her arms and bloody legs flailing like fish out of water.

"It's working," the druid said.

The dust cleared by increments allowing better view of the bodies. The lamentable howls of shades could be heard mourning their masters. The howls died out slowly and the shades lost their forms, finally being released to return to the Land of the Ancestors. Some Osseks who were still alive stumbled around in a daze, their faces covered in blood. Among them were a couple of Elders whose shades followed. Soon, they too would be released, judging by the state of their masters. Children wandered around crying for their mothers.

Lananell's heart hurt. She had grown close to these people and cared about them, especially Naton. But those thoughts were minor compared to the sadness she felt for Rosco.

"My husband," she whispered. "I love you." Tears streamed down her cheeks.

"He isn't dead." It was Sheena. Her eyes were open and she stared at her. She put a hand to her cheek. "Thank you."

Lananell stared into lavender eyes. The most beautiful eyes, hiding the most sadistic of intentions.

"He's not dead. But Kurin is."

Lananell turned to the druid. "My husband…"

"Will live. And if he doesn't, it was the will of the Weavers. We depart now. Both of you."

Sheena tried to stand but fell back on her bottom. The shade that had been nearly invisible was now easily seen. He was a tall skinny man of about thirty and his expression was downcast, defeated, almost ashamed. Sheena felt around her waist but what she searched for had been taken. Her violet eyes grew wide in comprehension.

"Where are we going?" Lananell asked.

"To Linnso," he smiled broadly as he offered a hand to Sheena and pulled her to her feet.

A hissing sound next to them formed a doorway in thin air, the bottom edge about waist height. The ease with which he created a doorway enraged Lananell. It had taken four people when they created the hole in space back in Ebro. Even now, with her power unblocked, it would be extremely difficult to perform such a feat.

Sheena trembled and moaned. The druid still held her hand and he offered the other to Lananell. "Shall we?"

Lananell grasped it and they stepped through, the shade included.

A SKULL AND A DRAGON

"WHY HASN'T THIS GODS-BE-DAMNED fog lifted?" Ragnar asked, mostly to himself.

The fog thickened with every league they sailed. The wind was non-existent and Ragnar had instructed his crew to man the oars. The steady *harumph, harumph,* pushed them forward but not too quickly. In this fog, that would be suicidal. It had been two days since they entered the mouth of the Othalla and the fog had been with them ever since. Occasionally, they heard the call of gulls and fishes jumping in the water. But never any sign of civilization or people. To the right, they passed the borders of Hawk's homeland, the Knotts. So named because of the distinctive red rock formations that jutted into the air as if pointing to the gods. The rocks formed bulbs, then shafts, then bulbs, like knots on a sailor's rope. The rock was soft and could be scraped with a fingernail. But this coastline did not harbor those wonders. It was the hot, sub tropic climate of the Knotts they passed, where a tribe called Spelon lived. From what Hawk remembered, they were active fishermen, in the river and along the coasts of the Southern Sea. But he neither heard nor saw them. Granted, not many men with sense would be sailing in this fog.

Occasionally, he would send out his mind to the animals in the area, mainly gulls, occupying their bodies for brief instances to discover if the fog covered many leagues. From what he saw, it did. Once, while in the body of a gull, he soared high above the fog where the sun shone as a hazy white globe. The white blanket of cloud seemed to cover the entire earth. Whatever was causing the fog would just have to be waited out.

The fog was only one of their worries. Ragnar's crew grew restless.

"We should set anchor," said one particularly authoritative pirate. "It's insanity rowing in this fog."

"The captain is enamored of his new lover," laughed another man with missing teeth and greasy hair.

"This is suicide. The river gods are not favorable to such wanton disregard for the fog spirit," said another who spat on the deck in the direction of Hawk.

He didn't blame them. Ragnar had promised booty from the Triad. And from the legendary tales, there was a lot of booty to be had. Perhaps he should confront the pirate and insist they anchor until the fog lifted but that would delay his reunion with Sillisnae and perhaps cost her life. He couldn't risk that.

Ragnar seemed oblivious to his men's discontent and that was dangerous. Mutiny was notoriously common among pirates, unlawful and treacherous as they were, their bloodlust the stuff of legends.

"Lo there!" someone called.

In the dark water, only a few yards from the hull of the ship, human heads protruded from the water.

"Are they alive?" Hawk asked.

An oarsman picked up a piece of wood and threw it at the shoulder of one when he got close enough. The head turned and revealed a burnt face and blackened eye sockets.

"They're all like this," said another. And indeed they were. But their positioning was wrong. Instead of floating in a reclined position, they bobbed as if something was holding them that way.

Ragnar must have felt the oddness, too, because he shouted, "Man your oars! Get us out of here!"

"Captain, we can't see a quarter league in front of us!" the man with the missing teeth pointed out.

"He's right," Hawk whispered to Ragnar so the others wouldn't hear. They were standing at the bulwark, gazing into the water.

"Those bodies are not right—" Ragnar began.

"I know," Hawk interrupted. "But driving the ship into the fog is not the answer."

The pirate captain turned to him, his dark eyes stormy. "What would you suggest then?" he asked, clearly irritated. "Delve deep into your vast knowledge of seafaring. These…things in the water are not normal. The Black Art is afoot here and I don't like it. Give me merchant's ships guarded by swords and bows, give me fast running galleys manned by muscled warriors with axes and clubs. By the gods, give me wild, raging salt water and krakens, but the Black Arts strike fear into the heart of every pirate that does not possess the Talent. And none of my men possess it."

"But I do, Ragnar. Have you forgotten?"

"You're a shapeshifter."

"I've seen through the eyes of gulls that this fog goes on forever. If you like, I can call up the river monsters and have them eat these bodies but what good would that do? They're only dead bodies, albeit in a strange position. We must carry on but slowly. We must keep our heads. I agree that this is the working of Adepts, but it seems they are gone now."

Ragnar rubbed his beard. "Your words are wise, Knottian."

For the next few hours, they continued on at the slow pace. The fog never lifted but at least no more burned bodies were spotted. The humidity was oppressive and Hawk wiped sweat from his brow only to have it reappear within seconds. Strange sounds were heard within the fog. Once Hawk thought he heard Sillisnae calling to him.

"It's a grotto, Hawk. A massive cave...and Nominthe..."

Other voices came to him.

The voice of Lananell... *"My husband!"* she cried in agony.

Rosco... *"All I wanted was to save her, Hawk. Why did you leave us?"*

"Who's there?" he asked the fog. But it didn't answer.

"I'm sure we've passed the Triad by now," Ragnar informed him. "If the calculations I've done in my head are correct, we are beyond the Triad and deep within Osseka."

"But how could that be? The Triad is a damned place full of

hungry ghosts with legends abounding about their attacks upon any ship that passes."

"Perhaps this fog was a blessing in disguise. Perhaps the Black Arts I feared so much were done purposefully in our favor."

Sometimes Ragnar surprised him with his insights. But Hawk had seen too much to allow for optimism.

"Do you hear that?" He asked Ragnar. A gurgling, swishing sound amplified somewhere ahead in the fog.

Ragnar held up a hand "Halt the oars!" He leaned over the railing, listening. "Yes. I hear it. It sounds like waves lapping against something...or..."

The ship suddenly lurched starboard as if a strong current took it by surprise. The fog swirled around them driven by a powerful wind but it did not dissipate, only thickened where Hawk could no longer see Ragnar clearly. The gurgling sound was now so loud, Hawk had to shout. The ship tilted to port and several of the crew slid along the incline of deck, piling against the port railing.

"By the gods!" Ragnar shouted.

A powerful wind came out of nowhere, swirling the fog into a vortex just above the river. The fog turned a reddish-purple color.

"It's a gateway," Hawk shouted into the fog.

"A gateway to where?" Ragnar shouted back. Somehow he had gotten behind Hawk and was splayed out on his stomach, holding a crack in the wooden deck by his fingers, the wind now whipped up to storm force. "We're being pulled into it!" he screamed, "Man your oars! Man your oars, by the gods!"

But his commands were futile and fell on deaf ears or at least ears filled with the howling wind that had come out of nowhere. His commands were also dangerous. If any man stood in this wind, he would immediately be knocked over. There was nothing they could do. They were trapped and the vortex sucked the ship along with massive amounts of river water. Sea gulls squawked in protest as they too, were sucked within the purple vortex. Its power was so ferocious that the stern lifted out of the water. Hawk slid down the tilted deck but was able to maneuver his feet onto a square wood box that had been nailed down. Some of Ragnar's men slid past him, grabbing frantically at anything with their hands.

Water sprayed onto the deck from all sides, soaking his clothes and skin. Someone sliding by grabbed his outstretched hand. It was the toothless man, his mouth working but Hawk could not hear him. In addition to the howl of wind, another sound now emanated from the center of the vortex. It was a low hum that carried a strong vibration. The toothless pirate let go of Hawk's hand to cover his ears and slid farther down to join other pirates' bodies congregated at the bow. The hum grew louder with each passing second and Hawk decided it was time to take another form. He did not want to die on this ship.

A loud crack sounded behind him. The ship was splitting in two. Two men jumped over the bulwark of their own volition. Through the hum he heard someone scream. He lifted his head to look behind him and saw Ragnar still clung to a crack in the deck. He mouthed something and Hawk strained to hear.

"What?"

"…shift…die…"

"What?" Hawk shook his head.

"Shapeshift and save yourself! We're going to die!"

Another wave crashed over and drenched them in whitewater. For a brief second, Hawk thought the water had unloosed Ragnar's grip and his friend was lost forever, washed overboard into a torrent of water which would be sucked into the vortex along with the ship and all animals within proximity. But the water only washed him to port, where he huddled beneath the bulwark.

The truth was, Hawk would never leave his friend. He felt an intense pang of guilt but it was quickly replaced as the purple light grew intensely bright within a matter of seconds, surrounding them all. Its intensity was such that Hawk had to close his eyes. It was like staring into a violet sun. The humming stopped. The crashing of waves stopped. The squawks of gulls stopped. The screams of terrified pirates ceased. He floated in complete silence. And the light, the blinding light.

Is death upon me? He thought. *Will I die here in some mysterious vortex on a river?*

The ship seemed to right itself. There was a lurch backward then a splash. Through his eyelids, he noticed the intense brightness wink out. He slowly opened his eyes.

He lay on his back staring up at the ceiling of a limestone grotto. Craggy rock formations hung from the ceiling. He stood and saw the ship rested in a pool of turquoise water. The grotto seemed to go on forever with fingers of limestone protruding like an underwater hand getting stuck on its ascent. An underground smell permeated the air, an earthy smell of sulfur and something else Hawk couldn't identify.

"What happened? Where are we?" Ragnar asked. He was back on

his feet. His crew stood from where they took refuge, their eyes wide and mouths gaped in shock.

"I...don't know." Hawk immediately sent out his mind to search for the animals in the area. A few fish entered his consciousness but that was overwhelmingly overshadowed by another presence, something mysterious and unknowable, but oh how the waves of power flowed from that consciousness. He felt distinctive humans or...no...not humans but something human-like about them...

"What are they?" a pirate named Moscan asked from behind him. He was Ragnar's first mate and unusually quiet for a pirate.

Light that seemed to emerge from the water reflected off several pairs of eyes hidden within the crevices and ledges of the grotto. The eyes belonged to little men, most of them would barely reach Hawk's waist. They were uniform in their height but not in hair color or dress. Their noses resembled those of pigs, short and pushed in, their lips were pert and fleshy and their skin was rough, their cheeks red.

"They're gnomes," Hawk told the men. "Earth elementals. They won't attack."

"Why do they carry axes and clubs, then?" Ragnar pointed out.

"We're strangers. Perhaps they can tell us where we are."

The ship sailed slowly through the turquoise water, pulled by an invisible force as no wind existed. It meandered through the jutting crags with an elegant grace, never touching them. The gnomes tentatively emerged from the shadows and into the light, curious about their visitors.

Hawk held up his hands and then folded them over his heart in an ancient greeting of the Jaanaarians.

"We come in peace!" he called out in the True Tongue.

Two gnomes on a ledge of limestone, whose beards reached nearly to their knees, exchanged glances. Hawk knew they were the leaders. Among gnomes, the Elders let their beards grow and sometimes braided them.

In the manner of the Jaanaarians, Hawk tapped his heart with his hands.

The gnomes nodded and the most Elder of the two, with the longest beard, pointed ahead in the direction they currently sailed. He took it to mean they were on the right course.

"Do you understand the True Tongue?" Hawk asked.

"Yes," the eldest responded in the ancient Jaanaarian language.

"What is this place?" Hawk repeated.

"It depends. Where have you come from?" The elder gnome's voice was a deep baritone. He spoke the True Tongue with a strange accent.

"Why does it matter where we came from?" Hawk asked.

Laughter erupted from the elder gnomes with slight titters from their compatriots. "Where did you come from?" he repeated though bursts of laughter.

"From the Triad. We sailed the Othalla."

At once all laughter stopped. Hawk didn't like that and neither did Ragnar or his men.

"Let's kill these insolent little buggers," Ragnar growled into Hawk's ear, drawing his sword.

Hawk rounded on him.

"No, friend. You won't do that. They cannot be killed because they are elementals and if you attack, they could bring this entire cave down on our heads."

Ragnar pursed his lips. "They don't look like they could do much." But instead of pursuing it further, he sheathed his sword.

"If you come from the Triad, continue and we will inform him," the eldest said.

Hawk didn't know who they referred to but hoped he could tell them where they were. The gnomes seemed to have decided not to give out any more information. They were retreating back into the darkness of the cave.

The ship continued on and the gnomes all but disappeared.

"The water is getting darker," Ragnar observed.

He was right. No longer translucent turquoise, the water was now dark blue. And getting darker. The ceiling of the grotto was also getting higher and as they moved forward, it eventually disappeared into darkness.

"This place, it be cursed," said one of Ragnar's skinny oarsmen. "We should put oars to water and reverse."

Hawk sensed Ragnar was contemplating such a thing. His old friend had a very uneasy expression on his face. And truth be told, Hawk felt uneasy himself. What exactly was propelling their ship through the water? There was no breeze whatsoever.

The craggy fingers of rock that jutted out of the water became less and less frequent. The walls of the cave expanded and now it appeared as if they were sailing an ocean with a dark, starless sky above. The last column of rock Hawk could see clearly had someone standing atop it and he was not a gnome.

Ragnar drew steel as they approached. The man who stood there was tall, taller than any Jaanaarian Hawk had known. He was dressed entirely in black, his cape swirling around him and the sheen of it appeared kaleidoscopic, as if it was enchanted. His hair was wavy, black, and brushed back away from his face. He was clean-shaven except for an oiled mustache that turned up slightly at the corners. His skin was unnaturally pale. When they got close enough, the man held up a hand and the ship came to a gentle stop.

Hawk made the Jaanaarian gesture of greeting. He and Ragnar walked to the bow and when they got close enough, he saw the man's eyes were red with vertical black slits for pupils. And Hawk felt the strange animal presence in his mind.

It suddenly hit him.

...*Kefkinala*...

This man was a dragon in human form!

The man leapt over the railing of the ship with such grace that gravity seemed to have no effect upon him. The presence he exuded made the ragged pirates step back, some of them gasping in awe. He was twice the size of the tallest of them.

"I am Hawk, son of Niall and this is Ragnar, the captain of this ship."

He didn't answer but stared at them with his demonic eyes. Most of the crew had backed far away. Hawk heard them whisper among themselves.

"Hawk of the Knotts, we have been expecting you."

The man never opened his mouth. Hawk heard the sentence in his mind, just as with other animals. Just as with Renfala. As Kefkinala communicated with him, the dragon's eyes glowed and sparkled.

"You are…" Hawk said aloud.

"Kefkinala."

Again, he said it in Hawk's mind, just like an animal would. Just like a dragon would. A brief thought of Renfala ran through his mind.

Ragnar gaped back and forth between them, as though he sensed some form of communication was taking place.

"This is…?" Hawk thought.

"Mount Moirae, the home of the Weavers."

"Why are we here?"

Kefkinala raised an eyebrow. In the distance Hawk saw something rise out of the water, another finger of rock, only much wider and taller than the others. He could not see the top. When he returned his gaze to Kefkinala, he intuitively understood that was their destination. The sound of trickling water was unmistakable. The ship slightly bobbed up and down in the water as if something moved underneath. The water suddenly rose as they sailed closer to the giant rock finger. A wall came into view and Hawk saw massive amounts of water running down it, filling the chamber.

Ragnar's men drew their swords and waited as the ship rose slowly upon the water. Hawk saw the top of the rock finger was flat and formed a small island in the rising water. When the water was nearly level with it, he saw a group of men standing in a strange formation, two of them very tall, as tall as Kefkinala. It took a few seconds before he realized one of them was a woman with auburn hair.

Sillisnae!

Forgetting himself and any caution he might harbor in such a situation, he leaned over the railing.

"Sillisnae!" he called. "Sillisnae!"

She turned and saw him for the first time since they parted in Westernaphalia, since he sent her back to the Crystal Palace with the Fire Globe. Recognition dawned on her face.

"Hawk!" she screamed. Her face quickly went from recognition to terror. She waved her arms in front of her as if shooing him away. "Go back! Go back! It's a trap!"

Hawk instinctively tried to shapeshift but couldn't. Only a few yards of water lay between the ship and the island. Without another thought, he dove into the water. It was frightfully cold and shocked his muscles and skin. He ignored it as best he could and swam with all his might toward Sillisnae.

While he swam, he had the fleeting thought; *the tall men appear Jaanaarian...*

When he reached the edge of the island, the giants were there to pull him up. Their strength was immense. He struggled against their grip but it was useless. He tried to call upon his power and shapeshift but it was gone. They pushed him to his knees in front of Sillisnae and held him there. That's when he saw the man with the strange contraption on his head. The man lifted it off and Hawk had an uncanny feeling of déjà vu. He knew this man. A few seconds passed before he realized who it was: The Maeltipian he had saved in the

Renfala Forest! Was this the Prince of Maeltip? The thing that had been on his head was a transparent skull.

The Crystal Skull...

Hands closed around his head. They were big hands, probably belonging to one of the giants. He heard Sillsinae scream, "Hawk! No, don't!"

Men shouted and Sillisnae screamed his name as he lost consciousness.

He lay on the ground, the cold stone hard against his back. A face appeared over him. He recognized the man as Jaanaarian by his eyes but did not recognize his face, and there was a tattoo of a winged disk in the center of his forehead. The image tickled Hawk's memory but he could not bring it to full realization. Suddenly, hands were under his shoulders, lifting him up to a sitting position.

Time must have passed because the Prince of Maeltip wore the Crystal Skull and Sillisnae sobbed in front of him.

Why were Jaanaarians dressed in black with the Linnsonian symbol on their chests? Another stood behind Sillisnae holding her in place with his giant arms.

Why hasn't Kefkinala shapeshifted into a dragon? Doesn't he guard the Skull?

"Do it!" a dark-haired Linnsonian shouted. "Do it now!"

The Crystal Skull encasing the head of the Maeltipian prince shot out bright white beams of light that twirled and meandered like small, slithering snakes. The prince grabbed Sillisnae and hugged her close. A column of light spun around them, its source the Crystal Skull. The circumference of the light expanded, eventually reaching the spot where he lay. The light was alive, with small particles dancing within beams. When it touched him, he saw a female form hovering above Sillisnae and the prince. She flickered and wildly struggled against something, forcing herself into physical manifestation. Her hair and face would take shape and then lose shape again. Hawk recognized her at once.

But how? Her heart is safe within a crystal in a Jaanaarian hillnon.

"Where is he?" the Linnsonian shouted at the Jaanaarians. "It won't work without the heart."

They had no answer for him. Nominthe's image continued to flicker and make an unnerving howl that shook him to the very bone.

So there are no Weavers. It was all just a legend...

The thought managed to make it to the surface of his mind, right before he heard the roar of a dragon. The light column around Sillisnae and the prince glowed so brightly Hawk had to close his eyes. A roar of wind, like that he felt before entering the purple vortex, was the only sound he heard before Sillisnae's scream reached his ears.

...Sillisnae...I am so sorry...

Everyone suddenly disappeared, including the *Tawdry Maiden*, the water it had risen on, even Kefkinala. They just winked out of existence in a millisecond. He was alone on the rock island and he was exhausted. He wanted to sleep but the nagging thought of Sillisnae was the only thing that kept his eyes open. He twisted his head in every direction, fighting against the tiredness, to see where he was and how to get out.

"Hello?" he called. "Is there anyone there?" He struggled to move his arms but they would not budge.

"...*Sleep*..." he heard a voice say. "...*Rest*..."

"Who are you?" he mouthed but barely any sound came out.

Somewhere behind him he heard footsteps.

"Who are you?" he repeated.

Someone put their fingers to his temples and said "Shhhh." He looked up and saw the most ancient face. A woman's face. It was more wrinkled than crocodile skin, the animal that inhabited the lakes and rivers of the Knotts. The eyes were black, shiny beads with folds of skin hanging halfway over them. Her nose was long, with a fleshy bulb at the end of it. Her hair was gray and long, still thick for a woman her age. She was the ugliest thing he had ever seen, even uglier than Sheena when she lost her youth and beauty.

"Shhh..." the woman whispered. "Sleep..."

And Hawk slept.

EPILOGUE

"WHAT HAPPENED?" KRYST ASKED. She cradled his head in her hands. "Where am I?"

Sillisnae looked around, some of her auburn hair stuck to her tear-stained face. "I don't know. It's a marshy wetland. They won't tell me anything."

"What happened?" he asked again. He barely remembered. Only bits and pieces came to him. He saw the man who had saved him in Renfala Forest. After that it was fuzzy. A ship appeared on waters that rose unexpectedly.

"You...you...fainted," Sillisnae said. "After they put the Crystal Skull on your head, the druids used it to manifest someone, a goddess."

Nominthe!

"Did they succeed?" Kryst asked through bitter lips.

"No," she sighed and looked around. "They've left us in this place.

I don't know where they went."

When she said *they*, he assumed she meant the Jaanaarians and Captain Oscan. His head pounded. Now he remembered the light and screaming in his mind. The screaming of a woman.

He sat up. They occupied a heather-laden, hilly field. Small, twisted trees dotted the landscape here and there, but it consisted mostly of long, yellowish grass, heather and steel gray rocks. A steady wind blew, freezing him to the bone. It smelled of salt and fish.

"I've never seen this kind of landscape in Corvasa," he remarked.

"Neither have I."

He heard fear in her voice. She tried to cover it up. Her face was wet and her eyes red from crying.

"Did you know that man? That shapeshifter?" he asked her.

She nodded and wiped away a tear. "His name is Hawk. He was the one that got me out of Minosae not so long ago."

"He saved my life," Kryst said. "He was the man that pulled me from the thorny trees in that accursed forest."

"He did?" Sillisnae sniffled. "That was before I met him. You've known him longer than I have." She gave a little laugh and he was glad to hear it.

"My body...it feels..."

"Tired?" she finished for him. "When I woke up here, I thought I was paralyzed. I couldn't move. Slowly, feeling returned."

"Where is the Crystal Skull?"

"They took it with them when they left."

"Where did they go?" Kryst stared out at the barren, hilly terrain. "Did they leave us alone you suppose? Abandon us here?"

"They didn't say. They saw I was awake and did not speak but walked off in that direction." Sillisnae pointed. "I believe it is north. We'll just have to watch the sun and see."

The sun. It was a roundish white haze in the opposite direction of where she pointed. Kryst longed to feel the sun, not the bone-chilling cold of the perpetual wind that plagued this barren landscape. Sillisnae resumed crying. She did not sob but let out barely audible gasps of air.

He wanted to put an arm around her, comfort her. But something stopped him.

"If they went north, perhaps we should go in the opposite direction, toward the sun."

Sillisnae nodded and pulled the threadbare blanket she clutched around her more tightly. If they did not get warm, they very well could freeze to death when the sun dropped below the horizon.

He tried to stand but his legs were weak and he fell back onto his bottom. A sudden thought occurred to him. "Where is Locklin?" He couldn't believe he didn't notice the absence of his friend earlier.

"Dead." She wiped away her tears. "He tried to feed me to monsters on the side of Mount Moirae but they had something else in mind. They attacked him instead of me."

"I see..." Kryst felt sad even though the Corvasan Healer had betrayed him. It seemed the man got himself involved in things far too powerful for him to control.

Sillisnae seemed to read his thoughts. "We buried him where he was killed. Very few can say their final resting place is on the side of Mount Moirae."

After a few moments, Kryst stood and walked without falling. They decided to go south. Perhaps there was a river somewhere and a river would lead to people.

Kryst found a long branch and used it as a walking staff. They descended in silence but only came to a small stream. Sillisnae threw some water on her face and drew away, amazed.

"The water is hot," she said.

"A hot spring!" Kryst exclaimed, taking off his shoes. "This will warm us to our bones. This annoying chill will now be remedied." He stripped down as naked as the day he was born and stuck his toes into the stream. She was right, it was piping hot. He slid in as Sillisnae turned away, her cheeks burning red.

"Wet clothes in this cold cause the wet lung sickness," he told her.

She didn't answer but waited by the side of the spring. The water was deliciously warm, working out the kinks and stiffness in his muscles, and most importantly, warming him.

When he was sufficiently warm, he got out and dressed, all the while staring at Sillisnae's back. The voice he had heard on occasion, the outright hatred he felt toward Sillisnae when the voice spoke, had not been heard since the time with the Crystal Skull which made him think of something else.

"There were no Weavers. Nor a dragon. Only a skull. It seems the ancient legend that all of Perthia learns at a young age is just a myth. You can turn around now. I've dressed."

She did and he saw she had been crying even more. Her auburn hair was tangled and matted, her clothes were torn in places and dirty but she was still an exceptionally beautiful woman. He had another overwhelming urge to comfort her but refrained. The last time he touched her, he saw Nominthe's face and experienced her rage. He never wanted to feel something like that again.

"There was a dragon," she said. "At the very end, before everything went black, I heard the roar of a dragon."

"Did you?" Kryst asked, confused. "I did not. I have heard it once before and will never forget the sound."

They continued to walk slowly, following the stream. His mind raced with questions as more memory of their ordeal poured in.

"Why would the Linnsonians want to manifest a goddess that kept their male ancestors in bondage?"

She glanced at him sideways. One thin finger scraped away a strand of auburn hair, blown there by the wind. "She is their blood. Her divine blood mixed with that of mortal men, creating a new race of people, a semi-divine race. Even if she kept them in bondage, she is their ancestor and the power of magic rests in blood."

Kryst was intrigued. They came upon small ponds and saturated bog land. The croaking of frogs rose up in a melodic chorus. Here and there, small brown rodents darted between crowberry shrubs. Kryst smiled. If they had to be out here longer than the passing of a day, there would be plenty to eat.

"So the talent is inherited?"

"Yes. In Minosae, they taught it was a lot more prevalent at one time, but no more. Those with the talent are less and less with each generation."

The smell of smoke wafted into his nostrils. He crouched down instinctively and motioned Sillisnae to do the same.

"What is it?" she whispered.

"There are people nearby. I smell smoke."

She sniffed the air and nodded. Kryst pointed. A plume of smoke rose over the crest of the next hill. He stood again. "I believe we've found some living people!"

They crested the hill and gazed down upon a hamlet with the houses spewing smoke from their chimneys. A few men were feeding and herding pigs, while some women scrubbed clothes.

"Hallo!" Kryst called out and waved his hands. "We come in peace!" he said in Corvasan.

All of them looked up at once, taken by surprise as they were. The women immediately ran inside the houses. Sillisnae stopped mid-wave when she saw that.

"We come in peace!" he repeated as three men walked up the hill to meet them.

All three were very tall and muscular. One was old, perhaps near sixty and the other two were young men in their prime. They wore work clothes of thick fabric and their trousers were held up by suspenders. All were clean-shaven, and one of the young men resembled the older one more than a little. The same close-set blue eyes and wide, chiseled jaw. The old man's hair was silver and dark gray, wavy and long. His son—Kryst was sure the younger man was his progeny—had wavy blond hair held back by a leather tie. The third man was not as handsome as his compatriots. He had a nose that appeared to have been broken more than once. His cheeks were unnaturally red, like he was fond of wine and mead. His eyes were greenish brown, underneath a prominent brow and one bushy, black eyebrow. His teeth bucked out and his cheeks were hollow.

As a matter of instinct, Kryst moved in front of Sillisnae. There was something in the men's eyes when they looked at her that worried him.

"I am Kryst of Maeltip," he introduced himself. He thought it prudent not to reveal who he was right away. "And this is Sillisnae of Corvasa."

The ugly man nodded. "We are Maken." The man pointed to himself. "Ramos"—he pointed to the young blond—"and Klen."

Maken spoke in the same heavily accented Corvasan as Master Oscan.

"Can you tell us where we are?" Kryst asked.

"Why do you stand in front of the woman?" the young one called Ramos asked.

Kryst sensed Sillisnae stiffen. He had no weapon and her power was blocked. "No reason," he replied trying to keep his expression as neutral as possible.

"We have not seen her before," Klen said. "You are in the north of Linnso. Have you lost your way from your merchant ships?" They all laughed at that.

Kryst did not know what to say. Merchant ships? How else would they have arrived at an obscure island in the North Sea? "Yes, we lost our way."

"Most Perthians do not bring their women here unless they mean to sell them."

"She is not for sale," Kryst said firmly. "She's my cousin."

"Well, you're too far away from your comrades, my friend." Maken said. "We'll be relieving you of your duties for the female. You are, of course, welcome to our bread and wine. But we'll be having a little fun with your lass while you wait."

Sillisnae gasped behind him.

"No, you won't. Like I said, she's my cousin. I cannot allow—"

"You're not in a position to allow or disallow anything, Kryst of Maeltip." Klen said.

"I am the *Prince* of Maeltip," he corrected. But they just laughed at him and Maken lifted an axe he carried on his back. Klen reached for a dirk attached to his breeches.

"This can be easy for you, Prince Kryst," Klen began. "We'll take her and you can enjoy our hospitality, even that of our women"—he winked—"or we'll take her and you'll die, alone on the heathered moors."

Behind him, he heard Sillisnae run.

About the Author

LV Barat discovers tales in the most unlikely of places: in the ancient spiritual literature of India, Greece, Scandinavia, Britain and Ireland. An extensive study of the occult in several different cultures led to an awakening of the power of myth in her mind. Myths are woven in the imaginations or collective unconscious of peoples worldwide and the connection to the archetypes can weave tales that inspire!

LV Barat has been writing fiction and non-fiction for twenty years. Epic fantasy is her genre of choice whilst some suspenseful mystery has managed to worm its way into her opus corpus.

Jane Eyre was the first novel she read as a prepubescent. Its gray, mysterious moors and subdued emotions that raged under the surface of its characters called to her longingly, convincing something deep within her to become a writer.

LV Barat lives in the Rocky Mountains, the spine of North America, an enchanted place of glistening pine needles, massive boulders, jutting gray crags, stealthy red foxes and antlered elk.

Please visit her website at WWW.LVBARAT.COM